James Page has blown his sister's TV to hell with a shotgun and chased her into her room with a firewood club. There she will live or die on a diet of apples and a lurid fantasy of illicit drugs, kinky violence, and casual sex . . .

"ROLLICKING, RIBALD, TRULY IMAGINATIVE THE WAY DICKENS, FOR EXAMPLE, IS IMAGINATIVE AND REAL."
The Washington Post Book World

**Also by John Gardner
Published by Ballantine Books**

GRENDEL

THE SUNLIGHT DIALOGUES

NICKEL MOUNTAIN

THE WRECKAGE OF AGATHON

THE KING'S INDIAN

FREDDY'S BOOK

OCTOBER LIGHT

John Gardner

Illustrated by Elaine Raphael
and Don Bolognese

BALLANTINE BOOKS • NEW YORK

Library of Congress Catalog Card Number: 76-13718

ISBN 0-345-29298-7

This edition published by arrangement with
Alfred A. Knopf, Inc.

Manufactured in the United States of America

First Ballantine Books Edition: January 1978
Fourth Printing: June 1981

To my father

To turn to the news of the day, it seems that the cannibals of Europe are going to eat one another again. A war between Russia and Turkey is like the battle of the kite and the snake; whichever destroys the other leaves a destroyer the less for the world. This pugnacious humor of mankind seems to be the law of his nature, one of the obstacles to too great multiplication provided in the mechanism of the Universe. The cocks of the hen yard kill one another; bears, bulls, rams do the same, and the horse, in his wild state, kills all the young males until when he's worn down with age and war, some youth kills him.

I hope we shall prove how much happier for the man the Quaker policy is, and that the life of the feeder is better than that of the fighter: and it is some consolation that the desolation by these maniacs of one part of the earth is the means of improving it in other parts. Let the latter be our office; and let us milk the cow, while the Russian holds her by the horns, and the Turk by the tail.

Thomas Jefferson to John Adams, June 1, 1822

Acknowledgments

The passage in this novel which is entitled "Ed's Song"—along with other details sprinkled throughout the book—is largely drawn from Noel Perrin's *Vermont in All Weathers,* with photographs by Sonja Bullaty and Angelo Lomeo (New York: The Viking Press, Inc., 1973), and is used with Mr. Perrin's kind permission. James L. Page's ruminations on the words *up* and *down* are adapted, with the author's permission, from an essay by Julius S. Held, "Gravity and Art," published in *Art Studies for an Editor: Twenty-five Essays in Memory of Milton S. Fox* (New York: Harry N. Abrams, Inc., 1975). I've of course borrowed from numerous other writers, ancient and modern, but I forget which ones. The smugglers' story which Sally Page Abbott reads, I wrote in collaboration with my wife Joan.

Most of the places I mention in the real-world sections of this novel are actual, and many of the characters are real people, living or dead, introduced into this book by their real names—among others, Ethan

Allen and Jedediah Dewey, John G. McCullough, Charles Dewey, Andre Speyer, Kayoko Kodama, Norman Rockwell, Chief Joe Young, George and Peg Ellis, and Mr. Pelkie. I have also borrowed some fictitious people from other people's novels, notably Judah Sherbrooke and his barenaked wife, who were originally invented by Nicholas Delbanco in a novel called, in the manuscript I've seen, *Possession*. If anyone is offended by my having put them or their inventions in this novel, I apologize.

"I was in the State House Yard when the Declaration of Independence was read. There was very few respectable people present."

CHARLES BIDDLE, 1776

1

The Patriot's Rage, and the Old Woman's Finding of the Trashy Book by the Bedside

"Corruption? *I'll* tell you about corruption, sonny!" The old man glared into the flames in the fireplace and trembled all over, biting so hard on the stem of his pipe that it crackled once, sharply, like the fireplace logs. You could tell by the way he held up the stem and looked at it, it would never be the same. The house was half dark. He never used lights, partly from poverty, partly from a deep-down miserliness. Like all his neighbors on Prospect Mountain—like all his neighbors from the Massachusetts line clear to Canada, come to that—he was, even at his most generous, frugal. There was little in this world he considered worth buying. That was one reason that in the darkness behind him the television gaped like a black place where once a front tooth had hung. He'd taken the twelve gauge shotgun to it, three weeks ago now, for its endless, simpering advertising and, worse yet, its monstrously obscene games of greed, the filth of hell made visible in the world: screaming women, ravenous for refrigerators, automobiles, mink coats, ostrich-feather hats; leering glittering-toothed monsters of ceremonies—for all their pretty smiles, they were vipers upon the earth, those panderers to lust, and their programs were blasphemy and high treason. He couldn't say much better for the endless, simpering dramas they put on, now indecent, now violent, but in any case an outrage against sense. So he'd loaded the shotgun while the old woman, his sister, sat stupidly grinning into the flickering light—long-nosed, long-chinned, black shadows dancing on the wall behind her—and without a word of warning, he'd blown that TV screen to hell, right back where it come from.

It might've been a tragedy. The old woman had shot up three feet into the air and fainted dead away and gone blue all over, and it had taken him close to an hour to revive her with ice-water. Though the TV was hers, the old woman—the puffy widowed sister who'd come here to live with him, now that her money'd run out—hadn't been so brave or so crackers as to try and get another. She'd dropped hints in that direction two, three times, maybe more, and so did all her friends when they stopped in and visited, chattering like magpies, their eyes lighted up like they had fire inside, but they'd never dared pursue it. He was a man of fierce opinions, meaner than pussley broth, a whole lot meaner than those bees he kept—he ought to be locked in the insane asylum—so his sister maintained, shaking like a leaf. But he'd known her all his life: the shaking was pure cunning. He'd told her right off, first minute she'd moved in, that if she wanted TV she could watch it in the shed with the tractor.

He'd been generous enough in every other respect, or so it seemed to him. He'd even been willing to hole up in his room like some drunken hired man out of the County Home when she had friends in—old Estelle Parks, who'd taught school many years ago and played "Smoke Gets in Your Eyes" and "The Beautiful Lady in Blue" on the piano, or old Ruth Thomas, who'd been forty-some years a librarian. He'd done plenty for his sister, had walked his mile and a half and then some. But he had, like any man, his limit, and the limit was TV. God made the world to be looked at head on, and let a bear live in the woodshed, he'd soon have your bed. It was a matter of plain right and wrong, that was all. The Devil finds work for empty heads. "Did God give the world His Holy Word in television pictures?" he'd asked her, leering. *"No* sir," he'd answered himself, "used print!" "Next thing," she said, "you'll tell me we should only read words if they're carved on rocks." She had a crafty tongue, no use denying it. Might've been a preacher or a Congressman, if the Lord in His infinite wisdom hadn't seen fit to send her down as a female, to minimize the risk. He'd told her that, once. She'd preached him a sermon off television about the Equal Rights Amendment. He'd been amazed by all she said—shocked and flabbergasted, though he knew from magazines that there were people who believed such foolishness. "Why, a woman ain't even completely human," he'd said to her. "Look how weak they are! Look how they cry like little children!" He'd squinted, trying to understand how anyone could've *missed* a thing like that. She'd thought he was joking—he'd never been more serious in his life, Lord knows—and gradually he'd realized, his amazement increasing, that they might as well be talking different languages, he might as well be trying to hold conference with a horse. She'd seemed as astonished by it all as he was, so astonished to discover what he thought that he almost came to doubt it.

Well, fierce and foolish opinions they might be, but he'd held them for seventy years and more (he'd be seventy-three on July the fourth); he was hardly about to abandon them. Though he was never a great talker —certainly not in comparison to her, she could lecture your arm off—he knew a significant fact or two, knew, by thunder, a *truth* or two—as he mentioned to his grandson, grimly poking a crooked, cracked finger at him—a truth or two that was still worth getting out of bed for. Such knowledge was as rare these days as

3

golden parsnips. He was the last, could be, that still possessed any real, first-class opinions.

The old woman, his sister, whose name was Sally Page Abbott—she thought she was royalty, her husband had been a dentist—was up there in the bedroom, furiously pacing, locked in the bedroom by her brother's hand, away from the boy, where her foolish ideas could have no influence. She believed in "changing with the times," she'd said—believed in, for instance, atomic-bomb power plants, since the Government claimed they was perfectly safe and eventually, one way another, they'd get rid of that waste. "Who knows about such things if not the Government?" she'd said, flustered and offended. She'd seen some program about "feeder reactors," hope of the universe. "Lies!" he'd said. From the look of her he might've been a Communist Chinese. Well, he knew what he knew, he'd told her, and smiled at her like poison come to supper. He was, he reminded her, a taxpayer. She wept. She believed there was no harm in mass production and business efficiency, even agribusiness; an opinion that lifted off his shingles. Agribusiness was the enemy of the nation, he'd informed her in no uncertain terms, thumping the arm of his chair for emphasis. Agribusiness was squeezing out honest small farmers by the thousands, making them go to work in pencil factories, stand in soup lines, turn into drunkards. He'd see them in hell, those tycoons of the ten-speed tractor, and that devil in a skin Earl Butz with 'em. The old man's cheeks twitched and jerked as he spoke; he was shaking head to foot, like a goat that's eaten lightning. She also believed in supermarkets (got that, too, from TV), and in New York City and Amnesty for the War Resisters, even believed it was society's fault when some crooked little snake committed murder. She was a cotton-headed fool who confessed, herself, that she had faith in people, though she was eighty years old and ought to know better.

The brother—"James L. Page is the name," he'd say—was never one to argue, except on occasion at a Bennington Town Meeting. He'd settled the business

4

by driving her upstairs with a fireplace log, sister or no sister, and had locked her to herself in her room; let her think things over. "Insane, drunken devil!" she'd bawled as she retreated, stepping upstairs backwards, holding up her spotted, crooked talons for protection. "Insane drunken devil my ass," he might have said. She could thank her sweet Saviour he was a Christian and didn't care to pop her one. He was a patriot, and foolishness like hers was destroying this great country.

If James Page was crazy, as his sister maintained— and there were some on the mountain who'd be inclined to agree, to say nothing of all her friends—it was not for lack of study, not for lack of brooding over magazines and papers, or listening to people's talk. Except for his morning and evening chores, or patching up the barn when a board blew off, or shoveling through shoulder-high drifts now and then to let the milktruck up, and cutting ice from the roof, or sometimes sorting through potatoes in the cellar, culling out the rotten ones, squishy to the touch and more foul of stench than politics, foul as the bloom of a rat three weeks dead in the cistern, or Social Security— except for what trivial work wandered in between the second killing frost and sugaring time, James Page, for the length of the whole Vermont winter, did practically nothing but sit pondering books (his daughter in Arlington, mother of the boy, had joined him to a book club—history books—and subscribed him to four different magazines) or reading his newspapers—grimacing angrily, baring the upper front teeth in his foot-long, narrow head, leaning toward the window in his steel-rimmed spectacles, the brittle, dry-smelling, yellowed lace curtains softening just noticeably the mountains' light, white as his hair. Between times he'd drive to the village in his pick-up and sit with his hat on in Merton's Hideaway, nursing a Ballantine's and listening, full of gloom, to the talk.

She'd spoken of corruption. The best social programs in the world, she said—the powder-white wings of her nose aflicker—could be made to look bad by corruption; that wasn't the program's fault. She'd got

5

feistier by the minute since the evening he'd shot out that TV. When he'd thumped his fist on his chair-arm she'd quickly pulled her chin back.

"I'll tell you about corruption, by tunkit," he said now, bending toward his grandson, squinting like an Indian, nodding his head, white hair glowing.

The grandson sat perfectly still, his hands, pale as alabaster, folded in his lap, his blue eyes as wide as two quarters. The black and white cat, curled up casually asleep under the old man's chair, was used to such commotion, as was the dog, watching sadly from the corner of the room. It would be hours, the boy knew, before his mother would come get him. He was nine and, as always in his grandfather's presence, he was terrified. His grandfather, the boy had heard people say when they thought he wasn't listening, had had a son who'd hanged himself and another who'd fallen off the barn and broke his neck when he was little. The one who'd hanged himself had been twenty-five and had a house across the road. It had since burned down. The boy had seen the graves at the cemetery in the village. That was why the boy wouldn't sleep in this house, or anyway not unless his mother was with him. He was afraid of the noises in the attic.

"Benjamin Franklin," his grandfather said, still bending toward him in a threatening way, "was a nudist. Used to walk around his house nights barenaked. I bet they never leahnt you *that* in school."

The boy shook his head, smiling eagerly to save himself from harm, and shrank from the old man's eyes.

"Faddle's ah they teach," said his grandfather. "Bleached-out hoss-manure." He took a puff from his pipe, blew out smoke and said, aiming the pipestem at the middle of the boy's collarbone, "Sam Adams was a liar. Your teachers tell you that? When Sam Adams organized the Boston militia, he told 'em the port of New York had fallen, which was a damn lie. He was as bad as a Communist agitator." He smiled again, glinty-eyed, like a raccoon in the orchard, and whether he was feeling indignation at Sam Adams or at somebody else—the old woman upstairs, the boy himself, the gray-brown whiskey and specks of ash in his glass—it was impossible to tell. "Ethan Allen was a drunkahd. When he moved through these pots"—or perhaps he said *parts*—"with his roughneck gang of Green Mountain Boys, he got drunker at every house he stopped at, and that's God's truth. It's a holy wonder he made it up the cliffside, at Ticonderoga, him and his boys and them drunken wild Indians. It's a wonder he could remember the names of 'The Great Jehovah and the Continental Congress' when he told 'em to surrender."

He sucked at his pipe and grew calmer for a moment, thinking of Jehovah and the Continental Congress. He stared with nothing worse than a malevolent leer into the fireplace. "They was a rough, ill-bred lot, for the most pot, them glorious foundling fathers. But one thing a man can say of 'em that's true: they wasn't fat pleasure-loving self-serving chicken-brained hogs such as people are nowadays."

He looked at the ceiling, and the boy looked up too. The old woman had stopped pacing. The old man squeezed his eyes shut and lowered his head, then opened them, staring in the direction of his knees. He pursed his lips and sucked at his teeth, and his bushy white eyebrows were red in the glow of the firelight. Perhaps for an instant he felt a touch of remorse, but if so he got rid of it. He nodded in thoughtful agreement with himself. "They was a rough, ill-bred lot— 'filthy rabble,' as General Geahge Washington called 'em—but there was things they believed in, a sma' bit, ennaway: a vision, you might say, as in the Bible. It was *that* they lied for and fought for and, some of 'em, croaked for. What will people lie for now, eh boy? Soap and mattresses, that's what they'll lie for! Coca-Cola, strip-mines, snowmobiles, underarm deodorants! Crimus! Thank the Lord those old timers can't be hollered back to life. There'd be bloody red hell to pay, believe you me, if they saw how we're living in this republic!"

He groped for the glass beside his foot and chuckled, still full of lightning but maliciously pleased at the ghastly idea of the foundling fathers coming staggering from the graveyard—hollow-eyed and terrible, their blue coats wormy, musket-barrels dirt-packed— and starting up a new revolution. He glanced at the boy and saw that, hands still folded, he was looking up timidly at the ceiling. Not meaning it quite as an apology, though it was, the old man said: "Never mind, do her good," and waved his long hand. "She be asleep by now." He sipped his whiskey, and when he'd lowered his glass to the carpet beside his iron-toed shoe again, he discovered his pipe was out. He reached into the pocket of his shirt to get a match, struck it on a stone of the fireplace, and held it to his pipebowl.

The boy could not help understanding that the rant was serious, nor could he help knowing—though he couldn't understand it—that he himself was in some way, at least in the old man's eyes, in alliance with what was wrong. Staring at the flames, finding forms in the logs—an owl, a bear with its arms extended— the two were not seeing the same thing at all. The old man had been born in an age of spirits, and lived in it yet, though practically alone there, and filled with doubts. When the windows of his house, on a cold winter morning, were adazzle with flowers, forest-scapes, cascades and avalanches, he believed—except if he stopped to think—that Jack Frost had done it, best painter in the world, as James Page's sharp-eyed old uncle used to say. The grandson, who lived in a warmer house, had never seen such windows. The old man believed, except if he stopped to think, in elves and fairies, in goblins and the Devil, in Santa Claus and Christ. The boy had been told since he was small that such things were just stories. And in the exact same semidark level of his mind, the old man believed in that huge old foul-mouthed bear of a man Ethan Allen, whose spectacles lay yet in the Bennington Museum, along with his account at the Catamount Tavern, which he'd lived next door to, the brown writing firm and unmythic as the writing of Jedediah

Dewey, hellfire preacher, whose great-great-great-great-grandson Charles built fine eighteenth-century furniture for friends and could be seen here and there throughout New England with his matched black team and one of his buggies or his high, polished sleigh, sitting there grinning in the forty-below weather when cars wouldn't start. The old man believed—as surely at least as he believed in Resurrection—in Daniel Webster, who'd spoken to four thousand people once in a natural theater, a great swoop of valley walled in by green mountains, now a forested stretch on John McCullough's estate. He believed as surely in Samuel Adams, that angry, crafty old son of a bot, embarrassment to Franklin and the Continental Congress, indispensable as Death to the Sons of Liberty, and not much more welcome at an Easter party —believed in him as surely as he did in Peg Ellis of Monument Avenue in the village of Old Bennington, who had, by way of her late husband George, who had them from his grandfather, who had them direct from the addressee, faded copies of Sam Adams' letters, the few he'd been unable to get back, at the time of the Burr scare, and put to the torch.

But it wasn't mere myth or mere history-as-myth—exalted figures to stir the imagination, teach the poor weighted-down spirit to vault—it wasn't mere New England vinegar and piss that made the old man fierce. Though he was wrong in some matters, an objective observer would be forced to admit—cracked as old pottery, no question about it—it was true that he had, off and on, real, first-class opinions. He knew the world dark and dangerous. Blame it on the weather. "Most people believe," he liked to say, "that any problem in the world can be solved if you know enough; most Vermonters know better." He'd seen herds of sheep die suddenly for no reason, or no reason you could learn until too late. He'd seen houses burn, seen war and the effects of war: had a neighbor, it was nearly thirty years ago now, who'd hunted his wife and five children like rabbits and shot 'em all dead—he'd been a flame-thrower man, earned a medal for his

9

killings in Germany. He, James Page, had been one of the neighbors, along with Sam Frost and two others now gone on, who'd walked the man's pastures and woodlots, looking for the bodies. He'd seen a child killed falling off a bannister once, and a hired man sucked into a corn-chopper. He'd seen friends die of heart attack, cancer, and drink; he'd seen marriages fail, and churches, and stores. He'd had one son killed by a fall from the barn roof, another—his first-born and chief disappointment—by suicide. He'd lost, not long after that, his wife. He was not, for all this, a pessimist or (usually) a thoroughgoing misanthrope; on the contrary, having seen so much of death—right now, in fact, there was the corpse of a black and white calf on his manure pile—he was better than most men at taking it in stride; better, anyway, than the man sealed off in his clean green suburb in Florida. But he understood what with stony-faced wit he called "life's gravity," understood the importance of admitting it, confronting it head on, with the eyes locked open and spectacles in place.

He was a man who worked with objects, lifting things, setting them down again—bales of hay, feed-bags, milkcans, calves—and one of his first-class opinions was this: All life—man, animal, bird, or flower—is a brief and hopeless struggle against the pull of the earth. The creature gets sick, his weight grows heavier, he has moments when he finds himself too weary to go on; yet on he goes, as long as he lives, on until the end—and it *is* a bitter one, for no matter how gallantly the poor beast struggles, it's a tragic and hopeless task. The body bends lower, wilting like a daisy, and finally the pull of the earth is the beast's sunken grave.

James Page was never a man of many words, but words were by no means without interest for him. They too were objects to be turned in the hand like stones for a wall, or sighted down, like a shotgun barrel, or savored like the honey in a timothy stalk. He wrote no poems—except one once, a prayer. Even when angry, at a Bennington Town Meeting, he'd be hard pressed to make a political speech. But he noticed words one by one, as he might notice songbirds, and he sometimes made lists of them, crudely pencilled into his Agro pocketsize farm record. He knew about *down:* a man, a horse, a rooster has times when he feels *down*hearted, *down*trodden, *down* in the mouth, plain *down,* and in the end *down* and out. He turns *down* offers, he turns thumbs *down.* And James Page knew, needless to say, about *up:* he would at times feel *up*lifted, *up* to a thing, *up* to someone's tricks, *up*right, or if barely on his feet, hard-*up*. A man, he knew, looks *down* on the people he considers beneath him; he has *high* or *low* ideals and opinions, *high* or *low* spirits and morale; his spirits *rise* or get a *lift* whenever things look *up* for him; in time his spirits *fall,* like a conquered city, a woman deflowered, a season. Even language, James Page understood—*low* speech—suffers gravity.

Call it a curious and idle opinion, it nevertheless had, at least for James Page—who was a thoughtful man, a moralist and brooder—sober implications. It was bone and meat that the world pulled downward, and the spirit, the fire of life that pushed upward, soared. It was sin, slavery, despair that hung heavy, freedom that climbed on eagle's wings to cliffs transcendent, not common rock. "Give me your tired, your poor, your *huddled masses* yearning to be free . . ." Everything decent, James Page believed, supported the struggle upward, gave strength to the battle against gravity. And all things foul gave support not to gravity—there was nothing inherently evil in stone or a holstein bull—but to the illusion of freedom and ascent. The Devil's visions were all dazzle and no lift, mere counterfeit escape, the lightness of a puffball— flesh without nutrients—the lightness of a fart, a tale without substance, escape from the world of hard troubles and grief in a spaceship.

He believed sure as day in those airy cliffs—not heaven, exactly, but a firm, high place luring feeling and ambition past existence as it is; not the Oz of the fairy tales his wife Ariah had read in the living room to his daughter and sons (James Page, in his spectacles, pretending to read the paper), not an emerald city where dreams come true, but some shadowy mountain calling down to intuition, some fortress for the lost made second by second and destroyed and made again, like Mount Anthony seen through fog.

Because of this opinion or general set of thought, the old man—almost without thinking, almost by instinct—was violently repelled by all that senselessly prettified life and, in his own dark view, belied it. He hated the Snoopy in his grandson's lap, hated Coca-Cola and the State of California, which he'd never seen, hated foreign cars, which he identified with weightless luxury and "the Axis," hated foam rubber, TV dinners, and store-bought ice cream. At Christmas, when the stores in the town of Bennington were jubilant with lights, and shoppers' voices, breaking through the muzak and feathery snow, were as clear and innocent as children's cries, James Page would pause, blanching, his hands in his overcoat, his ears sticking out, and would stare in black indignation at a glittering white astronaut doll in a window. Whether or not he could have said what he was feeling, and whether or not it would have mattered to the world or the company that runs it, the old man was right about the meaning of that doll. It was there to undo him, both him and his ghosts. Whether or not it was true, as he imagined, that once in his childhood he'd heard angels sing, and had seen them moving in the aurora borealis, it was undoubtedly true that the muzak made certain he would hear them—if in fact they were still up there singing—no more. It was hard to believe that any soul, however willing, could be uplifted by the conflict of recordings rasping through the snow-flurried air; hard to believe that the nodding, mechanical Santa in the Bennington Bookstore window could be drawn to the house by the magic of a Christmastree cut with an axe on Mount Prospect's crest and sledded, the children all squealing, to the woodshed door.

He did not of course, when he stopped to think, believe in elves or believe that bees can talk with fairies or pigs with wind, or that bears are visitors from another world; did not believe in Jack Frost or even, with his whole heart and mind, Resurrection. Though he muttered spells from time to time—though for luck he spit left or made a circle to the right, and carried with him everywhere he went a small stick (a stick of ash) and a rattlesnake's skull, protection against changelings—in even these he did not, when he considered carefully, believe. He believed in the most limited natural magic, the battle of spirit up through matter, season after season; and he believed that his ghosts, insofar as they were real or had the power of things real, were allies in the grim, universal war, as were the huge crayon paintings—the work of some nun of the Bennington Convent, years ago—that he liked to take people to see, now and then, at the Bennington Museum. He knew many such allies in the struggle toward ascent—church music, for instance, or Ruth Thomas's poetry, even his own life's work caring for dumb animals: horses, dairy cows, bees, pigs, chickens, and, indirectly, men.

He glanced at the boy, feeling guilty, as if the child were his judge. "Never mind," he said aloud. He thought of a phrase Estelle Parks used, one of Sally's friends: "Very fragile, this world." He nodded, full of gloom. *His* world, he knew for pretty sure, was beyond fragility. Smashed. Well, tell it to the bees. Yet he listened to the wind even now, unconsciously, for some faint suggestion of articulate speech, and he glanced uneasily at the ceiling again, imagining his sister asleep, sunk into an absolute loneliness like death, just short of oblivion, molested by dreams.

He was reminded of his wife, then of her tombstone, down in the village cemetery, glossy. "Oh James, James," she would say to him. He sighed. His anger was foolishness, tonight as always. All life was foolishness, a witless bear exploring, poking through woods. He couldn't remember very well how his wife had looked when they were young. Even when he studied the picture album—a thing he rarely did—it was no help. He remembered one single moment—picking her

13

up in his buggy one afternoon; an instant of emotion like a snapshot. The air had been yellow.

He gazed into the fire, hunting some sharper recollection in its flickering light.

Concerning his sister, as it happened, the old man was wrong. She had paused above the table beside the bed, weeping hot, pinkish tears of indignation and spite, planning out her definite and terrible revenge—she was a demon for revenge, he ought to know that by now—and happening to look down when she'd just rubbed the tears away, pushing her hankie past the bottoms of her blue plastic spectacles to her eyes, she had noticed on the floor below the table, and had bent down to pick up for closer inspection, a dog-eared paperback with what looked to be pinpricks or possibly tooth-prints and ugly bits of grit and dark stain on the cover—coffee grounds, or maybe wet-and-then-later-dried-out bits of oat-grist. It was torn half to pieces, as if it had been run over, and the binding glue was weakened so that the pages were loose and great chunks of the story were fallen away. It was probably one of her niece's books, the boy's mother's, she supposed—though why the girl had saved it, ruin that it was, only the good Lord knew. Anyway this was where the niece had fixed her make-up, before leaving for her meeting—little Dickey watching her, promising to be good—and it was the kind of book that girl *would* read, no doubt: common drugstore trash, you could tell by the cover. *The Smugglers of Lost Souls' Rock,* it said, and above the title, in big white letters: *"A Black-comic Blockbuster"*—L. A. Times.

She turned the book over, clamping it tightly to keep the pages in, brushed futilely at a stain, then squinted, reading what it said in red letters on the back.

"Blows the lid off marijuana smuggling, fashionable gang-bangs, and the much-sentimentalized world of the middle-aged Flower Child. A sick book, as sick and evil as life in America . . ."
—National Observer

She lowered the book, then half-absentmindedly raised it once more to reading range, her hands still trembly—the book was so dried out and bleached and cheap it was lighter than nothing—and opened it indifferently to "Chapter 1." Lips puckered with distaste, brushing away dirt with the side of her hand, she read a sentence, then another. The print swam and blurred and the sense drifted up through her brain like smoke. She tipped up her blue plastic spectacles again and dabbed at her eyes with her hankie. She had, of course, no intention of reading a book that she knew in advance to be not all there; but on the other hand here she was, locked up like a prisoner, without even her sewing to occupy her mind (it was down on the table by the ruined TV). Forgetting herself, almost unaware that she was doing it, she eased down onto the bedspread and went back to the beginning. She let her mind empty, drift like a balloon, as she would when she sat down to television. She read:

1

THE DROWNED MAN

"Snuff it, baby," he'd hissed at the world, but the world dragged on.

After thirty-three years of insipid debauchery—balling and whiskey and dreary books (poetry and novels, philosophy and science), more foreign ports than he could now remember and, between them, endless weeks at sea, where he shoveled his head fuller yet with books —Peter Wagner had come to the end of his rope or, rather (this time), the center of his bridge. All life, he had come to understand, was a boring novel. Death would be boring too, no doubt, but you weren't required to pay attention.

"Isn't it the truth!" Sally Abbott said aloud, head lifting as if someone had spoken to her. Why she said it she could hardly have told you—except that it was something she'd occasionally said to her late husband Horace when he'd read to her, years and years ago. The truth in the novel she was looking at now was a trivial one at best, she was partly aware—even downright silly. But she wasn't thinking with any care just now. She wasn't really thinking at all, in fact, merely hovering between fury at her brother and escape into the book. Edging back toward fury, she held her breath and listened past the ticking of the clock for some sound from downstairs. Everything was silent—from outside the house not a cluck, not a whinny, not the grunt of a pig, and from the living room below, not a murmur. James was no doubt reading some magazine, little Dickey fast asleep. Heartless, both of them. She sighed bitterly, glanced down with distaste at the paperback book, then raised it again into reading range.

His death was to be a grand act, however senseless. He'd drop without a sound through pitch-dark night to be swallowed by the Old Symbolic Sea. He'd read the grisly tales—suicides gruesomely, foolishly impaled on the radar antennae of passing ships or splattered obscenely on pilings or rocks—and had planned ahead. He had examined the span by daylight and had marked his spot with an unobtrusive X in light green paint. Now the hour was at hand, in a sense the toughest of his life. He was extremely drunk

16

and had to walk the bridge three times to find his X. By the time he found it, there were red and yellow lights flashing on and off at both ends of the bridge—they had found his car—and the suicide squad had its sirens going. He climbed over the rail where the X was and hung there waiting for the squad cars to pass. They didn't. They too knew the perfect place. For a panicky second, he thought of dropping immediately, but good sense prevailed, as it always did with him, or he wouldn't be here committing suicide. What could they do when they saw him there, hanging by his fingertips? Shoot him?

"Ha," Sally laughed, tentatively amused. But she at once changed her mind. It wasn't funny, it was irritating, and again she raised her eyes, listening past the clock, focusing on a door panel, lips pursed. She had half a mind to throw down the book and forget it, half a mind even to throw it out the window, where it couldn't contaminate her bedroom. It was base, unwholesome. That nonsense, especially about suicide proving a man's "good sense." People might say such stupid, irresponsible writing did no harm, but you could bet your bottom dollar, no one who'd experienced the tragedy of the suicide of someone near and dear would ever in this world dream of saying such a thing. If anyone had dared even hint such a notion, back when Richard had died, a man still young, everything still ahead of him—a young man so gentle that it simply broke your heart—well, she hated to think what she'd have done to him.

Her heart churned and for an instant she remembered how everywhere she'd looked, just after her nephew had taken his own life, the world had seemed inert, like a half-fallen, long-abandoned barn on a still, cold day. She remembered the feeling, though not the details, of how she'd flown up the mountain in her late husband's Buick, after James had phoned, and how he'd stood in the doorway stunned to vagueness. When she'd reached to take his hand—trying to protect him as she'd done when they were children, she the big sister and he the poor helpless little boy with darting eyes—she'd been painfully aware of how cold the hand was, and rough from farmwork, unresponsive. Ariah, his wife, was behind him in the kitchen, watching from the sink, moving the dishcloth around and around a cup, in her cheeks no life.

"He hanged himself," Ariah said; then her throat constricted and she could say no more.

Sally had looked back at her brother and moaned, "Oh, James!", tightening her grip on his hand. There was no response.

She gave her head a little shake now, freeing herself from the flicker of memory—enemy to her perfectly reasonable anger at her brother's insane and savage ways. She at once raised the book. She'd been making a mountain of a molehill, no doubt. She'd never liked loose talk of suicide; but it wasn't as if the book was in earnest. She was on edge, that was all, and who could blame her? She hunted for her place.

. . . sense prevailed, as it always did with him, or he wouldn't be here committing . . .
. . . do when they saw him there, hanging by his fingertips? Shoot him?

Sally Abbott nodded; that was where she'd stopped.

With the intense vision of the very drunk, he watched the door of the white car fly open and saw two booted feet hit the pavement. "There he is!" someone shouted, and the sound seemed, amusingly, to reach him from behind, from the thick night and fog. It came to him that if he were hanging from the bottom girder of the bridge, as he'd meant to be, he couldn't see the squad cars. Gripping tightly with his right hand, he let go with his left and groped for something lower. It was farther down than he would have expected, but large, with wonderful flanges. He gripped it with all his might, and lowered his right hand. He swung, or else the bridge yawed—by mathematics he could support either theory—but the grip of both hands held. He made his legs into dead weights to stop the swinging.

Sally Abbott read without commitment at first, just a hint of curiosity and a tentative willingness to perhaps be amused. But quite imperceptibly the real world lost weight and the print on the page gave way to images, an alternative reality more charged than mere life, more ghostly yet nearer, suffused with a curious importance and manageability. She began to fall in with the book's snappy rhythms, becoming herself more wry, more wearily disgusted with the world—not only with her own but with the whole "universe," as the book kept saying—a word that hadn't entered Sally's thoughts in years. Life became larger, in vibration to such words, and she, the observer and container of this universe, became necessarily more vast than its space, became indeed (though she would not have said so) godlike. By degrees, without knowing she was doing it, she gave in to the illusion, the comforting security of her vantage point, until whenever she looked up from the page to rest her eyes, it seemed that the door, the walls, the dresser, the heavy onyx clock had no more substance than a plate-glass reflection; what was real and enduring was the adventure flickering on the wall of her brain, a phantom world filled with its own queer laws and character. She read—at first doubtfully, but with increasing abandon:

20

He could see all San Francisco now. It was beautiful, rising, slightly bleary, out of fog. Interestingly enough, his whole body felt limp, muscleless, yet he was hanging by, essentially, only three fingers of each hand, only two knuckles involved on each finger, or six knuckles in all, approximately. It was incredible. Also, it was incredible that they'd found his car so quickly. Civilization was a marvelous thing. He thought of the Babylonians, the Romans. "Hang on!" someone yelled. He hung on, for reasons of his own. There was great commotion now on the bridge above him.

"I'm Dr. Berg," a voice in (it seemed) the fog above and behind him said. It was a gentle voice, deeply concerned, professionally friendly. It was a veritable musical instrument, that voice. Peter Wagner in his drunkenness smiled, almost giggled. He knew by experience how such voices could sweetly groan, like cellos, seduce like double-stopped, mourning violins, suddenly lash out in anger, like a snare-drummer's rim-shots. He'd had a dozen psychiatrists, as had his wife—all excellent, capable of baffling him with terrible clarity, like a loving parent. (He was well off; a trust fund from his father's estate.) Peter Wagner was no one to disparage such skills, the virtuoso music of an accomplished brain-bender. It was mortally depressing that such voices, warm and human as an uncle's, one might have thought, were precision-built, cool scientific devices that could engage and disengage the gears of the will by precise neuro-chemical formulae, laboratory-tested and repeatedly proved "psychological strategies" that no human consciousness, even the most obdurate, could indefinitely resist (the effects of adrenocortical fluids, ureic acid, and ingested alcohol were as predictable and controllable as acid in a battery, dishearteningly dependable as the drool of a witless Russian dog at the tinkle of a bell); and it was no less mortally depressing when they "played it by ear," as they liked to say, cunningly hiding in the dark, husky center of the language of the masses —trying now this shrewd approach, now that, fishing, in this case, for some last feeble tittle of vulnerable, smashable humanity in the would-be suicide—played it, that is, not by ordinary ear but by finely tuned, educated nuance-perceptor, quicker to respond than young lovers, indifferent as transistors, chilly as dead snakes.

"I'm Dr. Berg," said the voice a second time, mellow, firm as cable, reaching down to him with calculated universal love, man to man, a voice to lean on, to depend on or from, emblem of unguessed reserves to be called upon, model for his weakness and confusion to reach up to, grasp toward: "I have survived this cesspool," called the guardian in effect, teeth clenched, eyes mild with experience overwhelmed (he had, clearly, no beautiful sister turned vegetable, no misfiring glands, no ex-Christian rage), "so can *you*, my son!"

"Hello," he said.

The voice called down: "I'm your friend. I'm a psychiatrist."

He listened to the foghorns mournfully groaning to the universe *B.O.* The sirens were still going, and he couldn't tell where, in the blackness below his dangling shoes, the ships were. His fingers, though he couldn't feel them, were like steel. He tipped back his head to look up (he was unable—because of the bunched-up shoulders of his overcoat—to look down or anywhere else except level-and-straight-ahead, like a horse in blinders, sometimes called blinkers, or, laboriously, up). Among the bridge-lights, drifting double images to his eyes' dis-focus, there floated a mushroom-white, bearded face with a hat. "Tell them to turn off the sirens," he called.

"Turn off the sirens," Dr. Berg said, softly fulminant, basso profundo.

Despite the rolling, ruminating fog, the night was suddenly still, it seemed to him: majestically peaceful. It was as if, exploding outward to the farthest, filtered star, the invisible edge of the ocean horizon, he had himself become— had mysteriously subsumed—the night, containing it like a bell-jar. Call it enlightenment, subject and object in perfect interpenetration. The colored lights of San Francisco, stretching for miles, bloomed vaguely in the fog like emotions lost, or here and there cut sharply through open air like a few childhood Christmases. Far, far ahead of him and slightly to his right, a huge scrawl of neon that he couldn't read, though he remembered it faintly, went on and off, and he was aware all at once of the distance he must fall, the distance he had come, the magnitude of things, God's grandeur. He was alarmed from the tips of his fingers to his toes: miracles on every hand, seagulls and the brilliance of squadcar lights, the stability of steel, the intense physicality of fog-swirled space, space he would penetrate in a moment, probably with a yell. The world was a magnificent, mysterious thing, thrilling as a dance on a volcano rim, charged with unspeakable, unnameable powers that rose up out of earth and came plummeting from the night, invisibly colliding and exploding all around him, rushing, inaudibly roaring, to the ends of the universe. He was the center of it, hanging by six knuckles from his girder, high priest and sacrifice, objective and dispassionate, churning with emotion (*ah!, air, pride, plume*), ultimate perceptor of cosmic nuances, core of "the *ambiance*."

23

Directly underneath him, a foghorn loud as an earthquake exploded from the watery stillness, startling him so badly that he almost lost his grip.

"Listen," Dr. Berg said. "You can let go any time you want to, but until you do I want you to listen. Will you?"

Oh yes, life's guardian, light of my darkness, clarity to my miserable soul's confusion, he was on the point of saying, drunkenly giggling as he thought of it, but he caught himself in time. It would give Berg a clue. ("Ah, you're an intellectual, a student of books!" the man would say.) It was one of life's mortally discouraging facts that if a psychiatrist understood you, he could beat you. "Yes sir," he said.

"Can you hang on?" Berg said.

"Pretty drunk," he said.

"Let me hang onto your hands."

He smiled, drunkenly malevolent, at San Francisco. "Yes, good." He could feel the big ship sliding past underneath him. Another foghorn, higher in pitch, was coming in from his right. Berg's hands came around his wrists, gentle as a fairy's, and clamped on. No, he realized then, not Berg's. Leather-gloved.

"You tricked me," he said. It came out badly and he tried again. The leather gloves began pulling at him and he clamped his knees under the bridge.

"The shithead's got hold of something with his legs," the policeman said. "Lend a hand."

Some more gloves came. He smiled. "I lift weights," he said carefully and slowly. To himself, at least, he sounded sober as a judge.

"Also, he's psychotic," Dr. Berg said. "They have amazing strength. You can tell he's psychotic by his eyes. Look." He pointed down. "He's got eyes like a couple of vaginas."

Peter Wagner pursed his lips, deeply offended, his anger rising. It was not so much the slur against his eyes, though that was outrageous, in fact. He had beautiful eyes. He'd been told it a thousand times, in a thousand ports, and it was true: his eyes were otherworldly, they had mysterious glints and depths, odd shadows, the stillnes of clear, dark pools in a German forest. To describe them as Dr. Berg had done was tasteless, blasphemous. But what offended him most was the slovenly diagnosis. It was shoddy medicine, such practice as the world had left over for the poor and dispossessed—the weeping mad maiden in her upstairs room, the whiskered drunk in his Fillmore Street gutter, the sixteen-year-old black bow-legged whore. To calm his wrath and stall for time, he yelled, "Purity of heart is to will one thing!"

Sally Abbott stopped a moment, touching her lower lip with one finger, and read the line again. *Purity of heart is to will one thing.* In her mind's eye she saw silent, gray-bearded uncle Ira, a small, solid creature with animal eyes, an axe on one shoulder, on the other a gun. He stood for her memory as for a photograph, a picture in what would by this time be some discoloring old album, his snowshoes brown against the yellow, dead snow. He came out of the past like a creature from the woods, his reluctance and strangeness absolute, hostile; and beside him now stood her brother James in a lumberman's cap, long coat and snowshoes—James who had loved him, in a way even worshipped him, unless perhaps, as her husband had suspected, it was an unwitting trick James had played on himself, twisting fear of the man to intense admiration as little Dickey sometimes did (so it seemed to the old woman) struggling to pacify this older James.

"Grampa," little Dickey had whined to him once, his breath steaming in the deep-winter cold. (She had watched it all from the back-room window.) The old man ignored him, and the boy touched his sleeve, cautious as a city man reaching toward a horse. "Grampa, what does it mean when you say 'cold as a cane'?"

"Kind of hail," her brother answered, pushing him back out of the way of his axe, "sticks instead of stones. Coldest thing there be." He would say no more, miserly with words as with everything else. James, chopping wood, had only thin wool gloves on.

Dickey said, after a reasonable wait, "What's pussley broth?"

"Nubbidy knows." He gauged his stroke, squinting, and brought the axe down hard. He was splitting blocks of elm. Only two weeks in a year was it cold enough for elm-splitting. Most people said you couldn't split elm at all. "Trick to 't," he'd say, and would say no more.

Dickey said, "Grampa, what's 'tunkit' mean?" He danced to warm his feet.

The axe came down again, clean as the sound of a stone against a stone—it was twenty below zero—and the block fell apart as if opened by a spell. He brought the axe away, looking with self-satisfaction and casual ferocity at the boy. "Why do pigs sleep in trees?" he said.

Her brother was more like their mad uncle Ira than he knew, she'd mused. It was not a thing she planned to mention to him. He'd be flattered and maybe turn still meaner.

"Boy, go inside where it's wahm," James said, pointing with the axe.

"I ain't cold," Dickey said. He continued dancing, steam all around him, his mittened hands tucked inside his armpits.

"The hell you ain't, boy," the old man snapped, chaining him there by the pride in his voice. She had turned from the window, disgusted.

To will one thing.

She looked back at her novel—or rather, began to

pay attention again, since while her mind had wandered her eyes had gone on reading, dutifully moving
from word to word like well-trained horses through a
haylot. She drew them back to where the sense had
stopped registering and realized with satisfaction that
Peter Wagner spoke not, as she'd thought at first, in
earnest, but in anger and scorn, taunting the psychiatrist, taunting all the stiff, self-righteous world. Again
she saw him dangling in his overcoat, below him
churning fog and San Francisco's colored lights. She
imagined the psychiatrist, at the rail above, with baggy-
lidded eyes, the policemen like storm-troopers in a
World War II movie.

"Get the rope," someone said.
Looking down at the fog, insofar as he could,
was like looking at clouds from above.
"That's from Kierkegaard," Dr. Berg said
with sugary interest.
"You're an intellectual," he said.
A rope came down, with a grapnel on the
end, and they fumbled it toward him. He broke
free with his left hand, hanging only with his
right, and Dr. Berg said, "Lay off," then whispered, "Let me talk to him." Dr. Berg said,
"You think I don't know about suffering?
You're suffering."
"It's true. Christ." It was not true, except that
his fingers had lost their numbness and his
knuckles were in pain.
"You feel as if all life's a waste. You've read
the philosophers—hungry, hungry—and nobody's got a real answer. You're practically an
authority on existentialism, *absurdism!*" He
carefully spoke French.
"Christ, yes."
"Love is an illusion. Hope is the opiate of the
people. Faith is pure stupidity. That's how you
feel."

"Yes," he said. "Yes."

"Let him drop," Dr. Berg said coldly.

The gloved hands let loose but he hung on.

"Is there a ship underneath me?" he asked.

Berg laughed. "You're testing me, friend. You're a very complex person."

"Is there?" he said.

"No. Not right now."

"You're a very complex person too. If you can't win, you want me smashed on some fucking ship." He looked up and the mushroom face smiled.

"That may be true," Dr. Berg said. "It puts you in kind of a bind, doesn't it? You're too drunk to tell if there's a ship underneath you, and since I'm a professional psychiatrist, with a certain inevitable ego-involvement in the work I do, maybe I'd rather see you smashed on a ship than gently sucked out by the ocean if I've got to lose."

"That's true," he said. He began to cry, carefully listening to the foghorns. "The whole modern world is a catastrophe for the individual psyche. I've tried everything—love, drugs, whiskey, withdrawal to the Old Symbolic Sea, but everywhere I turn falsehood, illusion. I want to die." He glanced quickly at Dr. Berg, then down again. "Waaa!" he bawled.

"I know how you feel," Dr. Berg said, vastly gentle. "You think I haven't felt it? Listen. I'm married. A sweet, good wife, three sweet, good children. You think I'm ignorant of despair?"

"Where have we gone wrong?"

"That's what Tolstoy asked himself."

They had cars going over the bridge again now. It seemed a little unfeeling. How could they know Peter Wagner was not that poor mad weeping maiden, or the bow-legged prostitute, hardly more than a child? Yet all life is compromise, of course. The mail must get through, and the groceries; almonds to San Diego, squash to Pasadena. *God bless, God bless.* His father had made his fortune in sugar beets. A splendid man; frail and coughing, those last few years, but optimistic to the end. His rural background. "Europeans," he said, "know how to live. We're mites by comparison to the wise old Europeans." Everything he said was true, always, for the moment at least. Peter Wagner's respect for his father was boundless, his admiration downright religious, though he agreed with him in nothing. "Between them, big government and the unions are ruining this country," his father said, "and a few unscrupulous big businesses." It was not that what his father said was untrue; it was merely tiresome, like great art forever staring ga-ga at the black abyss. "Drink up, Andrew," his mother would say. That too was a tiresome philosophy. His uncle Morton had a book, which he was unable to get published, about "the great Negro-Jewish conspiracy." The rest of his childhood, so far as he could remember, had been bird-baths and elm trees and lawns. Sometimes at parties, to his horror, his stepmother spoke French.

"*Doesn't* it?" Dr. Berg asked sharply.

He realized his mind had been wandering. He wondered if arthritis was the feeling in his knuckles now. He called up, "If despair is the meaning of life, a man should seize it, clutch it like a god!" He felt his overcoat ripping at the armpits.

"That's true," Dr. Berg said. "Or anyway, it's as true as anything else. So drop."

"You're a very complex person," he said. "You make it extremely difficult for a man to drop." He felt openness below him. Another ship was moving in. A small one. Half a mile away there was a blurry searchlight, a Coast Guard cutter. Ah, civilization! Swift, swift! The cutter came on with incredible speed. It was too late already. He hung on. He said: "Death is as meaningless as life. You agree, Dr. Berg?"

"Of course. So what else? Listen. Come talk with me in my office. If you convince me that suicide is the only way, I won't prevent you. You believe me?"

"I do, I do!"

"Then let us pull you up."

"I don't want to."

"Then drop." He saw his mistake instantly. The ship had passed and the water below was clear. "Grab him!"

He dropped. The beautiful lights of San Francisco hung level for a time then sank upward, slowly, slowly. The rush of wind sucked his breath out. He fell and fell.

Aboard the *Indomitable*, Mr. Goodman turned with a jerk. "Man overboard!" he yelled, though it was not quite fitting. Whatever it was that fell, six inches from the larboard bow, went down like a boulder, throwing almost no splash. *Choong*, it went, and he yelled, "Full speed backwards!" A strange command. "You're crazy," Mr. Nit hissed. "If the Captain hears—" "It was a man," Mr. Goodman said. "I saw it." It wasn't quite true. He knew it was a man; he saw nothing, merely heard it come screaming like a bomb. The boat jerked and shuddered, then backed up as Jane reversed the engine. "There!" Mr. Goodman yelled. Jane cut the engine and the *Indomitable* was silent except for the trickle of a few small leaks.

"Jesus," Mr. Nit said, and glanced back at where the Captain would emerge if he emerged. But he could see the thing floating, sweeping out to sea, and, in his confusion, he threw a line to it. The Coast Guard cutter was turning, coming back. "Jesus," he said again. The *Indomitable* was loaded to the gunnels with marijuana.

"Switch off the lights," Mr. Goodman said.

"Switch off the lights," Mr. Nit called. The lights went off. The cutter crossed to starboard, the wrong side. Mr. Goodman had his shoes off now. He snapped back the rope and dived. He thrashed in the water, blind as one of Mr. Nit's eels, and in three, four minutes, absurdly, he found the body. It was certainly dead, but he clutched it by the hair and yelled, "Pull the rope!"

Mr. Nit was already pulling, though in the cacophony of foghorns and shouts from the bridge he heard nothing. Mr. Goodman, with the corpse, came up to the hull and understood that Mr. Nit could not pull them both up— could hardly have pulled up one of them alone, since Mr. Nit was a tiny man, fragile and quick as a monkey but no more substantial. Mr. Goodman looped the rope around the drowned man's waist, then shinnied. When he reached the rail he dug in and hauled. The drowned man came over the side; still no sign of the Captain.

"Jesus," Mr. Nit said.

Mr. Goodman lay down on the deck, panting like a whale.

"Jesus," Mr. Nit said, "what do we do with him now?"

"He's a human being," Mr. Goodman gasped. "We couldn't just let him die."

The Coast Guard cutter had passed and was circling back.

"Terrific," said Mr. Nit. "Human being. Terrific."

He did not look like one, it was true. His suit, striped shirt and tie were unsightly, and his shoes had come off. His hair hung over his face like seaweed, and whenever you moved him or pushed down on his stomach—neither Mr. Goodman nor Mr. Nit had had lessons in artificial respiration, though they were doing their best—water came out of him like juice from an overripe pumpkin. He looked like one of those pictures called *Descent from the Cross* (Mr. Goodman had once been a museum guard).

"Is he breathing yet?" Mr. Nit asked anxiously of Mr. Goodman's ear.

Mr. Goodman pushed hard on the stomach again. "Not that I can see."

Mr. Nit leaned still closer. "That cutter's coming right up our asshole, Jack."

Mr. Goodman sighed, pushed up from the body, hunching his shoulders in the cold wet salt-smelly shirt, and seized the drowned man's feet. "We better get him out of sight," he said. "Grab hold."

Mr. Nit grabbed hold and they rolled him into the fish hatch with the pot. "Now let's get out of here," said Mr. Goodman.

The cutter horn boomed and Mr. Nit jumped like a rabbit. "Yes sir," he said, as if the horn had spoken English, and he yelled, "Full speed frontwards!"

The *Indomitable* churned up white water a moment, then moved. The cutter's searchlight came over them like the eye of God—the cutter looked a mile long—and a man on the cutter yelled down at them through a bullhorn. *Rowrrrowrrow!*

"Yes sir!" Mr. Nit yelled, cupping his hands. "Yes sir! Sorry sir!"

"Get the lights back on," said Mr. Goodman.

"Lights!" yelled Mr. Nit.

They came on.

The bullhorn growled again, something about a drowning man. Mr. Nit and Mr. Goodman cupped their hands and yelled: "No sign of him. We been looking." The *Indomitable* was now running full speed ahead, bobbing up and down in the sea's heavy waves like a fisherman's cork; the cutter was standing still, the white eye of God staring after them as if baffled and slightly hurt. Mr. Nit and Mr. Goodman continued yelling until fog blanked out even the searchlight.

And now, riding easy in the quiet of the bay, bobbing more gently, the engine no longer groaning in spasms as it did in the waves of the open Pacific, the *Indomitable* slowed and Mr. Goodman struggled to figure out his bearings. He made out at last the on-off-on flashing of the beer sign.

"Christ," said Mr. Nit, "what'd we have done if the Captain come up, back there?"

They both turned at once. The Captain came out in his old black coat and his old black hat, his face greenish white from his sea-sickness. He steadied himself on the rail and inched toward them. He was barefoot, like the drowned man, and the crotch of his pants hung low. He was whiskered and bruised like one of those bums on Third Street. He had long white hair.

"What's going on?" he said.

"Drowned man, sir," Mr. Goodman said. "We pulled him aboard."

The old man's eyes widened and his lips sucked in and he decided not to believe it.

"It's true, sir," Mr. Nit said. "He was a human being, sir."

Captain Fist leaned over the rail and vomited. Then, turning as slowly as a ship, he went back to his cabin and to bed.

Half an hour later, after they'd docked, Mr. Nit and Mr. Goodman dragged the body from the fish hatch, scraped off the marijuana, and, failing to notice that it was breathing already, though fast asleep and possibly unconscious, tried to revive it. Jane came from the wheel to help, slipping off her glasses as she came. She was pretty, but rugged as a saw. "Jesus Christ," she said, and pushed them away. She pulled the drowned man's tongue out and sat down on his belly. About a spoonful of water came dribbling from his mouth. She pumped on his belly with her buttocks and moved his elbows up down and like wings. "It's useless," she said. "He's been like this for an hour by now." Nevertheless, she went on pumping. Mr. Nit and Mr. Goodman squatted beside her, watching, and after a long time the drowned man groaned. She put her mouth over his.

When Peter Wagner opened his eyes it was the story of his life. By habit, he closed his arms around her and returned the kiss. She seemed surprised, and struggled. He humped upward a little and her pelvis moved down to meet his. He remembered the bridge then, and his eyes came wide open. Beyond the girl he could make out two men, hunched down, one broad-chested and sad of face, with arms like a boxer's, a mouth oddly meek, the other small as a boy, with an axe-shaped head and the eyes of a coyote. In the greenish-yellow light behind them stood a man with an old black overcoat reaching to his shoetops and, on his shaggy, snow-white head, a wide-brimmed hat. His heavily knuckled hand leaned hard on a cane. Peter Wagner pulled his mouth away and the girl straightened up.

"Well," she said, "he's alive," and she swung up off him and put on her glasses.

It was the wrong thing to say. He jerked up, groping with his hands and feet, and made for the rail. Without expression, the old man brought up his cane and then brought it down. It felt like being clubbed by a baseball bat. He saw stars; then he saw nothing.

2
ALKAHEST'S CONVERSION

John F. Alkahest, sitting in his wheelchair

The old woman lowered the book to her lap, wondering, half-unconsciously, whether or not she was in a mood to continue. She was finding the story at least mildly interesting—certain little oddities of attitude and style awakened in her mind brief flickers of satisfaction. But even for an old woman imprisoned in her bedroom by a lunatic, there was no denying it was a waste of time, and since she knew in advance that there were pages fallen out—for all she knew, whole chapters might be lost—it was a more or less serious question. Yet it was not exactly in those terms that she framed it.

"That's what we're down to," she said half aloud, as if to someone in the room. She was thinking how, when Horace was alive, they'd sometimes gone down to New York City to some play by William Shakespeare. She remembered the city lights, the crowded sidewalks, the sudden excitement of entering the theater, stepping abruptly into a whole new world—new qualities of sound, red seas of carpet, red, velvet-covered chains on brass posts, the people all dressed in their finest. She thought of that moment, just after the lights dimmed, when the outer curtain rose, lifting like the skirt of a curtsying grand lady, and then the

36

second swept away, and there stood the set, unreal, magnificent, a lure to an even more magical kingdom where unreal creatures in spangled, bright clothes walked their stylized walks, making stylized gestures, faces brightly painted like the faces of dolls, intoning in a language never spoken by men,

> Now, fair Hippolyta, our nuptial hour
> Draws on apace; four happy days . . .

Sometimes, in the years since Horace's death, she'd gone down to the city with her friend Estelle, and though it wasn't quite the same, it was thrilling nonetheless, that magical step into a world all sharp color and high sentiment. How paltry these modern novels were, compared to that!

And yet it was not merely the excitement of the stage. What could be more humble—more ridiculous, even—than her friend the village librarian, Ruth Thomas, sitting on a milkstool behind her husband's cows, reading to him and to his hired men stories out of Edgar Allan Poe or Wilkie Collins? Sally had not heard it, actually, had only heard Ed Thomas speak of it, and sometimes Ruth; yet she had no doubt that the excitement was nearly the same. As he moved like a thoughtful bear from cow to cow (Ruth loved speaking of her husband as a bear, mimicking him as she did so, looking far more like a bear than he did, since she was large and lumbering), Ruth would read expressively, casting her voice above the milking-machine noise, and if he missed something Ed would call, "What? What?" and she would read the line again. So Horace, long ago, had frequently read to Sally Abbott. They had meant something then, works of literature. The world had been younger, feelings had run deep.

Yet even as she thought it, she doubted that it was true. With sudden vehemence and grief, she thought: Books have no effect at all, no value whatsoever.

Horace had been a voracious reader, as well as a lover of music and art. One might have supposed that it was there he had found his serenity and wisdom—

for nothing could ruffle him except, occasionally, her brother. But Richard too, Horace's nephew and all but son—certainly as dear to them both as a son could have been—Richard too had been a lover of books and good music. Shakespeare and Mozart and the rest had not saved him. With grim purpose, alone in the house where his parents had first lived, he'd drunk himself indifferent and gone up to the attic . . .

The old woman sighed, her mind flinching back to the commonplace. Where was Ginny?

It was an embarrassment to think of her niece at her Lodge meeting, sitting in a kind of imitation throne, with a satiny, sashlike thing slanting from one shoulder, speaking to her "sisters" in stylized mumbo-jumbo, making stylized gestures, exactly like characters in some tedious play without a story. It was all, in the old woman's opinion, shamefully low-class, artificial. In her mind's eye she saw them seated in their get-ups, prim in wooden folding chairs all around the room, the middle of the room left empty so that three or four of them—no doubt Ginny among them—could parade with their Christmasy dark blue and scarlet flags: pudgy, fat-hipped women moving carefully in step, furtively glancing left and right to stay in line, imitation soldiers on the march to God knew what. The very thought sickened her. Yet how much of life came down to that, really—mere dress-up, ridiculous make-believe!

She sighed again, more shallowly this time, her reverie drifting toward a sensitive place. Everyone was guilty, of course. (Now the old woman was safe again, though her expression was sad.) Even Horace, she thought, evading the tedium of life, the plainness and ultimately, hopelessness of it all, playing *Swan Lake* on his office phonograph while he picked at decaying teeth. Even she, Sally Page Abbott herself, drifting through this novel full of clever, weary talk—

Where have we gone wrong?

That's what Tolstoy asked himself.

—Tolstoy indeed!

It was covering, all covering, mere bright paint over

38

rotting barn walls. It was perhaps that that her nephew had realized, that night.

She remembered with a pang the annual Bennington Antiques Festival, where she'd first seen Richard with the Flynn girl. One single image came into her mind, and the emotion, dimmed by years but still sharp, that went with it. It was August, the time when all through Vermont every village had its fair, in those days, its battery of church suppers, its evening band concerts and firemen's demonstrations. It was a time of almost daily celebration of high summer and the beginnings of the harvest, one last communal fling before September, when the harvest came in earnest—apples, corn, pumpkins—and with it increasing signs of autumn, and then locking time, and then winter. She and Horace, that year, had taken Richard and Ginny—he was seventeen, Ginny perhaps ten, both of them golden-haired as angels and both full of life, always laughing and romping. The children had gone through the rooms of exhibits and the temporary shops with only casual interest, even Richard too young to understand the importance and beauty of old tables and lamps, wooden plows, old paintings that represented actual scenes of Vermont life seventy years ago; and while she and Horace lingered over hand-painted dishes and Bennington pottery, Ginny and Richard had gone on out to the lawn where there were games in progress and where, unbeknownst to Sally Abbott, the Flynn girl stood watching, heart fluttering, for Richard. When she and Horace emerged, arms loaded with packages—and this was the image that remained in Sally's mind—Richard and the Flynn girl were on the bright green slope that dropped gently toward the brook, holding hands and swinging each other around and around in a kind of wild primaeval dance. She had on a white dress, and her red hair was flying. Behind them stood pines and the dark greenish blue of Mount Anthony. Ginny looked up as she and Horace came out, her expression slightly furtive, knowing. "Richard's in love," she said. Her smile was

39

proud, proprietary, as if perhaps she herself had arranged it.

They stood still, looking; and after a moment Horace said, "With the Flynn girl?" He spoke as if bemused.

They'd been surprised to discover, the next instant, how fully little Ginny understood the implications. "Daddy doesn't know," she said.

"Would he mind?" Horace asked—disingenuous.

"She's Irish," Ginny said, and smiled again.

Horace had showed nothing. Sally had looked thoughtfully at her niece, not quite sure what her own feelings were, though part of what she felt was, of course, distress. To Ginny, clearly, it was all just delightful; and Sally had mused, half-unconsciously: how easily nature overwhelms stiff opinions, dead theories. Horace said, his nearly bald head tipped, his suitcoat bunched up from when he'd lifted the armful of packages, his mild eyes gazing past his load at the pair on the slope: "Well, well! Irish, you say!"

They'd stopped whirling now and stood laughing, still holding hands. Then Richard looked up and saw them and waved. After a moment the Flynn girl waved too. It took courage, knowing Richard, but he came up toward them, leading her, still holding her hand. He introduced her, stumbling on her queer old Gaelic name and blushing. She too blushed, so that the freckles were hidden for a moment, eclipsed. Horace bowed formally, exactly as he would if he were meeting a new patient, someone he wished to assure of his care and respect. He was shorter than the girl. Her beauty made him seem a mere dandy.

When they were in the car, later, starting for home, Richard watched, trying not to make it too obvious, until the bright orange hair and white dress were out of sight behind the trees.

Then Ginny said, looking up at Sally, "Isn't she *pretty*?"

"She's beautiful," Sally said. She studied Richard's face, smiling to herself. She added, "Don't you think so, Horace?"

40

He seemed lost in thought, his soft hands closed firmly on the steering wheel, his head still drawn back and tilted. She knew pretty well what was going through his mind. It wasn't good to intrude in another man's family affairs; but also young people had a right to fall in love as they pleased. It was the most obvious of all lessons of history. "A very nice girl, I thought," he said.

It was true, they'd learned as they later came to know her. She was a joy and a delight, gentle and quick-witted, passionate, full of fun—though she also had a temper, and when she chose to, she knew how to sulk. They had valued her none the less for it. If she dared to contend with James L. Page, she'd need all her weaponry. Little by little Sally and Horace Abbott had become implicated in the lovers' schemes. Sally, for one, hadn't minded. She would do it again.

She looked down at the book, staring through it, still gazing at that elegant dance on the lawn, the Flynn girl's red hair flying. No, not a dance, she corrected herself, feeling sudden irritation: the natural exuberance of young people in love.

But it was also a dance. An artifice. An illusion. She half closed her eyes, studying the image more critically, watching the stylized gestures, listening to the voices.

It was a curious reverie, Sally Abbott realized, awakening with a start. It was as vivid in her mind as the pictures that rose when she was reading the book—and probably not much more true to life. But what was strangest about it, she realized now that she'd noticed what she'd been thinking—what sadness she'd been savoring—was that the thought, the whole mood, was so unlike her. She'd always been an optimist, a person who enjoyed life. She was never one to brood: she cleaned house, cooked meals, took hold of things firmly and did her best with them. Why these doubts of the obvious, this ugly cynicism? It was an effect of the novel, she had to suppose. An unhealthy effect, no question about it!

No question about it, she thought again, but her

41

fingers were trembling. Sally Page Abbott had been a handsome woman once, well married and well off, wonderfully proud of her nephew and niece, though sorry, of course, to have no children of her own. When she looked around her now . . . She glanced away from the page, then back, snatching a little breath.

She was staring at the print, and it came clear to her that she did intend to go on reading, merely to pass the time—merely to escape the stupidity, the dreariness, the waste of things. Never mind how foolish the book might be, how artificial. Her niece's meetings were right, in the end. Mumbo-jumbo; flags. By all means, throw up a screen! Sing hymns! Speak verse!

She glanced in annoyance at the light above the bed, soft, overshaded, then at the ceiling globe, hardly brighter. They'd certainly never been designed for reading. She could do as well lighting up the kerosene lamp on the commode.

She thought, for some reason, of James' wife Ariah, pretty-faced and witless, dead now for years—a kind of cancer. The whole house, this house in which Sally had grown up, bore yet the stamp of Ariah's sweet, soft character. She remembered her putting up lace curtains in bright sunlight, singing. "You have a lovely voice," Horace had said. He'd always been especially polite to ladies. It had to do, partly, with his dentistry work. Ever after that time, whenever Sally and Horace had come up to visit, Ariah had found reason to sing to herself. It was annoying.

The old woman returned, somewhat abruptly, to her book.

2
ALKAHEST'S CONVERSION

John F. Alkahest, sitting in his wheelchair at
the polished rail of the Coast Guard cutter,
peered down through his opera glasses at the
fishingboat below. The whole evening had made
his heart race—it was his first ride on a Coast
Guard cutter—but this was beyond his wildest
dreams. The word *suicide* had shogged through
the night, and now Guardsmen, pumping elegant, animal muscles, chins poking forward
with glorious intent, hurried back and forth,
prepared for self-sacrifice and wide heroic gesture, though mostly they had nothing to do.
John Alkahest was not a Guardsman but a medical doctor—an ex-brain-surgeon, who had had,
in his day, an excellent reputation. He was now
eighty-three. Several things stood out about
him. First, he was paraplegic. He'd been in a
wheelchair since the age of nine, when his
father, disordered by a tumor and hard to live
with in any case, had shot him in the back. Second, he looked like a man dressed as Death for
some macabre party. His head was like a skull,
as white and devoid of sheen as chalk, and his
hands were so ashen you'd have sworn he carried in his vessels not blood but formaldehyde.
Along with the paleness went a curious hyper-
sensitivity, a gift for precise sensory definition
highly unusual in elderly persons: he was—as
he sometimes remarked himself—like one of
those characters in gothic tales who could hear
a dead woman's shroud rustle many rooms
away. He had a nose more delicate than a hunt-

43

ing dog's, and his sense of touch was extraordinary. Only his sense of sight was inferior. His glasses were thick, a smoky yellow-brown. And whether because of his myopia or for darker reasons, Dr. Alkahest's eyes, set deep in his head, had a glitter that even old colleagues who'd known him for years found unnerving. It was to counteract the effect of those eyes that

he smiled, whenever he remembered, his death's-head smile. He was, it goes without saying, vain. He wore dark, natty suits, funeral ties hand-made in Italy, a ruby stickpin, and, tonight, a great Austrian overcoat with a black fur collar. His motorized wheelchair was a luxury model, a Mercedes-Benz among wheelchairs: a black leather seat, silver spokes, and black leather arms. He had a handsome purple lap rug draped over his knees.

The reason for Dr. Alkahest's presence on the Coast Guard cutter was a remarkably powerful feeling he'd developed, in recent months, that his life was a pitch-black, bottomless pit devoid of all pleasure, all direction. He needed thrills, he thought; quasi-sexual thrills, the kind he'd gotten, for a while at least, after hiring his cleaning woman Pearl, who'd been raped. Though once notorious among the English set and a sometime celebrated frequenter of gay bars, old Dr. Alkahest had been inactive for years. He had lost all sense of . . .

"Drat," Sally Abbott said. There was a leaf missing, pages eleven and twelve. She looked through the other loose pages in the book, but it was lost completely. It occurred to her that maybe it was still on the floor, where she'd found the book, or had slipped under the bed. She put the book on the table, open to her place, and got out of bed to look. She bent down—still spry for all her years—and with her left hand raised the dust-ruffle. The page was not there. She straightened up again, scowling out the window toward the road.

"If you had any sense, you'd drop the silly book and get some sleep," she said, more or less to her reflection.

The trees in the front yard were motionless and dark—rather strangely dark considering that by daylight they were all in their brightest autumn foliage. Over by the fence something moved. She jumped. It was nothing, just a chicken, yet even after she'd identified the movement she was uneasy, as if like her crazy uncle Ira, long years ago, she believed an animal might be more than it seemed. She considered reading on, never mind the two pages, then decided to get into her nightie first. She started for the bathroom to wash her hands and face, and remembered only when she pulled at the knob that her brother had locked her door. She stood motionless, sudden hot anger flushing through her, then breathed deeply and drew back her hand. She needed to use the toilet, but she was a woman of stronger than average will, as her mother had been, and her grandmother; she could last all night, if necessary. And in any case, when her niece came home all this foolishness would end.

She undressed, slightly trembling, holding in her wrath, hung her dress in the closet, put her nightie on, tucked her hankie in her sleeve, put her teeth in the waterglass, and got back into bed with her book. She breathed deeply again. Still no sound downstairs. She read:

. . . two figures on the deck of the fishingboat, waving, pointing at the water. While they were still shouting, their boat began to move. Soon the searchlight picked out nothing but tumbling fog.

Then something happened. It felt at first, to Dr. Alkahest, like sunstroke, or like one of those attacks one gets sometimes when one is short of vitamins, or unduly keyed up. The canvas hoses and polished brass fittings, the studded bulkhead, the too-clean deck, the rail, the Guardsmen's uniforms, took on an intensified, unnatural "presence," in the painter's special sense—the not quite alarming but startling thereness of normal vision in early childhood. He snatched at his flask, believing he might faint, but even as he did so his refined senses closed on the delicate impression as an

ordinary man would take hold of an axe. Then,
like a violent eruption in his mind, the whole
thing came clear. It was the smell of cannabis!
It churned up out of the sea beside the ship as
if the whole belly of the world had disgorged it.
It lifted him heavenward like a scent of new-
mown hay. It brought back his childhood, his
first kiss, his Summa Cum Laude. It made him
want to sing. He made a tentative peeping noise
and, after a moment, crazed by the narcotic,
he did, in fact, sing. His head fell back, his
mouth gaped wide. *Io Pagliacci!* Sailors up near
the bow turned and looked at him. He wavered.
He bit off the note, apologetically leered. He
hummed to himself, choked off even that, fumbled with the cap of the flask, and drank. He
hummed again. He giggled, then immediately
put on a sober face. His whole reason for coming on the cutter had dropped out of his mind.
"I'm so *happy!*" he thought. He shook his head
—his hands shook too—in amazement. But
now the officer was coming toward him, looking
rather odd, and he got hold of himself in
earnest. He put away the flask. "Dee dee dee
DUM" he sang, then finally, irrevocably,
stopped himself. Even so, the scent was everywhere, that beatific smell. He could smell it
through his pores. It was incredibly like hay—
but hay transmuted, glorified, dubbed Knight.
Surely they too must notice! He'd smelled pot
before, of course, and had thought it quite
pleasant, as the smell of weeds went. But this
was something else. They must have had tons of
it aboard, those "fishermen." *God bless them,* he
thought. *God bless them every one!* To his right
and behind him, out toward the sea, foghorns
moaned, and, somewhere toward land, a bell
clinked four times. Tears filled his eyes. Pot
was in the wind! God was in his glory! What
sport for the Sons of Liberty! He wept.

The officer with the bullhorn approached him, coming slowly, sliding his hand on the rail as would a child. He seemed not quite sure what to say, if anything, about old Dr. Alkahest's behavior. The officer was a big, burly man, an Italian or Greek, but in his confusion he looked like a shy, self-conscious boy. Dr. Alkahest dabbed away tears with his hankie. He thought of mentioning the scent, then, suddenly shrewd, thought he'd wait. The officer stopped in front of the wheelchair, shook his head, leaned on the railing, thought a moment, then shook his head again. He jerked his head toward the bridge, finally, and said: "Suicide."

Dr. Alkahest nodded, then remembered to look grave.

The man shook his head. "We get hundreds of 'em off that bridge, ye know." He had a muscular face, small squinting eyes, a dimple. He pressed the bell of the bullhorn against his beer-drinker's stomach, squinting harder, and cocked his head. "You believe in flying saucers?" he asked.

"I beg your pardon?" Dr. Alkahest said. He smiled. The merest flicker.

"It all ties up," the man said. He pursed his lips, then nodded.

Dr. Alkahest tapped his fingertips soundlessly on the arms of his wheelchair. His skull eye-holes in their steel-rimmed glasses looked past the man's head into the drifting fog, and in what sounded in his own ears like a faraway voice, as if he were reciting some poem he'd learned many years ago, he said, "The sea, in its infinite gentleness, carries all things, good and evil, shit or otherwise."

The officer glanced at him.

Dr. Alkahest smiled, breathed deep. "It submits to all gods."

The officer glanced down, this time pursing his lips so hard it made his nose move.

But Dr. Alkahest smiled on, frail, fragile fingertips tapping the silver opera glasses that rested on the purple lap rug. He moved his head forward and down slowly, pursuing anfractuous questions of philosophy. He resisted with all his might the temptation to hum a little ditty, though it boomed in his head: *Have some Madeira, my dear! It's really much nicer than beer!* "I've often reflected," he said gently, thoughtfully, "that we should all of us try to be more tolerant. Close our noisy mouths and accept divergent lifestyles. After all, that's America! Truth has many faces, even changes her mind. We organize, you know, we establish splendid laws, but—" He paused, breathed more deeply, nostrils trembling. "New men will come, and not improbably with new ideas; at this very instant the causes productive of such change are strongly at work."

The officer mulled it over a moment, peering into the fog. At last he said . . .

More pages were missing. Sally Abbott looked up, listening, eyes narrowed, then sighed irritably and looked back at the book. "We're our own worst enemies," Horace had often said. (Now what on earth had brought *that* to mind?) She discovered that a line from the book was idly repeating itself in her head. *Close our noisy mouths and accept divergent lifestyles.* Horace would no doubt have agreed with that, though for reasons not quite pure. (She was no child; she could accept impurity of motivation. All of us hold back. We all "hedge our bets," as her friend Estelle's husband Ferris used to say.) As he grew into middle age —though he'd once been a talkative man—Horace had fallen more and more into the habit of silence, especially with her. When he came home from the office he'd do nothing but listen to his music and read, though perhaps inside his mind he talked endlessly to himself. Not that he'd been sullen! She'd never known a more contented man. He was quiet, merely. Men frequently grew more quiet and withdrawn as they got older. It had been the opposite with her. She'd started out a quiet one, but now in her old age she liked nothing better than a little conversation when the mailman came, or the insurance man, or when she met old friends at Powers' Market.

She could remember well how hurt she'd been at first by Horace's unwillingness to talk. She'd been jealous, in a way, and hadn't been altogether wrong to be. It had come to a head as they were speaking one night—or rather *she* was speaking—about her sister-in-law, about Ariah's cooking, actually, and about cooking in general, though what was in the back of her mind was an image of Horace wiping dishes, up at her brother's house, some weeks before, joking with Ariah and little Richard. Horace was at work tonight on his map of next year's flower garden; Sally, here in their own kitchen, did the dishes alone. Horace seemed to listen to her talk of Ariah without interest, speaking not a word. "My," she'd finally said, *"you're* certainly the quiet one tonight!" She'd put her fists on her hips, smiling hard, giving him no choice but to say something.

He went right on working with his map and colored pencils, and after a minute he said, "Are you aware that we have on this planet, or used to have, something like ten thousand languages—maybe more?"

"That's a great many," she'd said, studying him, putting up her guard.

He nodded. "Yes sir, it's the last frontier." He eyed his map, for a moment holding it away from him. "You'd think we'd all get together and try to speak one language, wouldn't you? It would improve understanding, advance the cause of peace." He glanced at her and grinned, pleased with himself, secretly remote.

50

She'd said nothing, still studying him, smelling a trap.

"Well, we never will," he'd said, shaking his head, still grinning that private, insufferable grin that wasn't meant to be understood—putting down the yellow pencil, picking up a blue one. "Children will continue to say 'I and him,' scold them all you like, and your brother will continue to say 'Here I be.' Peace and understanding—" He looked over her head, thoughtful. "That's the dilemma of democracy."

She hadn't been fooled by his fancy talk, and in a sudden flash of hurt feelings and indignation she'd lashed out, still smiling: "Why don't you just run *away* with her?"

He hadn't pretended not to know who she meant. "I never said that's what I want, Moogle." (It was one of the pet names they'd called each other.)

"Everything she makes tastes of onions," she said.

He shook his head, smiling, saying something in French. He knew she knew no French. After that he would say nothing, and gradually it came to her—it made her scalp prickle—what it was he'd meant: people had all those languages in order *not* to be understood. They were castle walls. She had cried that night, understanding that there were things about her that he did not want to know, and parts of himself he would hide from her, wall off, even if he spoke of them. She'd learned to accept it, though it was natural to be watchful and suspicious. It was at about that time that he'd begun to read aloud to her. What she thought of it she wasn't quite sure, though she'd quickly grown used to it.

She pursed her lips, eyes narrowed again, then abruptly looked down at her book. After the gap of missing pages, it continued:

. . . him that he slid down awkwardly in his chair and couldn't pull himself up.

"Doctor," the officer said.

But he waved him away, gasping with laughter, and leaned forward to say more. He had a sense that he was speaking very rapidly, though as a matter of fact an omniscient observer could have told him he was not. "I survive, of course. My cleaning woman makes little remarks—I embarrass her, no doubt. Working for a lunatic crippled pervert soils her reputation. But I survive. I can't help myself, you know. I tease people in uniforms the way monkeys climb trees, or chickens lay pigs." (There was something wrong with that, he felt at once; but the more he thought about it the better he liked it.) He'd slid practically out of his chair by now, and realizing this, he felt sudden panic. The pot smell strengthened. Then the lights all went off.

He woke up in a white, white room. A man in a white coat looked over at him and nodded to show that all was white. The officer stood leaning on the studded white doorway, his face fixed in a wince.

"This happened to you before?" the man in white said.

Dr. Alkahest stretched his eyes open wider. Hours might have passed. Days.

"You seem to have fainted," the man in white said.

"Ah," he said, growing clearer. He tried to sit up, felt faint—sickish woozy—and lay back again. He seemed to be floating above the table. The officer came over from the door, and Dr. Alkahest suddenly remembered. He asked urgently, craftily, lifting his head, "Why do you suppose those people had their lights off?"

The officer glanced at the man in white, the ship's doctor.

"The fishingboat," Dr. Alkahest explained, irritated, his old heart racing, and at last the half-wit officer understood. He sucked in his breath, puffed his cheeks out, patted his belly.

"Good question," he said. He lowered his head, squinting. "I'll tell you my theory," he said. "My theory is they must've heard him go in. *Splat!* They shined their lights around, but the fog reflected it, you know, and they saw that the lights was more harm than good, so they switched 'em off. But no luck. Gone."

"Ah," Dr. Alkahest said, and closed his eyes. But he was still unsure how much they knew. "Why do you suppose they left so suddenly—while you were still talking to them on that—" he struggled for the word, but it refused to come. He waved his hand. "That horn."

"You don't know fishermen," the officer said. He rolled his eyes heavenward and grinned.

Dr. Alkahest said nothing.

"Well," the ship's doctor said, "you get some sleep, that's my advice, and when you wake up you'll be as good as new."

"Yes, good," Dr. Alkahest said; but he looked up at the officer again. "What are the chances of that fellow's surviving that drop?"

"The suicide? Zero!" He waved the idea away; his hand was like a soft brick. "Practically zero. The water's like concrete when you hit it from that far up. And then there's the current." He laughed, only partly rueful. "Also, the fall takes the air out of you. You drown just like that." He snapped his fingers. He sounded quite pleased. "A lot of them die of a heart attack before they even hit."

Dr. Alkahest moved his head in a subtle nod, then closed his eyes. "What fishingboat *was* that, by the way?"

"I don't know," the officer said. "Just some boat, I guess."

"You don't know?" This time he did sit up. The room yawed and swung. Both the officer and the ship's doctor looked at him as if he'd gone crazy and reached out to catch him.

The ship's doctor put his arm around his shoulders. "Take it easy, there!"

"You didn't ask?" Dr. Alkahest said.

The officer grinned *(Stupid pig! Moron!)* and said, "Too much going on, Doctor. They called us to come look for a body, you know. When you're looking for a body, in weather like this . . ."

"You ought to have noticed," Dr. Alkahest said. By pure chance, by the wildest of accidents, he had made the most important discovery of his life, and their squeezed-shut, piggish little brains had blooched it. He clenched his fist, understanding with a terrible shock how utterly alone he was: who among his medical friends could get him marijuana—not a piddling joint, a paltry pipeload, but a mountain of it, a load like the load they had in that boat, that could bring him back *WHAMMO* his youth? Some people might in their frosty superiority—spouting Boethius or Augustine or Carlyle—make light of his anguish. Some people might shrug off his insight as senility. But a man lives only once! He comes wriggling, howling with pain and terror into the chilly, indifferent world, and all too soon he goes trembling-like-a-leaf and howling, bawling, out. No trace of him remains, and no heaven snatches (let us face these things) the failing electrical impulses of his brain. Scoff ye who will! Dr. Alkahest thought, *I'm a pitiful, miserable crippled old man without a friend in the world except my cleaning woman—who, God knows, hates my ass. Who scorns me and worse. Who ignores me! Now happiness is planted—behold!—within my reach! and, the very same instant, it's kicked out of sight like a football! Laugh! Laugh on, ye stony distancers! Someday you too will be ridiculous and full of woe! Half my certain inalienable rights were shot away when I was nine years old. No wonder if I cling with all my might to what little remains!*

54

"You could at least have noticed what fishing-boat it was," he whimpered.

"Maybe somebody else did," the officer said. "I'll ask around."

But nobody had.

Dr. Alkahest closed his eyes, clenched his fists, and made a vow. Life was precious, never to be repeated, despite all the wide-eyed memories of the transmigrationists. He would do what he must; it was decided. The man unwilling to fight for what he wanted did not deserve what he wanted. He smiled, eyes still closed. His jaw was firm now; a change had come over him. He could not but lament the impending calamities; nonetheless, his sleep was sound.

Meanwhile, at its pier in San Francisco, a vague shape in the tea-brown fog, the *Indomitable* sits waiting, moving a little like something alive, with the gentle lappings of the water supporting its bulk. Old Captain Fist appears on deck, holding his overcoated belly with one hand, leaning with the other on his cane. He is still very sick and walks with the greatest care, as a kindness to his stomach. After a moment the girl, Jane, appears beside him, wearing jeans, a man's workshirt, and an oil-grimed baseball cap, red, white, and blue. She stands balanced and wary as a cat. "All clear?" she asks softly.

From the dock above, Mr. Goodman answers, "All clear."

Captain Fist makes his way carefully, carefully to the side and stretches up a trembling hand. Mr. Goodman reaches down, takes the Captain's hand and gently pulls, almost lifts, him to the dock. Jane climbs after him lightly.

"Wait here," Captain Fist says, without troubling to glance at Mr. Goodman. His old eyes stare like two bullet holes into the city.

Mr. Goodman waits. The Captain and the handsome young woman in the patriotic cap move away toward the lights.

> "The cause of Liberty is a cause of too much dignity, to be sullied by turbulence and tumult."
>
> JOHN DICKINSON,
> "Letters from a Farmer in Pennsylvania," 1768

2

The Old Woman Finds Trash to Her Liking; and a Chamberpot Sets Off a War

It was a little past midnight when the old woman was roused from her reading by the squawk of a chicken and the thunderous rumble of her niece's car pulling up into the driveway. She couldn't believe so much time had passed, or that the novel, mere froth that it was, had so held her attention. She was always fast asleep by eleven at the latest, except, on occasion, when friends came to visit and Estelle played piano or Ruth recited poems; and even allowing for the way he'd upset her and, come to that, nearly killed her, that brother of hers—he was insane, that's all; always had been—even allowing for the way he'd gotten her all riled up, treating her like an animal, depriving her of her most ordinary human rights till she was trembling and shaking and so weak at the knees she'd been afraid, coming up the stairs backwards, protecting her face with her hands, that she'd collapse and fall on him, and serve him right (she was shaking again now, remembering)—even allowing for all that, it was hard to believe it was fifteen minutes past midnight!

She put down the paperback, opened to her page, on the white-painted square-topped wicker table beside the head of the bed—higher than the bed, an awkward, foolish excuse for a table if ever there was one, wicker-wrapped legs angling out past a useless little shelf down underneath (the table, she was sure, was a remnant from the years her niece Virginia had occupied this room)—and got up to go over to the clock on the desk to make certain she was seeing right. She was, it seemed.

It was a grayish-black clock made of onyx, or something made to simulate onyx—it weighed twenty-five pounds if it weighed one ounce—with ostentatious pitted gold pillars on the front, Roman columns, and Roman numerals so unevenly spaced it took study to be sure of what hour it was, let alone what minute. It stood in front of the mirror on the top of the closed oak desk, to the right of the glassed-in bookcase, level with her eyes. She couldn't help noticing, looking above her blue plastic spectacle-rims at the hands on the clock, that her eyes, in the mirror behind it, were red, ruined by her weeping, and perhaps made redder still by all that reading. She was not a great reader, she'd be quick to admit—certainly not a person who ordinarily read trivia! That's what he's brought us to, she thought, and her lips and white, white cheeks began to tremble. By "us" she meant herself and her late husband Horace.

Horace, her husband of thirty-five years, would never have read such a book as hers. He'd read only the finest literature, authors like Nathaniel Hawthorne, John Dos Passos, and Thomas Wolfe. She had not read them clear through herself, but she knew, if only by the fact that *he* read them, that they were profoundly serious-minded authors, "heavy," as they say, full of difficult philosophy and memorable prose and keen insights into human nature. It was wonderfully comforting, hearing him read her memorable passages just as she was drifting off to sleep, prose that rolled over her dimming mind like the ocean over tumbling wrecks at sea. Sometimes as he read he would choke a little with emotion. She would pat his elbow. Heaven only knew what he would think of her—gentle Horace Abbott with his mild gray eyes and soft dentist's hands—if, standing, ghostly, at her shoulder, he should find her reading trash. Her eyes filled with tears, not so much of self-pity as righteous indignation, for she was thinking again of her television set, and, taking her embroidered hankie from the sleeve of her nightie, where she'd tucked it, she angrily blew her nose. "We'll get even, Horace, you wait and see," she whispered to the empty room. Her husband had been dead for twenty years—twenty years exactly this Halloween. Dead of a heart attack. Someone had been in the room with him; they were gone when she got there.

Her niece's car was still rumbling, down below, though Virginia was in the house now; the old woman could hear them talking. It was odd, she thought, that Virginia'd gone and left the engine running, eating the gas up at sixty cents a gallon; but then she remembered. Sometimes when they turned off the motor the car wouldn't start again. Last Sunday afternoon when they'd come over after church (Sally's church, not theirs; Lewis was an atheist), they'd had to work two full hours to get the old thing running. It was a terrible car, a Chevrolet four-door (she and Horace had had Buicks). But Virginia and her husband were poor, of course. Virginia's husband Lewis—Lewis Hicks— was shiftless and dull-witted—or at any rate that was Sally Abbott's opinion, not that she condemned him; it was a free country. He had just a little touch of Indian in him. His great-great-great-great-grandfather had been a Swamp-Yankee. It was well known. Lewis had never gotten past eighth grade and was now just a handyman, a painter of porches, fixer of old pumps, shingler of barn and woodshed roofs, installer of screens and storm-windows, and in the winter, a gluer of old broken pictureframes and caner of chairs. He'd worked for her some, years ago, when she'd sold antiques. The Chevrolet, bluish-gray with brown patches, was a menace: she, for one, refused to ride in it. To take the thing out on the highway should be a criminal act. There were great rusted holes you could put your whole leg through, the front left headlight had been smashed out for months, and the back had been crashed into by a hit-and-run so that they had to hold the trunk shut with electric wire.

She stood twisting the hankie in her two hands, as if trying to wring it out, wondering what they could be saying so long, James and Virginia. She ought to get that Dickey home to bed; tomorrow was a school-day. Picking up the book, not noticing she was doing it, she went over to the tall narrow door—the door to the hallway, the one James had locked (there were two other doors, the closet door and the one by the foot of the bed that went up to the attic)—to see if she could hear what they were saying. She couldn't. Even with her good ear pressed to the wood, all she could catch was a faint rumble and vibration in the wood—ordinary chat of the kind you might expect in the middle of the night, her telling him, no doubt, the gossip from her meeting of the Rebekahs, or whatever, him saying just enough to keep her there, the way an old man will when his daughter comes by, and over by the fireplace or on the overstuffed plush couch, little Dickey curled up asleep with his deformed, one-eyed Snoopy.

In her mind's eye the old woman could see her niece Virginia as clear as day, all dolled up in rouge and lipstick, artificial black lashes, the stiff, half-dead looking dyed-blonde hair teased high over her head in a wide bouffant, cigarette between her fingers—she was a nervous wreck, and no wonder, growing up with that mad fool James and her poor troubled brother who had killed himself, and then marrying that Lewis! —nails dark red, same color as the lipstick not quite following her lips—there would be lipstick too, lined like a fingerprint, on the filter of her L&M. Virginia was pretty, for a woman of thirty-eight. She luckily hadn't drawn that long, narrow Page head but, instead, the short, wide one her mother, Ariah, had—James' wife—and that same double chin. Ginny was a good girl, always had been, just as her poor simple mother had been, one of the Blackmers. You could be certain James Page hadn't told her yet that he'd gotten drunk on whiskey and chased his own eighty-year-old sister up the stairs with a fireplace log and locked her in the bedroom like a madwoman! Virginia'd have something to say, all right, when she heard about that. And no doubt he was working up to tell her, that old mule. Likely's not he'd pretend to be proud of it—maybe *would* be proud of it, you never knew. Anything he did, he'd confess it right away; that was the way he'd been since he was old enough to talk. Thought it proved him honest. She pressed her ear to the door again. They were still blabbing on quietly. She pulled her head away and straightened up, lips compressed, annoyed, absentmindedly slapping the paperback book against the palm of her left hand, thinking again about revenge.

The room smelled of apples. He had twelve bushels of them upstairs in the attic, where in the winter it would be cold but not too cold. She didn't give a hoot about the smell just now, but when her mood was better she liked it, sometimes even opened the attic door to let it float down the narrow wooden stairs and drift around her bed while she slept. It reminded her of her childhood, in this same house. This had been James' room, in those days. She'd slept downstairs in the room off the pantry. Even then the floor—the wide, softwood boards—had been unlevel, so that at night the furniture would incline to slide toward one corner. The same old drop-leaf oak desk with glassed-in books to the left of it had been here then, though the books had been different—heaven only knew where these had come from, perhaps James' poor wife's mother: *Little Journeys into the Homes of the Great, Coe's Cyclopaedia, The New Pharmacopeia, The Blithedale Romance* by Nathaniel Hawthorne, *Training Vicious Dogs,* and a dozen ragged hymnals. The grayish-black clock had been kept downstairs in those days, on the fireplace mantel, and the chimes, back then, still rang.

She noticed she had the paperback book in her hand and thought, How odd, and shook her head. She was half-inclined to read a little more in it. The grayish-black clock said twenty to one now, but strange to say she wasn't sleepy at all. It must be she'd gotten her second wind; or perhaps the truth was she never really slept much anyway, anymore, just fooled herself, laid her head against the pillow, closed her eyes, let her mind drift, and passed it off for sleeping. Yes, she *would* read a page or two more, she decided. She wasn't some child, going to be corrupted by a foolish book. Which was worse, come right down to it?—a book that made you smile from time to time, though it spoke about certain things better left unmentioned, such as bedroom things, and suicide, or a book full of gloomy opinions and terrible forewarnings in memorable prose that was all hogwash anyway? "Show me, Horace Abbott," she demanded sternly, "a book that's got insights into human nature that an eighty-year-old woman hasn't thought of!" The ghost kept mum. Yes, then: she'd tuck herself in and poor Horace could just look the other way.

But just as the old woman was taking the first step in the direction of the bed, the commotion broke out downstairs. With a look of what could only be described as manic glee, she darted back to the door and flattened her ear to it.

For once in her life, as it happened, the old woman was wrong in her prediction about her brother. The old man had fully intended, in point of fact, to tell his daughter just exactly what he'd done, and he'd repeatedly moved the conversation in that direction; but somehow or other he had never quite said it, had merely stood there like a Stoughton bottle, and when she'd got up and picked up her Dickey to carry him to the car, he'd decided to let the thing slide. It was thus his grandson Dickey who told Ginny what the old man

61

had done. They were halfway to the car, Ginny carrying the boy in her arms, his long legs dangling, his
pale eyelids closed, one elbow clamped on Snoopy.
"How's my good baby?" Ginny asked him, as she'd
been asking every night since they'd got him from the
adoption agency. "Mmm," he said, as always, and
brushed his cheek against her hair. Ahead of them in
the darkness, just within range of the light falling over
the leaf-covered lawn, the grayish Chevrolet with its
smashed-in headlight was rumbling and clanking and
sending out such thick brown clouds of exhaust one
might have thought at first glance it had been parked
near a pile of burning leaves. They were just out of
range of the old man's hearing when the little boy
said, "Grampa chased Aunt Sally up the stairs with
a stick."

Virginia Hicks stopped walking, mouth opening,
eyes widening, and with an expression more like sorrow and terrible weariness than anything else, turned
her head, slightly drawing it back, to try to see her
son's face. She could only see his neck and ear. Not
in disbelief—in despair, more like—she said, "With a
stick?"

Dickey nodded his head. "It was a fireplace log. He
locked her in the bedroom."

Ginny turned, child and all, eyes swimming in tears,
to face her father. "Oh, *Dad*," she wailed. She saw his
back straighten and his long jaw stiffen, prepared to
be belligerently defensive as usual, and the same instant she felt Dickey tense up with alarm, realizing
too late that now he was in for it from his grampa.
Both Dickey and the old man spoke at once, her
father barking, "She had it comin! She stotted the
whole thing!" and her son: "Mommy, I want to stay
in the car."

"You can't stay in the car," she snapped. "The
damn fumes'll kill you." She started back with him
toward the house.

"Now Ginny you mine your own business," her
father said, self-righteous and whining at the same
time, standing his ground in the doorway though both

of them knew he'd back off if she pressed him. "This is between yer aunt Sally and me, and nobody else's got a pot in it."

"Holy Christ," she said, and moved straight on toward him, unconsciously using Dickey as a human shield, and the old man backed out of the doorway. She went straight to the living room, put down Dickey on the couch, mechanically stuck the red sateen pillow under his head and Snoopy in his arms, then went striding back to deal with her father. He was still standing in the kitchen, looking hawk-eyed and sullen and crazy as a loon, his hand on the white doorknob, holding the door open. She closed the door to the living room behind her. "Just what the hell," she asked, "is going *on* here?"

"This is my house," her father said, "and if Sally don't like the way I live here, she can damn well move right on out of it."

"It's the family house," Ginny said, throwing her head forward, fists on her hips. "She's got as much right to it as you have."

"That ain't so!" His indignation was more confident now, for about this there could be no question. "It was left to me and I've lived here ah my life."

"Well it shouldn't have been left to you," she yelled, "it's not fair and you know it. Why should one child get everything and the other one nothing?"

"Sally was rich. She had her dentist." He sneered childishly.

"Well she don't now, does she? If they'd known he'd die young and Aunt Sally would live on years and years past him, they'd have left it to you both. Fair's fair."

He was less confident, all at once. "Fair is fair and law is law," he said.

"Shame on you!" she barked. She saw him wilt a little, puckering his wide, almost lipless mouth, glancing left and right like a cornered rabbit; and furious though she was, her heart went out to the old maniac. He'd never in his life been a man to defend the indefensible, and both of them knew she had him dead

64

to rights. He noticed he was holding the door open, letting in October, and abruptly closed it.

"Go let her out, Dad," she said. A muscle was jerking in her right cheek, and with a start she realized that the exact same muscle was jerking in his. It for some reason gave her heart a wrench. She wanted to cry, throw her arms around him as she'd done as a little girl. Oh God, she thought, things are so terrible! Tears squirted into her eyes. She thought then: Christ, where are my cigarettes?

He crossed his arms across his chest, fingers on each hand hanging over his elbows, thumbs hooked inside —crooked, stiff fingers, with huge, arthritic knuckles; a farmer's fingers: knuckles barked and scratched, one finger cut off just below the fingernail, from an argument with a baler. She remembered when his hair, snow white, had been brown as shoepolish. He said nothing, biting his lips together and not meeting her eyes, staring a little cross-eyed at the yellow wall beside her. He could stand that way all year if he took a firm notion.

"Dad," she said still more sternly, "go let her out."

"*No* sir!" he said, and snapped up his eyes to meet hers. "Sides, she be asleep." He turned and stalked straight across the room to the cupboard, practically stamping in those iron-toed shoes, and got a glass out. He looked at it critically, as if expecting Aunt Sally would have left it streaked and spotted, though a better housekeeper never lived, and he knew it. He took it to the icebox and got out ice from the blue plastic tray, then carried the ice-filled glass to the upright cupboard in the corner where his whiskey was.

"Don't you think you've had *enough?*" she asked.

He tipped his head sideways and stared at her in rage. "I've had one damn glass ah night and that's *ah*," he said. It was true, she knew. For one thing he'd never told a lie in his life, and for another he was not a hard drinker; he'd been through it and he'd stopped. She bit her lips together, watching him pour the whiskey, then the water. What time is it?, she wondered, and where the hell did I leave my cigarettes? She'd

65

had them, she remembered, just before she went over to the couch to pick up Dickey to carry him to the car. She saw her hand putting them on the fireplace mantel. Without a word, she opened the living-room door and went to get them. Just as she was picking them up—Dickey was fast asleep—the phone rang. Lewis, she thought. Oh, Jesus.

"That'll be fer you," her father called from the kitchen.

The phone was on the murdered television. She shook out a cigarette as she picked up the receiver. "Hello?" she said. She got a match out and hurriedly struck it. On the cover there was a picture of the Boston Tea Party. Everywhere you looked, it was the Bicentennial. Did people have no fucking shame? "Hello?" she said again. Her hands were shaking.

"That you there, Ginny?" Lewis asked. He sounded baffled and only half awake, as if it were she who'd called him.

"Hi, Lewis," she said. She took a quick suck at the cigarette. Thank God for cigarettes, she thought, and then, thinking of her father and Aunt Sally, Thank God for cancer! Softly, trying not to wake Dickey, she said, "Honey, I'm still up at Dad's. There's been a little trouble, and—"

"I can't hear you too good," Lewis called to her.

"There's been a little trouble," she said again, more loudly.

"Trouble?" he called.

"It's nothing serious. Dad and Aunt Sally—" She stopped, a sudden chill running up her spine. It took her a moment to register the cause: out in the yard, the car had died.

"Ginny? You still there?" Lewis asked.

She took a deep drag on the cigarette. "Yes, I'm still here," she said.

"Ginny, your cah's died," her father called in to her.

She clenched her left fist and rolled her eyes up.

Lewis asked, "Are you all right, Ginny?" Not exactly critical—that wasn't his nature—more in the way of offering information that might be new to her, he said, "It's half past one in the mahnin."

"Yes, I know," she said. "Look, sweetheart, I'll be home just as quick as I can. You go to sleep."

"Dickey's not sick, is he?"

"No no, Dickey's fine. You go on to sleep."

"Well ah right, sweet-hot," Lewis said. "Don't be too long." It was not, of course, an order; he never gave orders, even to his dogs. It was merely good advice. "Goodnight, then, sweet-hot."

"Yes, goodnight, sweetie."

When she replaced the receiver and glanced over at Dickey, he had his eyes open, watching her.

"You go back to sleep," she said, and pointed at him. He clicked his eyes shut.

Back in the kitchen with her father, Ginny said, "Dad, are you going to unlock that door or am I?"

"Must be you are, if ennabody does," he said. He pursed his lips and looked down into the glass in his hand. He swirled the ice around.

It wasn't much but it was more than she'd hoped for. "Where's the key?" she said.

"Likely as not it's in there in the dish on the TV," he said, "where it always is."

She went and got the key, then came back into the kitchen and started for the door to the stairway. As she was opening it she paused and looked at him and asked, "What did she do that you thought was so terrible?"

"Talked," he said.

"Talked," she echoed. She waited. She listened to the hum of the clock over the stove.

"Said a lot of things not fit for a young child's ears," he said. He took a sip of the whiskey. He held the glass awkwardly, elbow straight out, as if he'd be a bit more comfortable with a dipper.

"Like for instance?"

"It's not woth discussin."

"I'd really be interested to know," Ginny said, eyebrow cocked. She tossed the key in her hand, the same hand that held the cigarette. But she knew that smug,

67

self-righteous look. Doomsday could come and go, and he'd stand in the wind like a cornshock and tell her no more.

"You can lead a hoss to water but you can't make him drink," he said.

"Or a mule," she said. She started up the stairs. When she'd unlocked the door she turned the handle and gave it a tug, then pushed inward. Nothing happened. It was bolted on the inside.

"Aunt Sally?" she called softly.

No answer.

She thought a moment, then rapped lightly on the door. She tipped her head to listen. "Aunt Sally?" she called again.

"I'm asleep," Aunt Sally called.

"Aunt Sally you're *not* asleep, you're talking."

"I talk in my sleep."

Ginny waited. Nothing. After a time she called, "Aunt Sally, your light's on. I can see it under the door." Again she stood with her head tipped, listening like a bird. She thought she heard the floor creak; otherwise nothing.

"You're *both* crazy," she said.

No response.

She had half a mind to lock the door again but thought better of it. "All right," she said, "sulk then. When and *if* you decide to come out, the door's unlocked." She waited half a minute longer, but the old woman wouldn't speak, so she walked down the hall, stopped and used the bathroom, then went back downstairs. Her father was not in the kitchen now. She went to the living room and put the key in the dish, then changed her mind and slipped it into her pocket so the old man couldn't use it to lock the door again —not that that would stop him if his stubbornness hung on. He could nail the thing shut. She wouldn't put it past him.

"Dad?" she called.

"I'm in bed," he called back. He had the bedroom in back of the living room, the room that, when she was a child, had been used for the ironing. She went

68

over, past the couch where Dickey lay, and tried the door, opened it two inches, and looked in. It was pitch dark. "You won't be in bed long if I can't get my *car* started," she said.

"If you can't stot the cah, you just run up and sleep with Aunt Sally," he called. "He hee!"

"Like God damn *hell*," she said. "You'll hitch me up the horses."

"Don't fahget to turn out the lights," he said.

Above, they heard Aunt Sally sneaking to the toilet.

The car, for some reason, started the second time she turned the key. She went back to the living room for Dickey, turned off the lights, put the screen over the fireplace—her father never used it, "Steals the heat," he said—carried the child and Snoopy back out to the Chevy, and started for home.

The old woman, up in the bedroom, listened to her leave. She smiled wickedly, exactly like a witch on TV—she was aware of it herself, and relished it. What had it ever actually gotten her, those years of trying to be a Christian, fair and decent? A television set with the works shot out of it, a crooked old bedroom she wouldn't have put a hired girl in if she still had her house in the village, a bedroom that, whenever the wind was strong, was so troubled by drafts that the doors rumbled, and so unhealthy, for some reason, that her coleus in its green ceramic cart—a plant that had nearly taken care of itself when she'd lived in town—was now half-dead, and nothing she could do seemed to help worth a Hannah cook. No, she would read her trashy novel; they could think what they liked.

She opened the paperback to the place she'd left off, closed her eyes for just a moment, and at once fell asleep.

It was morning when she awakened, and James was knocking, calling to her at the door. Through the window she could see the mountain, garish pink with sunrise. The air in the room around her was crisp. It smelled of winter.

"You planning to get up and have breakfast?" James called. Meaning, she knew: "You planning to get up and get *me* breakfast?" Ha! Before she'd come here to cook and keep house for him, he'd been sick all the time on account of the way he ate—nothing but fried foods, never any vegetables, so that he was constipated both day and night, and walked bent over at the waist with cramps. She saw him again, in her mind's eye, waving that stick of firewood at her, eyes like a wild drunken Indian's, prepared to kill her, his own blood sister without a friend or protector in this world.

"Sally? You hear me?"

She decided to keep silent, as she'd done with Ginny. It was a fact of life that if people knew what you were feeling they could work you around.

With a little start of joy, she remembered the apples in the attic. She could get by on those, for a while at least. She didn't *need* to cook him breakfast. In her sudden happiness, she forgot her resolve to keep silent. "I'm not hungry, James," she called. When he was out doing chores she'd sneak down and poach herself a nice egg, and make herself some toast. "I'm just not hungry this morning," she said.

That stopped him a minute. She could see him, in her mind's eye, standing there pulling at his long, whiskered chin, bushy white eyebrows lifted, eyes staring straight down his nose. He said: "You've gotta come out of there sooner or later, if it's only to go to the potty."

She thought about that. It was true enough, and it would be more like sooner than later. She could use the bathroom while he worked at his chores; but the rest of the time . . . Then her gaze, restlessly roving around the room as she groped for a rejoinder, landed on the washstand in the corner, beyond the attic door, and she realized with a start that she *had* him! Down inside that washstand, tucked in among old towels and washcloths, lay Ariah's old bedpan, and right there on top, under the wooden towel-rack on its oaken lyre, peeking out from behind the kerosene lamp, sat

a whole box of Kleenex! If he wanted war, war he
would get. She could outlast any siege he could mount!

"All the same, I'm not hungry, James," she called
brightly.

There was another minute's silence. She held her
breath, smiling.

"Well I be cussed," he said—more to the doorknob,
she imagined, than to her. Now she heard his footsteps moving away, hay-foot, straw-foot, maugering
slowly toward the head of the stairs, just past the
bathroom, and then down the stairs into the kitchen.

"Well I be God damned," said James Page to himself, down in the kitchen. The cat ducked out of sight.
It was all very well for the old woman to play games,
he told himself, but the facts of the matter was as they
was. He was willing to admit that by rights the house
was as much hers as his, now that his daughter had
called it to his attention—though they was many a
man he knew would never been so generous. It was
him had the deed in the Courthouse. So far as the *Law*
was concerned, she damn well had the clothes on her
back. Well, tell it to the bees; law was law and fair
was fair, as he'd said himself. He was willing to grant
she had a certain, as you might say, moral right. But
by the same token, *he* had certain rights. Did she think
she could take away his house from him and, like
some scoundrel on Relief, just lay there in her dad-
blame bed like a pig in a pughole? They'd see about
that!

He frowned, head thrown forward, stroking his
chin, his left hand fingering the snakehead in his
pocket; then, reaching his decision, went into the living
room for the key. He smiled when he saw it was missing from the dish that held the others (the dish held
also a thimble and some coins and buttons). He
should've known right off his daughter would've taken
it. And *she* should've known he'd have another one.
There was always two keys to everything; that was one
of the unalterable rules of the universe. And in this
case, the second was in his shoebox, in his upper right
desk draw.

Sally, in her bed, with her teeth in now, was still smiling with self-satisfied, malicious delight, like a foxy old general—or like wicked Captain Fist in the novel she 'was reading—when she heard her brother James coming back up the stairs, then down the hall toward her door. She was puzzled, a little. It was unlikely that he'd beg; even more unlikely that he'd stoop to persuasion. Then what?, she wondered. The footsteps stopped outside her door and she leaned forward, listening. After a minute, she heard—her heart fluttered—the lock click! She continued to smile, but her eyes were thoughtful, even a little troubled, as his footsteps went back to the head of the stairs and then down them. Soon she smelled bacon and eggs frying.

She got up and used the bedpan (thank God for the bedpan!), then turned the stiff winglatch on the attic door, pulled the small china knob until the door came unstuck, and went up to get two apples. She polished them on her nightie as she brought them back down, and, after she'd re-latched the attic door, took them to bed with her, along with her book. She heard James whistling as he went out to milk the cows—tunelessly chirping, not a trouble in this world!—to torment her. Well they'd see about that.

By now the pink had nearly faded from the clouds, and the mountain had settled to the various reds, yellows, purples, dark greens, and browns of high autumn in Vermont. She did love autumn. Always had.

She could last on apples—they were big, juicy Winesaps—as long as *he* could last, too stupid or set in his ways to cook a vegetable or nibble at a fruit. She remembered how sorry she'd felt for him when she came, seeing him doubled over with the constipation cramps. Sally smiled.

She found her place in the book, got her pillows adjusted, and settled down serenely to her reading.

3

IN WONG CHOP'S RESTAURANT

Captain Johann Fist was a terrifying old man. Sometimes at night when he climbed into an occupied taxi by mistake people would glance at him once and have a stroke. Jane did not like him, by any means, but she was not so childish as to blame him for things he couldn't help. He was an Aries, born with Saturn in the ascendent. "He's an unfortunate man," she'd written to her mother, feeling it was better not to give too much detail. "He has no family, no friends, not even a pet—though he used to have a parrot, he tells me, but it bit him. I pray for his soul, but I don't really think it will help much."

Jane was a wonderful letter writer, for which her mother was grateful. Every time she got a chance, relaxing out at sea, she would write a good long letter to her mother or, sometimes, as they called him, Uncle Fred. She never said what she was thinking; just loving chat and news. She would put all her letters in envelopes and stamp them, and the first time the *Indomitable* put in, she would mail them all off—all she could still find. Sometimes there were nearly a hundred in a shipment. Her mother was right to cherish them. Since it would be awkward to tell what the real news was, Jane made things up. Sometimes, when she was tired, she copied things from books.

Tonight, walking with the Captain toward Chinatown (he had a habit of hurrying from doorway to doorway, peering around corners before daring to step out), Jane's mind was troubled. Perhaps she had made a mistake somewhere, she was beginning to think. She had been all her life a decisive girl, quick to think and act, though she fooled people by her casual smile and the innocence of her large blue eyes. She had come to California and had sized up the situation instantly: Aeronautics, that was where the future was at. You could tell by just glancing at the black, roaring sky. She'd gone to a place where they gave flying lessons, had craftily extracted two twenty-dollar bills from the hundred dollars Uncle Fred had given her—a whole lot of money for a hired man to have put by in Nebraska—and she had set the forty dollars on the counter and said to the man, "Can you teach me to fly for that much? It's all I've got." The man had grinned. "Not a chance, lady." He was a red-headed, freckle-faced man with a dimple. She'd looked at him like a lost child, letting her innocent blue eyes do their work— besides he was the kind of man you couldn't help but like—then had slowly drawn back the money from the counter and, like a lady she'd seen in the movies one time, had tucked it in her bosom, giving him a little glimpse. She let a tear slide down her cheek. "Oh hell," he'd said. She'd let him put his arm around her when he was talking about buttons and gauges, and once or twice she'd made no remark when his gloved hand came to rest, as if accidentally, on her thigh. She'd proved no ordinary student. Breaking horses in Nebraska, she'd developed one especially valuable trait: she never panicked. She was looping the loops in no time, and he'd given in to her every new, more outrageous demand—instrument training, multiengine . . . She'd paid him well enough. As soon as he'd agreed to let her go to twin engines, she'd let him initiate her sexually, so to speak. She owed him at least that. He was a Sagittarius. She'd been eighteen when all this happened—four years ago now. It was two days after she'd gotten her air-transport rating that she'd met Captain Fist.

She was leaving the airport, walking toward the bus stop, when she saw a billfold lying on the sidewalk, the edges of some bills showing. She bent down, hardly thinking, and just as she was about to close her hand on the billfold, it moved. It moved about four feet, off the sidewalk into the grass, and stopped again. She felt her face going beet red: someone was pulling it by a string, children no doubt, as a joke on her. Any minute she'd hear their laughter. But though she waited, grinning at the bushes where she knew they must be, no laughter came. Cautiously, tentatively, secretly baffled though she continued to smile, she went over to the billfold and reached down for it again. Again it moved. "Now look here," she said to the bushes. Still nothing. She got a brilliant idea. Quickly, but as if indifferently, she walked over to where the billfold was now, glanced up at the sky as if to see if it might rain, and, faster than a rattlesnake, stamped her foot down beside the billfold where the string would have to be. Sure enough, the billfold bumped into her foot and stopped. She reached down to grab it.

"Your name's Jane, I believe," a voice said. The voice was so horrible she felt faint. It was the kind of voice cobras would have if they talked. Every leaf of the bush was suddenly distinct, every branch sharply outlined. She stared in stark terror, perfectly certain by the prickling of her skin that in a minute she was going to die. The birds had stopped singing. There was no sound anywhere. She saw herself as she would be shown in the newspaper photograph, naked in the bushes, or headless, lying in a pool of blood. In a few short seconds, she had crossed from the world of people to whom nothing ever happens into the world of perverts, maniacs, murderers—and she, she was the victim!

Then her heart stopped dead. She was staring straight into two pale eyes, unmistakably the eyes of a serpent—unblinking, dusty.

"Don't be frightened," the horrible voice said. "You're a lovely girl. Nobody's going to hurt you!"

She wanted to get up, run from him; but her muscles wouldn't move. "What do you want?" she whispered.

"I want to make you an offer," the voice said. "My name's Johann Fist. I'd like to make you rich."

She said nothing, breathing hard. She was giddy.

"I want you to fly my airplane. You wouldn't believe how well I'm willing to pay you."

"Why?" she said. "Where?"

"To Mexico and back, on regular runs. It's Paradise, Mexico. I'll pay you a thousand dollars a run. You'll be richer than God." He laughed, a heavy rippling sound like sewers overflowing.

She thought about it. It was a lot of money. She was young, beautiful, full of ambition; also, she had her relatives to think about. They'd scrimped and saved all their lives for her. If God hadn't meant for her to take the opportunity, why would He have sent it? Also, a thousand dollars was a lot of money. She peered into the dusty, unblinking eyes. "Is it illegal?"

"Come, come, my dear."

She was satisfied. It would be different, she reflected, if she agreed to it *knowing* it was illegal. "I'll do it," she said. She laughed.

And so she had done it. It was a fat brown World War II cargo plane so big you could drive huge trucks up into it. It creaked and shuddered with every gust, and the engines were so noisy she had to wear ear-plugs; but it flew. Or flew until one awful night over the Mojave. It was their fourth run. Some noise came over the radio—it didn't work—and the next thing she knew the United States Air Force was shooting at them. "Keep driving," Captain Fist said, his revolver at her head. All four engines were on fire. "I can't," she said. "Look out the window." He looked out, saw the engines, sighed, and put the gun away. They parachuted down, Captain Fist, Mr. Goodman, Mr. Nit, and Jane. The plane crashed a half-mile upwind of them, and as they stood, then sat, then lay, smelling the burning marijuana, they became close friends, for the time being, and told each other stories of their lives and in the end made love. She told of Uncle Fred—sweet fat old Italian who'd been derailed on the way to the California vineyards and refused, after that, to budge from Tomb City, Nebraska. "Dis America, she's-a beautiful! She da rock of Ages," Uncle Fred liked to say. He had a suitcase full of Caruso records. Her mother made him play them in the chicken house. Toward morning, as they were stumbling hand in hand across the Mojave, startling bats and tortoises and owls, Captain Fist said, "What we really need is a boat." They'd gotten the boat, for two thousand dollars, from the California Salvage Corporation.

She no longer pretended to herself that Captain Fist's business was legal or her personal relationship with the three men strictly proper. Her poor mother and Uncle Fred would be shocked, no doubt. But what was right in Nebraska was not necessarily right for California or out on the Pacific. Also, as she sometimes reminded herself, it was perfectly possible for a person to begin badly but mend his ways later, when he saw the light. Meanwhile, the pay was good, her friendship with Mr. Nit and Mr. Goodman, at least, was comfortable—no one could accuse her of puritanical hang-ups—and she was getting, it might be, valuable experience. More than most anything, she wanted to *be* something, *make* something of herself. She wanted to be so rich she could do anything she wanted, anything she could think of; but it wasn't just crass materialism. She wanted to be famous, do things that would change the world. She'd talked once, in a grubby little bar, to a girl with red hair and a smudged face who was planning to assassinate Dr. Kissinger. Jane's heart leaped. She would never do anything like that herself, she wasn't the type, but she could understand the feeling—the eyes of the whole fucking world upon you! star of the Walter Cronkite show—beautiful eyes flashing, clenched fist raised . . . "Are you really going to shoot Dr. Kissinger?" she'd said. "Keep it down, will ya?" the girl had said. "Half the people in here are fuzz." Jane had looked around, more awed than ever. Yes, she would definitely do something like that, except something more reasonable, something her mother and all her friends back in Nebraska would be proud of, it was hard to think what.

Or so she had told herself until tonight. Tonight the stranger had dropped into their lives as if out of heaven, and everything was changed.

What would they do with him? They couldn't very well just let him go, with his clothes stinking of marijuana. Sure as day the police would trace him to their fishingboat. On the other hand, the longer they kept him aboard, the surer the man was to find out their secret. They'd just have to keep him as their prisoner forever.

The thought blew her mind. She saw him chained up, getting gaunter every year. He'd grow a long beard, like the man in a movie she'd seen one time. She would sneak little presents to him—a bird in a cage, a book of sad poetry, one perfect rose and a cap of LSD, if he liked such things. They'd have whispered conversations. —No, on second thought, she would be, to him, like the Dragon Lady. He would reach out to her, in an anguish of indecision . . . —No, he would finally force her to see what had become of her: she would weep, facing the stark, awful truth, clinging to his knees. It was *she* who was in chains; he, in his iron shackles, was truly free. Like the play in San Francisco. She imagined him rubbing her back very gently, as Uncle Fred had done when she was a little girl and had been frightened by a nightmare. The stranger would smile, and she would know she was forgiven, both here and in the life hereafter.

They were in Chinatown. Chickens hanging in darkened store windows. Boxes and cans with Chinese writing. Chinese theaters emitting their weird tinny music. *Kee-yong, ka-waiyong, kee-yo, kyo, kyonnnng*. Tourists milled on the sidewalks and in the street; little Chinese in business suits bobbed past them. Captain Fist darted from doorway to doorway, his hat-brim pulled down so that nothing showed but his blackish potato of a nose and his eyes. When they came to Wong Chop's restaurant he darted in and ran upstairs. Jane followed. At the head of the stairs stood a large American flag.

She found him in the last booth in the upstairs room, his back to the doorway, his hat sitting level on his shoulders as if, like a turtle, he'd pulled in his head. She took a chair at the side of the table, and as soon as she was seated he turned away as if everything were her fault. She sighed, removing her glasses. She wondered if the stranger, back on the ship, had come to yet. Perhaps the old man had killed him with that blow.

Music came through the wall. Gongs and something that sounded like tin cans on a string.

"Captain Fist," she began. She put on her glasses.

He shrank from her voice, and she changed her mind, took her glasses off, and kept still. What was she doing here—a nice girl really—in this den of recooked leftovers?

Then, without a sound, Wong Chop appeared in the doorway, big as a mountain, dressed in gold and scarlet, with tassels. He smiled and bowed. "Good evening, fliends." He held a menu in front of Captain Fist. Captain Fist pretended to study it, then reached out, his hand shaking violently, and pointing to something. It was the signal, Jane surmised. Now Wong Chop bowed, deeply gratified, and slipped an envelope to the Captain. Even though she was watching for it, she almost missed the pass. Quick as an electric spark, it went from Wong Chop's hand into Captain Fist's pocket. Wong Chop bowed again, deeply and slowly, and then, as if he had been an illusion, vanished. Captain Fist sat quiet as a mossy stump. Ten minutes expired.

At last, unable to help herself, Jane leaned toward him. "What's going to happen to the stranger?" she whispered.

He gave a jerk, as if he'd been asleep. "Be still," he croaked, and raised a trembling finger to his lips.

"I won't be," she whispered. "You've got to free him."

He shook his head. "Impossible."

Everyone in the booths around them had stopped talking and sat perfectly motionless, heads tipped or turned, listening with all their might; the waiter, a few booths down, had his hand inconspicuously cupped to his ear. All federal agents, probably. Too softly for them to hear, she whispered, "But you can't keep him with us forever. Think!"

"I have," he whispered.

"Suppose they got onto us. Suppose—" she hung fire, visualizing it herself clearly for the first time. She put on her glasses. "Suppose they send out a destroyer or something and sink us! You'll be a murderer."

Captain Fist smiled. She looked away and wished she were back on the farm with the chickens and tractors and dear Uncle Fred.

"I can't let you," she whispered. "It's not ethical." She whispered it so firmly, so courageously, that it gave her a little thrill. At the same time it occurred to her that she'd done all she could. The murder would not be on *her* hands. "And then too," she said, "there's the *Militant*. What if—"

The Captain went white. "Don't mention them!" he whispered. His shudder made the floor shake.

"If the *Militant* attacks us, and the stranger is killed—"

"Be still!" he whispered. He clutched his hands together; sweat popped out on his forehead. His eyes rolled and his mouth shook, but he managed to bring out, "He'll be dead already, stupid girl. Do you think he was joking when he jumped off the Golden Gate Bridge?"

"We can't let him," she said.

"We can't stop him," he hissed. "If I don't miss my guess, our visitor's dead as a doornail right this minute." He jerked out his pocket-watch and glanced at it. It had stopped. He thumped it against his palm.

She studied him, light with alarm. Only now did she fully realize how pleasant the stranger's kiss had felt, when she was reviving him. "What do you mean," she whispered, "dead already?" It came to her that Mr. Nit was still on the *Indomitable*. He always came ashore when they hit San Francisco. He loved the city, would never have missed it for the world, unless . . . They had whispered, she remembered. She had come upon Mr. Nit and the Captain in the passageway below, by the engine room door,

81

and the minute they saw her they'd stopped whispering and looked guilty. Now it was all coming clear to her. *Murder!* she thought. Her face felt on fire. It was one thing to smuggle, to steal a little gas in an emergency, or to slow down the harbor police boats with mines, but cold-blooded murder, even if that was what the handsome stranger wanted . . . He was a sick man, a pitiful person whose life had gone all wrong or he would never have jumped, and they, who should have been his saviours and restorers . . .

"I quit," she said. She felt reckless, suddenly pure and invulnerable. Astonishingly, the stranger really had become her redeemer, had brought her proud, wicked heart to submission. She stood up, radiantly beautiful, she knew—it was exactly like a thing she'd seen on the Wednesday Night Movie. She was free of him. As free—even if he whipped out his pistol and shot her dead—

"Sit down," he hissed. "Don't be stupid."

"Never!" she said. Then, glancing at his eyes, she reconsidered; it might be best not to overdo it. "I need to go to the ladies'," she said, and slipped her glasses off.

As soon as the ladies' room door closed behind her she was up on the sink in a flash and climbing out the window. It opened onto a flat roof high above the street. The lights were beautiful, below: deep reds, sharp blues and greens. It was as if she were seeing the neon signs for the first time, all transmuted to a new beauty by the harsh ugliness of the roof with its clumsy chimneys and antennae, desert plants on a strange planet. She slipped her shoes off, to cross the roof more quietly. She felt light, as if born again. She'd gone only two steps when a blocky shape detached itself from the chimney.

"Good evening," a voice said. She couldn't

see the man's face, but his bow was Oriental.
He had on a turban, or an incongruous silver
Afro. She put on her glasses. In his right hand,
casually stretched toward her, he had a knife.
She went back to the Captain.

"Ah," he said, "you're back. As you see,
dinner's served."

She sat down. "I'm not really hungry," she
said. She put her hands on the table, getting
herself steady.

The Captain smiled. His teeth were like a
carp's. "Ah well," he said.

It was still more than an hour before they
could return to the boat. She thought frantically,
snatching about for some stratagem; but there
was no possibility of escape, he had her cold.
Surely Mr. Goodman would never allow . . . But
he would never know, she realized. He was as
innocent as a baby. She would rush back, go
below at once, and she would find . . . nothing.
The body would be gone. Her eyes filled with
tears. *The poor man*, she thought; but she was
weeping for herself, the Nebraska farmgirl
that was lost—ah, lost forever!

"You should read more philosophy," Captain
Fist said.

She listened to the queer, half-musical noises
that were coming through the restaurant wall.
Drums. Gongs. Tinkles. A long human wail. It
sounded to her, in her troubled state, like some
weird blood-sacrifice.

"Personally, I read philosophy all the time,"
Captain Fist remarked. "Ask me about Hegel."

She met his dusty, soulless eyes, as close together as shotgun barrels. "Evil man," she whispered. "Wicked demon!"

"Eat your seaweed," Captain Fist said. "Or
whatever it is." He sighed.

———

It was the end of a chapter.

Sally Abbott smiled. The book had improved, it seemed to her, though perhaps it was just that her mind was fresher, her brother's attack on her receding in time and the morning clear and beautiful, crisp. She hadn't spent a morning in bed reading since heaven knew when. She'd been missing something! Also, the battered old paperback was oddly comforting, though she couldn't exactly put her finger on why. The impishness of it; perhaps it was that. The delicate way the writer mocked all those foolish things her brother James, among others, set such store by. The flag in Wong Chop's restaurant—that was a wonderful touch! —and all those government spies! Or the stupid false piety of the girl from Nebraska! Ah, but hadn't she known such people!

She smiled again, blessing the fine weather, the sunlit room. James would be livid, if he could know what she was reading, know what wickedness she was thinking. James was a Veteran—had gone off to World War II though he was nearly middle-aged and didn't even have to, as a farmer. "Duty," he said. He'd been a Seabee in the South Pacific. She poked her chin out, mimicking him, and saluted, then smiled at her antics and at James. Every Veterans Day, there he'd be in his ridiculous VFW cap—it was all that still fit, now that he was old and shrunken. He and Henry Stumpchurch would lead the parade, James, as the oldest, carrying the Colors of the United States of America (she saluted again), his eyes smouldering as if he imagined he was marching it through China. Henry Stumpchurch, a huge man, looking equally stern, would carry the flag of the VFW—he had enormous curling eyebrows and a round, bald head, sun- and windburnt below the sharp line of his normal wide, floppy hat; the skin above—revealed in near nakedness under the gray VFW service cap—was as pale as your bottom, boiled looking, like a cabbage. Behind them, grimly on the watch for Jews and Democrats, came William Peabody Partridge, Jr., and Samuel Denton Frost, and then the younger men, mostly Irishmen and Italians

(Democrats!). The old ones thought of themselves as descendants of Vermont's Green Mountain Boys. Her Horace had smiled. "That's odd," he'd said, all innocence. Round faced, cherubic. "I'd understood they were nearly all killed." He'd wisely gone no further— James had come alert and was prepared to pounce— but she knew her husband's full opinion, which he'd read in some book: after the Revolution, there was practically not a man left in all the East except cowards and Tories and, here and there, an Indian. Ethan Allen himself ended up with only twenty live men.

Oh yes, he was your True American, her brother James. He could be downright dangerous if you got him on the subject of immigrants, or workmanship, or almost anything else. More than once she and Horace had fallen silent before James Page's wrath. More than once they'd had to sneak and lie to save young Richard from his opinions, especially when he'd been courting the Flynn girl—"an Irish and a Catholic," as James had called her, his eyes bugging out with indignation. It was a tragic story; her brother would never know the half of it. It was mostly at their house, or at Horace's office, that the two would tryst. She was eighteen, a tall, frail looking slip of a thing, with large, strange eyes and some queer Irish name— a beautiful girl except perhaps just a little bit knock-kneed—and when they met it was like iron and a magnet, you could feel the pull.

He was tall and shy, her nephew Richard. One year older than the girl. They would sit on the couch in the living room (Sally's living room), far apart but holding hands, listening to the music, Horace smiling and nodding to the beat, and after a while her Horace would yawn and say, "I don't know why I'm so tired tonight," shaking his head as if it baffled him; and then, not long after, "Well, *I* give up. Sally, you ready for night-night?" Richard would lean forward, as if willing to go home, though you could see his reluctance all over his face, and as for the girl, she looked downright panicky. "No, no," Horace would say, "don't let me drive you off! It's early yet."

Once, when they were up in their room, sitting up in bed, side by side, Horace reading, she at her knitting, Sally had said: "Have you thought what would happen if James should come by some night and find them?"

He'd looked up over his glasses, staring straight ahead, and the strength of resolve she'd glimpsed that instant had frightened her. "I've considered it," he said.

She'd breathed a little prayer that his resolve need not be tested.

She knew for certain, as it happened—Horace only guessed—what it was that they did down there alone. One night when she'd gone down for a glass of milk she'd glanced in at the two, half by accident—the music was still playing, the lights were turned low—and she'd seen that Richard was lying on top of her, she had her legs spread for him, though they both had all their clothes on. Her skirt was hiked up, just a foot or so, so that her knees showed. Richard's face had been turned away, blond hair shining, so that he hadn't seen her looking in. The Flynn girl hadn't seen her either, at first. Her eyes were closed, her mouth slightly open. She was breathing heavily. If they weren't making love Sally Abbott was hard put to find a better word. Then the Flynn girl's eyes had popped open and stared straight at her, as wide and dark as the eyes of a deer. Her face was expressionless, helpless and resigned, her eyes like those of an animal surprised by a hunter and no place to turn, no course but surrender. Their eyes had met for a long moment, hers and the Flynn girl's, and a mysterious emotion had passed through Sally, a recognition for which she had no words—a sudden hushed knowledge. Frail as she was, the Flynn girl was a woman, exactly as Sally was —for an instant it was as if they were the *same* woman —and Sally felt a thrill of, what?—perhaps love mixed with terror. Though he hadn't been moving, so far as she could see, Richard seemed all at once more still than before, as if by some means, through the girl's body, he'd become aware of her. Quickly, without a sound, Sally had fled like an evil shadow—that was how she felt—from the doorway.

"Horace," she'd said upstairs afterward, worried as a mother, "what if the Flynn girl gets pregnant?"

"It's more like a question of *when*," he'd said.

Now, staring at her book, she saw again, through it —as if the paper and the print were a frail screen—the Flynn girl's eyes. Such was woman's lot, the lot of all victims of the world's high righteousness: to sneak and cower and forever lie below. Not defenseless, quite. There was always guile. There was always conspiracy, secret insolence, the comfort of the victim's hidden scorn. Once Horace had spanked her. (He hadn't been perfect; she never said he was.) It was common in those days, husbands spanking wives. Horace had been better than most, in fact; he'd never beaten her, as James would beat Ariah if she ever dared look at him cross-eyed. "Yes dear," Sally would say to Horace thereafter, smiling sweetly, whispering black murder inside her mind. And there were always stories to give women secret comfort, like the legends of old Judah Sherbrooke's crafty young wife.

It was that that gave her pleasure in the paperback novel, she realized. To all that would tyrannize—the flag and religion and the domination of men—the novel smiled sweetly, like a loving wife, and . . . She hunted for the image and, with delight, jumped it: *smiled sweetly and let a little fart.*

She read on.

4

SUICIDE AND RAPE

Dr. Alkahest was no fool. He guessed at once that the first place to look for that "fishingboat" must be Fisherman's Wharf, and if he didn't find it there, he must search the surrounding wharfs and docks from San Francisco to the

87

ends of Sausalito. The cargo, after all, must be coming in, not going out. All the back gardens in the city could hardly have yielded such a load as that.

Enfeebled though he was by his night's excitement, he leaned toward the taxi driver's ear —he was an elderly black man with steel-wool hair—and called, slightly whining, "Cabby, let's drive around the docks awhile. I have a kind of thing about old fishingboats." The driver nodded and leaned sideways to look at him in the mirror. Dr. Alkahest added, "I think I'd like to see *all* the docks, all around the Bay—if I don't get tired and tell you otherwise." He leered. If that boat was docked anywhere, he'd smell it.

The driver said, "That'll take a week, old man. Wheah you wanna start?"

Dr. Alkahest gnawed at his lip, distressed. "Well," he said, "what I especially like is those *big* old fishingboats, the kind that go out to sea for days and days, you follow? I like the kind that list a little, old trash-heaps you wouldn't think a sane man would go and risk his life on. It's the texture, ye see. In my younger days I was a photographer."

The driver laughed. "You shittin me, man. You workin for the FBI and you lookin for dope."

Dr. Alkahest smiled from ear to ear, terrified. "A man my age?" he said.

The driver laughed happily and turned left into a narrow, pot-holed road that went up into some trees and at the crest of the hill looked down over San Francisco Bay. For all Dr. Alkahest's fear, the man drove harmlessly . . .

Here again several pages were missing. The novel resumed:

. . . he knew it was hopeless. His heart was racing from the unusual exertion, and his head and lungs were filled with the thick stench of diesel fuel and fish. Dr. Alkahest leaned once more toward the driver and gave him the address of his home. Then he leaned his head back, and the next thing he knew, the driver was gently lifting him from the taxi to the wheelchair, already set up on the sidewalk, asking him was there anything more he could do for him.

"No no, thank you," Dr. Alkahest said, and got out his moneyclip. For no reason, he burst into tears. The cab driver leaned toward him, reaching across the chasm of race and class to lift him by the armpits and set him up more straight. "You want me to wheel you in?" he asked.

"No no," Dr. Alkahest said, and bit back a whimper. "Thank you. You've done more than enough. How much is it?"

"Eighty dollars," the man said.

He was startled at that, but after all, they'd driven for most of the night. He gave the driver ninety.

"Thank *you*, sir," said the driver, and saluted.

Alkahest returned the salute and pushed the right turn button, starting in.

When he reached his floor, the ninth, he hardly even glanced at his cleaning girl, Pearl, though on many occasions he had watched her for hours, looking subtly past a book he was pretending to read or peeking through a keyhole, thinking about the rape of the Trojan women, the million raped women of Bangladesh. No two ways about it, that little Pearl was a juicy number, born to be a queen, or the wife, perhaps, or better yet, mistress, of some rich black lawyer in Chicago, or better yet, white. That someone should sooner or later attack her had been practically inevitable.

But his thoughts, this morning, were not primarily on his cleaning girl. Old John Alkahest had lost all hope, all reason for living. It would take him days to find that boat; he was convinced of that now; and the boat, of course, would not *be* there for days.

He drove the wheelchair to his bedroom and closed the door behind him. On the far side of his large brass bed, French doors opened onto a concrete-balustered balcony, which had plants all around it—flowers and ferns and an enormous rubber tree—and just enough room for him to sit in his wheelchair and take the air. Tired as he was, and sick with confused and turbulent emotions, including a background awareness of Pearl, he drove to the balcony and sat gazing down.

"My life has lost all meaning," he said aloud. It was not so much a question of *whether* he ought to kill himself as *how*. He could, if he liked, ram the wheelchair forward and throw himself onto the concrete railing and, desperately scrambling, grunting and panting like an elderly lover, pull himself over it and fall, flailing, easily piercing the clean light and air to smash through the sidewalk. He leaned forward to look down through the balusters, and felt woozy. Better to use pills, he thought. He remembered an acquaintance, a famous intellectual, who'd killed himself years ago by drinking lye. He'd had his expensive, red velvet curtained apartment cleaned, and he'd carefully gone around and set up black candles, and he'd set out poetry here and there for his friends to find—touching sentiments from Rossetti and favorite works of his own—and he'd put on his velveteen smoking jacket and, with as much elegance as possible, considering, had rammed down the lye with a brandy glass, after putting in a phonecall to his friends. When they came they found tables tipped over and the velvet curtains torn down, the candles knocked akilter, and everywhere the filth of the miserable body's indignation, girlish resistance, and reluctant sleep.

Dr. Alkahest, crying now, pale hands trembling, backed off the balcony, closed the French doors and white silk curtains, then drove, breathing hard, to the telephone by his bedside. SUI-CIDE, he dialed, and while he waited for someone to . . .

Here again she found one of those infuriating gaps. Two pages later the story went on:

. . . farther from my mind. Who have *I* to get even with? No, this is a reasoned suicide. I'm the loneliest young man in the world."

"You're *young?*" she said. She seemed faintly excited.

"I'm disguising my voice," he said, and found he was a little excited himself. He imagined her breasts.

"You're kidding me," she said. "You're old."

"Why would I kid you? I'm at the point of death. I phoned you, didn't I? That must mean I want help, so why would I fool around with you?"

"You're really young?—disguising your voice?"

He imagined her crotch. "I've already told you twice."

The fool was convinced. "You're very good, you know that? I mean, are you an actor?" Her excitement was increasing. He was discovering, for no clear reason, the will to live.

"I *am* an actor, actually. I'm amazed that you got it so quickly!"

"But you're out of work," she said with deep sympathy.

"That's it! Right on!"

"But surely, with a talent like yours—" She let it trail off, perhaps hoping he'd speak. When he said nothing, she continued, "Are you an actor I might have heard of? TV?"

"Movies, actually. You've heard of me all right."

"Not *Brando*," she whispered.

"My God," he said, "how do you *do* it?" Noisily, he hung up. Yet even as he laughed with rackety glee, he was not amused—felt increasingly depressed. He'd forgotten how inadequate women were to a person's needs—like the world. That was why, in the Middle Ages, they'd been the Church Fathers' great symbol of "the World." No wonder preachers railed against them, and conquering armies raped and slaughtered them! He indulged himself with a brief, dead serious fantasy of seeking her out, this Judy of SUICIDE—lying in wait for her, a pipewrench in his hands. He felt, simultaneously, exhilarated and despairing. In secret he couldn't deny to himself that her girlish voice had touched and distressed him with a hunger for the perfect, for heaven's glory and absolute justice, for the girl-faced, golden-winged angels of his childhood, things he'd known for years he was never to have in this world—in this or any other—so that, hungering for the possible, he could think only of filth and death: the deflowering and smashing of beautiful young women, or suicide, which was the same. There was no third choice, metaphysically, except perhaps waking sleep—sweet mystic Mary Jane! He saw himself floating, as in a sportscar ad, or an ad for toothpaste or shampoo, his wheelchair surrounded by flowers and beautiful young

women and effeminate young men, Judy of
SUICIDE, leaping toward him through tall yellow grass in slow-motion, CONCEPTROL
printed in the blue sky behind her.

That's my dream, thought Alkahest, bitterly
weeping, wringing his fingers, not making a
sound. *That's everybody's dream, the whole
length and breadth of America. And not to be
had!*

As old Dr. Alkahest sat weeping, something
came to him from nowhere. Perhaps it was illusion—he was tired enough, certainly—but then
again, perhaps it was a memory, buried in his
consciousness and peeking out only now,
timidly, like a lizard from behind a rock. It
seemed to him that—faintly, so faintly he
hadn't noticed at the time (if it was not in fact
a dream)—a voice had said, down in the darkness below the cutter, "He's a human being. We
couldn't just let him drown." It was all Dr. Alkahest could recall from the exchange, but now,
going over it in his mind, he was so excited his
brain began to tingle and he thought he might
faint. The fellow who'd jumped from the bridge
had been picked up by the fishingboat! Perhaps
he was still alive, then! Perhaps he could still be
found!

It was a slim lead, but reason enough to go
on living. He'd start at once, not a moment to
lose!

But he was faint with exhaustion. The white
of the morning was like steady lightning, hammering at his eyes, and the vacuum cleaner, in
the tower now, was like thunder or the roar of
a surf. Incredibly—considering how much was
to be done—he found himself slipping physically and mentally, sinking toward nothingness,
heavy of brain and body as a stone. By desperate effort, he drove himself into the elevator,
away from the monstrous suggestion of the bed,
rode up to the tower and out into the white,

octagonal room, meaning to ask Pearl to get him coffee, pep pills, tobacco—bring him back to life.

"Pearl!" he tried to call, but his voice was inaudible. "Oh *no!*" he wailed inwardly. It was unspeakably unjust—intolerable! But the dimming continued, as when the electricity falters and fails in an old hotel, and at last Dr. Alkahest gave in to it—helplessly endured the obscene violation, abandoning his rights.

It was the end of the chapter, but Sally Abbott was enjoying herself now, and she had nothing but time. She went on without a moment's hesitation.

5

MR. NIT

Peter Wagner awakened to a foul, green darkness that seemed an intensification of troubles in his stomach. Things moved, ugly shadows as in a William Burroughs novel; he couldn't focus them. Black things began to impinge on the green, now weed, now seaweed, so that he couldn't tell whether he was drowning or merely in hell. Mouth open, eyes squinting, he thought of his wife, source of all misery and cruel disenchantment; never mind that he was, for her, the same. Once—maybe half of that first year of marriage—when he'd looked at her he'd seen her, as he'd seen all the world, integral and transcendent, like a lemon in sunlight, and he'd been indivisibly, unthinkingly one with her as a child and a day in July are unthinkingly one (or a lemon and sunlight). That was long past, now; might have been a dream. He saw now, discrete as numbers, her tics and oddities. When she turned her hand palm up, holding her dark brown, pencil-thin cigar, he saw the gesture in perfect isolation, raised from the life-giving mulch of its surroundings and logically finite, as if the hand were severed at the wrist.

So it was in everything these days. He had reached—and it seemed to him everyone had reached—the decadent age of analysis. Eden's bright apple had turned in his mouth to dust and blowing ashes. Like his wife, like what he'd once thought of fondly as his country, life had turned trivial-minded and bitchy, filled with unreasonable complaints. He closed his eyes, felt sicker—his head was pounding—and slept again.

The next time he awakened he was in a large cabin, mysterious as Ben Franklin's tinkering room, thick with alchemistical smells. He felt at once the familar hovering of a docked ship —a gentle, more-than-physical restlessness, speculum of Peter Wagner's world: an eagle trying forever to land on the limb of a forever falling tree, a sentence snaking ominously downward in Spengler's *Decline of the West*. Through his blood and bones came, from time to time, the thud of the boat's outer wall against a wharf. He could feel the heaviness of the water beyond the iron hull, silt and sewage, old condiments and condoms, pages from popular psychology books, and he could feel, or imagined he could feel, the slippery bump of, hopefully, dead fish. He was lying on a wooden bunk suspended from the bulkhead by chains. He moved his arm. It was stiff. He lay still, oppressed by a sense of *déjà vu*, then remembered: all that was happening had happened in some novel he'd read about a hoax.

Then the smells came over him more heavily. Like a zoo. He tensed himself to identify the smell, and suddenly remembered, with strange joy, the Reptile House in St. Louis. The alligator pit and, somewhere nearby—was it peavines?

At last he saw well. A second officer's cabin, once well fitted out, black now, decayed. There was a wooden table, once a mess table, he guessed. It was so close to his bunk he could have reached out and touched it. There were things on it, vaguely alive. Five feet or so beyond the table there was a desk and, beyond the desk, a wall of books. At the desk there was a man. The light was dim, only a Coleman lantern above the man at the desk. Once more, Peter Wagner closed his eyes, this time to think.

He was not dead. Nor was he ruptured, so far as he could tell. He remembered all at once the woman who had revived him, and immediately thought again of the man behind the desk. Small, with the wide mouth and red, button eyes of a monkey. Black cap, black sweater. Peter Wagner opened one eye experimentally. The monkey eyes came at him like a pair of nails.

He scratched his head, pondering, then raised up by little jerks, uncertainly onto one elbow, and prepared to speak. *Where am I?* he thought of saying, but he changed his mind. "Pig's ass in hell," he said. He squinted at the man.

"My name's Nit," the man said. His eyes were red at the edges, the color of steamed lobsters.

The outlines of things were clearer now. The things on the desk were electric eels. They lay side by side, a few inches apart, apparently nailed down to the table in some way, and they were connected by wires. Just in front of their heads, carefully lined up so that the tips of their noses made a line as straight as a ruler line, there was a wooden thing like the paddle on a butter churn, with a crank at the end like the wooden crank on an ice-cream freezer, apparently designed so that all the eels could be bumped on the nose at once. Peter Wagner rubbed his eyes, then looked again. They were still there. There were other things—stacked up pieces of electrical equipment cluttered with wheels and dials and knobs, old pieces of rope, and under the table, coils of insulated wire.

"My name's Nit," the man repeated. He added, this time, "Jonathan Nit." He smiled exactly like an eel.

Peter Wagner now thought about this for a time, compressing his lips, then nodded. "My name's Peter Wagner." When he tried to sit

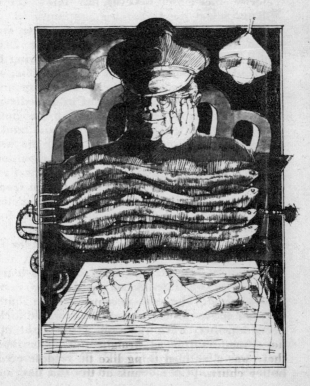

up he discovered that his legs were tied from the ankles to the hips like a roll of carpet in a warehouse. He threw a look at Mr. Nit, who went on smiling, the shadow of his turned-up nose growing longer and shorter as the hanging lamp swung beside him. The smile did not hide the fact that Mr. Nit was distressed, for some reason disappointed and perhaps at the same time, paradoxically, relieved.

"Jesus," he said. "You been sleeping like a dead man." He gave a laugh. His face was heavily lined, and under his eyes there were great gray sacks like dead things hanging by the hooves.

"How come you tied up my feet?" Peter Wagner said.

Mr. Nit's hands clutched at each other and began frantically popping his knuckles. "Oh that," he said. He rolled his eyes up, trying to think of an explanation, but nothing came, so he went on sitting with his eyes rolled up and his head to one side like a saint in a medieval painting. Peter Wagner pushed up on both arms, threw his feet over the side of the bunk, and began untying the ropes. Though he was not looking at Mr. Nit now, his whole attention was focused on the man, listening for the first sign that Mr. Nit might try to prevent him from freeing his feet. Mr. Nit made no move. Peter Wagner stood up, leaning toward the table for balance.

"Don't touch the eels," Mr. Nit said, as if involuntarily.

He caught himself and drew back his hand in the nick of time. A surge of panic went through him. The eels were wired like lightbulbs in series. Touch one and they would kick back, together, a charge that would light up the whole West Coast for minutes. When the first instinctive horror passed, he remembered his latest attempt of suicide and saw in a flash of inspiration that here lay the perfect instrument; a jolt, a flash, a smell of burning flesh that he would probably miss, and Zero. He smiled grimly and reached toward the eels again. But he happened to look up. Mr. Nit sat bent over and sideways at his desk, tightly covering both eyes with his hands, except that the left eye was peeking through the fingers.

"You *want* me to!" Peter Wagner said, shocked and, in fact, somewhat hurt.

"Oh no!" Mr. Nit said, throwing himself so violently into the look of innocence that he nearly fell off his chair. "I warned you, didn't I? Wasn't it me that—"

But Peter Wagner wasn't fooled. "You don't even know me!" he said. He could have cried. "You *want* me dead. You pull me out of the fucking ocean and you waste my time and inconvenience me, and then you try to get me killed on a fucking eel!" He was suddenly furious. He clenched his fists, dangerous weapons, he knew from experience. "God damn you, it isn't right," he said. "I'm a human being!"

The words had a powerful effect on Mr. Nit. Tears flooded down his cheeks and he popped his knuckles wildly. "Human!" he said, and laughed, sobbing. "Human. God knows! Terrific!" He popped his knuckles and shook his head from side to side and drew up his knees in spasms. Peter Wagner calmed himself and covered his mouth with his hand, thoughtfully, watching the strange performance. "You're crazy," he said.

"I'm crazy," Mr. Nit said. It sent him off into peals of tragic laughter that tipped the chair over backward, leaving only his jerking feet in sight. Cautiously, Peter Wagner made his way around the eel table and went over to bend beside the desk and study Mr. Nit. The little man wiggled and jerked and writhed, laughing as if heart-broken. At last he stopped. They studied each other, their faces no more than two feet apart, Mr. Nit looking thoughtfully up from the floor, with bloodshot eyes, Peter Wagner looking thoughtfully down, like Zeus at Sarpedon.

"You all right?" Peter Wagner said.

Mr. Nit pursed his lips, thinking, then nodded.

"Let me help you up."

"I've been under a strain," Mr. Nit said when he was back in his chair. He corrected himself: "I'm under a constant strain." He glanced furtively at Peter Wagner to see if he believed him. "I'm an atheist."

"I see," Peter Wagner said.

Mr. Nit looked away, folded his hands, resisted the temptation to pop his knuckles. "It's very comforting, talking to you." He slid another glance at Peter Wagner, then away.

Peter Wagner's mouth smiled sickly.

"Actually, what's got me so upset—" Mr. Nit struggled to find words, bit his lips together, and squinted. He looked so guilty, all at once, that Peter Wagner glanced around half expecting to see the old man in the long black coat sneaking up once more to brain him. But there was nothing, or nothing but the table of eels, the electrical equipment, and the smell. Or smells. Two distinct smells, it came to him now. The zoological smell and something else, the smell of . . . He strained, and at last it came to him: pot! He breathed deep, confirming the suspicion, and Mr. Nit's eyebrows lifted in alarm.

"I'm a scientist," Mr. Nit said. He snatched at Peter Wagner's sleeve. "That's my joy and my curse. Can you imagine where civilization would be without science? Inventors have taken the place of God in the modern world. Are you aware of that? Come look!" He jumped down off his chair and ran over to the table of eels. "Look!" he said again, spreading his arms and stretching the sides of his mouth out and downward. "Eels," he said. Lovingly. "If we could harness that power . . ." He turned some knobs. A red light came on. "Watch that dial," he said, stretching his arm toward a dial to Peter's left. The dial had a range from zero to fifty thousand volts. "I merely turn this crank and bop their noses—" he turned it, "—and *zap!*" The machines all suddenly hummed, and the dial went nearly to the top.

"Whooey!" Peter Wagner said.

"Yes," he said, rubbing his hands. The eels writhed a little, then lay still. "Terrific animals, eels. They can live either in water or on land, they're cheap to feed, they make no great mess —" He sank into thought, smiling darkly.

"That's very interesting," Peter Wagner said. They were ugly things to look at: snakelike, sharklike, flat-bellied as snails, the color of a rushing subway train going through smog.

"A man would be famous if he could harness that power. More famous than Benjamin Franklin," Mr. Nit said.

"I imagine he would." Then, politely: "You should do it."

"Hah!" He pushed his hands down into his pockets and looked grim, just a touch sly. "Not as easy as you think." From the twitch of the little man's jaw Peter Wagner saw he'd hit a sore spot and tried to circumambulate. "Well anyway," he said . . .

"Mr. Wagner," Mr. Nit said. He turned to go over to his desk, where he stood, hands folded behind his back, his back turned to Peter Wagner. "Inventing is a God damn discouraging business. Degrading. Like everything else. Ah, I could tell you! How thrilling it seemed, the idea of inventing, when I was a young little donkey, full of beans! Roger Bacon, Faraday, Franklin, Watt— those were names to conjure with, like the rustle of yer dear love's skirt or the ineffable syllables describing her parts."

Mr. Nit's head turned, his small eyes dimmed. "Has it ever occurred to you that every discovery mankind has ever made was accidental?"

"Actually, no," Peter Wagner said.

"It's a fact," he said. Mr. Nit's back looked angry. His trousers were as rumpled and crabbed as his face. He shook his fists as if working up a tantrum. "Some stupid caveman banked his fire with copper ore, and that was the end of the stone age. We have records of such things. Believe me, it's depressing! The invention of glass, for instance: it's recorded in Pliny. There was this Roman merchant ship with a cargo of natron—that's a washing powder. It was driven ashore on a beach of white sand, and the crew lighted a fire on the sand to cook their food, and since they couldn't find rocks they propped up their kettle with some big lumps of natron. *Kavoom!* They'd invented glass. I could tell you a hundred stories like that. It suffocates the soul."

"I see what you mean," Peter Wagner said.

"Louis Daguerre, for instance." He began to pace back and forth from wall to wall, banging one fist into the other, faster and faster. "He worked for years on the idea of fixing an image on a surface, but no luck. Then one day he laid a silver spoon on a metal he'd treated with iodine, and when he picked it up he found its image printed on . . .

Sally Abbott had come to another gap, several pages this time. "Oh, *tunkit!*" she said. Again she had half a mind to quit. The farther she read, she could see in advance, the more pages she'd find missing. She stared at the top of the page beyond the gap, trying to reach some decision. Without quite meaning to, half-dreaming, she read on.

. . . "Actually," Peter Wagner said.

But the man was unstoppable, a looney. He might have been talking of pestilence, earthquake, death. "Thomas A. Edison," he rushed on, "invented the phonograph in eighteen seventy-seven when he was trying to invent a telegraph-repeater that could make a needle record dots and dashes on a revolving paper disk as they came in over the telegraph line. When the needle passed over the indentations at high speeds it vibrated like a tuning fork, and that was the secret of the Victrola! In eighteen thirty-nine Charles Goodyear discovered the secret of curing rubber when he clumsily dropped a sticky glob of uncured rubber into sulphur. And then there's Acheson's ridiculous discovery of—"

"How come you locked the door?" Peter Wagner said.

Mr. Nit turned, looking uncomfortable, wringing his hands. "Oh, that." He seemed to sort through explanations that might pass. He found nothing. At last he said, animated again, fiercely rattling some door of his own, "Worst of all—Gramme's discovery of the motor. In eighteen seventy-three Gramme entered a number of dynamos at an industrial exhibit in Vienna. By mistake, a workman reversed the connections between two dynamos, and to the astonishment of everyone looking on, the armature of the second dynamo began to revolve: the electric motor was invented." Mr. Nit stamped and slapped his right fist into his left hand harder than ever by way of comment.

"How come the door's locked?" Peter Wagner said. He jerked the wooden handle illustratively.

"What's the difference?" Mr. Nit said. Sweat popped out on his forehead and his wrinkles twitched. "One minute you want to drown yourself, and the next you want to go up and take the air. You should try and be reasonable."

Peter Wagner thought about it. He had bitten to the bone of history, chewed to the hirsute pits of metaphysics, and yet he'd remained, at least much of the time, a harmless man, nonviolent. How much did the world require? "I *am* reasonable," he said. "I just don't like to be locked up with a bunch of eels. They smell." He added, "For one thing."

Mr. Nit grew increasingly nervous. He smiled briefly, like distant lightning flicking on and off, then wiped his forehead on his sleeve. "So ironic, this piddling little human rage for freedom. So short-sighted and misguided, set against *true* freedom, that is, sacrifice. So the door's locked, you say. So what door isn't? It makes me laugh." He laughed, experimental, exactly like a goat. "Human freedom. What a laugh!" He laughed again. "Pride of a pissant! What is, I ask you, Mr. Wagner, *man?* The great technologist? The star-stepper? Birdpoop! You know what we are? We're the late evolution of a stick. Fact! You think human reason came down out of its tree and perceived the potential of the stick? Of course not! A man swung a stick by accident and the stick improved his mind. Exactly! There's an article about it in the *Science Digest.* I think I may still have a copy here someplace." He turned as if to look, then abruptly changed his mind. "We do nothing, Mr. Wagner. Things *happen* to us."

There was a thump above, then another. Someone coming aboard. Mr. Nit's despair became more urgent. He leaned forward, clutching his hands together. "You were right to want to kill yourself. It's not too late, you know. It was a brave, brave thing you attempted. I mean *morally* brave."

Peter Wagner smiled wanly, feeling it was true but feeling, also, suspicious.

Mr. Nit glanced past him at the door. Now there was more than one person above. Peter Wagner tried to separate the footsteps. The shuffle of the old man, then younger feet—the girl's, the muscular man's, perhaps. Were there more than that? The suicide squad? Was it illegal to kill yourself in California?

"To be or not to be," Mr. Nit said, stretching his arms out, "*that* is the question!" He'd snatched a jackknife from somewhere and was holding it up in front of his face, looking at it cross-eyed. Peter Wagner took a step toward him in alarm, then hesitated. It was clear that Mr. Nit was not going to kill himself before finishing his speech. "Consciousness, that's our tragedy," he said. "We watch ourselves, we watch the world, and we perceive in horror that we're no more free than, so to speak, the physicist's ball on an inclined plane—except in this, yes! We're free at least to say 'No, Universe! No, no, no, no, *no!!*' " He jerked his arms as if to stab himself but hesitated, looking at the blade. It was rusty, perhaps not sharp. He made a face. "That's why I admire you."

Outside the door and upwards a little, a voice said, "Yes it's all unloaded. Let's clear out."

Mr. Nit blanched. Quickly he said, "We'll kill ourselves together! We'll make a pact!"

Peter Wagner frowned. "How come you people had marijuana on this boat?"

Mr. Nit made a fast swipe at his forehead with his sweater sleeve, then again clasped his hands around the jackknife, holding it in front of his belly now, ready for the plunge. "You do it on the eels," he hissed. "I'll use the knife. One . . . two . . ."

But Peter Wagner turned away a little, eyeing Mr. Nit intently. "You want me dead." And now it came to him. "They told you to kill me,

105

that's why you're so nervous." He thought about it and saw it was true. Mr. Nit was shaking. Peter Wagner said, "Because of the marijuana, that's it? You're smugglers, and if you let me off this tub—" He moved a step toward Mr. Nit, smiling at last. He understood it all.

"You *see*?" Mr. Nit said, throwing his arms out and backing up a step. "You see how ridiculous the whole thing is? One moment you want to drown yourself, and the next moment you think someone's trying to kill you and you want to bash their brains in! That's humanity! Idiots! Fart-heads! We're supposed to be the idealists, vectors for all the world, us Americans—you and me. Where are our ideals? We live for nothing, not even filthy materialism. What true materialist would settle for a McDonald's hamburger? We're filth, dead garbage and creators of garbage! For the love of God, can *no* one rise above it?"

Peter Wagner stopped advancing on Nit and frowned. Mr. Nit had a point. He had long ago given up any hope of improving himself, much less the whole grisly race. He said, stalling, "You should see the kind of life I lead." His face puckered, and Mr. Nit's face mirrored it. "Awful," Peter Wagner said, and he felt again how serene it would be to be dead—physically, no longer just spiritually dead. There were certain women to whom he had made certain promises, not in so many words; there were certain bills he had allowed to mount up; above all, there were certain dull mechanisms he had observed in himself, impossible for him, at his age, to change. There was, incidentally, the matter of his sister Clara.

Mr. Nit nodded eagerly, eyes slanting downward, filled with grief. "All our glorious civilization is like this leaky ship, Mr. Wagner! Cargo of artificial joy, five-cent oblivion, now emptied, and for guidance, only a sea-sick, half-cracked

106

landlubber Captain that can't tell which way's larbard."

"Larbard?" Peter Wagner said.

Mr. Nit looked embarrassed. "Whatever that may be." He explained in haste, "Actually, none of us knows much in the nautical line. We're better with airplanes."

Someone was coming below now. He could hear the creak of wood and a heavy man's breathing. Mr. Nit became urgent. "I'll tell you the truth. The Captain may not be too happy with me if he walks in and finds you alive and well. You see, it's awkward, you see. You *know* now. About our business, that is. And even if you didn't we couldn't let you leave the ship. Somebody'd ask you how come you didn't drown, and sooner or later they'd turn up the *Indomitable*, and they'd come visit us, to ask questions, say, or give us medals or something, and maybe one of those officials would have a nose on him, and he'd get a little whiff of the *fish* we carry, if you see what I mean—find us out by blind accident, the way human beings do everything, and poof!, whole thing up in smoke."

Peter Wagner nodded.

"In other words, I've been asked by the Captain . . . It's not the kind of work I like—a scientist, you know, and a family man. But it's a living, you see. When your Captain says he wants X done, if you want to keep your job you do X. I don't mean I'm a murderer. Heaven forbid!" He threw his hands up, shocked at the idea. "I just thought, you see, if what you really wanted—that is, if after considered thought you went up there on the bridge tonight, if you follow me . . ."

Peter Wagner looked down, considering the eels.

"My hope was, actually, that you'd wake up,

still half-unconscious, and get up and start to take a step . . ."

He understood, now, the tied feet. If all had gone well he'd have gotten up and pitched into the eels. He wouldn't have known what hit him. The whole thing was queerly touching. Nit was odd, certainly odd, but he had a devious humanity about him. Most people did, when you really got to know them. That, in a way, was what made the whole thing so depressing. But Peter Wagner had no time to think that through. Mr. Nit had been talking faster and faster, hands fluttering like birds, now to the sides, now back to each other to make knuckles pop. Mr. Nit was scared. Because of the Captain, of course. *Poor devil*, Peter Wagner thought. He wondered about Mr. Nit's family, but there was no time to dwell on that either.

"So if you wanted to save us a lot of trouble," Mr. Nit was saying, his eyes imploring . . . "If you cared to be, for one brief moment in your life, a real American, a servant of others in the highest sense . . ."

The key turned in the lock and the door creaked open. Peter Wagner glanced at the eels, but he couldn't do it, not just like that, without even one good deep breath. And so it was too late. The old man stood peering in, incredulous, outraged, leaning fiercely on his cane as if to crush it. He came slowly, unsteadily into the room, and looked from Peter Wagner to Mr. Nit. Peter Wagner backed toward the eels.

"What's this?" the old man croaked.

"Nothing, sir," Mr. Nit said.

The Captain looked back at Peter Wagner.

And then the other two were there—the girl, Jane, and the muscular man, kindly looking, exceedingly distressed. He saw at once that those two had not been in on the Captain's scheme. They could save him, and would; he had no doubt of that, if he wanted to be saved. But looking at the girl, with her fine square jaw, her cowgirl stance, her comic-book blue eyes and granny glasses, he decided, with sudden vehemence, on the eels.

The Captain watched him with eyes like fires at the city dump.

He would do it. They could toss him like a burnt potato chip into the sea.

Hand over heart, eyes raised toward heaven, Peter Wagner said, "Farewell, cruel world! Another poor sailor goes down to Davy Jones."

"You're a sailor?" the Captain said, screwing up his eyes.

"I was Merchant Marine."

All four of them dived on him at once, and though he threw his arms with all his might, he could not quite get his hands on the nearest of the eels.

———

6

PETER WAGNER'S VISION

"God bless you, sailor!" the Captain bellowed, pounding him somewhat violently on the back.

Sally looked up, smelling cooking. Lunchtime already? She listened to her brother clumping around the kitchen, the cat meowing at his heels. After a moment she put her novel on the table and got up, slipped her feet into her slippers, and made her way up the attic stairs for three apples. She put the apples on the table beside the book, used the bedpan and tucked it away out of sight, then went over to the door and pressed her ear against it. James was whistling as he'd done when he went out to chores this morning. She scowled.

"We shall see what we shall see," she said aloud, squinting fiercely, half crooning it, sing-song. She smiled, distracted by her witch imitation, thinking of her friend Ruth Thomas crooning impishly-wicked poetry to children at the library. She had a wonderfully expressive face. She could do idiot looks, greedy looks, pompous looks—she could make her face do almost anything. Her eyes seemed to slant, and you'd almost have sworn that her dog-teeth grew longer when she recited the wolf poem.

> The Wolf is a very good watchdog, it's true;
> The only trouble is,
> He considers all he protects, and you too,
> His.

Ruth and her husband Ed had a cabin—more like a hunting lodge—in the mountains above East Arlington. Ed was one of those well-off farmers who could get away when he liked. Often she and Horace, and sometimes Estelle and Ferris Parks, had driven up there for a day or two. In the evening sometimes they would sing. Ed Thomas had a wonderful voice, of course; he was one of those Welshmen who would sing all day on his farm tractor, sing while he was milking or bathing in the tub, sing harmony with Ruth as they drove along the road. He was in church "every time they left the door unlocked," Ruth liked to say—she was a great joker—"thumbing through the hymnal and tuning up his throat." Estelle's tall, handsome husband Ferris had a bass voice, thin compared to Ed's but a pleasure to listen to, all the same. Horace's voice was ordinary. She smiled. The cabin had no electricity. The Thomases had put up large Japanese lanterns, and they had candles, of course. They would all sit on the full-width porch in front on a cool summer evening, the dark, shallow river driving past them, rattling—it had always been a river just jumping with fish—and she and Horace would hold hands, as would Ferris and Estelle, and Ed Thomas would talk of the weather or of things he'd seen. She'd never known anyone like him for talking of the weather. It was like poetry. He would speak of otters playing in the river—otters as big as large dogs, he said—or he'd describe precisely how locking time came, here in the woods, or he'd speak of the past. He told of the British spy who painted murals, over near Marlboro village, and of the pig-iron days in Shaftsbury and halfway down Prospect. They would sit hushed, entranced, and once while Ed talked she had been aware that Ferris Parks was looking at her. She'd been a beauty in those days. Stood out in a crowd. Aware of his watching her, she'd smiled just a little, pretending she still listened, and she'd slipped off her shoes, and crossed her legs, moving one stockinged foot rhythmically, and she'd let tall, quiet Ferris Parks think whatever he might please.

She put the apple to her mouth, lined up her dentures, and bit. Juice sprayed. Carefully chewing, she set the apple down and climbed back into bed. She pulled up the blankets and took up her book again. "Now where were we?" she said, and adjusted her glasses a little. Into her mind came an image of Mr. Nit, in his black cap and black sweater, talking of atheism and accidents. She saw that she was picturing him as her Ginny's husband, Lewis Hicks, and it made her smile. And who was Peter Wagner? Sally couldn't say yet, except that he was tall, with beautiful, sad eyes, and blondish.

6

PETER WAGNER'S VISION

"God bless you, sailor!" the Captain bellowed, pounding him somewhat violently on the back. And then, apparently to those around him: "He's alive. Just a bump on the nose where he met with the floor, ha ha!" They laughed, as filled with joy as the risen saints.

Peter Wagner felt spray and headway wind. They'd brought him up on deck to revive him.

"If we only had some whiskey to pour on his face," the girl said.

"There's cold coffee in the galley," Mr. Nit said.

"Good!" the Captain said. "Get it!"

Hastily, Peter Wagner opened his eyes and got up on his elbows. They were buried in fog, the engines running Full Ahead and nobody up in the wheelhouse.

"He's coming around," Mr. Goodman said, leaning down, hands on knees to look at Peter Wagner.

Peter Wagner groaned and wiped his mouth with the back of his hand. It came away bloody. He instinctively tensed himself to fight, but caught himself.

"That was a nasty fall, sailor," the Captain said. "Here, smoke this." He reached down his pipe.

Peter Wagner sniffed, winced back like a cat, then reconsidered. It was pot. He took a puff. A more than physical calefaction spread through his broiling chest and head, and the contrasting chill of the breeze and fog made him shudder. All four of them saw it, watching him like seahawks. "He's cold," "He's shivering," "Get him inside," their voices all said at once. Before he could avoid them, Mr. Goodman and Mr. Nit had his shoulders and legs and were carrying him up onto the bridge. He was too tired to resist. He let his arms drag, and puffed in and out, in and out, on the pipe. The violence in his heart evaporated.

Then he was in a dim room—the Captain's cabin. There was a flag on the wall, the red and blue slightly faded.

"Welcome aboard, sailor," the Captain said heartily. The others echoed it, and they slapped Peter Wagner's shoulders so cheerfully that he would have fallen down if they'd given him room to. "Sit here," the Captain said, and they forced him to a chair. Now they all had pipes. Blue smoke rose around him, thicker than the fog out on deck.

"This is Mr. Goodman," Mr. Nit said. "Mr. Goodman's who saved your life."

Mr. Goodman beamed, childlike, and his pipe-charge burned bright red.

"We're like a family, here on the *Indomitable*," the Captain said.

"We have our little disagreements, of course," Mr. Goodman said quickly, earnestly, as if it were very important that things be kept straight.

The Captain laughed like an alligator and Jane patted Mr. Goodman's musclebound cheek.

"We're like a society in small," the Captain said, growing more philosophical, leaning back in the chair Mr. Nit had produced. A foghorn boomed, dangerously close. No one but Peter Wagner seemed to notice. The Captain appeared to be far away, almost invisible in the smoke. It was excellent pot, quick-grabbing.

"Mr. Nit represents technology." The Captain chuckled, delighted with himself, then pointed with his pipe to the smoky shadow of Mr. Goodman. "Mr. Goodman here is our moral guardian, as his name implies. The clergyman, the humanist, in his small way the artist."

It flickered dimly through Peter Wagner's mind that in German "Fist" was "Faust." Very interesting. Then he forgot again.

"I believe," Mr. Goodman said apologetically, as if slightly alarmed, "we should do unto others as we would have others do unto us. That's the only true law, I feel."

The Captain chuckled wickedly. "And Jane here—" he began. He paused, seemingly at a loss, and leaned forward until his snaky eyes emerged from the murky smoke. "What was Guinevere to King Arthur's court, or the Virgin Mary to the Christian religion? The coronet! The jewel that gives it all meaning!" He laughed till he coughed.

"I see," Peter Wagner said. It was fascinating, astounding, like an insight into modern physics. He was stoned. When he closed his eyes he saw brightly lit clouds with glodes where wide beams of sunlight burst through, and standing on the sunbeams, waving to him like people in home movies, angels. Now there was music, some patriotic hymn, and the Statue of Liberty strode into the picture, carrying not a torch but the American flag, which was flapping grandly in the technicolor wind. He was standing on the wide, gleaming deck of some ship—he saw the name in red and gold on a snow-white life-saver: *The New Jerusalem*. He opened his eyes. The room was dark and distorted and filled with smoke. Jane was sitting now on half of Peter Wagner's chair, looking slightly cross-eyed down her pipe. She had her arm around his shoulder.

"And you, sailor—" The Captain's eyes were now inches from his own. His tone became ominous, as if brought from the midnight depths of the sea where unimaginable fish preyed on whales. "All is not well with the *Indomitable*." He slid his eyes sideways, as if watching for ghostly spies. The others' eyes slid sideways too, all inches away from Peter Wagner's . . .

Other things happened at the Captain's party, but nothing Peter Wagner would remember.

He dreamed that night that he slept with his wife, with whom he hadn't slept in a year or more—except that, as sometimes happens in dreams, it seemed she both was and was not his wife. She stood naked in front of him, radiating light like Tinkerbell, as dream-women

114

will, her breasts erect and pinkish with desire. He put his hands on her hips and pressed the side of his face against her belly. He had forgotten how it felt. Her lower hair was silky and, surprisingly, black.

"It's been so long," he said. She tipped his face up and kissed him, then straightened up slightly and guided his lips to her nipple. The next moment (something had happened to time) he was between her legs, plunged deep inside her, his open mouth locked, laboring, on hers. The moment after that, as if it were the same moment, she was talking to him, murmuring gently in his ear as she had done when he'd first known her.

"Why the bridge?" she seemed to say. "You're so beautiful, so gentle. What made you feel you had to? Are you a Pisces?"

"I don't know," he said; "it's not the first time. Maybe it's a habit." He pretended to laugh. Groan, groan, groan. She laughed too, but lovingly, as if completely unafraid of him. She had changed. She was like a living *Playboy* foldout. "Tell me about it," she said.

It was as if they had met in some neutral place—a medieval garden with grass and flowers like a featherbed, and, over their heads, interlocked limbs drooping hazel and oakmoss. It was a place where they might try, for once, for an honest truce, a new beginning. "Rapist," she had called him. "All men are rapists." It wasn't, he felt, true. Certainly he was more often the seduced than the seducer. Nor was her general thesis true. The Indian brave raping the wife of the soon-to-be scalped white settler, the settler raping the wife of the soon-to-be-massacred Indian, that was no proof, as she claimed —pompous and professorial and mired deep in facts—that womanhood was always the ultimate victim, the final enemy of Everyman. It made the woman the enemy's chief revenge, his ultimate insult to the husband. With the same mad leap of the pervert heart, the Vikings had torn down cathedrals. She, his wife, had been thoroughly unpersuaded. Men beat their women, she pointed out, echoing, he knew, some women's-center dyke; and men's laws, for five thousand years, had forgiven it. "In Russia, peasants beat their ikons," he'd said.

"I want all the lives that are possible," he said. "Not only for me. For everybody. I want to live everything that's possible to live, a hundred thousand novels. I want everybody to. It's—" He tried to focus her, but the dream-woman wouldn't come clear. She was not, it seemed to him now, his wife. Her fingers moved, infinitely gentle, over his testicles and penis. It felt, as dreams will, too real to be a dream. He moved his hands on her breasts. She moaned with pleasure and again, little by little, he grew hard.

"And what happened?" she murmured in his ear.

"Long drunken talks late at night," he said, "each of us trying to explain to the other, both of us feeling imprisoned and betrayed. Arguments; fights. I'd come to myself and she'd be lying on the floor, out cold, and I'd think she was dead. It was horrible; stupid. I never wanted to hurt her. I just wanted to live, wanted everybody to live—free, trying to find happiness, as innocent and simple as Dick meets Jane— live like crazy, like squirrels or deer or lyric poet, because everything around us was retreating." The phrase gave him a subtle thrill, the rushing sensation in the plumbing of the chest that would lead, in a child, to tears. "But I couldn't explain it, even at the moments when I believed it was true, because the possibility was always so obvious that maybe it was a lie, mere childish selfishness. 'Do you love me?' she was always asking, sometimes angrily crying, and I honestly didn't know. She was always talking, disagreeing, quoting articles. I would storm off and leave her sometimes, late at night, when I'd drunk myself stupid and I knew there was bound to be a fight, or else we'd already have had the fight, I'd kicked her black and blue in some neighbor's yard. I remember waking up in an old friend's house once, staring at an unfamiliar ceiling as you do when you're a child and don't know where you are. The ceiling was papered, a rented house, and the design was busy, vulgar, faded—gray and silver, I think it was—and directly above my head there was a light fixture, harsh black metal. I started, and then suddenly I remembered where I was, and I felt free. Free enough to soar. I thought of friends I could visit that she hated. Thought of riding the motorcycle I'd just bought maybe a month ago, over her dead body—almost literally. Thought of living the way I was born to live, loose as a tramp, independent as a hermit, fornicating—like a rapist, you may say. The phone rang, and I heard the friend I was staying with talking in his bedroom. He told me that morning that it was my wife who'd called. She was crying, he said, and he dropped it. But I remembered— oh, bitterly!—all the times she'd cried, all the times it seemed to me that I was all she lived for—and all she lived *on*, like beetles on an elm —despite the other times . . . So I went out and took some sleeping pills—don't laugh, though I admit it's somewhat funny—and I laid myself down on the railroad tracks, and when I woke up the train was roaring by and some whiskered old drunks were leaning down over me, tisking, pouring water on my face."

She rolled over on top of him and lay kissing his eyes and nose and lips. She became still.

"I used to be religious," she said. "I'm still religious, some of the time, some ways. Anyway, I worry about it. Sometimes. Have you ever been to a party of freaks?"

"That too," he sighed.

She said, "The first freak party I went to, the people all got undressed. Or some of them. They sat and lay around the floor smelling incense and playing strange instruments, a lot of them things they'd invented themselves. Two girls made love to one man, right there in front of us all, including this bearded Arabian with a turban. I went into another room—I still had my clothes on—and a boy named Berner and some girl whose name I didn't hear were looking through this telescope at the stars. They told me they had his sperm on the lens, and they wanted for me to come look. I felt strange—horrified and disgusted—and yet I looked. It was ugly, grotesque, I thought. And yet I also thought it wasn't. It was . . . strange. There were colors. I went back inside, and everything was crazy. There were people on the floor, doing things, you know, but also there were people sitting up in chairs, smoking and talking, ignoring the others—or not even that, dismissing all they did in what seemed a friendly, indifferent way. It blew my mind. There was a woman reading palms. I wanted to get out of there and I was ashamed to leave. A man in a suit with a lacy white shirt out of some other century came over and said, 'My friend, you seem tense. Can I get you something?' I shook my head. He looked at me, sort of friendly, harmless, for a long time. All at once he smiled and said, 'Are you afraid the police will come?' I hadn't realized it was mainly that, but it was. I wanted to have a good record, you know? I nodded. 'I don't think they will,' he said. He touched my hand. 'But don't stay if you're afraid. Nobody here will be insulted if you leave. Nobody's going to judge you.' I laughed, because I believed him. It wasn't true, actually.

There were people there who were judging every second, but he wasn't one of them. 'Does this embarrass you?' he said. I said, 'No. I like it. I just don't want to do it.' He started talking about the public schools, about busing girls to school when there were only boys. He had three children. We talked until the sun came up and it was, you know, nice. Part of the time he held my hand. Then his wife came—she'd been in one of the bedrooms and still had her clothes off—and the three of us talked. After a while they left, and then I left. I knew it was wrong,

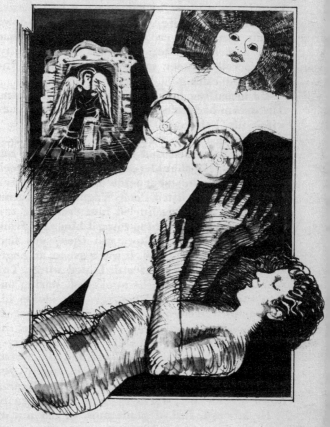

or something. I mean, it wasn't *normal*. My mother would have died if I'd written her about it. She thinks if you smoke pot you'll inevitably jump out of a speeding car. She hates the modern world. Filth and violence in the movies, dirty books, the pill . . . But I liked that party, when I thought back to it. I wished somebody would invite me again. It was like learning to swim, or flying—only scary in the beginning."

There were tears in her eyes, he dreamed. He felt guilty again that he'd abandoned her, for now it seemed to him again that she was the wife he'd loved, as sometimes it had seemed to him that his wife, when he was falling-down drunk and they were making fierce love, had been somebody else; such was life's fidelity. "No secrets between us anymore," he said "no anger, no hitting."

He heard her laughter, too real for a dream. The dream had turned nightmare. "I'm not your wife, silly," she said. "I mean, *Je*-sus!"

He clung to her, struggled to focus her face, and now it seemed that she wasn't his wife but some man, big-shouldered, with eyes like steel. The huge man, sharp-nosed, wearing steel-rimmed glasses, lifted Peter Wagner in his arms and, like a wrestler, hurled him down. He saw the wrestling mat coming toward him as if from hundreds of miles below, and there was fire-green grass at the edges. It was a grave, an angel sitting at the head of it with folded wings. The moment before he hit he awakened, staring out into some pitch-dark room. He was alone, his body bathed in sweat. "Margaret," he whispered. She stood, in his memory, erect as a steeple, tits like Akhaian breastplates. He clenched his eyes shut. All his fantasies, the best and the worst, were trash. He reached out suddenly, angrily, for the eels. The table was gone. His hand came down on the soft, warm flesh of some woman. He labored, full of panic now, to rise out of

the dream. A black, furry hand came toward him, extending a red-glowing pipe.

———————

Sally Abbott set the page number in her mind, closed the book and laid it on the blanket beside her. She'd reached a chapter end; she needed to relax her eyes.

The room was bright and cheerful with early afternoon, yellow glints in the faded wallpaper, the leaves outside her window colorful and gently fluttering, stirred by a faint breeze; yet for all the light and warmth, she discovered she was being drawn down, for no reason she could pinpoint, by an undertow of anxiety. She closed her eyes for a minute—the brightness still came through—and for a time, perhaps half an hour, she rested. If she dreamed, she was not aware of it.

When her mind rose toward thought again, she found herself brooding, eyes still closed, on Peter Wagner's marijuana dream. She could have no idea, of course, whether or not the description was true to life, never having smoked or even seen marijuana, so far as she knew. She had never even been drunk, in fact, though sometimes she and Horace had had a drink or two, Canadian Club, or sherry with Estelle and Ferris Parks. She felt the draw of anxiety building in her, an emotion that seemed to be groundless, yet increasing rapidly; and then, abruptly, as if the emotion had summoned the image instead of the reverse, she saw the open door the night of Horace's death. She saw, in sharper detail than in any photograph, the red and yellow leaves, the crooked sidewalk, the streetlamp, the lighted jack-o-lanterns on the porch across the street, and in memory she heard again the stuck needle on the gramophone, a phrase like an ironic question. The whole scene was caught in her brain as if snatched out of time. She knew that in a moment she would turn and see Horace in his chair, his mouth forming an *O* as if of slight surprise, and

121

she would cry out and run to him. But she didn't turn yet, perhaps knowing already that Horace would be there, unless the prescience had crept into the memory later, after she knew. Every line in the room was as sharp as a razor cut—books, glass-topped table, hat-rack by the door—and for an instant it seemed there was a smell, exaggerated by memory but elusive as ever. Someone had been there, someone from her past, perhaps her childhood. All this she had told the police, later, going over it and over it in meticulous detail. "What did it smell like?" "I don't know. The woods," she said. "Decaying leaves. Like a zoo." In the end they had concluded, and she had agreed, that he'd died of natural causes. She believed it still. But she was filled, again now, with anxiety, and she suddenly believed she knew what, all along, she'd been afraid of.

She had at one time understood her brother as fully as she understood herself—though she didn't always, perhaps, understand him now. When they were children she'd been more like a mother to him than like an older sister, at least most of the time. It was because she could control him when no one else could that Ariah had called her, the night he burned the house. Ariah had been sick at the time; in fact—though Sally had not known sarcoma could be so swift—Ariah had been dying. That had been partly what had made James snap, that and his son's death a year before, and the whiskey. Ariah had said on the phone, feebly, too drugged even to be clear-minded about her fear, "If you could just come up and . . . talk to him . . . Sally—"

"Where is he?" she'd said.

"He's at the house." A pause, then: "Richard's." Another pause, her voice growing weaker: "Burning it."

She'd said that earlier, but only now did Sally understand that it was true. "I'll send the police," she'd said.

"No!" Ariah begged. Sally waited, and across the ten miles of telephone wire she could feel Ariah

122

fumbling, struggling to clear her wits, unclog her tongue. At last she said hoarsely, "Don't send . . . police." There was a silence for a moment, or silence except for the roar of the line, and then there was another sound, which it took her a moment to identify: Ariah's crying.

"Is Ginny with you?" Sally asked in alarm.

Ariah tried to answer and at last brought out, "Yes."

"Are you all right, Ariah?" And then: "Has he hurt you?"

The answer was unintelligible, and she broke in, "I'll be there as soon as I can. Stay where you are, and keep Ginny with you. Do you hear me?"

She could catch no answer, only Ariah's crying—hopeless, not quite human—and the roar of the line. She hung up. She threw her coat and hat on, pulled on her overshoes, grabbed her purse, drawing the keys out as she walked, and hurried to the car. It was dark, lightly snowing, and there was ice on the roads. She drove as fast as she could, wondering all the way whether she should have called the police, whispering to herself, listening with intense concentration, for some reason, to the grind of the motor and the almost inaudible swish of windshield wipers. Halfway up the mountain she saw the glow of the burning house. Her heart chilled. She had believed Ariah, but it was as if she hadn't understood her. She drove more slowly, accelerator-foot shaking, and she was deathly afraid that by some accidental jerk of her arm she'd swerve the old Buick out over the drop-off.

When she came abreast of the burning house she saw there were cars there, parked beside the road, watching. One of them belonged to Sam Frost, from a little down the mountain. She slowed as if to stop, looking over at the house and the lighted trees, and by one of the trees she saw her brother, standing with his hands over his face. The sight so shocked her— the look he had of brute sorrow and confusion—that she pressed down hard on the accelerator, swinging and skidding, then driving on. Half a mile higher, when she came to the family house, she pulled in, turned the motor off, and sat for two minutes breathing deeply. She had a pain in her chest, like fire.

Inside, Ariah was in the downstairs bed, Ginny tucked beside her. Ariah was wasted to a skeleton, her arms like sticks, eyes enormous.

"Ginny, you go sleep upstairs," Sally said, taking off her coat. The child opened her mouth to protest, but Sally snapped, "Go!" and drew the covers back. Ginny slipped out and went quickly toward the door. "And brush your teeth!" Sally said. She took her hat off, then pressed her palm to Ariah's forehead; it was warm but not hot. "Ariah, we've got to change these sheets," she said. She drew them away, gently, and prepared to lift Ariah to the chair.

"Thank you," Ariah said, and could bring out nothing more. Tears washed down her cheeks.

"Never mind, now," Sally said, "everything's all right. In a jiffy we'll have you in nice clean sheets, and maybe a nice bath and your hair brushed—" She talked cheerfully, loudly, her heart slamming. She'd had no idea. Dr. Phelps ought to have told her. Then she wondered the next moment if he knew himself. When had he last been here? There were pill bottles on the tallboy, at least a dozen of them, and on the typed labels stood Dr. Phelps' name. She took sheets from the drawer—clean-smelling, not ironed—carried them to the foot of the bed and began putting them on. No doubt James wouldn't call him, as long as he had pills. Two weeks might pass, she might shrivel up to nothing, and James would imagine he was doing all he could; he'd always been a fatalist, drunk or sober, and he'd been doctoring sick animals all his life. Never mind. *She* was here now. Meanwhile, as she put on new pillowslips and blankets, heated water for a bath, and laid a clean nightie out, Sally chattered, talking of how wonderfully Ariah was holding up, how obedient Ginny was becoming these days—talking of every light and trivial thing that came flitting into her head. Ariah—whispering "Thank you, thank you," understanding none of it—wept.

When James came home, Ariah was white and shivering, clenching her teeth in pain, refusing to cry out. He stood in the kitchen doorway, reeking of smoke and gin, red-eyed, staring at Sally, his expression both belligerent and defensive. "I burnt the house," he said.

"I know," she said. "Ariah needs her medicine."

He turned his head slowly, blood draining from his whiskered cheeks, then stumbled toward the living room and the bedroom beyond. She followed, keeping enough distance to avoid offending him—he'd been a big man then, dangerous—and she watched as he fumbled with the pills. Ariah opened her mouth for them eagerly, like an animal, and he dropped them in, then lifted her head with his left hand, carefully, and with his right gave her the dusty water that had been standing on the bedside table for, probably, days. When she had swallowed she closed her eyes, and he laid her head back into the pillow again, then sat holding her hand, Sally leaning in the doorway, until Ariah was asleep. He stood up, looking around vaguely, baffled by something that hadn't quite registered; then he saw what it was, that the sheets had been changed and that even without his clothes on he'd be black as soot.

"I'll sleep on the couch," he said.

She nodded. "I'll sleep up with Ginny."

He looked at her. "You stayin?"

She nodded slightly, not otherwise answering, moving away toward the kitchen and the door to the stairs.

He said, too loudly, "I burnt Richard's house." She said nothing—for the moment.

In the morning he couldn't say why he'd done it—in fact he didn't even remember, at first, that he had done it. It was hard for Sally Abbott to believe that people could do violent acts and not remember, as Peter Wagner had done in her novel and James had done in life. She never could do violence and forget it; she was certain of it. Yet she couldn't believe that James was lying about forgetting. It was all far in the past, admittedly; he hadn't gotten dangerously

drunk in years; she oughtn't to be frightened. To tell
the truth, even when he'd chased her up the stairs
with the log she hadn't really been frightened, just
alarmed and—mostly—furious. But now she was
beginning to have second thoughts. More than she
realized, her brother was a stranger to her—possibly
even to himself.

She stared at the wall for a time, thinking nothing,
at first with an expression of sadness and compassion,
then with a sterner expression. Her jaw became firmer,
her eyes more fierce. Then, with a quick little shake
of the head, Sally returned to her book.

7

THE PHILOSOPHY OF RANK

He woke up with a queer, not entirely unpleasant sense that he had lost days, perhaps months,
out of his life. He was in a bunkroom he'd
never seen before, its peeling walls trembling
with the shudder of engines somewhere aft—
not far, he guessed; perhaps on the other side
of the bulkhead he leaned on now as he thought
about getting up. There were four bunks: his
own, one above it, another that was clumsily
made up with Army surplus blankets, and the
one above that piled high with boxes, folded
clothes, two jars of olives, parts of a record
player, and a coffee cup, cracked. He remembered, dimly, that someone had spoken poetry
—Mr. Goodman. A dream, perhaps? He remembered that someone had sung hymns, and
he'd enjoyed himself, but the memory would
not come clear in detail, not even the cabin it
had happened in.

A sound to his left startled him and he turned.
It was the bunkroom door swinging open. The
passageway beyond was bathed in sunlight com-

ing down through the hatch like a shaft from heaven, and suddenly, for no reason, he knew where he was and what had happened last night, or some of it: the Captain's cabin, the pipes of pot, the singing, talking, handshaking. He jumped up and crossed to the door quickly, as if thinking of escape. The galley door across the passageway opened by itself, exactly as the bunkroom door had opened, as if some absent-minded ghost were looking for his glasses. The galley was empty except for the sink, the refrigerator, the stove, and two inches of water sloshing on the deck. Someone had left out bread and peanut butter, and the sink was full of cups and plastic plates. He went forward down the passageway, came to the engine room door. The girl Jane turned and smiled at him. She had a shielded mechanic's lightbulb hanging down through a hole in the decking, and a pipewrench in her right hand. There were grease smudges on her forehead and nose and cheek.

"G'mornin, Cap'n," she said brightly.

He said nothing, snatching wildly in his mind to get his bearings. She went on smiling, then puckered her lips, blowing him a kiss. He remembered, suddenly, the dream he'd had, and knew it was no dream. He blew a kiss back, joyful and full of sharp panic, then abruptly pulled his head out and closed the hatch. He went up the ladder and stood a moment blinking, adjusting to the sudden and absolute change in the universe.

The sea was serene; the sun was directly overhead. He felt stupidly at peace. It meant nothing, of course; another proof that all human emotion, all experience, is meaningless mechanics. So days grow longer and in chemical reaction the feathers of birds grow brighter and their joys increase. He did not approve of what had happened to him. To Peter Wagner, it was a matter of high indignation that a man eating lunch, approached by a female panhandler, was almost certain to give money, because it was programmed in his genes: centuries ago, in some African cave, sharing the kill with some female had meant getting between her legs. It was an outrage—on occasion a matter for tears—that the noblest human altruism, the young man who throws himself down on a grenade to save his comrades' lives at the expense of his own, was similarly programmed, as surely programmed as the altruistic self-destruction of that walking bomb of the insect world, *Globitermes sulfureus*, who to save his tribe from the invading ant could, and sooner or later would, explode himself, sending the splash of his poison in every direction. But even as he scorned the way he was pulled to and fro by the universe, driven by his ancient, monkey past, enslaved by every tremor at the edges of space, he could not deny the fact that he was boundingly happy. The girl was pretty and in love with him, such a playmate as only the gods ever catch; he had sea beneath his legs, sky on all sides of him: he was king of the ocean-faring apes.

"G'mornin, Cap'n," Mr. Nit said. He touched his black wool cap but did not stir from the canvas chair where he was sitting with an old *Science Digest* on the deck.

"Morning," Peter Wagner said. He glanced up at the wheelhouse. Mr. Goodman was there, smiling down at him like an old, old friend. Mr. Goodman touched the front of his hat.

"Go ahead," Mr. Nit said, "look the ole tub over."

Doubtfully, but full of bliss, Peter Wagner went up the bridge steps, past the radio cubicle and the engine room skylight. He'd gotten used to the smell of pot now and was beginning to catch other things—old steam and the acid in the batteries stored in the louvered box between the *Indomitable*'s stacks. And something else: a kind of a toadstool and duff smell, as if the old can had lain for years half sunk in some forest. At the entrance to the Captain's cabin he glanced at the bridge. The engine room telegraph was as green as the dome of a public building, and the bridge itself was thick with oily dirt. Sandbags barricaded the wheelhouse, half rotten, seeping grit where someone had poked holes in them—or maybe shot at them.

Captain Fist was asleep in his bunk, his hands at his sides. He went on snoring, undisturbed, when Peter Wagner poked his head in.

It wasn't much, as captains' cabins go. Between the head of the bunk and the washstand opposite, the communicating door to the chartroom swung open and shut with the motion of the boat.

Just as he was drawing back his head the Captain's snoring changed, and a moment later Captain Fist jerked up. "Ah, Captain!" Captain Fist said. He stretched his eyes, tasted his mouth, coming the rest of the way up out of sleep.

"Now wait a minute," Peter Wagner said. A merry, queerly boyish and indifferent indignation surged up in him, then dissolved in the general warmth and light, the end-to-end-of-the-universe dazzle of love. Now he was certain of what he'd suspected before: it was not mere good humor that had made the woman, and then Mr. Nit, call him "Captain." Something curious was going on.

"Just dozed off for a minute," Captain Fist said, "while I was waiting for you to awaken." He chuckled, horselike, and whether it was evil or just apologetic, Peter Wagner couldn't tell. The Captain threw his legs over the side of the bunk—he was fully dressed except for his shoes and hat—and pushed up into sitting position.

He swept white hair away from his eyes and put his hat on. "Captain, let me show you around," he said, and grotesquely smiled.

"Now hang on," Peter Wagner said. Still half-grinning, he clenched one fist, then relaxed it. Though he knew better, he said, "What's this 'Captain' business?"

"Why, my dear boy!" Captain Fist exclaimed. He got up and staggered to the door to take Peter Wagner's hand. "You agreed! The whole crew shook hands to it!" His smile was like a snake's. He even weaved a little, head thrown forward. It was true that they'd all shook hands on something. Peter Wagner smiled uncertainly and waited.

"Let me show you around the ship," the Captain said.

Discounting the rotten smell and the dirt, the chartroom was standard: chart rack on the ceiling, chart table to the right with drawers underneath, etc. The two compasses were stuck, the protractor and parallel ruler on the chart table were museum pieces, and the ship's sextant was so old its silver scale had been worn down to brass. The chronometer in its padded box was not running.

"Everything all right?" the Captain asked nervously.

For the first time in months—unless it had happened last night, when he was stoned—Peter Wagner laughed, without irony, from the heart. He went back through the connecting door to the Captain's cabin and out onto the bridge. He was still laughing, like a boy, like a bridegroom. The Captain came behind him, worried, his fingertips stuck in his pockets. "Is everything all right?" he said again. His back was so crooked his head came straight out of his chest.

"Where are we?" Peter Wagner asked, still

130

grinning, brimming with childish brainless joy.

"*I* don't know that," the Captain said.

He laughed again. He took the binoculars from the shelf where they had been lying for, perhaps, years. They were so moldy they worked like tandem kaleidoscopes, but he wasn't really looking for anything anyway, so he peered into them, facing first one direction, then another. "How in hell do you usually make it clear to Mexico?" he asked.

His smile was perhaps infectious. In any case, the Captain grinned back. "We stick close to shore, normally. But that's dangerous, of course. Now that we've got *you*, Captain—"

As nearly as Peter Wagner could tell, without compass or stars, they were heading due west. He said, "How long we been out?"

"All night," the Captain said, and smiled again.

"And you expect," he said—but he couldn't finish, because a fit of laughter took him once more, so severe that he had to bend double and hold out the binoculars to the Captain for fear of dropping them.

"Is everything all right?" the Captain said.

"Everything's wonderful!" Peter Wagner said. "I'm going below." Another laughing fit. "Let me know when we get to Japan." He started for the hatch.

The Captain stared after him without a word, leaning on his cane with both hands, for perhaps three seconds. Then abruptly, angrily, he called out, "See here!"

Peter Wagner turned, looked at the furious old cockroach, and again bent over laughing.

"See here!" he said again—a roar, this time. "You're the *Cap*tain of this vessel, boy! You're responsible!"

Peter Wagner went on laughing, staring down the bore of the Captain's pistol. Young male chimpanzees in love, he'd read somewhere, sometimes went without eating for days, in their jubilant stupor, until they fainted. The pistol was shaking; the Captain was in a fury. And that, for some reason, was so funny that Peter Wagner sank to his knees. "My dear Captain," he gasped and, after thinking about it, went down on his hands and then over on his back, rolling like a bear. "My dear Captain, we're all——" His body convulsed, and though at first he had been at least partly clowning, by now the laughter was in such earnest that he couldn't catch his breath. "All dead men!" He hooted with laughter. The pistol hit his face. He laughed and laughed, though now he was crying too.

"He's crazy," Mr. Nit said. "We're lost in the Pacific with a lunatic."

Captain Fist hit him with the pistol again, but not as hard as before; he was feeling unsure of himself.

And now Mr. Goodman was there, Peter Wagner made out, peeking through weeping, nearly closed eyes.

"Let me talk to him," Mr. Goodman said. No one answered, and Mr. Goodman kneeled down beside him. "Mr. Wagner?" he said.

Peter Wagner smiled, groaned, felt himself at the edge of another laughing or maybe crying fit, and caught himself.

"Mr. Wagner, sir," Mr. Goodman said. "I understand your feeling, since you wanted to kill yourself anyway and we seem to be playing right into your hands. But Mr. Wagner, I beg you to think a minute. We're family men, Mr. Nit and I. What will become of our children? Think about it, sir. And then too, there's Jane, who's a fine young woman and *counting* on you. If we go down, sir——" he paused, for some reason flustered. Peter Wagner smiled, or grimaced—he could hardly have said himself which it was—and the Captain moved his pistol to within inches of his nose. Mr. Nit bent over, holding out his billfold. There was a picture of a wall-eyed girl of six or seven. Mr. Goodman got out his billfold too. He had three boys, two girls, and two cats. He lived in Sausalito, up on the mountain. Even the headache where the old man had hit him couldn't hold down Peter Wagner's spirits. He was reminded, by the way they were holding out those snapshots, of something else he'd read about those chimpanzees. When the leader males had a fresh kill of monkeys and young baboons, the rest of the chimps would approach and beg for morsels. They'd touch the meat and the faces of the males, whimpering and *hoo*ing, holding out their hands, palms up, in supplication. Grandly (sometimes) the males would drop food into the outstretched hands. Such was life's generosity.

Peter Wagner closed his eyes, and even now the dream that had proved no dream filled the world with dazzle. "We're on the Ship of Death," he said. "The Lord be with us." Another line, he remembered, from the novel about the hoax.

Captain Fist cocked his pistol, but Mr. Goodman bent down closer. "Why?" he said. "*Why?*"

"Metaphysically," Peter Wagner said, leering, tears still falling, "that's a difficult question. But in practical terms, you're way out at sea with no radio, no telegraph, no compass that works, no sailors, and no pilot."

"*You* be our pilot!" Mr. Goodman said.

Peter Wagner smiled blissfully and said nothing. They too were silent. At last he opened his eyes. The sea was serene; the sun directly overhead. Mr. Goodman's look was full of idiotic woe.

Captain Fist said, "You're a philosopher! 'Metaphysically,' you said. I'm a philosopher myself—phenomenologist!" He put his pistol away in clumsy haste, as if to cancel his ever having drawn it. He had his hands around Peter Wagner's shoulders, pulling him up. "Help him up," he hissed to Mr. Nit, "he's a philosopher!"

Mr. Goodman looked reverent. His children were forgotten.

Peter Wagner sat up.

"We'll do anything, sir," Mr. Nit said. There were tears in his eyes. "Just tell us what to do!"

Peter Wagner sighed again. The sea was serene. "Fix the radio," he suggested. "Take the compasses apart, to the last little screw, and clean them." Mr. Nit jumped like a monkey and darted to the bridge.

"You'll do it, then! You'll save us!" Mr. Goodman cried.

Peter Wagner got to his feet slowly and shook his head. Impossible as it might seem, he felt peaceful, joyful, thinking of Jane—it was as if she had become the sea-smell, the sunlight, the rumbling and shuddering of the ship —and at the same time, he felt he had never been more depressed. Perhaps even that, it crossed his mind, was genetic. He was thinking again of those chimpanzees, generously giving food, and of the soldier throwing himself on the grenade, genetically chosen. "Kin selection," it was called by sociobiologists. The family of the sacrificial lamb survived, saved by him, passing on his genes—the brothers and sisters, if the lamb had no daughters or sons—and so, little by little, the world grew more sublime and pathetic. And so now he had been chosen saviour of this groaning, floating little Eden. Saviour, not leader, there was no mistaking that, "Captain" him and "sir" him as they might. Pride and Damnation were their leader; agent: J. Faust. It was the Fausts of this world that the genes chose for kings and generals, black-hearted and soulless, infinitely cunning, cruel and selfish as bulls. And yet he'd chosen, or accepted the choice of his genes, Peter Wagner saw. He would take them to Mexico, to confront whatever law or competitive outlaws he must face there—had chosen just like that, without a flicker of thought, as it seemed he always chose. *Fool!* he thought, and thought no further.

In two hours the radio was fixed. Four hours later the compasses were clean and Mr. Nit was working on an electro-magnet which would remagnetize the compasses and serve as a compass itself in case of emergency. There was no point in fixing the engine room telegraph. Any message that came would be Greek to the gold-winged angel down below. There was a speaking tube, not very effective since it had an obstruction of some kind—seaweed, bird manure, he couldn't tell—but it worked if Jane kept close to it. They were no longer headed west. His first order had been to turn the old can around.

A little before dark he decided he'd better give the ship a few tests. God only knew what he'd be required to demand of her—or it: for all his time at sea, it was hard to think of the reeking, patched up hulk as a she. ("Rapist," his wife said, crying, in his mind.) He called down through the tube, "Dead Slow, Jane." The *Indomitable* slowed down. Eyes drawn to slits, ear close to the tube, he listened to the engines. He jumped when Jane said, standing at his elbow on the bridge, "Was that right?"

"Holy cow," he said.

"Was that what you meant by 'Dead Slow'?" She smiled, full of love, and touched his arm.

"Yes, fine," he said. She moved her hand softly, sweetly on his arm. He seized her by the elbows and kissed her, dizzy with joy, then, gravely, said, "Get back down there, Jane. It'll be dark soon." She nodded, radiant, kissing him again and pressing her body close, then ran down the bridge steps quick as a boy, one lovely hand holding on her patriotic cap,

135

and danced over to the hatch. When he was sure she was back in the engine room he called down through the tube, "Take back the revolutions till we're barely ticking over." She did so and called up through the tube, "Was that right?" "That's fine," he called back, stupidly proud. Then, to Mr. Goodman in the wheelhouse: "Take her up a point." And then again to Jane: "Ring her up to Full." They obeyed. "Steady as you go!" he yelled to Mr. Goodman.

After dark he took an easy reading of bearings—not a cloud in sight—set his course, and put Mr. Nit on watch, letting Mr. Goodman rest. At the door of the Captain's cabin he said, "All ship-shape, sir. Relatively." He smiled.

At the radio cubicle he paused and, after a moment, went in to look the old instrument over. He switched it on, playing with the tuner. For a full minute he got nothing but static. It wasn't much of a radio, and they were still a long way out. But for some reason he kept at it, the old nautical sixth sense, perhaps. And then, quite suddenly, loud and clear a voice came through. "*Indomitable*. Calling *Indomitable*." His mouth was open to answer before he remembered and switched off the mike. Captain Fist appeared behind him, eyebrows lifted. A second later Mr. Nit was there, and then Mr. Goodman and Jane.

"Don't answer!" Captain Fist whispered.

"I *knew* we should never have fixed it," Mr. Nit moaned.

Jane pressed her head in, cocked as if to listen to the radio tubes. "Who could it be?" she whispered. "The Coast Guard, you think?"

"Not way out here."

"Then who?"

They looked at one another.

"We'll never know unless we answer," Peter Wagner said. Line from some novel.

Captain Fist put a finger to his lips.

"We had a plane once," Jane whispered. "We heard some static on the radio, and the next thing we knew the United States Air Force was shooting us down on the Mojave."

"Could be the Navy, all right," Mr. Goodman said.

"Calling the *Indomitable*," the radio said. "Come in *Indomitable!*"

Peter Wagner flicked the switch. "This is the *Indomitable*," he said. "We read you. Identify."

Captain Fist leaned hard on his cane with one hand and hard on the bulkhead with the other.

"Hello *Indomitable*," the radio said. "This is your old pal the *Militant*, baby! We'll see you in somethin like a hour, you dig?"

Then static.

Captain Fist's cane went out from under him and he went down like a fat, greenish baby. "Get the lights out!" he croaked, still sitting.

"You giving the orders?" Peter Wagner said. He drew Jane toward him, for some reason, as if to shield her.

"I tell you get those lights out!"

"You said I was Captain," Peter Wagner said. The familiar churn of anger bloomed up in him. The smell of Jane's hair in his nostrils gave the anger strength. "Divide . . .

Sally Abbott had come to another large gap. She sighed and closed the book.

> "Passion governs, and she never governs wisely."
>
> BENJAMIN FRANKLIN, February 5, 1775

3

The Spat Between the Old Man and the Old Woman Turns More Grave

She was not a fast reader. She liked to take her time and savor what she read, even when she knew what she was reading was hardly worth a speck. Moreover, whether it was because of the softness of the pillows behind her back, or the crispness of the bright, October day, or the unimportance of the writing—Horace, she knew, would have wondered at her continuing on with such a book: life was too precious to be idled away, he'd always said—her mind kept wandering and from time to time she would nod and drop off; and so, when she laid the book aside, not yet half finished, and looked over at the clock on the desk, it was mid-afternoon.

It was hunger that had roused her again from her story. She looked around in surprise, reality flooding in—or another reality, so to speak; the book, for all its foolishness, had convinced her exactly as a dream might do, she'd seen those people and that ridiculous old fishingboat as plain as day, as plain as the pictures on *Hawaii Five-O*. She glanced at the cover—the half-naked girl and the horrible old Captain (not at all as she herself imagined them)—and shook her head. "Well that does take the cake," she said. The Captain was supposed to have eyes like bullet holes, and the girl's hair was dark. As if from another time and place, the memory of her battle with James came back. It seemed silly now, cranked up out of nothing like the troubles in her book, and considering the leaves outside her window and the blue-as-blue October sky, she had half a mind to call him and let bygones be bygones. It occurred to her that maybe, one of those times when she'd nodded off, he'd come up and unlocked her door.

She got up to see. The floor was so cold it was like walking on hard snow, and despite her curiosity about the door, she stopped to put her slippers on, and then, as an afterthought, her gray cardigan sweater. In the back of her mind she heard the phone ringing. Now she went to the door and tried it. Still locked. "Stubborn old fool," she said aloud. The phone rang on. He'd be outdoors somewhere, collecting the eggs, cleaning the stables, feeding the pigs and horses, or whatever. Well, she thought, there was nothing *she* could do about the phone, locked in her bedroom like some poor old madwoman in a novel. She went toward the attic door, planning to smuggle down more apples. She could smell the bedpan, which she'd pushed in under the washstand after she'd used it this morning. She frowned, trying to think how to empty it. Maybe there was some old pail or empty trunk in the attic. But she was standing looking out the window toward the road as she thought the problem through, and abruptly she seized, almost without consciously thinking of it, the simplest solution: she opened the window and unhooked the screen, then, nose wrinkling, carried the bedpan over and dumped it on the bushes down below. Then she went up to get the apples.

When James came back in from watering the stock

and gathering eggs, the phone was ringing. He had a pretty fair idea who it would be. He picked up the receiver and called, "Ay-uh?"

"Hi, Dad. It's Ginny."

"I thought it might be you, Ginny."

"I just thought I'd call and see how everything's going."

"I thought you might do that."

He could see, in his mind's eye, her gathering frown.

"Well?" she said.

"Well what?"

"How is everything going?"

"Oh, fine. Everything's fine over here. How's everything with you?"

She said, "How's Aunt Sally?"

"Aunt Sally? Oh, she's alive, far's I know."

There was a pause.

"What does *that* mean?"

"Well, Aunt Sally didn't get up today. Slept in."

"She didn't get up at all?"

"Not that I know of. Course I ain't been listening at the keyhole."

"Didn't she eat?"

The old man tipped his long head back, studying the leaves on the lawn.

"Dad?"

"No, I can say for pretty certain she never et a thing."

In his mind he could picture her reflecting on that, probably fumbling with her cigarettes. At last, perhaps after a drag on the cigarette, she said, "That's impossible! She never left her room?"

"Never once," he said, nodding thoughtfully at the leaves. "I can say that for pretty near certain."

"Dad," she said, "you've nailed the door shut!"

He shook his head. "Nope, just used the other key."

There was a silence. Then: "I'll be right over."

"Now Ginny, don't you do that! You mine your own business. I *had* the door open, but she wouldn't come out. She wouldn't do a stitch around the house

140

all day, wouldn't even fix breakfast. What's a man supposed to do, a case like that? She thinks she can move in and live off my sustenance and never do a lick, pollute my parlor with her dad-blame TV, clutter up the air with her dad-blame chatter—"

"Just don't do anything more," Ginny said, "I'll be right over." She hung up. James Page hung up too, and refused to feel guilty, though he could see pretty well he was in for it. Nevertheless he was well within his rights. He'd been working from sun-up to well after sundown for sixty-odd years, paying his taxes, keeping the place fit, and in she'd come like some immigrant, barging in on everything, talking about *her* rights . . .

A mile down the mountain, Samuel Frost was also just hanging up his phone.

"What are *you* smiling at?" his wife Ellen said. She too was smiling, for Sam Frost's good humor was infectious. He was bald except for a shadow of gray hair that had once been red, and he was fat, though solid as a treetrunk.

"You know I'm not one to tell tales," he said, still grinning from ear to ear, hardly able to contain himself.

"Fiddlesticks," she said, "people use a party line, they should mind their talk."

"Mebby so," he said chuckling, holding his belly. "But there's nothin to tell. If old James Page locks his sister in the bedroom, it's certain he's got some good reason."

"He didn't!" she said, eyes widening in disbelief and glee.

"Mebby not," he said, "mebby I heard wrong." She stared a moment longer, flabbergasted, and then both of them laughed till tears ran down their faces.

He mentioned it that night at Merton's Hideaway, sitting with a fat, freckled hand closed tight around a Ballantine's. He was drinking from the bottle, though as usual, out of some queer stubbornness, Merton had handed him a glass. Leave the thing clean as a whistle, Merton would still wash it; all part of the price. It

141

was early, but dark as a pit outside. When they happened to look out, turning from the oval wooden table near the bar, it seemed to them all, one way or another, a surprising and vaguely unnatural thing—though they'd seen it every year of their lives—that sudden contraction of daylight in October, the first deep-down convincing proof that locking time, and after that winter and deep snow and cold, were coming. Whether or not they cared for winter—some claimed they did, some claimed they didn't—every one of them felt a subdued excitement, a new aliveness that was more, in fact, than the seasonal change in their chemistry.

Summer, for all its beauty on those mountain-slope farms, meant back-breaking work, long hours on the tractor where you struggled against the stiff upgrade pull of the steering wheel and fought till you ached against the jerk and jab of the plow-lift lever as the plow-points skittered over stones. And then later, in July, it meant heaving bales in the still, dead heat, with bees all around you, first-cousins to the fairies, but nothing magical about a swarm of impinged on bees in a dry, hot haylot in July, no magic in anything except, perhaps, to the tourists who came like a plague of locusts and had time to watch the otters in the high mountain streams, or the foal in the shadow of the barn. August was cooler, though still high summer, so cool in the morning and evening, at times, especially those mornings and occasional evenings when mist filled the valleys, that it was best to have a fire in the woodstove; but August meant even more work than before—still hay to get in, but also sweetcorn, potatoes, and tomatoes, and now wheat and oats, grainsacks to throw, your eyes and ears and nostrils full of dust, harsh chaff in the cracks around your neck. Late August, although still grain-harvest time—it would drag through September—was the time of carnivals and village fairs, church suppers, all-day auctions, and demonstrations by the Volunteer Fire Department. It was the time of respite before the air turned winy and the field-corn came in and then the busiest harvest of all. Apples. The State had been rich in them since long before the Revolution. Even in deep woods you'd come across old apple trees still bearing away, half-forgotten species like Pound Sweets and Snow-apples. Now, in October, the farmwork was slackening, the drudgery had paid off: the last of the corn went flying into the silo with a clackety roar and a smell as sweet as honey; the beans were harvested in half a day, like an afterthought; on the porch and out by the roadside stood mountains of pumpkins. The trees turned—those along the paved roads first, dying from the salt put down in winter—sugar maples orange, pink, and yellow on one branch, elm trees pale yellow, birch trees speckled with a lemony yellow, still other trees carmine and vermilion and ochre, red maples as red as fresh blood. Soon—anytime from mid-October to the end of November—it would be locking time.

It began as a suspension of time altogether. Rudyard Kipling saw it in Brattleboro, in 1895, and wrote: "There the seasons stopped awhile. Autumn was gone. Winter was not. We had Time dealt out to us—more clear, fresh Time—grace-days to enjoy." There'd be nothing to do but chores, load pigs for butchering, chop firewood, or walk through the dry, crisp leaves of a canted wood hunting deer. The air in the cowbarn would be clean and cold, but when you bent down between them for the milking, the cows would be as warm and comforting as stoves. Sometimes an Indian summer would break up the locking, sometimes not; but whatever the appearances, the ground was hardening; every now and then a loud crack would ring out, some oak tree closing down all business for the season. If it was warm and mild on Monday afternoon, Tuesday morning might be twenty degrees, and you'd find the water in the pig-trough frozen solid. By Thanksgiving the locking would be irreversible: the ground would be frozen, not to thaw again till spring. When the first good snow came, maybe three feet of it, maybe six, they'd call it winter.

This darkness now, fallen unnaturally early, as it

always seemed every year—fallen like a thick tar-paulin around the Hideaway—was to them all, in their blood if not quite in their conscious minds, obscurely magical, a sign of elves working. If it had not been for that strangeness about things, Sam Frost might perhaps not have mentioned what he'd heard on the telephone, that old James Page had confined his sister to her bedroom.

"He never did!" Bill Partridge said, leaning toward Sam Frost. "Locked up old Sally in the bedroom? He must be daft!"

Giggling and blushing, his eyes filled with tears, Sam could only nod.

"No doubt he had plenty provocation," Bill Part-ridge said. His voice had the high, thin whine of a buzzsaw. He sat with his hat on, his nose long and red, below it big folds—where there were still a few whiskers—drooping past his mouth and small chin.

"She's got mighty strange opinions," Henry Stump-church said—serious-minded, enormous and whopper-jawed, though by blood part Welshman—watching Sam Frost for some sign that he might know more.

Sam Frost nodded, still smiling and blushing. "You can understand his feelings," he said. "Works all his life, puts his money in the bank, and there she comes with her hands held out, and he does what's right and the next thing you know she's got him hog-tied hand and foot, even runnin his cussed politics."

"She don't!" Bill Partridge said.

Sam was still nodding. "She's a Democrat," he said.

They waited, watching him, none of them admitting quite yet that the tale had gone somber.

Sam nodded again, eyes crinkling as if for a grin, but the grin was unconfident and failed. "Wife Ellen calls up about the Republican fund drive, and old Sally says to her, 'James ain't home.' Twant the truth, point of fact. You could hear him in the background, hollerin to know who's on the line."

They stared, only gradually understanding the ter-rible implications.

"He'd ought to shoot her," Bill Partridge said thoughtfully, and filled his glass.

By this time Lewis and Virginia Hicks were at her father's house, trying to negotiate a peace. They'd left Dickey with a neighbor in Arlington, had come up Mount Prospect as fast as their rattle-trap car would climb, and in no time at all Ginny had persuaded the old man to unlock that door. It proved to be no help, as the old man had known it would be or he'd never have given in. "Two stubbaner people never lived," Lewis said, not to anyone in particular. The old woman had the door-bolt shot inside and she'd rather be dead, she told them, than come out where that maniac was. Ginny and Lewis stood in the upstairs hallway, pleading through the door, the old man downstairs in the kitchen feigning indifference, but with the stairway door cracked open, allowing him to hear. Ginny grew angrier and more tearful by the minute, Lewis more despondent.

Lewis Hicks was a small man, and though he was going on forty years old he was thin as a boy. He had on the gray coveralls he'd been wearing when he came home and Ginny was making that phonecall to her father. His hair was cropped short and was by nature dry as dust and approximately that color; he had practically no chin, a large adamsapple, and on his upper lip a brown, insignificant moustache. He had one blue eye, one brown eye. "Aunt Sally," he said, for out in the driveway his car was running, swilling down the gas, and also he was paying that baby-sitter, "this is costin good money." It was entirely unlike him to assert himself so, and as soon as he'd said it he glanced over at Ginny. He could see himself that it was petty and not likely to persuade. Ginny gave him a glance and he looked hastily at the floor. All the same, people asked a great deal of him, he thought. If crazy old brothers and sisters had fights, what concern was it of his? She'd come out, all right, when she got hungry enough; and if not, well, they could cross that bridge when they'd come to it. He glanced

145

furtively at Ginny, then away again. He was rarely brought conviction by even his own most sensible reasoning. Life was slippery, right and wrong were as elusive as odors in an old abandoned barn. Lewis knew no certainties but hammers and nails, straps of leather, clocksprings. He had no patience with people's complexities—preferred the solitude of his workshop down cellar, the safe isolation of a maple grove he'd been hired to trim, or some neighbor's back yard, where he'd been hired to rake leaves—not because people were foolish, in Lewis Hicks' opinion, or because they got through life on gross and bigoted oversimplifications, though they did, he knew, but because, quiet and unschooled as he might be, he could too easily see all sides and, more often than not, no hint of a solution.

Ginny crushed out her cigarette in the stippled glass ashtray she held in her left hand. As always when she was angry, her face was a trifle gray and puffy, putting him on guard, making him droop more than usual and run one finger across his moustache. "Aunt Sally," Ginny said, "I want you to come out of there." She listened, and when no answer came she flashed a look at Lewis as if her relatives' craziness were all his fault, then called again: "Aunt Sally?"

"I hear you," the old woman called back.

"Well, are you coming out or *not?*" she demanded.

"Not," the old woman said. "I told you that. If I'm going to be treated like an animal, I might's well be penned up like one."

"Ha!" Ginny's father broke in from downstairs. "Animals at least got some use in the world."

"You see what he thinks of me?" the old woman whined. Possibly she was crying.

"Animals at least earn their keep," he called.

"I don't ask any keep," the old woman called back —half convincing herself, the way it sounded—"just a little room to die in."

"Aunt Sally," Ginny called, "you've got to come out and *eat* something." Her voice was sharper than ever now, annoyed, maybe, by the sentimental talk about dying.

"Don't want to," the old woman called back just as sharply.

It sounded final; Lewis had a feeling they'd be hearing nothing more from her. Ginny perhaps had the same feeling. She looked at him for help, then changed her mind and decided to light another cigarette. When it was going she said, "Aunt Sally, I'm going to bring a tray up here. I'll leave it by your door. When you get hungry, you come on out and eat something."

There was no answer for a moment. Then Aunt Sally called, "Wouldn't bother, I was you."

"What?" Ginny called.

"I wouldn't bother if I was you. I won't eat, and after you're gone he'll just feed it to the pigs."

Ginny took a deep breath, mostly cigarette smoke, or so it seemed to Lewis. He'd always been a worrier, and Ginny's smoking was the chief of his worries, though he rarely spoke of it. We ought to be getting back, he thought. She knew well enough the situation was hopeless, but she kept at it. Lewis shook his head, miserable, picked at his moustache, and then, catching himself, pushed his hands into his coveralls pockets. "We ought to be getting back to Dickey," he said casually.

"I *know* that," she said, and as if he were surprised that he'd spoken the offending words aloud, he lifted his eyebrows, tipped his head, and focused his attention on the chipping, cream-colored paint on the bedroom door. Without thinking he raised his left hand and with one square fingernail picked experimentally at the edge of a chipped place. A larger chip came off. Ought to be scraped to the wood, he thought, and knew if it were done it would be he who'd have to do it, and then he'd have to do the rest of the doors, and the moldings, to make them match, and then new papering—for no money, because he was a son-in-law, and old James Page was tighter than a snakeskin. More than before he felt guilty and depressed. Now that he'd noticed the chipping paint, he had a feeling it was his duty, in a way, to fix it.

Aunt Sally was saying, full of righteous indignation

and self-pity, enjoying herself, "It's a free country. Just you tell him that. I have rights the same as the next person."

"Any time she wants," Ginny's father called, "she's free to pack her bags and go live where she damn well pleases."

"That's the way he thinks!" Aunt Sally said. The way she pounced on it, even a perfect stranger would have known it was an idea she'd been over and over in her mind. "It's a free country to die in, that's all! You ever hear him talk about Welfare?"

"Aunt Sally," Ginny began, but she knew it was useless. They all did.

"You get him on Welfare and that man will stutter and foam at the mouth like a rabid wolf. You just try it. 'Welfare's the ruin of this country,' he'll say. 'Let the people that's fit to work eat, and let the rest go hang!' "

From the bottom of the stairs Ginny's father shouted, "Let the people that's *willing and able* to work eat. You get it wrong on puppose."

"Same thing," she snapped.

"Ain't the same at ah!" But he bit off all the rest of what he had to say, how it wasn't child labor he was asking for, or turning a deaf ear to the whimperings of the sick, but if a healthy man was too fussy to take a job when it was offered him—and so forth and so on, they'd heard it many times, so that even Lewis Hicks, who agreed with the old man, was glad to hear him stop. Yet at the same time, confusingly, Lewis was sorry to see the truth choked off, as it so often was in this miserable world, it seemed to him. He could see old James Page, in his mind's eye, with his mouth clamped shut like a snapping turtle's, arms folded tight across his chest, down there at the foot of the stairs, his eyes aglitter with cold fury.

"Just get him onto Social Security," she said. The old woman pounced on that subject too with malicious glee. She knew her brother. It was no case of "tensions raised by misunderstanding." Struggle as he might, bite his false teeth together hard as he pleased, hop on one foot with his eyes shut, he couldn't help answering. "I'd rather see the Government rob banks than have Social Security," he cried out.

"You see?" she shrieked.

Lewis could picture her with her hands squeezed together, behind that door, lips violently trembling, her smile like the smile of an axe-murderer. Without thinking he said, as if he thought he was in heaven and reason might settle the whole dispute, "Social Security's a terrible thing though, you got to admit it, Aunt Sally. You pay all your life, and then when you retire it ain't enough to live on, and if you go get a job you ain't eligible for your own damn money. It's dollers down a rat-hole."

"Oh, *Lewis*," Ginny said.

"Well, it's true, sweet-hot." He spoke gently, eyebrows lifted, not insisting on the point, just appealing to common sense.

"What's true has nothing to do with it," she said.

That too, he realized, was true. He turned from her, feeling, as usual, stupid as an Indian, and absently picked another chip from the door. He'd had things to do tonight. Jack up the kitchen. Repair the woodshed door.

"A person can believe what he pleases in a democracy," Aunt Sally said firmly, "and say what he pleases, and live as he pleases, and watch whatever television programs he pleases, or read whatever books. That's the law of the land."

"Not in this house," Ginny's father shouted up, then went silent.

The old woman, too, went silent now. Ginny waited, watching Lewis, hoping perhaps for some suggestion. Nothing came. He could hear the old woman moving about, slowly, stiffly, in her bedroom slippers.

He might have thought once it was an easy question, what rights a person had when they moved into somebody else's house. But nothing was simple. That was the only thing he'd learnt all these years, though he'd been born, could be, with an intuition of the fact. You heard all your life about people who moved in with relatives, how they kept to themselves, did whatever bit of work they could think of to do, washed dishes, cleaned storm-windows and sap-buckets, helped with chores; and the relatives would say they were no trouble at all, though occasionally the relatives might briefly complain, with great pains making nothing much of it. That was all—or so he'd more or less taken for granted—how things ought to be. His grandmother had lived with his parents for years, and that had been, generally, how it had been then: an old woman for the most part invisible as a ghost, darning socks, dusting floors, warming baby bottles—more like an old, inefficient family servant grateful to be kept on, happy to be of whatever small use, than like a grandmother, someone who had once been a wife and mother, with a life of her own. Lewis nodded, encountering the same thought again: nothing's simple.

Picking at the paint, only half aware what he was doing or thinking, he saw his grandmother again—she'd been dead for years—her yellow-white hair in a bun on her head, clamped with amber pins, her brown eyes quick as a squirrel's or a doe's, and he realized he'd been fond of her; and mixed with that image, distinct and clear and yet a part of it, joined with it as images join in dreams, he saw the furniture he'd had to help move from Aunt Sally's when she'd finally sold off the last of it. It had been expensive once—more expensive, anyway, than anything Ginny and he would be able to afford in this Vale of Tears. A rocking chair, for instance, of inlaid mahogany; an old cherry table with hardly a scratch; a standing lamp of brass, with etched glass bowls for the light-bulbs; a tallboy of pearwood. The furniture had been sold, the house soon after. With a few trunks and bags and a shawl around her head, she'd come away from the place like a refugee. Even if the thing had been her fault, it would hardly have been fair, somehow; and it had not been, so far as he could see, her fault. Ten years ago or more, she'd tried to make the house an antique shop. She'd been unlucky. She knew nothing about antiques, and had no real way to find out about them. People who knew more cleaned her out when she had good things and sold her mediocre things for more than they were worth. He'd repaired old tables and chairs for Aunt Sally, from time to time, and whenever he went into her living-room shop he'd had a feeling, clear as a chill, that things were out of hand. She'd been in business, if one could call it business, less than two years, then finally had resigned herself to living on her savings and the insurance and, now and then, some housecleaning work. But she'd lived too long by a good ten years, and besides, she'd been generous, giving to political campaigns and charities as her husband had done, though she knew, Lewis Hicks suspected, nothing much about them. Perhaps he could have helped her, somehow another. But she was too proud to reason with, he'd known without trying, and who was he to give anyone advice, the unluckiest man he knew? So he'd shook his head, wondering what would come of it all, no surer than any of the rest of them how much money she had left, and one morning—it had seemed at the time just that sudden—they'd found out Aunt Sally was a pauper.

"It's useless, Lewis," Ginny was saying now, stubbing out a cigarette. "We may as well go home. Let them fight it out themselves." She was turning toward the head of the stairs when she paused and frowned. "Sweetie," she said, "look what you're doing to that door!"

He'd peeled away patches up to three inches round, six or seven of them, maybe more (he didn't count), revealing there, beneath the cream-colored paint, shiny green. It looked like the door had some dangerous new kind of chicken pox. He smiled ruefully at his guilty left hand, turning it, looking at the dirt cracks.

"Well, come on," she said, and led on toward the stairs. She called back to Aunt Sally, "When you're ready to come out, Aunt Sally, come out. And try to behave yourself."

"He'll lock it as soon as you're gone," Aunt Sally called back, and seemed thoroughly pleased.

"No he won't. You be reasonable and he'll be," Ginny said.

Lewis Hicks doubted it but said nothing.

When they reached the kitchen, her father said, getting up from his chair at the formica table, "Right's right, that's ah." It seemed he intended to say no more.

"Nothing's simple," Lewis said thoughtfully, as if to himself, and nodded. He saw, too late, it put him squarely in the wrong—put him with the Liberals. The old man pointed at him, eyes narrowed, hard as flints. "That's what *you* say, boy. But suppose *you* had a house, and some woman come into it and turnt it end for end? She's got a right to live ennaway she pleases, she says. But what about me, now? That's ah I want to know. I been living the same way for sixty-odd years, paying up my taxes and obeyin ah the laws, keepin my mind clear of lies and foolishness, and now, because *she's* had a little hahd luck, I got to change my ways till this life's just not woth gettin up for."

Ginny was over to the door by now, as eager to get out of there as Lewis was. "You know it's not that bad," she said.

"I know no such thing. Meaner than a wasp, that's what she is. Soft-headed as a cheese. We read in the paper, sittin right here at this same kitchen table, some woman over there in Shaftsbury has been breakin and enterin, stealing people's things, and by tunkit Sally stots tellin me how society's to blame. You and me! *We* done it! I never said it's a picnic to be poor, ye know, but the way she talks wrecks my supper, and that wrecks my sleep nights. I got work to do, ye see? When a man has to get up in the mahnin for milkin, it ain't healthy to be lyin awake nights, sick."

Ginny had her hand on the doorknob but still didn't turn it.

"Well," Lewis said, nodding in the general direction of her father, venturing no definite opinion.

"And now," the old man went on, "there she is on strike. That's the long and the shot of it. Let her go back where she come from, then, that's ah *I* can say."

"Dad, she *can't* go back," Ginny said.

The old man said nothing, merely stood puckering his lips in righteous anger.

Ginny let go of the doorknob and turned again to face him. Unconsciously, she was opening her purse and reaching in. She said, "Maybe she should come live with us for a while."

Lewis frowned almost unnoticeably.

She saw it all right but pretended not to, getting the cigarette between her lips now and lighting it. "We could keep her for a *little* while at least, sweetie, till we think of something better." She blew out smoke.

He could see the old woman moved in at their place, bumping into Ginny in the kitchenette, where there was hardly room for two mosquitoes to pass, sleeping on the sofa, with her bags piled around her, or on a mattress on the dining-room table, maybe. He mentioned aloud, his eyebrows lifted thoughtfully, "It's a pretty sma' house."

"We could figure something out." Her hand was shaking. He hadn't seen Ginny shake this bad since the night after they'd been inspected by the people from the adoption agency.

He mentioned, as if thinking aloud again, "We wouldn't have room for her things, course. Mebby a suitcase, one or two."

From upstairs, Aunt Sally called—she'd apparently opened the door to listen—"I wouldn't go where I'm not wanted, thank you."

"You think you're wanted here?" Ginny's father called.

Ginny's eyes filled with tears, and the cigarette she drew to her lips shook violently. "Oh the hell with the both of you," she said. "Lewis, let's go."

"Now, Ginny," he said vaguely.

But she'd opened the door. Cold air rushed in. He nodded to her father, apologetic, gave a left-handed wave, and followed her out. When he reached back with his left hand to close the door behind him— Ginny was already in the car and had turned on the headlights to hurry him—her father was holding the

153

door on his side, pulling against Lewis. Lewis nodded awkwardly, let go, and went on toward the car. The old man called after them, "Don't worry, now. I'll straighten this out." His voice had such determination that Lewis, hurried as he felt, had to pause and look back one more time, uneasy. Then Lewis gave his left-handed wave again and walked to where Ginny sat waiting, blowing smoke like a chimney.

Sally Page Abbott sat listening in her bed, waiting for signs that her brother had finally gone to sleep. She got nothing of the kind. No sooner would the house become quiet for a moment, leading her to believe that before long she'd be free to sneak down to the kitchen where the food was—a little something just to stave off diarrhea—than there it would be again, the clumpings and shufflings of his moving around, hay-foot, straw-foot, coming up the stairs, breathing hard, the way he breathed when he was carrying things. What he was up to, Great Peter only knew. She was tempted to go open the door a crack and look, but it was impossible to be sure he wasn't watching from somewhere, or listening and she was bound and determined to give that man no satisfaction. He would come down the hallway and move past her door, hay-foot, straw-foot, not pausing for a moment, though the hallway went nowhere, only to the closet beyond her room, and the place where the plaster of the wall was cracked from the chimney heat. She heard him grunting sometimes, and whistling just under his breath in a way that seemed curious, somehow cautious—whistling as he might when he was doing some moderately dangerous work such as electrical wiring. He worked for more than an hour after Ginny and her husband what's-his-name went home. (She squinted, trying to remember that man's name—she knew it as well as she knew her own, of course—but all she could think of, now wasn't that something?, was "Mr. Nit.") Much of the time he worked so quietly she began to doubt he was still there. Then one time James said, shuffling away toward the head of the stairs, "The door's still unlocked, Sally, case you're wonderin." She heard him go into the bathroom and close the door and, after a long time, come out, the toilet flushing—a sound unnaturally loud in the otherwise still house—and then she heard him go slowly downstairs, heard the door pulled closed at the foot of the stairs, and then silence except for the grunt of a pig once or twice and the ticking of her clock.

She sat up straighter to listen harder, her sharp-beaked head tipped forward and sideways like an eagle's. There was still not a sound, but he'd left the hallway light on, it came to her. Tight as he was, he'd never have gone off to bed and forgot there was a light on. She smiled and went on waiting. For the second night in a row, she saw when she looked at the onyx, Roman-columned clock, she'd been up past midnight. She couldn't have felt better, more young for her years, more wide awake. She tapped the bedspread with the paperback book, too excited and impatient for reading. "You see what it's come to, Horace," she said. She hadn't the faintest idea what she meant, or even that she was speaking; it was merely a fragment of a daydream surfacing, diving again before she noticed.

It came to her then that perhaps her brother had gone to sleep after all. He'd be sitting up waiting, that was how it was, trying to surprise her when she sneaked into the kitchen—trying to starve her to submission as did all those tyrants of old—and before he'd known it he'd nodded off. She could just walk right down and . . .

That was it, yes, certainly: he was trying to lay an ambush. He'd done that with his poor son Richard, she remembered. Spied on the boy and jumped him when he was guilty. If he skimped on cow-feeding, as boys will do when it's fifteen below out and Jack Armstrong is playing on the radio, one day suddenly there James L. Page would be, stepping out grimly from behind some beam, pointing like an Angel of Judgment at the job left half done. If Richard came home late after an evening with the Flynn girl and tried to sneak into his bedroom with his shoes off, there James L. Page would be, waiting like the sheriff. "Your watch workin, Richahd?"

It was true of course that Richard had a tendency to sneak and play twice and was not always "forthright in his story-telling," as Horace used to say, and true too that Ariah was far too soft on him, spoiled that child rotten, as a matter of fact; but after all, as Horace also said—Horace had been especially fond of Richard—*no* one was as forthright as James L. Page, "not even God," as Horace put it, "or He'd never have given us the word in such a language as Hebrew." Horace was furious whenever he heard of those ambushes her brother would lay for the boy, and though he knew well enough it was none of his business how James raised Richard, it was all poor Horace could do to keep from bringing it up, letting James know his mind.

She stared at the open book in her hand as if reading it, but her eyes went through the print, still studying what James had done to Richard. She didn't mean to say—she would be the *last* to say—that James was responsible for what that poor boy had done, how he'd gotten himself drunk and hanged himself. As well lay the blame on that silly, whimpery Ariah, meek as a fieldmouse all her life, and plain besides—all the Blackmers were plain, though hardly one in a century was ever simple as a nit, like Ariah. Not that Sally hadn't been fond of her, and pleased that she could make James happy. She shook her head, remembering how proud—and openly skeptical —her parents had been the day James got engaged to a Blackmer. Her father had flatly refused to believe it. He'd said nothing, as usual, glancing at Uncle Ira, who also said nothing, as usual—two peas in a pod, her father and Uncle Ira, glint-eyed and bearded, still as a pair of Stoughton bottles when they weren't out working—and then finally her father had said, as if someone had mentioned to him blizzards in July: "Don't b'lieve it." Her mother had said, puzzled, "How *old* is this Ariah?" When they'd told her which one of

156

the Blackmers it was, she'd had nothing more to say. It was clear that she too would believe in the marriage when the rings passed. But the Blackmers had known a good thing when they saw it. With a girl as plain and simple-minded as Ariah, it was either a Page or some African, and after the engagement had gone on a while it was the Blackmers who'd bought them a house of their own, later Richard's little house across the road and down the mountain a bit, the one James had drunkenly burned that night, God knew why, not even for insurance.

Poor Richard! He could have been a glorious boy, if James had just let him *be*. Besides handsome, he'd been wonderfully quick, and charming—though never around James, which was a pity. James might have liked him better if he'd allowed himself to know him. Everyone liked Richard. Little Ginny had downright worshipped him, which was why she'd renamed her adopted boy Richard—much to Lewis's disgust. On that matter, actually, Sally had to side with Lewis Hicks for once. It was a dreadful thing, changing a boy's name from John to Richard when he was six years old. It was somehow unnatural, a kind of bad magic. All of them had thought so, in fact, except Virginia. There had been a great thundering row about it between Ginny and her father, or so she'd heard up at Arlington. The woman next door had heard the shouting. She knew no details, or at any rate, being a close-mouthed Vermonter, chose not to tell them. No wonder if James had been upset, of course. He'd never admit it this side of the grave, but everyone knew he'd detested that boy. Blamed him for his second son's death among other things—it had been Richard left the ladder against the roof of the barn. (Richard blamed himself even more for it. Horace had once tried to talk to him about it, hoping to set him straight; but no chance, the chance of a hankie in a hurricane. Richard had treasured his guilt, as Horace told her. It was the one thing his father had taught him and he'd got down pat.) But it was long before the death of little Ethan that the trouble had started. It was as if James had taken a dislike to the boy when he was still a little mite in his cradle. "Don't be a cry-baby!" James was always saying.

Absently, she smoothed the gritty pages of her book. They'd gone sleigh-riding once, she remembered, and it was cold. Richard was just seven; little Ginny wasn't born yet, Ariah was pregnant with her—"Big as a bahn," James Page said proudly. It must have been zero if not ten below, so biting cold that the snow squeaked when you walked on it. The horses were flying, the big sleigh rushing along the slant without a sound, and even snuggled up between Horace and herself, with the blanket up over his face, little Richard was freezing. She and Horace were freezing too, though they had too much sense to say so. Richard called out, "Mommy, I want to go home! I'm *cold!*" James turned just enough to call past his shoulder—he'd been a big man then, beefy, his face red and raw from the wind, but of course he didn't mind it, not James— "Don't be a cry-baby! Blow on your hands!"

Meek little Ariah said, "I'm cold too, James. Let's do start back."

"Hell," he said, and reached over to slap her leg— he was always slapping her, mauling her, hugging her; no doubt she was better than you'd have thought up in bed—"don't always stick up for him. When I was Richard's age—"

Sally had glanced over at Horace, whose face was pink and white, like a turnip, and whose glasses looked to be frozen to his skin. His scarf was wrapped around and around him, and his stocking cap was pulled down as far as it would go, but both the scarf and the hat were storebought, not terribly substantial—not at all like the bright red home-made things James wore— so no wonder if Horace had had enough of this January fun, though he was damned if he was saying so. He merely bit his lips together, staring hard at James' head. He cried out, as if he meant it as a joke, "When *I* was Richard's age I nearly died of pneumonia."

"Darling, it *is* cold," Ariah meeped, and put her mitten on his.

"Hell," he said, but he leaned far left in his seat and yelled *Haw!* at the horses, and around they came.

In the house, she remembered—or perhaps this was some other time—Richard had whimpered, sitting with his feet in the icewater, so he wouldn't get chilblains, and his mother rubbed his back and ran her hand through his hair and petted him like a dog, singing to him in a kind of half-wit voice (or such was Sally's opinion; to hear Horace tell it, Ariah sang like an angel out of heaven), and suddenly James had said, jokingly, but his eyes were angry, "When I was his age, I was out laying bob-wire for spring fencing with Uncle Ira. If I cried because my feet got cold, Uncle Ira would just say, 'Putty soon they'll freeze hard and stop huttin.'"

Horace said—only Sally and, possibly, Ariah had known exactly how angry he was—"I understand in the end he shot himself, your uncle Ira."

"It want because his *feet* was cold," James came back.

The memory made her realize what a chittering devil her brother had always been. It had momentarily slipped her mind. He was a kind of savage—even to the stick, the snake's head, the outlandish magic charms. He hadn't been that way as a boy, of course, though the seeds were no doubt there. She'd had to lead him by the hand to church or school, he was so shy and diffident; had had to protect him from the older boys; later had had to tease and cajole him or he'd never have made a move toward a girl. It was his uncle Ira that had changed him. He was a *strange* man, Uncle Ira. Not exactly human—he even smelled like an animal—as if his mother'd been brought low by a bear. No one would've been surprised, who knew her—Leah Starke, great-great-granddaughter of the famous colonel. "Boy!" Uncle Ira would say, voice low, and little James would leap. It was almost the only word the old man ever said.

She gave her head a little shake, as if the memories were dreams and she meant to awake from them. Still no sound in the house. Surely he was asleep—and sleeping like a log half buried in a pughole, if she knew her brother James. She'd find him there at the kitchen table, where he was waiting in ambush, and she could walk right around him and cook a Christmas dinner if she wanted and he'd never twitch his nose. She put the book on the white wicker table and dropped her legs over the side. At the door she stood listening again. Not a sound. Sally opened the bedroom door, and froze.

Aimed straight at her, suspended from the ceiling above the stairwell, was James' old shotgun, and all around her, stretched in some impenetrable pattern like the strands of a drunken spider's web, were strings leading up to the trigger. If she'd come out less cautiously, or happened to trip, James' shotgun would have blasted her head off. Her heart beat so painfully she had to gasp for air, pressing both hands to her chest. She couldn't believe it. He was worse than that horrible Captain in her novel! She touched the sides of the door to ward off dizziness, carefully stepped back, took one last, long and careful look, as repelled as she'd have been, perhaps, at sight of Mr. Nit's eels, then gently closed the door. "He's gone crazy, Horace," she said, and realized only now that it was literally true.

The thought of Horace, fully conscious this time, changed her mood—her husband gentle and generous to a fault, a man who'd been famous far and wide for his painless dentistry, a cultured man who'd had a record player in his office long, long years before muzak, a reader of serious and worthwhile books. His image rose up in her mind so strongly—his image and the bitter memory that he was dead, he who had done so much good in the world—that Sally, all at once, could think of nothing but violence and terrible revenge. She could see Horace sorting through the records on his table, his bald head tipped, glowing in the lamplight like an infant's head with its soft new hair, his soft lips pursed, his dimple showing; and when he'd chosen the records that would please him most and placed them ever so carefully on the spindle, he would push up his glasses with a quick, gentle motion, an absentminded flick of the middle finger of his immaculate right hand against the black plastic bridge, and he would stand looking down into the thick, hooked rug, his plump fingertips tucked into the pockets of his vest, listening happily to the first few measures, before striding—for that was how he walked, striding, though he was chubby and short—to his bookshelves to choose this evening's book, then carrying it back like a prize of war, where the teapot sat waiting on the marble-topped table, beyond which she sat, Sally Page Abbott, knitting—in those days still handsome, still a beauty. He was not a man who wore greens or blues. He wore brown, like the scant hair remaining on his head, the warm brown of dark, new-ploughed earth on a mountainside, or the lighter, still-warm brown of autumn oak leaves. He took cream in his coffee, and sugar: three lumps. He smoked tobacco which he kept in an amber-glass, copper-covered humidor. He had a curious, boyish habit, with which she never interfered, of chewing little pieces of the newspaper while he read it. He cried at movies, knew poems by heart, had a garden he labored over hour after hour. He was a sensualist, he'd said once to James, with a smile. It had never occurred to him that her brother James despised him.

Sally had a feeling that her husband's ghost was very near just now, and would sadly disapprove of the hatred in her heart. But facts were facts, and the fact was this: she could sooner make Niagara Falls run backwards than kindle the slightest spark of warmth in her heart toward her brother. With clenched teeth, glinty-eyed in spite of her tears, scheming murderously in the back of her mind, as if James her brother were solely responsible for the decay of all values, the coming of the *Militant,* death and decline throughout the universe, she used the bedpan, dumped it out the window, and, being too het up to imagine sleeping, returned some part of her attention to her book. Where the gap left off, she gradually made out, the *Militant*

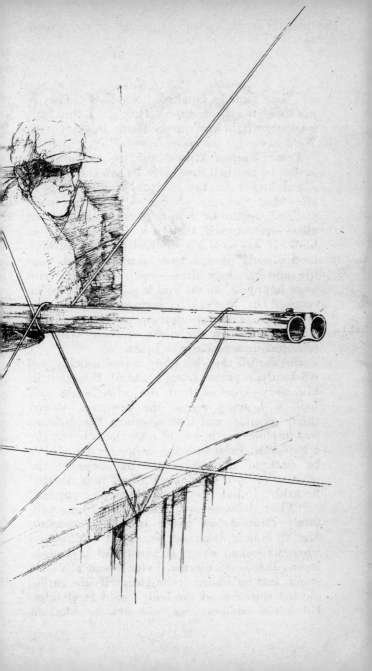

had not yet caught up with her friends on the *Indomitable*.

. . . The Captain laughed. "Not likely. They've got three times our speed. They got a tiny little boat, very light and quick. That's Dusky's style. We'd never get a hundred yards."

Peter Wagner started for the sextant, but just as he reached the bridge he saw their lights: a red flicker on the horizon, hardly lights at all—what was the phrase?—"darkness made visible." Again he felt he was something not alive—not himself, that is: a character in some book. It was as if his life had been somewhere meticulously plotted from start to finish—his life and all their lives—and even if the end were happy he would find it poisoned when he reached it: intolerable because brutally pre-ordained. He'd read too many novels, he understood; had taken the clicks of their well-oiled tumblers unnecessarily to heart.

But for all that, his body moved quickly and efficiently, separate from his head. He—that is, his body—ducked into the wheelhouse and took a bearing across the compass, waited thirty seconds, and took another. The *Militant* was angling north, would miss them by maybe a half mile. Even with the darkness, it wouldn't be enough. He went down the steps to the others. "They'll pass about a half mile north," he said. "Unless they're blind, they've got us."

"What shall we *do*?" Jane said. She unwittingly clapped her hands in her excitement. Mr. Nit looked disgusted, exactly as he'd looked when he talked about accident and invention. It was that same disgust, Peter Wagner understood, that he'd been feeling himself: the futile, idealist rejection of the body's cold mechanics. He felt a sudden urge, not new to him, to

164

resist every impulse of his bestial system, revoke his plot. Impossible, of course. They depended on him. "Wind up the engines," he said, "we'll head south."

"Aye aye sir," Jane said, and darted for the hatch and to the engine room.

They watched the *Militant* sliding toward them, Peter Wagner scowling, the others pale as ghosts. He glanced at his watch. Ten minutes at most to get away, and the engine still not running. Suddenly the sound of the *Militant's* engine—and the same instant, the *Militant's* lights—was gone, as if swallowed by a whale. Captain Fist hobbled over to the rail and shaded his eyes.

"They've shut down to listen for us," Mr. Nit whispered. "Thank God our engine's off."

Peter Wagner hollered down the speaking tube, "Don't start her yet, Jane!"

"Can they see us, you think?" Captain Fist called softly

"Not yet," Peter Wagner said. "We're pitch dark." He wiped away the sweat from his nose and forehead. If they were going to stop and listen from time to time, it would be hard to move the *Indomitable* out of range.

The *Militant's* lights came on again, and then the *chug-chug-chug* of the motor. Peter Wagner darted to the speaking tube. "Move it, Jane," he shouted. "Let's get out of here." That too, he was certain, was a line from a movie. He was feeling increasingly glassed in by the minute, mere shadow in a film.

Jane's voice came not from below but from the hatch, where she'd just stuck her head up. "It won't start," she said.

They all turned their heads to stare at her, then turned them again toward the lights of the *Militant*. "It won't turn over," she said. "Won't make a sound."

He ran for the hatch.

The starter of the *Indomitable* was a mechanism so complicated it seemed never to have been intended to be used. Its colored wires in their rusted iron box were as thickly intrinsicate as congressional by-laws, as impenetrable to the casual eye as the Truths of the Church. Standing in water that sloshed to their knees, Jane held the mechanic's bulb and Peter Wagner traced the wiring with his fingertips, swearing beneath his breath. He saw almost at once that it was hopeless, at least for him.

"Get Mr. Nit," he said.

She hooked the light over the patched, pitted tie-rod that held the hull together and hurried out the engine room door and away up the ladder. A moment later Mr. Nit was bending there, pulling at his earlobes and shaking his head. "Take us hours," he said. With trembling fingers, he drew out one of his cigars.

"It *can't* take hours," Peter Wagner said.

"True," he said. "But I can tell you it will. It's a very sophisticated starter, Captain, because the engine, y'see, is extremely complex. It's built so it can run on oil, diesel fuel, or gasoline. A heavy fuel, see, takes a *hot* starter, whereas a lighter fuel . . . So the wiring's what we call sophisticated." He gave a monkeyish laugh and felt in his coveralls pockets for the matches. When he found them, he lit one and made several quick passes—not watching what he was doing—at his cigar. At last, successful, he blew out smoke, then nodded, sucking at it quickly, as would a rabbit. "Sophisticated little machine," he said, and nodded.

"Lot of good that is when you're stalled in the Pacific," Peter Wagner said.

Mr. Nit was defensive, as if he'd invented the wonderful machine himself. "What do you expect, with all that water from the seam-leaks. See here? They're half under water. It's a perfectly good system. It's just those leaks."

Peter Wagner said, "Wires should be *sealed* against leaks, Mr. Nit."

"Boats aren't supposed to leak," said Mr. Nit and looked sullen.

Peter Wagner wiped his forehead. "Well, bail her out and get to work," he said.

But again Mr. Nit shook his head. His upper lip jittered and the wrinkles around his eyes twitched. "Can't do it, Captain. The pumps run off th'engine. I could bail her out with a can or something, but how you expect me to throw out the bilge? Carry it up the ladder can by can?"

"Figure something out," Peter Wagner said. He went up on deck. His heart banged, just behind his collarbone, when he saw how much nearer the *Militant* was now. She looked like a coal furnace floating through the night. He sent Mr. Goodman below, put Jane on watch in the darkened wheelhouse, and crooked a finger at Captain Fist, inviting him to the cabin. Captain Fist hung back at the doorway, still watching those lights. Peter Wagner closed his hand on the old man's flabby arm, urging him in, guiding him through the darkness to the chair at the desk. "Sit down," he said. The Captain groped behind him and carefully sat down. Peter Wagner himself, when he'd felt his way to it, sat down on the Captain's bunk. "As you see," Peter Wagner said, "they're practically on top of us. I think you'd better tell me what's happening."

The Captain sat, baggy with hopelessness, his face blooming from the darkness like blue cheese. He watched the doorway as if expecting the bow of the *Militant* to come through it.

"Who are they? Why are they after you?" Peter Wagner asked.

"What's the difference?" Captain Fist said. He looked toward the door as if to show that by plain inspection their evil was essential, beneath complexity.

"Who are they?" he said again.

Captain Fist sucked his breath in, ground his teeth, then brought out like an explosion: "Devils! That's who! I've scrimped and saved and sweated and slaved, building up this business, and just as I'm putting a little pittance by—" The outrage brought tears to his eyes and hushed his tongue.

Sally Abbott looked up, a discovery tingling at the back of her brain, then hurriedly read on.

"But *who?*" Peter Wagner asked, bending toward him.

"Parasites! Scavengers!" Captain Fist said. "People that want the whole world for themselves, and refuse to work for it! Nihilists, barbarians, Ostrogoths that destroy people's empires for sport! Lucifer's legions!" He banged his cane. After a moment he calmed himself. "They're smugglers," he said. "Small-time chiselers that resent my existence. I beat their prices, I beat their quality, I carry tons to their miserable kilos. Also—" he glanced at Peter Wagner, eyes flashing: "I was here *first!*"

"So!" cried Sally Abbott and, despite the shotgun in the hallway, laughed. How long, she wondered, had she been missing it? The novel was all about Capitalism—about those pious, self-righteous and violent True Americans who'd staked out their claim and, for all their talk about "Send me your poor" (or whatever the Statue of Liberty intoned), would let nobody else

168

in on the pickings. Captain Fist was exactly like her brother James. *That* was the reason she enjoyed him so. He thought he was the real, true American stock —An Hour's Work for an Hour's Pay, and Don't Tread on Me, and Semper Fidelis!—and what was he? What was he if the truth be told?

She laughed again. He was a miserable, snarling, brawling old smuggler, living off the scraps of the plutocrats' dream and hounded by the envious even lower. Her laugh this time sounded, even in her own ears, maniacal; a fact which she enjoyed. The Captain even *talked* like her brother James. "Parasites! Scavengers! People that want the whole world for themselves, and refuse to work for it!" It might have been James Page talking of Sally Page Abbott, come here to live with him and now gone on strike. Men of brute violence, both of them; mad as March hares.

She cleaned off her glasses, polishing them on the sheet, fogging them with her breath and polishing them again, and returned to her story, smiling a little, reading hurriedly now, wondering if what she had discovered had really been intended.

Now Jane was at the door, her lovely eyes wide. "They see us," she said.

"Then we're dead men," Captain Fist said. He tipped up his face and started praying. He had, as he prayed, an incongruous, crafty look.

"Did you hear me?" she said, and touched Peter Wagner's arm.

He got up from the bunk without answering and crossed to the door, morose, trapped in a battle for which he'd never volunteered. The *Militant* was now about half a mile away, bearing down, engines Full Ahead. Their searchlight laid out their roadway on the water. He went to the speaking tube. "You got that starter cleared, Mr. Nit?" No answer.

169

"Look," Jane whispered, closing her hand on his arm and pointing. On the *Militant*, just below the lighted American flag, they were winching something up out of the foredeck; he couldn't make out what. Captain Fist appeared in the doorway of his cabin, wobbly-kneed, clinging to his cane.

Peter Wagner snatched the binoculars from their shelf on the bridge and trained them on the *Militant*'s bow. He saw, at first, nothing but bleary light and the delicate patterns of glittering mold on the lenses. He fiddled with the range. And then suddenly, strikingly clear, at the exact center of the ring of mold like a jungle creature in a sunlit clearing, he saw a black, old fashioned cannon. It had wheels. They must have stolen it from in front of some public monument. He lowered the glasses, and the same instant he saw a white puff of smoke, a bloom of dark flame at the cannon mouth—the *Militant* bobbed like a cork—and then he heard the report. Something splashed, twenty feet portside. Jane ducked into the wheelhouse, scrambled on the floor, then in the corner, and emerged a second later with a rifle. Captain Fist aimed his pistol, steadying his right hand with his left. Peter Wagner looked around wildly for some weapon, then stopped, shocked. He was doing it again, slashing out crazily, like an animal.

"Don't shoot!" he cried out. He grabbed the Captain's pistol with one violently shaking hand, Jane's arm with the other. "Come with me!" He dragged them to the cabin. "Sit down, be quiet!" he said. The cannon boomed again, and again there was a splash, much closer.

"We'll die like foxes in a hole!" Captain Fist whispered hoarsely. He was indignant but also, again, distinctly crafty.

"Be still," Peter Wagner said. His heart was

whamming and his tongue tasted brassy. He'd read that that happened.

The *Militant*'s engines went off, and now they could hear voices. Holding Jane's hand, Peter Wagner crawled over to the door to peek out, just in time to see the cannon belch smoke and flame. The muffled report of the cannon and the crash, somewhere above his head, were almost simultaneous.

"We're hit!" the Captain whimpered, clutching his heart.

"Sh!" Peter Wagner said.

Then came rifle fire. Six shots, a pause, four more. The *Militant* was right alongside them now. If they fired the cannon it would knock the whole cabin off. The searchlight swung around and slammed the deck and bulkheads like the flat of a hand; every bolt or bar, twist of rope, slant of cable was like a razor cut.

"We surrender!" Peter Wagner shouted, then instantly ducked back—a premonition. They machine-gunned the cabin door.

Then everything was still. They listened to each other's breathing in the cabin. Except for the lapping of the water, it was all they could hear. Mr. Nit and Mr. Goodman, down in the flooded engine room, made no sound.

"Why don't they sink us?" Jane whispered. She lay pressed to the floor, sheltered under Peter Wagner's arm.

"Sh!" he said. But he too had been thinking about that and believed he knew the answer. He felt foolish, plotting like some cowboy in a thriller—felt revulsion, in fact, thinking of the alphas in biological laboratories, the animals that always won out because they thrived on challenge, stress—but he also felt, puppet of the universe or not, exuberant, bound to be victorious. "Give me your guns," he said.

"You're crazy," Captain Fist whispered, but he gave up his gun: Peter Wagner had snatched

it from his hand before the whisper was out.
Jane gave him the rifle. He rose up off the
floor cautiously, balanced like a gibbon, moved
to the cabin door, and tossed the guns to the
foredeck, one at a time.

"That's all we've got," he called. "Don't
shoot! I'm coming out!" He took a deep breath,
raised his arms, and stepped through the door.
He had a brief sense of noise and of being hit
in the chest, like a dream of death, and he felt

himself fainting for a split second, but nothing had happened. His innards were like jelly, but only for a moment. He stood waiting, and little by little his eyes adjusted to the reddish light. Three men stood on the *Militant*'s deck, two blacks and an Indian. Two had rifles, aimed at the *Indomitable*'s fore and aft decks; the third, a heavyset, bearded black man, handsome as a king, had a machine gun aimed at Peter Wagner's belly.

"We want to talk," Peter Wagner said. His throat closed with fear, such fear as not even the bridge had made him feel, though he'd been drunk then, granted. But this was a greater fear nevertheless, such fear as one feels of snakes or scorpions, things living and in some sense intelligent—such fear as the black feels of whites in an unfamiliar alley.

"What have we to say?" the black with the machine gun asked. He had dark glasses and a beard, and though he smiled, his face showed . . .

There was a gap. She leaped it like a spark, reading on:

. . . with a grapnel and threw it up onto the *Indomitable*. Before Peter Wagner could reach it to help, the Indian jerked it back with a whip-snap, and the grapnel dug in. In seconds the gunnels were lashed together and the three-man crew of the *Militant* was climbing aboard.

"Get us the gentleman who understands about engines," the leader said. The accent was not English, Peter Wagner realized, but universal Shakespearean. He stepped up onto the bridge and looked around, cradling the machine

173

gun in his left arm, the fingertips of his right hand in his suitcoat pocket; then he leaned the machine gun against the wheelhouse door. "But first, if you don't mind—" he nodded toward the bulkhead. Peter Wagner leaned on his arms to be frisked. When it was over he went back to the hatch, the lean black following him, and called down to Mr. Nit and Mr. Goodman. When he returned to the bridge, Captain Fist and Jane had their hands against the bulkhead and the leader was checking them for weapons, a pistol in his hand. He stepped back. "That's fine," he said. "You may lower your arms."

"Where's Dusky?" Captain Fist said.

"He died," the man said. "Made the great decision—

Whether 'tis nobler in the mind to suffer
The slings and arrows of outrageous Fortune,
Or to take arms against a sea of troubles,
And by opposing . . ."

"Died, you say," Captain Fist said.

"Deceased."

Captain Fist looked dubious.

Mr. Nit appeared in the searchlight's glare, popping his knuckles, the muscles of his face twitching as if separately alive. Mr. Goodman came a moment later, the black prodding him with his rifle.

"Good evening," the leader said with a bow, two fingers on the brim of his Tyrolean. The machine gun was once more under his left arm, casual as an umbrella. Peter Wagner thought of stories he'd read about smiling, sweet-talking murderers—the Jones-men of Detroit, the innocent-eyed Green Berets of Viet Nam who pushed captured enemies out of helicopters to make their comrades talk, or Mafia men who took friends out to lunch and carried home their bodies in the trunks of their Lincoln Con-

tinentals. Such things were unthinkable for an
ordinary man, even for Peter Wagner who'd
sailed the seven seas. Yet they happened in the
world, like other fictions; killers spoke their
trivial, predictable lines, laughed, offered cigarettes, talked about the weather; and then,
when the time arrived, out came the pistol,
or the acid or the knife, and one more poor
sucker, still laughing, was lightly blown away.
It was difficult to believe, though he carefully
fixed his mind on it. He was not so naïve as to
doubt that the trashiest fiction is all true, as
the noblest is all illusion. Yet for all Peter
Wagner's fear of him, the man in the Tyrolean
seemed too good for trash: his majestic looks,
his seemingly unstudied gentleness, his accent,
suggesting good background and education, his
Stratford gestures, they all hinted some story
more noble and interesting than the one he'd
apparently been chosen for. Yet one thing was
sure: he'd shot at them, and shot to kill. It was
purest luck that Peter Wagner had jumped
back when he'd fired his machine gun at the
door. So he too, Peter Wagner, was committed
to trash drama, if he intended to survive. Like
all the world, Peter Wagner thought. One
meets no King Lears in the ordinary world, no
Ophelias.

"Good evening," the leader said, more urgently, as if aware that his charm was uncon-
vincing, frightening—or, rather, frightening
because convincing.

Mr. Nit couldn't answer, tiny eyes darting.
Mr. Goodman merely whispered.

"Inside, please," the leader said. He took a
flashlight from his suitcoat pocket, switched it
on, and motioned with it toward the Captain's
cabin, automatically leading with his wrist,
again like an actor. The crew of the *Indomitable*
went in, single file. The leader of the militants
nodded them toward the bunk, then came in,

shadows flying out around him like birds, and sat, himself, in the Captain's chair. He laid the gun across his lap and shined the flashlight up and down, helping the fat, quiet Indian look for the lightswitch. When they found that the lights were dead—they depended on the engine— the leader set his flashlight on the Captain's desk. The shadows, settling at last, took on weight. At a nod from the leader, the Indian went back out onto the bridge and stood with the other man, watching the door. The leader called to them, "Perhaps you gentlemen would go below and check out those engines." They disappeared.

"Now," the leader said, getting himself comfortable. He sounded, just this moment, like a diplomat or a minister high in the establishment. He picked off the sunglasses and dropped them into his inside suitcoat pocket. He had large, handsome eyes, remarkably like a Pharaoh's. He smiled—warmly, or so it seemed at first—at Captain Fist. Captain Fist trembled, white as chalk, and said nothing. His hatred of the black man was as evident as a smell.

Peter Wagner squinted, thinking about that, thinking about the black man's exaggerated caution, his finger never straying from the trigger of the gun, the fingertip trembling, a tremor just visible, like that of, say, a plucked guitar string.

The man said, "Call me Luther—Luther Santisillia." As he spoke he turned sociably toward Peter Wagner, but only for an instant; then his eyes were back on Fist. "These people know me well enough. As for you, it's a pleasure to meet you."

He nodded.

"And your name?" Santisillia asked, and glanced at him.

"Excuse me. Peter Wagner." He was sorry to give it—sorry to give Santisillia any clue.

"Good. Excellent. How do you do." Then he was silent, watching Fist, mouth smiling, large eyes veiled. It was clearer and clearer, the fear of him, buried in the act. He was a mere man on a stage, fleshy sweating mortal in the costume of effortless heroics. Santisillia said: "I believe you were going to propose a deal?"

"Just this," Peter Wagner said, watching him. "We get the *Indomitable* running for you, and then you let us go."

The black man pretended to consider it a while. With a smile like a child's, he said, "Man, I'd have to be crazy."

"Why?" Jane said. She put her hand on Peter Wagner's arm.

"We could've returned your fire," Peter Wagner said. (*Returned your fire,* he thought. *Television talk.*) "We showed our good faith." (*We showed our good faith.*)

"You jivin me, man." He laughed, dropping into the Harlem language. He spoke it as if it amused him, pleased him like a toy. "We'd have sunk you sure, so you decided you'd just play it cool and come rip me off later." Then, returning to the elegant English, still smiling gently: "You have nothing with which to deal, it seems."

"You think you can get this boat going yourself?"

The black man smiled, head tilted, and considered it. The five of them, huddled in the bunk, waited. The water lapped softly, the gunnels of the two boats crunched together, a sound like garbage cans scraping on concrete. Outside the cabin there was dull red light; Peter Wagner could see a few large stars beyond, filtered. Then the tall, lean black blocked out the door, the Indian just behind him. Santisillia turned slowly. The black man shook his head, and after a moment Santisillia turned back to them and sighed.

"Ok," he said. He touched the machine gun. "You, mechanic—go down there, please."

"It's no use, Santisillia," Peter Wagner said. "He won't work out of fear if he knows you'll kill him anyway."

"Why would I kill a mechanic?" he said and smiled.

Mr. Nit got up from the bunk. *Ok*, Peter Wagner thought. His chest filled with misery. "*Eels*," Peter Wagner whispered to Mr. Nit. "We're on a wooden bunk."

Mr. Nit looked, puzzled, at the bunk.

"What's that?" Santisillia said.

"He can't fix it anyway," Peter Wagner said. "It's the *electricity*." He pushed the word crazily, hoping the idea would hammer down into Mr. Nit's frightened head. "The *electricity*," he said again.

"What you tellin the cat?" the lean black said. His rifle moved to aim at Peter Wagner's chest. The man's earrings jiggled.

"He'd have to hook up to a *secondary source*," Peter Wagner said. His heart beat wildly. It was clear that his plan was hopeless; it depended on Mr. Nit. He tensed, half believing he would jump the bearded black. Impossible, of course. Mr. Nit had half turned, looking wildly at Peter Wagner as if only Peter Wagner's madness threatened him.

"It would take a *live source*," Peter Wagner said, and then, to the man in the Tyrolean, "Interesting animal, electricity. Cheap to feed, it can live in either air or water—"

Mr. Nit backed away, but light was dawning.

"Take him down," Santisillia said. The lean man pulled Mr. Nit out the cabin door and they were gone. At a sign from Santisillia, the Indian stayed.

"Let me help him," Peter Wagner said. He started to get up.

Santisillia smiled. "Not a chance, baby."

They sat for perhaps five minutes, silent. Peter Wagner was limp now, unnaturally calm, still watching, cold as a machine. Jane's hand was on his arm. Captain Fist's breathing was uneven and hard, a sound like an old man's snoring.

Then, from somewhere in the belly of the ship, there came a boom like the noise of a cannon. Santisillia's face turned quickly for once, and the Indian vanished from the doorway, padding down the bridge steps and over to the hatch. A moment later the Indian reappeared. "Knocking a hole in the bulkhead," he said. His voice was like an adolescent's, soft, even girlish. "Man says got to run a wire to a secondary source. Be done in five minutes. Man says to give him a signal when you're ready."

Santisillia smiled. "Tell him I'll thump the deck."

The Indian gave a nod and vanished.

Santisillia said, "You were mistaken about your Mr. Nit, it seems." He turned his gentle smile toward Peter Wagner.

Peter Wagner nodded, closed his hands tight on the wood of the bunk frame and stretched his legs out, then lowered his feet slowly to the metal again.

Then the lean Negro was at the door. "Comin fine," he said.

Santisillia's smile was distant. He was thinking. He came out of it for a moment to say, "This is Dancer." The lean man bowed and came in a step. Santisillia's mind returned to whatever it was working on. The lean man, Dancer, watched him and occasionally glanced at Peter Wagner or Captain Fist. The lean man, too, Peter Wagner saw, was hypertense; a veritable walking bomb. It was curious that people so frightening should be afraid. Finally, Santisillia grinned. He'd showed no real sign that he was unsure of himself, for all his nervousness; no sign that, in secret, he had feared that Peter Wagner or, more likely, Captain Fist, might possess some advantage he couldn't penetrate; but now suddenly—no doubt having mentally bolted every door from which attack might come—he'd decided to be confident, expansive. "I've been telling our friends they were wrong," he told Dancer. "Wrong from the beginning!"

Dancer grinned. He was black as a coal except for the fluorescent green of his T-shirt. He came suddenly alive, as if stepping out on stage. Loose-hipped, graceful, he went over to the washstand then back to the door, as if for sheer pleasure in his ease of movement, delight at the swing of the rifle in his arm. It was all so smooth, so animal, you could see it had been carefully rehearsed. His left hand groped out, long-fingered, to touch things as he passed, and sometimes he tipped his dark glasses up to see more clearly. "They been wrong from the beginning, f'the beginning of time," he said happily, all rolling-eyed darkie. He delivered the line with magnificent style, perfect timing. Peter Wagner watched him in sudden alarm. He was far cleverer than he'd pretended. Dancer continued, theatrical eyebrows lifted: "They thought all our peoples was half-wit dumb subhumans!"

Santisillia smiled, just a touch aloof. He knew it all by heart; nevertheless, he watched on with critical interest.

"They walked on our necks with they highf'lutin words and they cibilization, and they believed it so much we believed it ourselves! But that's over. Done with!"

"Right on!" Santisillia said, widening his eyes in self-mockery, and chuckled.

"The oppressed peoples of the world has arisen, because they tine has come, the tine of rebolution, and the tine of rebolution is Reality and Troof! I said *Reality and Troof!*" He swung the muzzle of the rifle at them, Santisillia smiling, enjoying the show, though he was part of it—no longer enjoying it as once he had, perhaps; in his heart of hearts perhaps sick of the thing—but enjoying at least the art of it. Dancer bent down to shake his fist under Peter Wagner's nose. He was smiling with teeth as big as moons, the lenses of his sunglasses like a double vision of the sun's eclipse, and his theatrical joy was so fierce, apocalyptic, that Peter Wagner's chest went light and, suspending disbelief, he had the brief conviction that everything Dancer said was exactly so.

"Rebolution!" Dancer yelled. He pitched his voice higher, up and up, like a bright yellow frisby. "Understand what I said? And because you're about to go down to the hell that the white man's made up to make the black man tremble, I'm goin tell you the terrible facts, the truth that sets me free, understand—and the truth that's goin up Chuck's ass: You was wrong from the beginning, wrong about the whole fuckin universe, man, because *I* am the universe, and my brothers and sisters! I am reality and *we* reality and you the transient white debils that shall be exorcized! Hosannah! Reality is change, you understand? And you are a cibilization of tombstones and cathedrals and faggoty min-u-ets. Harpsichords! You are stiffness, understand what I'm telling you? I'm the dialectical method, man. I am the essential nature of bein, existence, ineluctable mo*dali*ty, Jack. I create! Creation and destruction, baby! I am the Everlasting News!" He waved the rifle in one hand and made noises with his mouth. *Tch-tch-tch-tch.* He ducked and stood looking up, smiling joyfully, aiming the rifle at the corner of the ceiling like a child picking off an imaginary cop. It was as if, through the dark glasses, he was seeing a vision, or acting, splendidly, a character who saw one. He froze in that position, half crouched, supremely impressive though absurd.

Santisillia—smiling, dignified and weary—clapped. Dancer bowed from the waist. Santisillia said gently, like a kindly old teacher: "You see, it seems you were mistaken, Mr. Wagner. You thought Mr. Nit would refuse to fix the engines. We, on the other hand, inclined to think he would, because engines are your friend's eternity, as Dancer has explained. Your poor Mr. Nit is in a cultural trap, blinded and grasping inside his white man's bag. You're victims, it seems—though perhaps I'm mistaken—of unrealistic ideals, inflexible genres."

"Commies," Captain Fist hissed. His face bulged and writhed like woodsmoke.

"No, it's Henri Bergson," Mr. Goodman whispered.

"All you say has a good deal of truth in it," Peter Wagner said. He leaned forward a little. "All the same, technological superiority—"

"I know, I know," Santisillia said, waving it away. "It's all so incredibly simplistic. But we're running out of time . . ."

It was true, Peter Wagner saw. Mr. Nit's five minutes to fix the engines must be up. Watching Santisillia's handsome face, feeling Jane's fear in the hand on his arm, Peter Wagner was of two minds, as if the lobes of his brain were disconnected. Why must they be enemies? Dancer and Santisillia were, heaven knows, no fools: he recognized with a leap of the heart, as when one sees an old friend, their morose ennui, their irritation with repetition. Yet in a matter of minutes, possibly just seconds . . . He gave his head a little jerk, driving out the wish that the conclusion might be nobler, the finale more dazzling—clearing his mind for the disgusting but necessary split-second action that was required of him by the plot. Below, if all was well, Mr. Nit would be seated on his high wooden stool, ready to bop the six eels on their noses. The charge would fly to the iron of the engines, up the metal bulkheads, across the metal decks. Dancer leaned on a bulkhead now, smoking a cigarette. Santisillia sat, feet planted squarely on the metal floor, machine gun resting in his lap. Peter Wagner sighed.

"I will say this," Santisillia was saying. "I've enjoyed our conversation. And now, if you'll come out on deck with me—" He got to his feet.

Mr. Goodman leaned forward obediently, but Peter Wagner put his arm in front of him, blocking him. "Why?" he said.

"We must send you on your way, I'm afraid," Santisillia said. He smiled, apologetic. "To dispose of you here, if we mean to use the boat afterward—" He shrugged.

"Do it later," Peter Wagner said. His mind raced, obedient to his chest. "You're right about our problem, our technological inertia, our generic traditionalism. I do want to know if the boat will run."

Santisillia smiled and shook his head. "I don't believe you," he said, "but needless to say, you don't expect me to." He put on his dark glasses, withdrawing from humanity like a visiting god. Softly, as if talking to himself, moving helplessly through old and familiar arguments, yet detached and indifferent, in a part of his mind —a professional killer with a deadly flaw, a weakness for language—he said, "How the foolish heart flails to live one moment longer! Mine too, you understand. But here we are, caught in these absurdities, creature against creature, victims of the world's most ancient rule. It would be pleasant, God knows, to be locked away safe from reality, like a doll in a toychest, a philosopher with his book. But here we are, for whatever reasons, guilty volunteers in the universal slaughter. What use to whine?" He brushed his hand across his forehead and compressed his lips. He continued: "I might have fled away to human goodness like the Eskimo, living in bare wastes where aggression has no use. So might you, of course. I might have crouched like an orphan in the safety of, for instance, a comfortable professorship. But for better or worse, as you see, I've made my choice. Not that I mean to defend myself. The bullet hole is no less red for my remorse. But we're familiar with the cunning of your Captain. Any slip we make will turn the tables in an instant. He's established the rules; we obey them." He was silent a moment, as if interested in an answer from the audience. At last he said, "Get up."

Peter Wagner closed his fingers on Jane's hand, pulling his arm free.

Perhaps it frightened her. "Please," she cried out, helping Peter Wagner's plan without knowing it, "what's the difference, just a few more minutes?"

"What the hell," Dancer said, weakening.

After a moment, Santisillia nodded. "All right. As you wish." He smiled as if slightly amused by his own sententiousness, and the smile was the most charming, the most boyish he'd given them yet. He patted the tiger-striped scarf at his neck, then lifted his left foot, preparing to stamp, the signal to Mr. Nit. He was still smiling, but again suspicion crossed his face, some sixth sense that, however absurdly, Peter Wagner half wished the man would pay attention to. Santisillia was one of the aristocrats, a beautiful creature whom it seemed bestial to waste. He *would* be a king if this were Africa, or the world were sane. Peter Wagner tensed, balanced like a cat.

The foot went down. *Boom.* A split second

later Peter Wagner threw out both his arms and slammed them into the bellies of the *Indomitable*'s crew, throwing them off balance on the wooden bunk. Their feet came up off the metal floor, and the same instant Santisillia raised the machine gun to fire, but too late. His face brightened like a dark cloud with lightning behind it.

"*Aw, shit!*" Dancer said, like a frustrated child, and fell.

Captain Fist, working from some script of his own, had found a pistol somewhere and—suddenly tipped onto his back—was shooting straight up.

Jane stared, mouth wide open, at the blacks, then screamed.

———————

Sally Abbott put the book down, indignant, then on second thought picked it up again, staring crossly at the next words, "Chapter 9," not yet persuaded to read on. It was ridiculous, killing those blacks like that, when they'd only a minute ago been introduced. It was probably more or less true to life—"Them that has gets," as the saying goes, even them that has relatively little, like the horrible Captain or her James. Nevertheless, she resented this turn for the worse things had taken—resented it partly, she would readily admit, because her own position in the scheme of things was like that of the people on the *Militant*. It was wrong for books to make fun of the oppressed, or to show them being beaten without a struggle. Of course it was mainly Peter Wagner's story, the age-old story of the man who in his heart of hearts takes no side. But even so . . .

She was extremely tired, though not sleepy. There was a barely perceptible ringing in her ears, and she had a curious sense of being terribly alone, as if hovering far out in space. It was long after midnight,

185

and except for the dim lights glowing in her room, there was probably not a light on for miles and miles. Again her nephew Richard came into her mind, it was difficult to say why, except for this: at some point in her reading—she had no idea when—she had begun to give Peter Wagner her nephew's features. There was really no similarity between them, unless, perhaps, it was the fact that both of them were victims, and tragically weak.

If it hadn't been for his suicide, you might hardly have known it, in Richard's case. She, Sally Abbott, was probably the only relative who knew the whole story. She remembered his standing in her dining room one night, three or four years after Horace had died. Richard was in his twenties. She'd been toying at the time with the idea of starting her antique business, and on the dining-room table she had silver things laid out —a friend of Estelle's had sent her a small box of odds and ends from London: a silver teapot with a carved ivory handle, cut-glass salt shakers with silver tops, knives and forks, little spoons, a pen set, an ornate silver dish. She'd just finished polishing them when Richard arrived. She was planning a kind of experiment: see how much mark-up the trade would bear, then decide on whether or not to go into the business. She'd offered him a drink—he always accepted—and invited him to come in and see.

He stood bent at the waist, looking excitedly from object to object, his eyes lighted up as if she'd shown him a pirate's treasure. "Aunt Sally," he'd said, "this is fantastic. Look! Is this really right?" He picked up a fork and the tag that had come with it. £1. "You can sell it for ten dollars easy—maybe twenty!"

She'd laughed. "We'll see," she said.

He shook his head in disbelief, and the light from the chandelier flickered in his hair. "Boy," he said, "I'd buy it myself!"

"How much?" she said.

He grinned. "Two pounds?"

"No siree!" she said, and laughed, "but I'll tell you what I'll do. I'll fill your glass."

"Done!" he said, and held it out to her. His hand was large, like James'.

Richard had been drinking too much in those days, and no wonder: the Flynn girl had thrown him over; and Sally had not fully approved of herself for offering him more. But she had no real choice. He was her guest, after all, and he was a grown man with a house of his own—he'd been living for some while in the house across the road and down the mountain from his father's. Even when he'd had a bit too much, he was never unpleasant or a careless driver. In the kitchen, fixing his Canadian Club and one for herself, she'd thought (it was bitterly ironic, as things turned out) how happy they all were, in spite of everything. She was used to her life as a widow now, in some ways even enjoying it, though the weight was always there. She was looking forward to this new adventure. Who could say? She might do well at it! She'd been annoyed that Richard had refused to go to college, but it seemed it had all been for the best, really. He was making good money at his stables job, and he was working for his father less and less. That was what mattered most to him, independence from his father, and heaven knew she couldn't blame him. Selfishly speaking, she'd been glad to have him near, able to drop in on her—and able to keep an eye on Ginny, who was then in her teens. She put away the ice-tray, closed the refrig, picked up the glasses, and started for the dining room. In the doorway, she stopped in her tracks.

He was holding a long-playing record she'd left on the buffet when she was straightening up. It had been Horace's favorite, *The Afternoon of a Faun,* and a pang of memory had made her leave it out, here in the dining room where she'd see it and remember to play it. Richard stood motionless, drained of all color —it was as if someone had slapped him—and she remembered only now that it was the record she too, the Flynn girl, had always chosen first. "Oh, Richard!" she said, heart shaking with pity, and she rushed to him, spilling the drinks as she went, and caught him in

187

her arms, still holding the drinks, and pressed her head to his chest. "Oh Richard, I'm so sorry!" They clung to each other like children and wept. How she'd loved that boy! There was nothing in this world . . .

It lasted only a few minutes. He gave a little laugh, drawing away from her, shaking his head and wiping his eyes, embarrassed. Head tipped, full of sorrow, she watched him compose himself, then handed him his drink.

"Richard, whatever happened between you two?" she said.

He smiled as if in panic, and for an instant it seemed he might cry again. Then he said, falsely brave, "I guess she found out about my faults." He smiled.

"Fiddlesticks," she said. "You have no faults."

"Ah, Aunt Sally," he said, "do I have faults!"

She'd pressed him no further, then or at any other time. She knew well enough what his fault was: cowardice. Or perhaps she should say half-legitimate fear of his father. He should have run away with the girl, of course. But no. "Soon," he kept saying. Even Horace had hinted that he was stalling too long; James was already half onto them, suspicious as a hen. "In the spring," Richard said, and seemed to mean it.

Looking around her bedroom now, the only light still on for miles, she had a sudden sense of how it must have been for him that final night, drinking in his kitchen, the Flynn girl married to another man, his Uncle Horace dead, Richard utterly alone in the only lighted room (or so it must have seemed) on the mountain. And now, abruptly, she saw in her mind's eye James' twelve gauge shotgun aimed at her door, and her heart, for a moment, beat more fiercely. "You'll pay for this, James," she said aloud. "All of it."

She closed her eyes to see if she was sleepy, felt fear shoot through her, a sensation like falling. Though she'd lost all faith in it, she decided again on her novel.

9
CHAINS

The east was pink.

It was only as Mr. Nit turned the crank that he realized he had perhaps made a slight miscalculation. He had wired the eels to the starter box, not to some solid metal bulkhead. It was too late now: the stage was set; the thump had come, his cue. The wooden paddle banged the eels on the nose and with a terrible hiss the charge went up the wire, burning it away like a lightning-fast fuse, and into the angle of starter wires—they went up like tissue-paper Chinese fireworks, though only the Indian was in the engine room to see it, standing in bilge-water nearly to his knees, so that if he saw it he never got to think about it. Mr. Nit scrambled down from his wooden stool quickly and ran to the engine room to see what his work had done. The Indian was floating, head down. There was nothing left in the starter box but melted plastic and ashes. On some odd impulse, an inclination toward neatness, he pulled the Indian up out of the water and draped him over the engine frame, then started up the ladder and met Peter Wagner coming down, face white as snow.

"Did we get them?" he said at the same time Peter Wagner said, "Where's the Indian?" They started over, and again both spoke at once, like clowns in some old-as-the-dinosaurs routine, so Peter Wagner jumped past him and looked through the engine room door. "He's dead all right," he said, a sort of croak. He would come to see later that he'd judged too quickly, they'd all judged too quickly; but

Sally Abbott widened her eyes in disbelief, and read the lines again:

"He's dead all right," he said, a sort of croak. He would come to see later that he'd judged too quickly, they'd all judged too quickly; but he believed it for the moment and started back away from the door, then stopped. He had seen the remains of the starter box. His whole face twitched. Mr. Nit, on the chance that Peter Wagner had gone mad, clambered through the hatch.

In the Captain's cabin the black called Dancer was motionless on his knees, like a Muslim praying. His toes pointed inward, his heels outward, his arms were flung out, and the right side of his face lay flat on the floor, one earring glittering. Santisillia sat where he'd fallen, in the Captain's chair, the machine gun on the floor beside him. His eyes were open, just slits.

"Whooey!" Mr. Nit said excitedly. He squatted down and gingerly picked the still burning cigarette from between Dancer's fingers.

Captain Fist stood over Santisillia, watching him as men of experience watch dead snakes. "Get 'em out of here," Captain Fist said hoarsely. "Throw 'em overboard, and then get those engines running."

Mr. Nit paid no attention, marveling at his work, walking slowly around and around it, so the old man waved at Jane and Mr. Goodman, sitting as if in suspended animation on the bunk.

"You hear me?" Captain Fist bellowed.

"Let them be," Peter Wagner said, leaning on the doorframe. "It's impossible to get the engines running. The wires are burned out."

Captain Fist twisted up his horrible face to

190

look at Peter Wagner. "Then we're ruined?" he said.

"There's still the *Militant*," Peter Wagner said.

Captain Fist nodded, stroking his chin, then smiled, showing his tooth-cracks. "Let's get out of here," he said. He beckoned Mr. Goodman and Jane. They stared through him. He bent down, waved his hands in front of their faces. "What's the matter with you people?" he said. He glanced at Peter Wagner, full of holy indignation. "What's the matter with these people?"

Peter Wagner sighed. He was limp, drained of feeling.

The Captain's fingers began clawing the air and he felt around him for his cane. It lay on the floor. He saw it at last and stooped for it. Then he felt better. "Stupidity," he said. "Stupid sentimentality. It was us or them."

"They know that," Peter Wagner said.

"But they don't accept it. Hah!" He was so outraged his voice became a hiss. "They defy nature. They deny reality. It's stupidity! I won't have it!" He raised his cane as if to hit them.

Peter Wagner shrugged. He wanted to sit down, but the chair was occupied and he was very tired, too tired to cross to the bunk. "They're unhappy," he said. "They don't want to live. Why should they?"

The Captain was angrier than ever, red as a volcano-top. "They should try to be more philosophical. Did I make the world? Did I create injustice? Did I ask these people to come steal my ship and get their fat black asses electrified?" He raised one arm and shook his finger, like a preacher. " 'For we are here as on a darkling plain, swept by confused alarums of struggle and flight, where ignorant armies clash by night.' Matthew Arnold. You see? *I* know about these things." He spit as he spoke, and

191

Peter Wagner wiped his hand across his cheek indifferently. "Now let's get out of here," Captain Fist said. "The sooner we're rid of these dead people the better." He snatched up Santisillia's machine gun and pushed past Peter Wagner and out onto the bridge. "To the *Militant!*" he said, and pointed, like Washington in the boat, but hunched over. He limped to the rail, climbed over it, and dropped awkwardly to the *Militant*'s deck. He landed loud as a box of bolts, and swore. Mr. Nit followed. "What about my eels?" he said. Fist ignored him. "Dusky," Fist called. "Come on out! I know you're here! You haven't got a chance!"

No answer.

Peter Wagner strained to take some action, but it was as if his mind had lost contact with his muscles. *I'm sorry*, he thought, too tired to speak. He had meant to be no one's enemy. But that was the structure of the universe: waves, particles in random collision, Platonists and Bergsonians, alphas and omegas. The lesson of what's-his-name's guppies. "All life is struggle," someone had told him so many suicides ago that it seemed by now some earlier incarnation. He had not fully understood it at the time; even in his misery he'd taken the mildly optimistic view. But he knew now about Time and Space; understood now the hideous implications of the fact that matter is motion, and God just an atom with a question. Stasis is nothingness; refuse an atom the time to establish its atomic rhythm, its molecule, and the universe would vanish, *click*, like that. But on the other hand all motion is pain, the ball striking out at the violent bat, and all rhythmical motion is tedium. (There were certain women to whom he had made certain promises, not in so many words; there were certain bills he had allowed to mount up, and certain violent mechanisms . . .) At the Captain's party, Jane had put her hand very gently on his leg. He'd been stoned. So was she. Two brute mechanisms, yes yes, yes.

He was startled awake by a clicking sound, and when he looked around the cabin in alarm he discovered he was snapping his fingers. Jane sat as before, hugging herself, staring. Mr. Goodman, beside her, had his hands up, covering his face. The dead—or rather what he thought were the dead—were as before. And then the engine of the *Militant* started up.

With the growing rumble, he rose to something approaching full consciousness. The old bastard would strand all three of them without a second thought if he didn't get Jane and Mr. Goodman to the *Militant*. He pulled at Mr. Goodman's arms, and when the man neither came nor resisted, Peter Wagner turned around, crouched, and pulled him up onto his back. He squeezed through the cabin door with him and staggered down the bridge to the rail, then dropped him like a sandbag to the *Militant*'s deck.

"God damn you, Dusky, where are you?" Fist was calling.

Peter Wagner puffed as he would do when lifting weights, then went back to the cabin for Jane. When he reached the bridge with her he realized that the *Indomitable* was moving. He stood baffled, straining to understand. Then Captain Fist came hobbling onto the *Militant*'s deck. He was shouting "Eureka! Eureka!" Mr. Nit came out behind him, popping his knuckles. "Fantastic discovery," Mr. Nit yelled up. "Fantastic!" Captain Fist, in his joy, threw his hat in the air. The breeze took it, and Mr. Nit went after it, two-thirds the length of the boat.

The discovery was an accident. They'd forgotten to unlash the *Militant* from the *Indomitable*, and they'd found that the *Militant*, small as she was, could haul the *Indomitable* like an oceangoing tug. They need not abandon the *Indomitable*'s cargo capacity after all.

"Help me up!" Captain Fist called. Why he insisted on riding in the larger boat, since they'd both be going pretty much the same place, was not clear. His dignity maybe; sense of theater, reality transcended. Peter Wagner ignored his appeal for help—hardly heard it, in fact. Mr. Nit bent over, Captain Fist scrambled up onto his back, grunting, and climbed back aboard the *Indomitable*. "What luck!" he said, smiling like a shark, "what luck!" Peter Wagner stood as before, with Jane in a fireman's carry on his shoulder. Captain Fist limped past him, shaking his head at his good fortune. Inside his cabin he called back, "Somebody throw these people overboard."

Down on the deck of the *Militant*, Mr. Goodman sat up, rubbing his head.

"Full Speed to Lost Souls' Rock," howled Captain Fist.

Mindlessly, robbed of will, Peter Wagner set the course. He was a man in a dream, his brain going over and over, as many times before in his life, the same unimportant facts. Tears streamed from his eyes, though he was aware of no emotion. He heard Santisillia's elegant, theatrical voice; saw Dancer's apocalyptic joy. He had lifted Dancer's body from the floor to put it on the Captain's bunk, and when the Captain said, "What are you doing? Get it out of here!" he had heard, had registered, and had immediately forgotten. It had seemed to him for an instant that Dancer was not dead after all, and the feeling was so strong that he'd leaned over to listen for a heartbeat. But then the Captain had shouted, and he'd forgotten what he was doing, moving from instant to instant like a drunk. The memory of his wife was smiling at him, her lip bleeding, her eyes rich with scorn. He felt, in brief panic, a need

—like the desperate need for a cigarette—for some book, some tale of high adventure.

Now, in the wheelhouse, he concentrated on the tremor of the compass needle as if the place they were going were important. But even the compass was more than he could fix on. It came to him at last that Mr. Goodman was beside him.

"You should sleep," Mr. Goodman said. He put his hand on Peter Wagner's shoulder.

It was a difficult concept. He concentrated on the ring of brass, brooding on *Ahead* and *Stop* and *Reverse*. His chest filled with panic. "Is Jane all right?" But he was thinking: *What of motion in all directions simultaneously?*

"She's coming around," Mr. Goodman said. "Go on in and talk to her. And get something to eat. Here, I'll take the wheel." Though his chest was wide, his face was undeveloped, ministerial.

The pink dawn was brightening, false as stagelight. Captain Fist had gone back onto the *Militant*, too persnickety to sleep with the dead.

"Someone should move the Indian," Peter Wagner said.

Mr. Goodman pushed his lower lip out and stared at the horizon. Then he nodded, turned with a shrug, and was gone. It would be dark and foul as a pit down there. There were still no lights on the *Indomitable*, and the leaks were still leaking. She was riding a foot and a half low. If he could remember he would have Mr. Nit rig a pump from the *Militant*'s engines, come daylight. (He could see Mr. Nit in the *Militant*'s wheelhouse, riding the course of the *Indomitable*'s steerage like the rear-end driver of a ladder truck.) The east was almost red. *Red sky at morning* . . . He thought of Jane, who had a claim on him. She'd saved his life, and even though he hadn't wanted it, it was a claim as powerful and burdensome as a parent's, or a hangman's. And also he had, of course, saved her life. So molecules are built, and ultimately the anguish of the stars.

Then, though no time whatever had seemed to pass, Mr. Goodman was once again beside him. "Go on in, let me take over."

He nodded and stepped back from the wheel. The east was blood red. They were now heading south, far off the southern California coast. The breeze smelled of land. On the deck beyond the *Indomitable*'s radio cubicle he could see the form of the Indian, wrapped in a tarpaulin. Peter Wagner stood still, thinking, looking. He turned to say over his should to Mr. Goodman, "I've been born again, you realize that?"

Mr. Goodman turned slightly, studying the deck.

"I've been given a new life, by pure chance—thanks to you and Jane." His voice was level.

"Thank Jane, not me," Mr. Goodman said. "I just happened to be near when you came flying down out of—" He pointed upward and laughed, then grew serious again, pulling his chin back, making it, once again, double.

"Just the same, here I am," Peter Wagner said. He stretched out one arm as if giving a blessing, playing the part to the hilt, papal—and it was an accident that he happened to gesture toward the form of the dead Indian. "Here I am, an innocent newborn babe, with all the frontiers of the *Indomitable* before me."

Mr. Goodman squinted.

He said no more. It was not, of course, Mr. Goodman's fault, this coffin of frontiers, empty options, Time stopped dead. Through the open cabin door, as deep red with the light of sunrise as it had been last night with the light of the *Militant*, he glimpsed some movement, some shift that his tired mind identified as the head-toss of a seal. He pressed his eyelids with his

196

fingertips and leaned through the door to look again. In the red light Jane was sitting on Dancer's belly. He was lying on the floor. She was giving him, it seemed, artificial respiration, sometimes pausing and slapping his arms with her left hand, his face—knocking it from side to side—with her right. Not with his mind, it seemed, but with some older, quicker faculty—something from that relic of the First Age, the brainstem—Peter Wagner understood that disintegrating wires had dissipated the jolt: the eels had merely stunned, not killed. He'd been granted, incredibly, a reprieve. It was like a telegram from heaven: *Rules all changed.* Time clicked in, taking hold like a gear. Then he saw that the body of Santisillia was gone. The same instant, violent pain shot through his head, and sound like a hurricane: Jane's scream. He must have been unconscious, and yet—one eye blinded by his own blood, his mind lit up as if by dynamite—he ran down the bridge, then staggered and fell and crawled on hands and knees to the tarpaulin and tore away the top to see the face.

The lifeless eyes stared through him like stones; nevertheless, he began slapping the Indian, trying to bring him to.

Luther Santisillia, with the pipewrench raised to hit him again, saw what he was doing and hesitated. He dropped, threw away the wrench, and began to help. Then Jane was there, pressing her ear to the Indian's chest, Dancer, looking dazed, just behind her. Her eyes widened, then widened more. "It's beating!" she said. Santisillia jerked forward and began hitting the Indian harder.

Thank heavens, Sally thought; but the thought had, strangely, no life in it. The truth was, she didn't believe the happy turn of events for one minute. It was only a novel of course. Nevertheless . . .

She glanced at the page she'd just finished, and read:

He'd been granted, incredibly, a reprieve. It was like a telegram from heaven: *Rules all changed.*

Curiously, the idea depressed her, and she wondered why. One of James' complaints about television was that it wasn't true to life, and—blinking the fact that what he really meant was that it didn't tell stories about life in Vermont, only stories about Utah, California, and Texas, the dullest states in the Union, surely, except for the scenery—or stories about the grubbier parts of New York City—the dullest place of all, if she admitted the truth—blinking all that, she had to agree with him that mostly it wasn't true to life. But that never bothered her, on television. Why should it in a book?

Running through, in her mind, the programs she knew best—*Maude, Mary Tyler Moore,* and *Upstairs, Downstairs*—it struck her that none of those programs ever touched real life at all. They were all about interesting characters, stage people, glittering and amusing exactly as characters were glittering and amusing in a Broadway play. That didn't seem to be true, somehow, of characters in novels, even bad novels. If characters in novels were entertaining, it wasn't in quite the same way. They might be a little like characters in movies—a good deal in her paperback reminded her more of movies than of life, and perhaps that was why, as she'd known from the beginning, it was trash, really, or at least not the kind of book Horace would read—but there was something, even in a novel like this one, that was more like life than any movie could be. You saw things from inside. You understood exactly why everyone did everything—or imagined you did—so that when something went false it seemed not merely silly but—what? A kind of cheat, a broken confidence. Well . . .

Her mind drifted. It was only a novel, and though it was true that, meaning to entertain her it had instead depressed her, that was no matter—though it would be different, of course, if the writer had intended it. She caught herself up, abruptly scowling, paying attention again. Suppose there were a writer so cynical and dishonest, so tyrannical, in effect . . . She stared at the locked door, thinking of the gun. Suppose, from pure meanness—or for her *good,* say—the writer had constructed the whole novel as a trap, intending in the end to embarrass her or mock her, jump her as James would jump Richard, those times when he'd skimped on his chores, or that vile Cotton Mather had jumped old women at witch-trials—for some high moral purpose, he supposed in his satanic pride.

She sighed and looked down at the paperback again. No, this was not that kind of writer; merely foolish and inept, like most people. What annoyed her in the chapter was merely that by accident it came close enough to life to remind her of it, and life was, Lord knew, a sad business.

Gazing at the print, sleepy now and thinking of putting the book away, she had, without noticing it, a kind of dream or fantasy, something that might have been a memory except that it was nothing she'd seen, merely a construction built of love like a mother's and the little she knew—those and the novel, which had triggered her gloomy mood.

She imagined Richard meeting the Flynn girl, some time shortly before his death. It was a hamburg place, Paddy's (it hadn't existed at the time), and the Flynn girl was eating at a table with her family, one child in a highchair, another in her womb, well along, bloating her body out of shape, draining the sheen from her red hair. The old woman imagined her nephew smiling shyly, looking quickly away, the Flynn girl's husband merely glancing at him, sullen, then growling at the child in the highchair to prove his mastery, and only on second thought nodding a greeting, final proof of his power, his absolute right, though now Richard wasn't watching. Richard walked on to the counter to order, a pink blush rising from his broad, stooped shoulders toward his straw-yellow hair. *So this is all it comes to in the end,* he was thinking. And, reading the menu on the blackboard above the shelves, he was aware of her fussing, covering her confusion, and smiled secretly, as they'd all seen him smile so often, panic in his eyes, as if James stood behind him with his arms crossed, wide lips clamped.

She saw Richard studying the girl behind the counter, noticing her youth, the childish lip, the high, too narrow forehead, unfocused eyes; saw him glance at her bosom, noticing the hint of womanliness there, thinking of the Flynn girl asleep in his arms, the room bathed in music, violins, trombones—thinking as he ordered his hamburg and fries, *So this is all it comes to.* And that night, again, alone in his house, sitting with a drink, tinny music in the background: *So it's all just this.*

Her hands began to shake, and she steadied the book on the covers in order to read.

10

ALKAHEST AGONISTES

For John F. Alkahest, M.D., it was a time of anguish. He sat in his tower overlooking San Francisco, not moving a finger, his wheelchair planted in the precise center of the octagonal room, on a real Persian rug that was mostly scarlet—and though he was now once more conscious, he could not rise. His cleaning girl, Pearl, appeared at the entryway door and looked in at him.

She disliked Dr. Alkahest, profoundly disapproved of him, but never before had she realized that she no more understood him than she understood spiders.

"You want somethin?" she said, though getting things for the old man was not one of her duties.

He said nothing, neither snarled nor simpered, and after a moment she came nearer with her feather-duster, and slowly, thoughtfully, dusted around him, showing no sign that she was watching him. He sat like stone. She dusted around the room: the antique clock on its flowerstand, the roll-top desk, the gin cupboard, the three stiff chairs. Still nothing happened. She looked cautiously down at the sunlit street. Hardly anyone out. A shudder came over her, which she did not stop to understand. One of the long-haired college students lay sprawled on the steps of the big gray house where a herd of them lived. Their Volkswagen was parked on the sidewalk, an American flag on the window. Down at the corner, by Llewellen's Market, a boy was leaning a bright purple bicycle against yellow crates of oranges, bananas, and yams on the sidewalk. Still no movement from Alkahest. She thought of touching him, then decided against it. If he was dead she would know soon enough by the smell.

As she stepped back into the entryway, she thought he said something. He still had not moved, but she became increasingly certain that he had spoken. The elevator door closed, the elevator started down. To her surprise, she was faintly disappointed that the man wasn't dead. What was wrong with her? If he was dead, who'd pay her? The familiar, brief panic came over her, and she made herself numb. *Slaves no more! Slaves no more!*, they'd yelled in Union Square as she walked timidly past them, primly dressed, carrying her shopping

201

bag. She'd been a teenager then. It was what she'd heard them yelling on television, and at San Francisco State when she'd gone there as a student. *Slaves no more!,* the elevator hummed. She was no longer fooled by slogans. Since the night she'd been sexually assaulted, she'd known she was a slave.

The elevator stopped, landing on nothing, and the door clunked open. She thought of Miss Pinky, in the ghetto of her childhood, whose daughter had buried her newborn baby in a coalpile. The girl's father, who did not live with them, killed a policeman, for no known reason, then sat staring at his linoleum until the police came in and found him. Had the policeman been the one, and had the father known? Pearl had followed for a year the trial of Joan Little, who'd been raped in jail. Every column she read of the story made her furious and afraid, sometimes violently sick.

It was not just the cold of the pistol as she remembered it against her temple. It was something huge, unnameable: the absolute violation of the center of her life. Once, earlier, her apartment had been robbed. She'd sat in the high wooden kitchen chair shaking, too weak-kneed to stand, and when the police spoke of the "intruder" the word took on suddenly, in her spinning wits, a terrible, half-supernatural sense: something not herself, not remotely of her world, had watched her movements, an invisible enemy, and had suddenly struck out of darkness and vanished, leaving her revealed, obscene. The rape had been the same, except a thousand times more terrifying, more final. He'd been white, in a dark purple jacket with orange sleeves, and calling her *Nigger, nigger, nigger,* he'd torn away her name, her very self, made her monstrous even in her own eyes, as she was in his. Even Mrs. Waggoner, who counseled her later, had hardly the faintest idea what rape meant. She wanted, like the police, a description. "Practical action, a step back to reality," she said. Pearl had seen only the jacket—dark purple, orange sleeves—and knew the cold of the gun. "I didn't look at him," she'd said. "I was afraid." Her counsellor had said, another time, "You must promise me you'll never feel ashamed, Pearl." Everyone assumes, the woman had told her, that nice girls don't get raped. It wasn't true. "Tell yourself that, Pearl. 'Nice girls *do* get raped.'" Pearl had nodded, in the end had dutifully repeated it. But Mrs. Waggoner knew nothing. The shame went far deeper than anything she'd ever understand. Pearl wished she could explain, but they were talking different languages. He had made her not human, not anything. Worse. He'd made her know that she'd never been human, it was all imagination, mere illusion. After that—she had no explanation for it, it was true, simply—when people talked, even jokingly, of stealing, or of breathing obscenities to some stranger on the phone, terror struck the pit of her stomach. She had learned—her whole life had taught her, in fact, though at first she'd ignored it—that the world is unspeakably dangerous.

Even among children born poor, she'd been unlucky, had witnessed from a safe psychological distance terrors to which, now that she'd escaped them, she would never return alive. "We just don't want no trouble," her father had said, poking his bald, back-slanting head through the living-room door. Or someone had told her that that was what he said. She remembered distinctly that there were men in the kitchen, opening drawers, but she no longer remembered if they were black or white. She was too young to understand. She had never understood it, and never wished to. It was odd that she should think of it, should from time to time be surprised by the memory, startled as she'd be by an animal at the window. She had other things to think of now. She had her own life. On free days she walked in the park or sat on the beach with her radio. (She had naturally wavy, not kinky, hair, and long, coal-black lashes. On Fillmore once, in the middle of the day, a middle-aged man had said to her, "Hey girl, you wanna fuck?" She'd looked at him in terror, and he'd laughed and had not pursued her. Men were forever touching her, patting her shoulder, even at church. She'd been having, lately, a recurring dream about Switzerland.) Dr. Alkahest, it came to her, was insane. Her eyes widened. She would never get paid.

The downstairs part of Dr. Alkahest's apartment was as neat as ever; nothing to do but dust, polish glasses, perhaps scrub the already glittering black-and-white tile of the small kitchen floor. She raised the duster toward the mantel, then hesitated. "No," she said aloud. She looked at herself in the oval mirror. She was like an old portrait, in the oakleaf frame. The light was gray-yellow as vermouth behind her. She looked like the long-dead mistress of some noble old house in a country where highborn ladies were born black.

When she was sure he could pay her, she would work. Not otherwise. A minute shock like a fever went through her. She went to the window and stood looking down with her arms folded, watching the street through her long lashes as if expecting it might, at any moment, open up and . . .

On the third day, John Alkahest was able to move again. He went first to the Bureau of Missing Persons. No luck. The man who had jumped from the bridge had left no trace but the car—no plates, no registration, no engine number, nothing but a paperback book in the front seat, something about an Indian. If the mysterious perfumed ship had saved him, it had sent no message back.

He spoke with the chief official, Mr. Fiorenzi. Fiorenzi sat like a huge, unhappy Maltese cat in a high-backed ox-blood leather chair with golden studs and walnut arms, on a square of scratched lucite, behind a walnut desk with a lucite top, an American flag to the right of him. Behind the flag, up against the door to some further room, he had a suitcase. On the walls there were pictures—Fiorenzi receiving a plaque, a medal, shaking hands with the Lieutenant Governor, shaking hands with . . .

There was a four-page gap.

. . . official began moving around the room, pulling hard at the bottom of his vest. "I can't even keep track of my own missing persons." He laughed, lamb-like. "I've got a daughter Teresa—she's the oldest, lives in Long Beach, married to a CPA. She's a lovely thing, that girl of mine. Graduate from college. But you think she writes? Three kids she's got, and I've hardly even seen 'em." Swinging near the desk, he picked up a photograph, a man and a woman and three black-eyed girls. "That's them," he said. "Beautiful?—Look at this!" He held up another of his pictures, a sullen young man in a uniform. "That's Joseph, my second. State Police up in Red Bluff. Hasn't been home since four years ago." He held up another of his photographs, boy of about ten. "This is Kenny, my youngest. It's an old picture, he must be twenty now. Hasn't been home since he was sixteen years old. We get postcards—Hong Kong, West Berlin . . ." He laughed again. "You didn't think I was that old, did you? Fifty-five. No joke! It's a funny world, I can tell you that. If my people came back from the grave, God forbid, they'd never believe it. House in Daly City, big white Caprice and a Gremlin for the wife—" He was looking at the suitcase between the door and the flag.

"Well, thank you very much," Dr. Alkahest said. He pivoted his wheelchair, more official than Fiorenzi, and shot away toward the door. There he paused, his hypersensitive nostrils filled with the chemical scent of the gray-brown carpet, the years-old government forms in the cabinets, Fiorenzi's Old Spice stick-deodorant. "Shame," he whispered. His weak eyes glinted.

Fiorenzi, some distance behind him, asked, "Do you believe in flying saucers?" A phone rang just then, and by the time Dr. Alkahest could turn around to look, the Bureau official had vanished.

The Police Commissioner was a busy man, putting off phone-calls, sorting through papers on his desk while he talked, writing notes to himself, poking his cigar at the ashtray beside him then back into his mouth then back at the ashtray. He was enormous: so bloated that the wire things that held on his glasses sank deep into his head. On his desk he had pill bottles, a dozen or more, all prescription. Brazenly Alkahest swigged from his flask, then slipped it back into his coat, but the Commissioner didn't notice. "Best damn Narcs in the country," he said, and hurriedly turned over a paper and wrote. "People don't realize. We make five, six, seven raids a week. Major raids, I mean. Not just Penny Annie. We burn it by the ton." He wiped his huge forehead.

"Where, if I may ask?" Dr. Alkahest asked.

But the Police Commissioner failed to hear him, coughing, then sucking at his cigar again. Dr. Alkahest tipped up the flask, hand shaking, and swigged. His fingers tingled and he began to feel dangerously impish. He put the flask in his inside overcoat pocket.

"People think it's just crazies and kids," the Commissioner said. "I could tell you different." He paused to pant. "Doctors and lawyers. Ministers. Whole country's gone to shit. Communist inspired. College professors." He snatched another paper from his pile and ran his eyes down it. "You wouldn't believe what goes on at those parties. Six, seven in a bed."

Dr. Alkahest remembered the smell for an instant, and his soul took wings; but then the smell was gone, fled to the depths of his being, and he couldn't get it back.

"As to what you ask," the Commissioner said, "can't sanction it. Sorry. Appreciate your interest. Glad to be reminded there's Americans left." He jerked out the cigar and looked at it, then quick as a cat popped it back between his teeth and reached for a pill bottle. "We get directives on these things. Don't know if you'd make a good agent or not, but we got directives." He took two pills. "Our undercovers are mostly young. Like college. Kind that can mingle and get in with that type. Kind that can grow big Looney-Tunes beards and look weird as the can in a whorehouse." He laughed. *Yaaa!* "You, now—" He shot a split-second glance at Alkahest, then looked back at his papers. "No chance," he said.

"I could mingle with the doctors and lawyers," Dr. Alkahest said. A miserable whine. He clutched his flask, his palm pressed to his heart. The cigar stench filling the room dizzied him, knotted his stomach.

"Sorry," the Commissioner said, blowing smoke. He slapped away the paper and started immediately on another. "They're not our prime target. Hard to get convictions. It's like flies," he said, "you don't swat the one on the edge of a cup, you swat the one on the wall where he's easy to hit." He blew smoke, gulped air. "So you see our situation. Appreciate yer offer." Suddenly, without warning, the Commissioner put down his cigar and stood up, like a whale breaching, and shot out his hand toward Alkahest. "Appreciate yer offer." Dr. Alkahest jerked his wheelchair forward and around to the side of the Commissioner's desk to shake. The impish malevolence was bubbling up more fiercely. Any moment now he'd do something intemperate and be thrown in the bucket where he couldn't do a thing about that boat. He held his breath. The Commissioner's fat hand squeezed his bones. "The way I see it," the Commissioner said, "not many Americans care about the law." He gasped in air. "I'd say nine-tenths of the people in this country is against the whole process. I tell my operatives: the few of us that's left—nothing but a handful—we got no choice but put our shoulders to the grindstone and preserve our American way of life—democracy and freedom for all— and put the rest behind bars." The Commissioner laughed, *gasp gasp*, crushing Dr. Alkahest's hand. Suddenly a coughing fit took Dr. Alkahest, and then a great spasm that threw him from his wheelchair and out onto the Police Commissioner's floor. The Commissioner, in his astonishment, did not notice that the cigar had fallen, or perhaps had been somehow pushed, from his ashtray into the wastebasket. "You all right?" he squealed, face red.

"I'm fine," Dr. Alkahest called up, coughing. "Happens all the time." A wild giggling took him, twisting his bone-white face.

The Commissioner quickly tipped the wheelchair right and lifted Dr. Alkahest, as if he were a small bag of feathers, into it. "Terrible," he said. "Call you a doctor."

"No, no!" Alkahest said. "I'm fine. I'm a doctor myself! No need! Don't bother!" He was already wheeling toward the door. The Commissioner hurried around him, almost at a run, to open the door and help him through. "Thank you! God bless you!" Dr. Alkahest said. He peeked back timidly, then quickly away. Flames shot up beside the Commissioner's desk.

It did not occur to the cleaning girl, Pearl, to pity Dr. Alkahest—not yet, that is—no more than it occurred to her to pity the lady who begged in front of I. Magnin's, placing her hand over her hat and piously saying "God bless you!" whenever a coin dropped in. She followed him merely because if he was crazy, as it seemed, she owed it to herself to find it out and start looking for new work. It was not the kind of employment a person threw away just like that. He paid well, it was a safe neighborhood, and the work was easy yet not dishonest. If the odds were that he would continue to pay her, she owed it to herself—and to him as well—to remain with him. Also, although his bathroom smelled, and though it turned her stomach to watch him eat (he sometimes had an oyster and a glass of white wine while she was dusting nearby)—and though she was practically certain that he watched her through keyholes—he made no effort to pat her on the fanny or snatch at her breast, for which she was, in her cool and sullen way, grateful. She knew about old white men.

But gradually, as she cautiously followed him from place to place—peeking around corners, hiding behind newspapers, exactly as in the movies—she began to doubt that the trouble was just insanity. The Bureau of Missing Persons, the Police Commissioner's, the FBI. She was frightened. She thought for some reason of female dope addicts, female bankrobbers, girls who made bombs. Though a law-abiding Christian to the soles of her shoes, she felt threatened. The world of Pearl's mind, now that what had happened was six months behind her, was a conditionally serene, brightly lighted tunnel where dark, jagged jungle things crouched, full of murderous intent, at the shadowy edges. She walked down the lighted path staring straight ahead. They called to her, *Pearl, what's happenin?* She pretended not to hear. Things mostly imaginary reached out to her, patted her buttocks, passed over her breasts like spiderwebs. She walked on, outwardly calm. But stories and memories once of no importance were important now: four boys shot by the Oakland police while playing cards. Black Panthers coming through high weeds with guns. She'd left Marin City at the age of twelve. She had taken piano lessons, sung in the choir. Sometimes, alone in Dr. Alkahest's tower, she stood, hands folded—drawn up before her belly like an anthem singer's—and looked across the city to where the sunlight struck the breast-like towers of the Russian Church, and had prayed for escape, total manumission, though she knew it was impossible. She knew where Dr. Alkahest's money was—in a black metal box in the gin cupboard—and one day stealing it had crossed her mind. The thought had merely come; she had not invited it, nor had she even for an instant entertained it. But it had come, and she'd felt queer, almost dizzy for a second, like a person looking down from a cliff. "Pearl, chile, you out of you mind," she'd whispered. Her grandmother's voice. Closing the cupboard, she had not even felt virtuous. There had never been a question of her stealing it. Her very bowels were against it, tightening in revulsion. But even so it was as if for an instant the jungle had darted nearer.

She sat on the wooden bench in the corridor, pretending to read a *Fortune* magazine. Pictures of United Nations buildings. On the doorway across from her and a little down the hall, a door with a frosted glass window and the words *Society for the Hindrance of International Trafficking*. Above the writing there were two large flags, a medical one and an American one, crossed like swords. She had no idea what kind of place it was. She had reached the corridor just in time—racing up the stairs while he came on the elevator—and had seen Dr. Alkahest's wheelchair darting in. It was a high, old fashioned corridor with a metal ceiling stamped in a design, squares and curlicues. The globes that hung down to give light were half filled with dead flies.

A man said, "Hey, what's happenin?"

She started, then instantly recognized him and, still frightened, smiled. "What's happenin?" she said. She sounded sullen, and tried to fix it. "You work here, Leroi?" It was Leonard, she remembered, not Leroi. She blushed, then shrank further, afraid he was about to do that hand-slapping thing, a thing she'd never learned.

"How's your mother?" he said. He leaned on his broom, wrapped himself around it like a python in a tree. His family had lived two floors up in Marin City. Six boys, all bad. Her mother would never let her speak with them.

"She's fine," Pearl said, and smiled. "How's yours?" Pearl's mother had been dead three years.

"She gets by," he said. He shrugged and made a so-so waggle with both hands. His smile was like a boy's, as if he'd never done anything shameful in his life. He was delighted—that much was true—to see her. She felt herself

211

blushing again, and pouting like a fool. "Well, shoo," he said, and gave his head a shake.

Before she knew she'd do it, she pointed at the door with the lettering on it. "Leonard, what *is* that place? You know?"

He turned to look, then smiled. He had a nose like an ocean liner and teeth like parked white trucks. "Ma'am," he said, "that's the American Medical Society's Special Organization to Prevent the Corruption of Our Youth into Horrible Addiction."

"Go on!" she said. A sudden white light flashed through her.

He nodded like a judge, then smiled again. "No foolin, baby, that's what it is. Whole lot of dudes with pipes and whiskers tryin to keep this country beautiful."

But he was talking too fast, and her mind was awash. Terrifying stories of drugs, murders; images of doors with five, six night-latches, heavy iron chains, dull black pistols in deal-dresser drawers. She remembered hearing shots, somewhere in her childhood. She said, "What's 'international trafficking'?"

He tipped his head, soberly, as if the question were natural. "International trafficking is The Mexico Connection——things like that. These dudes find out where some smuggler's at and they ride down on 'im wif their big black hosses and they bugles sounding like Jericho all over, and they yells, 'Burn 'em! Destroy 'em! Ride 'em cowboy!'" He laughed, momentarily closing his eyes, hands splayed out like a tap-dancer's. She felt a strange urge to touch him and drew back.

The door opened and she raised the magazine to hide her face. Leonard watched her. Dr. Alkahest came out and rolled right by without seeing her. She shot a look past the magazine. He pushed the elevator button. When he'd rolled the chair in, and the elevator had closed with a *whoosh* behind him, Leonard said softly, "You in trouble, Pearl?"

She shook her head but no words came. The magazine fell from her hands and struck the floor. She looked down, surprised. When Leonard bent over, starting to pick up the magazine, she had a sudden intuition that he was about to touch her knee. She froze, her back turning to ice, but the hand continued down, picked up the magazine, brought it up again. "You ok?" he said.

She had no idea. She was filled with panic. She didn't even like Dr. Alkahest, so what difference did it make if he was up to some terrible mischief? But her mind was unclear, full of guns and syringes, her mother turning toward the door, listening. On Twentieth Street, the place they'd moved next, there was a boy named Chico, about sixteen years old, two years older than she was. One day he was there and the next he was gone, and people said he'd OD'd on heroin. He was simply gone. She looked at the street, at the place where he'd stood the day before, grass coming up through a crack in the sidewalk, and he was gone and the place where he'd been was like a burn in film.

"Where you comin from, Pearl?" Leonard said.

The Jungle, she thought crazily, and the same instant her stomach jerked in as if to vomit the idea, the same revulsion she'd felt as a child at the movies. Barenaked Africans with drums and spears, bones in their noses, running around with crazy yells, killing people, shrinking people's heads. The corridor leaped toward infinity, floorless, and she seized the nearest thing to her, his arm, and held on for dear life. He looked at her from nowhere, notime, with frightened eyes, the left one larger than the right. Slowly, he raised the fingertips of his free hand to touch her hands, cautiously, lightly, and she knew it had never so much as crossed his mind that all flesh is imprisonment and filth.

"You pregnant?" he said.

She saw light bursting down the long corridor, and she was momentarily better. She drew away a little, even managed a foolish, apologetic laugh. "Not me!" she said. She looked at his face with sudden interest. It was the face of a coal-black mule, but intelligent and concerned. She said, feeling suddenly free, "*Me*, Lennie? You crazy?"

Dr. Alkahest, carefully unsmiling, entered Wong Chop's. He took a booth near the back, on the first floor, and a waiter, absolutely soundless, brought him a menu. The second time the waiter came, Dr. Alkahest said, an irascible whine, "There's nothing I like here. Let me talk to Mr. Chop." His heart raced, and he dared not look at the waiter. The waiter considered, face like a mask—he looked about eleven but was probably middle-aged—then bowed, exactly like a puppet, and flowed away. Two minutes later a large Oriental in a crimson robe came beaming in, his palms pressed together like a buddha. "Good evening," he said. "I Wong Chop." He bowed as if humbly but spread out his hands, palms up, as if nothing on earth could be more faultlessly joyful than being Wong Chop.

"How do you do," Dr. Alkahest said. "I'm John F. Alkahest, M.D."

"I deeply honored," Wong Chop said, his little eyes merry behind the thick green glasses. He bowed again, ignoring the hand Dr. Alkahest extended. "We glatified you come to our humble estabrishment, Doctor." Another bow. It was mere parody, of course, an act for tourists. Nevertheless, Dr. Alkahest was pleased.

"On your menu——" Dr. Alkahest began.

Wong Chop looked embarrassed, shamed beyond words, as if the menu were somebody else's work, a cross he could scarcely bear. "We have other thing, of course, Doctor," he said with a wave and another deep bow. "I venture say we allontee satisfaction." He smiled.

Dr. Alkahest smiled back wickedly, "What my friends recommended," he said, "was this." He brought the folded slip of paper from his pocket and pressed it into Wong Chop's hand. Wong Chop read it with no change in his smile, then folded it again, and, still smiling, sighed. "Ah, esteemed doctor fliend, you teasing poor Wong Chop!"

"Not at all!" Dr. Alkahest insisted. He began to tremble. "My friends assured me——"

"Some joke, must be," Wong Chop said sadly, compassionately. "They pray you a plank." He stood smiling down at Dr. Alkahest like a friendly red mountain. Then at last he said, "But perhaps I help you in some small way. Let me show you table you possibly find more congenial." He led the way, walking sideways, bowing, down a panelled hallway painted Chinese red to an arched door beaded and draped. He held back the drape while Dr. Alkahest wheeled through. It was a cubicle ambushed on all four sides by crimson. Paper lanterns hung from the shiny black ceiling, and below them stood a table for two, a linen tablecloth, candles, and two lacquered bowls. A stone Chinese lion saying *OM* kept watch in the corner. Wong Chop lit the candles.

"Now," Wong Chop said, and rubbed his hands. He pushed Dr. Alkahest's wheelchair to the table, then went around and sat in the chair across from him. He waved two fingers at a silent little man Dr. Alkahest had not noticed, and the man swept away. He returned instantly with a tray containing two green and gold, thin

cigarettes with golden tips. This time as he went
out the door there was a humming noise and,
turning to look over his shoulder, Dr. Alkahest
saw something solid move past the slit in the
archway drapery. A panel had sealed off the
room. Wong Chop smiled and held out a gold-
tipped match. Dr. Alkahest fumbled the cigarette
to his mouth and Wong Chop lit it. Almost instantly Alkahest's delicate brains were addled,
inspiring him toward song. Wong Chop lit his
own cigarette and, puckering his lips, breathed
in with enormous satisfaction. He laid one fat
hand on the table, and Dr. Alkahest seized it.

"Now," Wong Chop said again, and waited.
He had a large forehead and beautiful, womanly
features. An aristocrat, Dr. Alkahest surmised.
Man to be trusted. The plump fingers which Dr.
Alkahest clutched were dimpled like a girl's.
Sign of generosity.

"I want to get to the source," Dr. Alkahest
said. He leaned so far forward that he almost
fell out of the wheelchair. "I'm a wealthy man."
In his excitement he let it out as a yelp.

"As for that—" Wong Chop said sadly,
thoughtfully. With his free hand he waved the
marijuana joint. "I am humble restaurateur.
Now and then a little token may fall into Wong
Chop unworthy hands, but as to *source*—" He
seemed grieved that he couldn't be more help.
Dr. Alkahest was delighted, though of course
not fooled. Wong Chop was brilliant; they
would come to an understanding. Wong Chop
was growing larger, swelling gradually like a
balloon, and that too was delightful.

"Tell me about your friends," Wong Chop
said, momentarily forgetting his pidgin, "—the
people for whom you serve as agent." Behind
his little eyes lay tigers.

"With pleasure," Dr. Alkahest said. "In fact,
it's information that might be of some *use* to

216

you." He giggled, beside himself. Wong Chop's eyes narrowed, and Dr. Alkahest hurried on. "They are people, in fact, who are not what you might call *friendly* to you." Wong Chop's eyes narrowed more. "I'll trade my information for yours," Dr. Alkahest piped, believing he was falling though in fact he was not—not yet. It came to him that his chin was on the table.

"Information on smuggler?" Wong Chop asked, reserved.

Dr. Alkahest tried to nod. "That's what I meant."

Wong Chop pushed back from the table, musing, puckering his lips, drawing in hard on the cannabis. After a while he said, abandoning his pidgin, squinting thoughtfully, "The information would be useless to your friends. Better to deal, I suggest, with Wong Chop. Here today, gone tomorrow, that's how it is with marijuana smugglers. No 'ice,' you see. The rackets are in on the hard drugs, so the authorities get paid off. Marijuana smugglers, on the other hand, are mere peasants—foolish children and crazies. The police knock them off like flies. Good public relations."

"You're an honest man," Dr. Alkahest said, and meant it. Tears sprang to his eyes.

Wong Chop went on musing, eyes narrowed. He blew smoke through his nose. "Any smuggler I might name would be pinched, I assure you, before your friends ever got to him."

"I'll risk it! I'll risk it!"

Wong Chop nodded. "And in return—"

"Yes, yes!"

Wong Chop leaned forward, put his elbows on the table. "The *Indomitable*," he said softly. "Just off Mexico. Lost Souls' Rock."

Dr. Alkahest's heart beat crazily. With violently shaking hands he hunted through his pockets for pencil and paper. At last he found them, tried to write. He couldn't. Wong Chop reached over and wrote in swift strokes like knife cuts, then jerked back his hand. "Now, Doctor?" His whole face was suddenly a stranger's face, malevolent and keen, "these 'friends' you represent?"

"Oh, I don't *represent* them," Dr. Alkahest exclaimed. He couldn't tell whether it was his body trembling or the room. He raised one finger, like a teacher, and shook it, full of joy. "I got your name from the Society for the Hindrance of International Trafficking," he squeaked. "An organization of dedicated American doctors, he he he!, with whom, by merest chance—"

He had no clear idea what happened next. One moment he was looking at Wong Chop's face—it was swelling, turning purple—the next, the table was flying past his chin and he was falling through blackness, like a man in a dream. He looked up, saw a light, a blurry lantern. Then he was awash in some overwhelming stench, some sludgy liquid that carried him along through echoing darkness like a stream in the bowels of a whale. "You've misunderstood me!" he howled. And then, with his hypersensitive ears he heard, or imagined he heard: "Hello? This is Wong. Narcotics. Listen, it's another false alarm. If you could spare me a couple of men and a rowboat—" Dr. Alkahest gasped and fainted.

He woke up on a ledge, his trousers snagged on a comb of rusted pipes, his wheelchair beside him. Black sewage dribbled over him and trickled away with a soft noise into the ocean. It was a lovely day, seagulls and an infinitely gentle sky. Two old men in a rowboat looked up at him and sadly shook their heads.

Sally smiled and closed her eyes, meaning to put the book on the white wicker table in a minute, and also get up to turn off the lights. She was instantly asleep. Her mouth fell open. When she awakened it was early afternoon.

"The bees are as warlike as the Romans, Russians, Britons, or Frenchmen. Ants, caterpillars, and cankerworms are the only tribes among whom I have not seen battles; and heaven itself, if we believe Hindoos, Jews, Christians and Mahometans, has not always been at peace."

JOHN ADAMS, 1822

4

On Both Sides the Spat Is Further Escalated

1

She'd stood knocking for five minutes on her father's kitchen door, chickens looking up at her, and still no one answered. She'd never seen the door locked before tonight. She was beginning to be alarmed.

Lewis was behind her, standing dejectedly by the fat, silent Chevy—he'd turned the engine off—looking at the bright yellow maple leaves strewn across the yard, here and there a few bright red ones from the red maple by the mailbox. "He'd ought to rake these," Lewis said mostly to himself. It was a stupid idea and she was tempted to tell him so. The branches were still full; if her father were to bother with the leaves already fallen, there'd just be more tomorrow. Anyway, you didn't really need to rake leaves in the country. They'd be blown away before snowfall. But Lewis wouldn't know that, brought up in a prim little house with a prim picket fence in prim North Bennington—just four blocks away from Aunt Sally's old house—and she decided to say nothing, merely set her jaw tighter and frowned up at Aunt Sally's narrow window. She knocked harder and called, "Aunt Sally, you up there?" Still no answer. She looked over at Dickey.

He was standing with his hands in his coatpockets, the bill of his dark blue cap pulled low so that he had to tip his head back to see things straight in front of him. He was looking at the bushes under Aunt Sally's window. His expression was thoughtful. "Somebody went the bathroom in the bushes," he said.

"Oh Dickey," Virginia said, "for heaven's sakes."

But Lewis, from his angle, could see something she couldn't. He came over from the car to a little behind Dickey, looked for a minute at the bushes then up at Aunt Sally's bedroom window. "My God," he said.

"What's the matter?" Ginny asked.

Lewis half smiled, then sobered again. Matter of factly he said, "She been throwin her shit out the window, looks like."

"What are you *talking* about?" She turned from the door and went over to look. What caught her eye first was what appeared to be flowers on the lilac bushes, though the leaves on the bushes were withered to brown and bits of red. Nevertheless there were bits of white blossom, and not having quite registered what Lewis had said, though she had in fact heard it, she moved closer, scattering the chickens, and was suddenly assaulted by the stench. The bottom of her abdomen punched upward, trying to make her vomit, and she instantly covered her nose and mouth with her hands and backed away. She looked up at the window, horrified and enraged, so that her face, as Lewis and Dickey saw it, was not the Ginny they knew at all. She had bulging eyes, a sudden puffiness and redness of adrenaline—a kind of crackling look, as if she were shooting off electricity—and the sight made them cower, though they showed no outward sign. Looking up at the window Ginny saw now, despite the glow of sunset on the panes, her Aunt Sally standing there cool as a cucumber, saying not a word. Ginny drew in breath and bellowed, angrier than ever, "Aunt *Sally!*"

Now Lewis saw her too. Instinctively putting himself on Ginny's side, hoping for immunity from her wrath, he yelled: "Aunt Sally, look what you done!" He pointed at the bushes.

Still she said nothing, staring down through the red-lighted panes like a madwoman, murderously serene.

Now Ginny's face was taking on a new expression. Lewis saw the change, glancing at her furtively, but he no more understood it than Ginny did herself, or the child. She knew only that her anger had suddenly flashed hotter, and that it had to do with humiliation. These were *her* relatives, and the way Lewis stood, carefully not judging, made her face sting with shame. "Aunt Sally, you *answer* me," she yelled, white with anger, and then suddenly covered her face with both hands and cried. Lewis stood helplessly looking from Ginny to Aunt Sally to the lilacs, spattered with runny brown and the stained white of wadded Kleenex. Then the window opened, and Aunt Sally, standing in her bathrobe, a paperback book in one hand, called down: "If you want to see your father, he's out milkin."

Lewis said, not quite to his wife, "I *thought* it might be choretime."

Ginny gave him such a look of pure scalding rage that his heart quaked. "Then why in hell didn't you say so?"

He had no idea what he'd done to so anger her. "I'm sorry," he said, voice quavering. "I should've spoke up."

"Jesus," she spat at them all, and started toward the barn. Lewis, knees weak, caught Dickey's hand and followed.

Behind the house, where the back yard sloped down to the faded red barn on its rough rock foundation—

the dingy white hives of the bees just beyond—there
was only one tree, an old jagged hickory, most of its
leaves fallen, so they could see the full glory of the
crimson sunset above the mountain and the slope of
the pasture. Perversely, for all his grief, or because of
his grief, Lewis Hicks did see it, and registered that
it was beautiful. He saw how the stones and grass
of the pasture turned spiritual in this light, radiating
power, as if charged with some old, mystic energy un-
named except in ancient Sumerian or Indian—how the
forested mountains that had been a hundred colors
just an hour ago—blood red, wine red, pink and
magenta, bold strokes of orange, bright yellows and
browns, purples that Ginny would call garish in a
painting, and here and there, in blocks, dark greens
and blue-greens where there were stands of pine—
were now all suffused with the crimson of the sky,
transmuted. Lewis Hicks saw and registered how
even the old man's machinery was transformed by this
stunning light, the old yellow corn-chopper tilted
against the silo more distinct, more itself than it would
normally be, final as a tombstone, like the big Case
tractor, the paintless box-wagon, the lobster-red corn-
picker or the small gray tractor with its big square
faded umbrella. He had no words for his impressions,
but his misery intensified. He was wrong and wronged.
Wordlessly, caught at the intersecting planes of the
sunset's beauty and Virginia's strange anger—strange
to him even though he saw he'd been a fool, and all
she'd said was right—he suddenly wished his whole
life changed absolutely, wished himself free and in the
same motion wished for the opposite, or the same
perhaps, wished he were dead. All husbands wished
that, he supposed, from time to time, same as elves
and bears. And perhaps all wives. But how mysterious
that not even *one* could be spared, not even he, remote
from the world, in a barnyard in Vermont. Did even
cattle have such pangs of unhappiness? Grasshoppers?
    Dickey said, "Why's she so mad?"
    Abruptly, almost without noticing it, he was better.
His soul crashed inward from the sky, the sweep of

mountains like ocean waves—collapsed back to time out of timelessness—and he became a small man walking, holding his son's hand, moving again through a specific time and place, not a disembodied, universal cry but a sober-faced husband and father who had certain problems, certain groundless duties. In the trunk of the Chevy he had paint-remover and a scraper.

"She's upset," he said. "Don't worry about it."

They ducked under the electric wire of the gate, then he picked up Dickey to carry him, stepping carefully, not that his shoes were all that fine, from firm place to firm place, grass-tuft to grass-tuft, past mud and slime and cowplops toward the milkhouse. Ginny had already disappeared through that door, hurrying ahead of them. They could hear the *chuff-chuff* of the milking-machine compressor.

Having seen what she'd seen, Ginny was solidly on her father's side when she found him between two holsteins, putting on a milker strap.

"Hi, Dad," she said.

The old man jumped, then smiled, pleased to see her, yet somewhat grim. "Hi there, Ginny," he said.

"I knocked and knocked, up at the house," she said. "The door was locked."

It was a question, of course, but he pretended not to notice. "Wintah's just around the cohnah," he said. "*So* bahss"—leaning over to put the teatcups on.

"Have you seen what's happened to the lilac bushes?" Ginny asked. She had her arms folded, hands clamped in tight on each side of her bosom, because her father would allow no smoking out here in the barn.

"Can't say I have," he said, and tipped up his long face to look at her. She said nothing, and he finished adjusting the machine, absently batting away a fly with his right hand, then stiffly raised himself, helping himself up by grabbing the cow's sharp hipbone. When he was more or less erect—still bent over some, so that she was struck by the fact that her father had gotten old—he stepped back over the steaming, half-filled gutter to the walkway, placing the treads of his red boots carefully, to keep himself from slipping in manure or wet lime. He draped the strap from the cow he'd just finished around his neck. Ginny sniffled back tears. Though her father was strong from a lifetime of lifting and carrying, his flesh was wasting away, these last years, so that his rough red skin sagged and his bones stuck out like a half-starved animal's, especially the vertebrae in the back of his neck, his skull—unpleasantly prominent, lately, like the skull of a foetus—and the bones of his fingers and wrists. "What about 'em?" he asked, "—the lilacs?"

"Aunt Sally's been throwing her shit out the window," she said, and abruptly, jerking her hands up to cover her face, she began sobbing. Her shoulders shook, her voice came out in whoops. The old man stood with his knuckly hands hanging at his sides and couldn't think what to do. He hadn't heard what she'd said, or, rather, wasn't sure he'd heard correctly, and the crying was so extreme—as if somebody'd been killed—he could only stand fogbound and hope in a minute things came clearer. Ginny wailed, and what she said was even less distinct now, distorted by her sobbing. "Right there where everybody can *see* it, Dad. Anybody passing down the *road* can look over and—" The sobbing overwhelmed her and she could say no more, could only squeeze her face with her hands and gasp for breath, as she'd done when she'd cried as a little girl. He remembered when he'd spanked her out by the clothesline when she was something like seven, maybe eight, spanked her no harder than he ought to have done, but her sobbing, heart-broken, had filled him with anguish, and he'd held her and kissed her cheek—as now, awkwardly, he moved toward holding her, raising his stiff crooked hands toward her arms but unable really to hold her, because Ginny was grown now, and he was old, bent half double with constipation cramps. He remembered how she'd sobbed when little Ethan had fallen off the barn and broke his neck, their younger son, and was dead at just seven.

"Ginny, what's the *matter*?" he said now. "Honey, I can't understand you. What's happened?" Then, looking over toward the milkhouse steps, he saw Lewis and Dickey coming carefully toward them—they looked like fishermen crossing a shallow stream on rocks—trying not to step in the cowshit. "Lewis," he called, "what's happened?" Their faces lighted strangely as they came past the windows where the glow of the charged, crimson sky poured in. Lewis held Dickey's hand.

"It's Aunt Sally," Lewis said. "It looks like she's been usin the bedpan and dumpin it out the window."

The old man's heart sank. Sure as anything, they'd lay it all to him.

Lewis had come up to them now and stood three, four feet away, still holding the boy's hand, looking like a helpless little boy himself, miserably watching Ginny. James compressed his lips, still clumsily patting his daughter's arms on the fat place just below the shoulders, and could think of nothing to say but "There, there now, honey. There there, sweet-hot." It was time—more than time—to get the milkers changed, and if he didn't get down to it pretty quick, he thought, he'd have his milkers kicked clear past the barnyard. "Sweet-hot, I gotta change the milkers," he said. Ginny nodded, vocally drawing in breath, getting her crying in control at last, and he patted her arms two or three more times then left her, went over to the guernsey that was next in line and hung the strap over her back. He stooped to take the milker from the cow in the next stanchion, turned off the air, and stepped carefully across the gutter to dump the milk from the filled-up machine into the pail. By the whitewashed post six feet away the cats sat watching, soft and tame looking as pillows on a couch, though if you touched one you'd likely lose a finger. He went over to the cats' post and splashed a little leftover milk into their dish, an old dented lid from a ten-gallon can, then went back, still doubled over, to put the milker on the cow he'd just strapped.

Ginny, better now, came down the line to where he was working and was able to speak, though she wasn't entirely through crying. Lewis and Dickey came part way, too. She said, "How could she do it? She must be senile!"

Lewis said. "Could be that. When my gramp got old, he use to walk around the house with ah his clothes off, carryin a bucket."

"I just don't know what to *do*," Ginny said. Her head was stuffed up and she kept sniffing. "We can't put Aunt Sally in a Home. They cost a fortune."

James knew pretty well that he'd better speak up; but all he could bring himself to say at the moment was, "Oh, I wouldn't worry, if I was you, bout Sally bein senile."

"Well then she's crazy," Ginny said, "and that's worse." It looked as if she was about to cry again. Lewis was shaking his head, thinking God knows what. The boy was leaning far over, pulling Lewis's arm out straight, dangling a piece of straw over the cats.

James straightened up enough to walk and stepped over the gutter, hanging the strap around his neck as he walked. Little as he cared, right now, for that witch of a sister, it wasn't in his nature to leave the error stand. "I doubt that a doctor'd call her crazy," he said.

"I don't know, though," Lewis said, noncommittal, "you can't say it's normal, emptying your potty out the window, and in the front of the house."

"Prob'ly couldn't get to the bathroom," James said, equally noncommittal, and stepped back across the gutter to hang the strap on the cow due next. "So-o-o bahss," he said.

Ginny's head swung around. "You locked her in *again*?"

He pressed his forehead against the cow's warm belly. "Nope," he said. "Just saw to it she didn't change her mind about stayin in her room. Used the aht of pahsuasion."

They waited. When he said no more, Ginny asked, "Dad, what did you *do?*"

So again he was in the wrong. It was always nobody's fault but his. "Whant you go look for yourself?" he said. His jaw stiffened and his voice stepped higher with indignation and self-pity. His faith in laconic truth cracked and gave way like the wall of a haybarn now, broken by the weight of the injustices done him. "Look with your own two eyes and you'll know I ain't lying," he said. "You mistrust I chopped off her head, you two? Well mebby so. You go look. Ain't that the custahd, though? Sally can do ennathing she pleases in my house, and the minute I try'n put a stop to't, I be a criminal. No end to't! It's just like them terrorists. They can shoot the police like they was squirrels in a tree, and nobody says one blessed word, but let some Government shoot five convicted terrorists, and there be letters gonna come from all hell and gone! It's just like the Italians. Write down the truth about the Mafia in some book—how they'll shoot a man quicker'n they'll look him in the eye, even shoot John F. Kennedy, and the country can go knit —and before ye can say Jack Robinson they got you in court, fightin off the Italian League cause you made it seem some of 'em ain't honest." He had the milking machine on now, rhythmically chugging, and came back across the gutter. "Ah my life I been fair's I know how to be, and you know it, the both of you, and with Sally there was never but one thing I balked at, which is the root of all the rest, and it's that blame TV. 'You could've had her keep it in her room,' you'll say to me, but I tell you that ain't true, it want possible. I'd still have heard the rumble, and I'd've known what sickness and filth it was spewing through my house. You might as well tell me I should let people murder little children, long's they do it in their room. You'll say it ain't the same. Well I don't care to argue. I *believe* it's the same. I set there by the fire every night for two weeks and watched it, as fair as any man in a jury box, and I'll even admit I saw one or two things I thought was more-less hahmless. But on the whole I say it was filth and corruption: murderers and rapists, drug addicts, long-hairs, bosses and policemen till yer so weary ye could spit except your mouth's too tired. Half-naked women with microphones, stretchin out their long, limp ahms to you and puckerin and smilin with all their big, glassy teeth, singin you the damn foolest songs you ever heard, mostly bedroom talk. Quiz-shows where people go insane to get some money, news that goes jumpin around from one thing to another like a blame three-ring circus that's in a hurry to get struck, and no more attempt to make sense of what you're seein than a ten-cent get-well cahd from the drugstore. Sober conversations about the failure of America and religion and the family, as if there want no question about the jig bein up, and sober conversation bout how a man that's homosexual is just as nahmal as you or me—" A catch came into his voice and he broke off abruptly.

Ginny stared at him, shocked, her heart going out to him. She'd never heard such a tirade from him, never more than glimpsed the anger and helplessness now suddenly made plain. Even Dickey understood, standing by the wall with a guilty look, as if everything were his fault. As for Lewis, she realized glancing at him now that he'd probably understood from the beginning. She could only stand with her mouth open. Staring at the tremor in her father's cheek, watching him go past her, angry as a bot and close to tears, taking the pail of warm milk up to the milkhouse, she saw from inside him what it was like to be old and uncomfortable, cheated, ground down by life and sick to death of it. As if suddenly coming to, she started after him. "Dad, I'm sorry," she said.

"Of course you're sorry," he snapped back.

"Listen," she added quickly, "I'll fix you supper." Though his walk was slow, ordinarily, she had to hurry now to keep up with him. He moved bent over and tilted to one side, compensating for the weight of the brim-full pail, driving along swiftly and solidly like a hurrying, tipped tractor, one back wheel in the furrow. You might have thought he weighed tons.

Tears shone in paths down his cheeks, which increased his fury.

"You won't fix suppah," he said, "when you see what I done in there."

"You didn't hurt her?" she asked, but even that had now no accusation in it.

"No, course not, course not."

"I'll fix you supper," she said. They were going up the stairs now. The stairs were narrow and she had to drop behind.

"Don't want you to," he said. A little milk sloshed out and quickly went tan on the step. He pushed through the milkhouse door, where the light was suddenly bright and everything was clean, efficient, the icy air pungent with the smell of some powerful detergent, and he slid off the stainless-steel milktank cover and with both hands lifted the pail up to dump the milk in.

"You don't want me to fix supper?" she said.

"Wouldn't be fair, now would it," he said. "Give me an unfair advantage."

"What are you talking about?"

His eyes narrowed, brilliant icy blue in this bright, bright light. "It's a battle of the bowels, ye see," he said, and gave a quick, fierce smile though he was as angry and unhappy as ever. "There sits Sally up there on her hunger strike, provin if she can that I can't suhvive without her, tryin to bring me low the way Gandhi did the British, or unions do the companies. Fair enough, I say. We'll see who needs who! But I'll tell you this for certain: I'll outlast yer Aunt Sally as sure as I'm standin here, long as she don't cheat. And just to make sure she don't come sneakin to my kitchen and stealin food like a rat in the granary, breakin the agreement, I'm takin certain special precautions to see that she stays right there in that room like she claims she intends to."

"You two have *agreed* on all this?" Ginny asked.

"Not in so many words," he said. "But we ain't exactly strangers, Sally and me." He put the metal cap over the tank-hole again and started for the door.

Lewis and Dickey came in just as he was about to go out. He stepped back, making way, and Lewis and Dickey did the same. "Come on through," her father said, jerking his arm, and at once, sheepishly, they obeyed.

Ginny said, "Dad, if I make you supper it'll be over all the sooner. She'll see you've got others who can do for you if she won't."

He paused for an instant and slightly turned his head. "You plannin to come feed me for as long as I'm stubborn enough to stay here on the fahm?"

She blushed. "No, of course not. You know how far it is." She was getting out cigarettes; smoking in the milkhouse was all right, there was nothing here to burn.

"Then it wouldn't be fair. I'll beat her my own way, by tunkit." He started down the steps into the dimness, into the chugging of the milking machines and the oceanic rumble of the cows' chewing, and said not another word.

"That's an obstinate old man," Lewis mentioned, as if to the lightbulb.

"Dad," Ginny called, "let me take the house key."

The old man stopped, set down the pail, and, holding his trousers with his left hand, just below the pocket, wormed down in with his right to find the key.

Outside the milkhouse, to their surprise, it was dark now. The sky was full of stars. Up the hill, there was only one light on in the house, Aunt Sally's. A chicken ducked out of the way, looking up, and said something.

She'd been in her room now for two nights and days, without a single bite to eat, or so Ginny believed, yet Aunt Sally was unchastened. She was more stubborn than ever and wouldn't even answer when she was spoken to. Sometimes, intending to infuriate, she would hum a little. Ginny's father could say what he liked, it *was* at least a little bit senile, that behavior. And so was his, of course. Halfway up the stairs she'd glimpsed, at the rim of her peripheral vision, the trap that was almost directly above her, and she'd been so shocked she'd almost fallen—*would* have fallen, probably, if Lewis, coming up behind her, hadn't seen and reached forward to steady her.

"Lewis, we've got to get it down!" she'd said.

He'd pursed his lips, looking up, not completely in agreement.

"Make sure Dickey stays out of here," she remembered to instruct him then. "He mustn't see it."

Lips still pursed, the side of one finger brushing at his moustache, Lewis slowly turned, still looking up, then went back downstairs. She heard his voice rumbling in the living room, talking with Dickey, telling him, presumably, to get the blocks out and play. "Aunt Sally," she said sternly, "I'm warning you, I've just about *had* it with these stupid childish antics of yours." She listened. No answer. She felt compelled to add, for fairness' sake. "Dad's too. You're both acting like you've gone dotty or something. *Aunt Sally are you going to answer me or not?*"

No answer.

Lewis put his head in at the foot of the stairs. "Sweet-hot," he called, "I think I'll go out to the cah and bring in the tools."

"Tools?" she said.

"I thought I'd stot scrapin the paint off."

"What?"

"Be right back," he said.

"Lewis, we got to take this gun down!"

But he was gone. When he came back, three minutes later, with a cardboard box that had scraping knives and steelwool, cans and bottles, rags, a screwdriver, a hammer, and a putty knife, she decided for some reason not to mention the gun just this moment. It was wrong of her, she knew, and she half believed that in a minute she was bound to bring it up again; but for now she put it off. Aunt Sally was still refusing to answer, which made Virginia Hicks simply furious, as angry as she'd been, as she was growing up, when a cow got out and was so stupid it couldn't find the fence-hole and be driven back in. If she could get her two hands on the old woman right now, heaven only knew what she'd do to her. But it was more than that. Her father's extraordinary outpouring of anger and grief, out in the barn, was still fresh with her, and in Ginny's heart, whatever fairness might dictate, the choice between the two of them was no contest.

She heard the back door open and scrape closed again, her father coming in from the milking, moving slowly. Filled again with pity, she listened for his footsteps moving toward the kitchen, carrying tonight's milk for the house to the white porcelain pitcher in the refrigerator; but she could hear nothing now, the sound was drowned out by Lewis's scraper, gritching through the dry white enamel almost down into the wood. He was starting on the molding, taking off the old paint in two-inch wide strokes, making it look easy.

"Why are you doing that, Lewis?" she asked.

He pretended not to hear.

She let it pass. "Aunt Sally?" she called. She tapped on the bedroom wall, keeping back from the strings. "Aunt Sally, if we take this thing down, will you come and have supper?" She stared at the end of her cigarette and listened.

No answer.

"If you don't, you know, I couldn't care less," she called.

Lewis said, casting his voice above the scraper's noise, not turning, "She's a smot cookie, refusin to talk to us. Makes us feel more guilty."

It was true. Since Aunt Sally would say nothing, Ginny found herself saying in her mind what Aunt Sally disdained to say, thinking up justifications. She could understand well enough her father's hatred of television. He belonged to a different world and time than the rest of them did, even Aunt Sally, and the hatred he felt for all things shoddy, according to his lights, didn't even seem, in Ginny's mind, particularly cranky or unnatural, though she liked TV herself. What he said when he ranted and raved had a fair amount of truth to it. Once when their own TV had

233

come back after two months in the shop, she'd seen it for a while—perhaps two, three days—with entirely new eyes. She'd noticed how tiresomely gay things were if they were supposed to be funny, how tiresomely earnest if they were supposed to be mysteries, how program after program had boats or motorcycles in them, as if the same half-wit mind, or eleven-year-old mind, maybe, had written every single story. On any given night it was common to see three different programs in which people were murdered in exactly the same way, drowned in a bathtub or run over by a bulldozer; or three different programs in which a girl was threatened by urban witches; or three different programs in which someone said, word-for-word the same, *"Walter! Something's happened!"* or *"No use, she's dead";* and six in which someone said, *"Hold your fire!"* and maybe twenty in which someone said, *"Drop it and turn around slow!"* (She wondered if anyone had ever said that, ever even once, in the real world.) The commercials were no relief, buzzing in again and again like flies, sometimes in two hours one of them repeating up to five or six times until at sight of that waterfall or horse or snowmobile or slow-motion swing of some pretty girl's hair you felt your vital signs weakening, or your hackles going up like a tomcat's. And she could easily understand why her father thought them evil: they prostituted children, hard-selling Pop-tarts with a three-year-old's smile, selling washing soap or toothpaste or imitation orange juice by sweet displays of five-year-olds with footballs. It was all a kind of crime against decency and goodness, when you thought about it. You could never again see a white country church, or a cute little puppy or kitten, without thinking of some mouthwash.

But it was silly, all the same, to worry about it. For all its faults, she'd hate to have to live, herself, without her color TV. Perhaps it was true, as magazines kept saying, that somewhere in the world—in big-city ghettos, presumably, or in the suburbs where rich people's children all took drugs—there were people who did the things they saw on TV. If so that was too bad, but she and Lewis weren't about to snap matches into somebody's eyes because they'd seen it on *Kojak*. For them it was all harmless make-believe, trivial and insignificant as stovepipe potatoes, and they would stretch out in their chairs in the darkened room, Lewis with his bottle of ginger ale, she with her cigarettes and coffee, and they would rest after the wearying activities of the day, turn their minds from the bills that somehow never got paid, piled on the kitchen table, and the repairs around the house that would never be finished no matter how hard they worked, and they'd relax and let the noise and pictures bathe over them for an hour or two or three, drifting off occasionally, waking when the music got ominous or sugary to watch some character whose name and significance they'd failed to notice fall screaming off a cliff or be run over by a train or kiss some beautiful woman on the mouth and throat. It was a way of life, nothing more than that but nothing less, either. Having it taken away when you were used to it— as her father in his righteousness had taken it from Aunt Sally—would be a terrible deprivation. For Aunt Sally especially, when it came to that. TV was her link, almost the only one left, with life as she'd known it in North Bennington. They had concerts there, from time to time. (Ginny's father had never heard a concert in his life.) And in North Bennington people had all the latest gadgets. It was at Aunt Sally's and Uncle Horace's that Ginny had seen her first Saran Wrap, her first plastic dishes, her first dishwasher, her first TV dinner. Coming to Ginny's father's must have been, for Aunt Sally, like sinking back to the Dark Ages. Shooting her TV was like locking her away in a dungeon.

From downstairs came a cooking smell, her father making something in Crisco. "I guess I'd better go check on Dad," she said. Then, "Don't you think we ought to take that gun down before something happens?"

"Nothing'll happen," Lewis said, and went on working. "He ain't even pulled back the hammers."

She looked up at the gun but was immediately distracted. There was a car pulling into the driveway.

"Get it down, Lewis," she whispered. "Someone's coming!"

2

Estelle Parks had been a nextdoor neighbor of Sally and Horace Abbott's in North Bennington. For years and years she'd been an English teacher in the local school, a spinster taking care of her irascible old mother—her name had then been Moulds—devoting her life to others with selfless good humor, beloved by her students and even by the crabby old woman, her mother, who loved almost nobody else. Estelle was as happy as a bluebird on a fence, a bird she distinctly resembled. She'd once had headaches, it is true, and acid indigestion, which had gotten her into the habit of taking Bromo-Seltzer and had eventually led to terrifying nightmares, the typical bad dreams of a bromide addict; but Dr. Phelps—who was her doctor still, though retired years ago, and was also Sally Abbott's—had recognized the problem and changed her medication, and the bad dreams had stopped. It is true, too, that she'd had her share of sadness and frustration. She was a pretty woman, though a stranger might not notice it instantly, since her nose came to a point and she had very little chin; but sooner or later one could hardly help but see that Estelle had a pertness, a bright and uncriticizing eagerness of eye, a virginal sweetness and softness that made her almost beautiful. She'd always been careful of her appearance, not compulsively but strictly and dutifully, living as she'd been taught and believed to be right, and careful of her scent—which was stronger and more floral than absolutely necessary—just as she was careful about the appearance and scent of her house, which she kept, with her mother's help

(while her mother remained alive) spotless. It was a
house of dark panels; gleaming, rather spindly but
tasteful antiques; small, dark paintings of English land-
scapes and birds—she was a lover of birds and had
several of them in cages, all with classical names, Iphi-
genia, Orestes, Andromache—antimascassars on her
chairs; stained glass in the windows beside the door and
in the bathroom; mirrors—in the entryway and at the
foot of the stairs—with frosted fleur-de-lis borders.
She slept on a high brass bed with a pink flowered
coverlet.

She was, a stranger might have thought at first
glance, a classical type out of a certain kind of novel.
She knew it herself. No one read more novels than
Estelle Moulds Parks. Half the fiction in the town's
Free Library contained, engraved in blue, her EX ·
LIBRIS · ACCIPITRIS, ESTELLE STERLING MOULDS. But
the stereotype, to Estelle's discerning eye, was unjust
and petty-minded.

She had had, as the type was expected to have, her
unfortunate enamorments. A young man, for instance,
at Albany State Teachers' when she'd gone there many
many years ago. (She'd studied with the great Professor William Lyon Phelps, no relation, so far as
she knew, to her doctor.) The affair—not, of course,
in the modern sense—had been tender and sweet,
they'd read poetry together and acted in a play, but
its end had not been, as a novelist would make it, a
devastation. He had chosen someone prettier, a friend
of Estelle's, and Estelle had cried half the night but
after that it was over. He had not been, in fact, very
handsome. That was the error in the fictional stereotype. All the handsomest, cleverest men were always
taken by the cleverest, prettiest girls; people like herself got the seconds. Perhaps some young women, such
as she'd been then—sharp nosed, small chinned, with
a distinct overbite—wasted their affections on un-
attainable males; that would be sad, no doubt. But
Estelle had never been that sort. She'd been quick to
like people—had been gregarious all her life—but
moderation was her essence: even with the finest man

in the world she would not have been the first to
fall in love. She'd gotten along comfortably with her
second-bests, growing fond when all signs showed that
the boy had grown fond, and landing on her feet, as
a novelist would say, when it was over. Gradually the
inclination to grow fond had passed. Life went on and,
unlike the fictional character she resembled, she had
been happy. She had loved teaching. She had loved
not only the literature and the children but the money
as well. Over the years, having only herself and her
mother to support—and after the death of her mother,
no one but herself—she'd gotten on dashingly, as
Henry James might say, and had been able to take
trips to Italy and England.

"How," someone had asked her, "can you stand
to teach the same old poetry year after year?" Estelle
had laughed, taken by surprise. "But it's not to the
same *students* every year," she said, and then she'd
laughed again, because it wasn't that either. The
poems grew and grew on her, richer with every
decade—she was teaching, by then, her former students' children, seeing faces she half knew, as a woman
sees the face of her father in her son. Once a blond
boy of fifteen had chosen, as the poem he would mem-
orize, Wordsworth's "Lines Composed a Few Miles
above Tintern Abbey," and something rather odd had
gone through her—*déjà vu?*, a premonition?, it was
impossible to say—but then, weeks later, when he
recited the poem, she'd heard distinctly the boy's
father's voice, her student long before, and she'd covered her face with her hands, weeping happily, listening to the curious sweet irony in the lines, and she'd
wanted to laugh aloud or sob, in love with flying Time.

> *For I have learned*
> *To look on nature, not as in the hour*
> *Of thoughtless youth; but hearing oftentimes*
> *The still, sad music of humanity,*
> *Nor harsh nor grating, though of ample power*
> *To chasten and subdue. And I have felt*
> *A presence that disturbs me with the joy*

Of elevated thoughts; a sense sublime
Of something far more deeply interfused,
Whose dwelling is the light of setting suns,
And the round ocean and the living air,
And the blue sky, and in the mind of man:
A motion and a spirit, that impels
All thinking things, all objects of all thought . . .

So years had passed. She'd sailed across to Europe on the *Liberté* with her old friend Ruth Thomas, the town librarian, and they'd spent a month in Florence and a month in Rye, in a cottage around the corner from Henry James' old house, a cottage on the edge of the churchyard. She'd experienced unhappiness—the death of friends and friends' parents and children, tragedies of her students—and innumerable disappointments; but all the same, life had been good to her. She'd gotten her teeth fixed, correcting the unsightly overbite, and she'd taught and read and traveled, keeping in touch with everyone she loved, and little by little she had grown, without knowing it, beautiful. She had realized it only when Ferris Parks, a professor of mathematics up at Bennington College and a widower, a man she'd seen often at Sage City concerts—he reminded her a little of Gregory Peck—had asked her, one night, to have dinner with him. She'd blushed scarlet, or so he'd told her later. There followed what she liked to call, mimicking bad novelists, a "whirlwind courtship," then marriage. They'd been married eight years—the happiest of her life, playing bridge with friends, drinking sherry with Horace and Sally Abbott, traveling, when school was out, to Europe or Japan. Then one night coming across the mountains in midwinter, Ferris had been killed in a car accident. Her life reeled. If it hadn't been for Horace and Sally, she might never have survived it.

All that was, of course, many years ago. She was now an old woman: eighty-three.

Estelle knocked again, firmly but not imperiously, at James Page's door. A chicken watched her with its head cocked.

239

"Hello, James," Estelle said, smiling. Tipping her head, she looked in past him. "Oh dear me, you're having supper!"

"No, I be finished," he said. He backed away to let her in.

Now his daughter Virginia was at the foot of the stairs, just opening the door into the kitchen. She looked white as a sheet.

"Why, hello, Virginia!" Estelle said.

"Oh! Hi, Estelle. How nice of you to visit." She forced a smile.

Estelle smiled back happily, though she was not such an old dim-witted fool as not to have noticed there was something peculiar going on. She made her way carefully, leaning on her canes, far enough into the kitchen that James could shut the door. "Mmm, how nice and *warm* it is," she said. "Outside there it's cold as the dickens."

"I know," James said. "I been out."

She glanced at him, then smiled again. "Is Sally home, James?"

"I'll call her," Virginia said—it was a little like a yelp—and turned back to the stairs.

Estelle moved carefully, pushing down hard on her rubber-tipped canes, toward the table. James came along awkwardly beside her, reaching toward her elbow but not touching it. He looked glum as could be, she saw, glancing at him briefly. She gave him another smile.

"Aunt Sally," Virginia called, looking up the stairs. "Can you come down? You've got company."

Estelle heard the rumble of a man's voice above. Virginia, standing on the stairs, pulled the door to behind her, talking with him.

James had now brought over a chair for Estelle.

She hooked the two dark, wooden canes together and leaned them against the table, then lowered herself carefully to the edge of the chair. "That's it," he said behind her, "that's got it." She felt on each side with her gloved hands, got herself lined up, and carefully, heart fluttering, fell backward. "Oop!" she said, but all was well. She smiled. James pushed her, as though she were sitting in a wheelchair, closer to the table. "My goodness," she said, and laughed.

He went around the corner of the table to where his plate and glass were and picked them up. He said, "Your nephew bring you over?"

"My great-nephew, yes," she said. "Terence."

James studied the glass and plate, scowling. "He oughtn't t'ave to wait in the cah," he said. He carried the glass and plate over to the sink and turned the water on. He stood bent, washing them in hot water from the tap—rinsing them, rather—and Estelle smiled thoughtfully at the wide, gray X of suspenders on his back. She said, "Don't you mind about Terence, James. He's got the radio, you know." She listened to the hum of conversation beyond the stairway door. "Is Sally sick?" she asked.

"No, just cranky," he said.

It was not so much the words or the way he said them as the way he stood, like one of her twelfth-graders feeling picked on and furious, years ago, that made her ask, full of sympathy, "You mean she's cross with you, James?"

"Gone on strike, that's the fact of the matter," he said. He put the dish and the glass and some silverware in the strainer beside the sink. "Locked herself up in her room. What you think about that?" He turned to glare at her, wicked as a donkey. When Estelle only smiled, hardly knowing what to say, he reached down into his shirt pocket and got his pipe and tobacco, a bright red foil package, and clumsily, as if his fingers were wood, began poking the tobacco into the bowl. Estelle pulled her gloves off, delicately letting him know she was here to set things right, if she could, and no use his resisting. Her fingers were small and crooked but still supple, still usable, even on the piano, though hardly what they'd once been. He came toward the table. He was bent at the waist. Old.

"Poor Sally," she said, thinking what he'd done to her television. "—And poor James, too! How long has she been on strike?"

"Two nights and two days," he said.

Estelle's eyes widened. "My my!" she said.

The door to the stairway opened just then, and Virginia looked out, smiling falsely. At once the smile faded. "Dad?" she said. Her eyes shot guiltily toward Estelle.

"She asked how's Sally," James said, "so I told her. There somethin wrong with that?"

"Now don't be ashamed, Ginny," Estelle broke in quickly, "these things will happen. You mustn't blame your father—and you mustn't blame your Aunt Sally either. That's one of the things I learned in teaching. Trying to lay blame is a huge waste of time. No matter how it comes out, someone's going to feel cheated—and so would you, if you were in that person's place. It never fails." She smiled first at Ginny, then at James. "So let's agree no one's to blame and just try to get this settled."

Ginny looked doubtful, something between guilty and petulant, but came a step farther into the room.

"That's all very well to say," James said, "and I'm sure it works fine on schoolchildren, but it won't work here. I give you wahning." He lit his pipe.

"Why, James!" Estelle said, as though he were a favorite pupil in whom she was disappointed.

"Dad," Ginny said, "be reasonable."

The old man said nothing, his flat mouth shut tight, the bowl of his pipe sending clouds up. There were footsteps now on the stairs behind Ginny and after a moment Lewis appeared and came around her into the kitchen.

"Good evening, Lewis," Estelle said brightly. She'd always been especially fond of the Hicks boys. They'd patched screens and painted and mowed lawns for her for years.

Lewis nodded. "G'devenin, Mrs. Parks." He picked with two fingers at his moustache.

"What a mix-up!" Estelle said, and gave a little headshake.

"Yes'm," Lewis said. He looked over at Ginny for signals, but she was staring sullenly at the center of the table—or perhaps at Estelle's folded, liver-spotted hands—and didn't even glance at him for a sign that he'd taken the gun down. It was as if she'd turned everything over to Estelle, though she showed no great confidence that Estelle could do better than she'd done. Head bowed, Lewis glanced over at James. The old man looked as mean and firmly planted as an old white-headed billygoat.

Estelle was asking, "Why do you say it won't work here, James?" She asked it gently, and though it was clear she was trying to manage him, it was clear, too, that she would listen fairly and thoughtfully to whatever he might answer.

The old man seemed to consider whether or not he ought to speak. His eyes tightly narrowed, he took a puff from his pipe, then abruptly brought out, "Because she stotted it, that's why. It's all very well to say we'll lay no blame, but Sally knew the rules when she come here, and she wouldn't abide by 'em. It's all very well to say we'll stot right here from where we are, as if they want no past to the matter. But the fact is they *do* be a past to it. I told her the rules as plain as day and she wouldn't abide by 'em."

"I can see how you feel," Estelle said. She moved her left hand across the table as if to touch his hand and comfort him, though he was standing and too far away, his left hand hooked in his pocket, the other on his pipe. "Of course none of us likes to obey rules he didn't help make," she added.

He said nothing—not for lack of an answer, Estelle Parks knew. We're all born subject to laws we have no say about, starting with gravity. He was wrong all the same, but there was no point arguing that now.

243

"It hasn't been easy for you, James," she said. "That we all know."

Ginny said, blushing suddenly, glancing at Estelle and then down again, "It *has* been terrible for Dad, that's true." Tears came to her eyes. She was remembering his tirade in the barn, discovering again the emptiness and bitterness of her father's life, his anger at the shoddiness of everything these days, at least as it seemed to him. "I know how Aunt Sally loved her television, but you have to see it from my father's side. Here he's worked all these years, living by his convictions—"

"Of course he has," Estelle said. It was all even clearer to her, it seemed, than to Ginny. "Perhaps if I could just talk with Sally—"

"She won't talk," Lewis said, then quickly shut his mouth and raised two fingers to his moustache.

"She won't talk?" Estelle echoed, not at all judging, simply interested.

Ginny said reluctantly, flustered and annoyed that Lewis had mentioned it, "When we try to talk to her she won't answer. I guess her feelings are hurt."

Estelle drew herself up a little. "Well my goodness," she said. She began to struggle to get out of her chair. Automatically, looking worried, Lewis came around beside and a little behind her to see if he could help.

"You'll never make it up the stairs," James stated flatly.

"We'll see about that," Estelle said. "Thank you, Lewis." She gave him a slightly absentminded smile, standing now, fussing with her canes. She seemed unaware that she still had her coat and hat on. "Ginny," she said, "be a dear and come over beside me here. That's it, yes, good. Just steady me a little, like that, yes. And Lewis, you come over on this side." Before they could protest, they found themselves laboring up the stairs with her, Estelle Parks smiling with a look of slight alarm, telling them what to do, tortuously climbing toward Aunt Sally's room, calling ahead once or twice, "Yoo hoo! Sally!"

When they reached the top (the gun and the strings of the trap had vanished, nothing remained but the tack-holes in the wall), Estelle called more brightly than ever, "Sally, are you there?"

They waited.

"Sally?" Estelle called again.

Still no answer. Estelle—tiny and absurd in the hall-way, standing, bent with age, in her blue coat and hat—looked over at Ginny, pursed her lips and then, all at once, smiled impishly. "Well, I'll just talk with her anyway, keep the poor dear company, you know, let her see that she's still got friends." She turned back to the door. "May I come in, Sally?" She tried the knob, then shook her head, smiling again as if delighted, but squinting, thinking. To the door she said, "Well my my."

Ginny said, "Why doesn't Lewis get you a chair, Estelle."

"That's a good idea," Estelle said, "yes, Lewis, do."

Lewis turned and went down. He was back in a moment with one of the chairs from the kitchen. He helped Estelle sit.

"You know, Sally," Estelle called, "I'm surprised at you!"

They waited. Estelle looked over at them, eyes atwinkle, and gave a little nod as if dismissing them. Lewis squatted over his cardboard box of tools, picking out a scraper, trying to decide whether or not it would be right to get back to work. Ginny backed away toward the head of the stairs and, after watching a moment longer, went down. As she reached the door into the kitchen she heard Aunt Sally say in a feeble little voice, "Is that you, Estelle? Why, I must've drifted off!" Ginny shook her head, rolling her eyes up, and came out into the kitchen. She closed the stair-way door behind her, and without a word to her father went into the living room to check on Dickey. He was fast asleep by the fireplace, plastic building blocks closed in his hands and scattered all around him, green and yellow and red.

For half an hour Estelle did her best to talk sense into her friend, but with no success. It was an impasse, simply. They were both, James and Sally, stubborn idealists, and there was never any hope, she'd learned as a teacher, when you were dealing with stubborn idealists. "Well my my," she would say from time to time, shaking her head, glancing over at where Lewis was scraping the paint off the bathroom door. He would give his head a morose little shake in return and go on working. Lewis had the right idea, of course. Simply be there, on the chance that sooner or later you'd be of use.

She leaned toward the bedroom door again and called, "Sally, why don't you come out and at least get some food in your stomach? It might be you'd see things differently."

"That's all very well for *you* to say, Estelle," the old woman called back, "but there are some things a person can't just forgive and forget. When a situation's downright intolerable, what good is it to throw up your hands and just leave it to the bees? Too many people in this country have been doing that too long."

Estelle sighed. "Oh Sally dear, what's the *country* got to do with it?"

Sally's voice was haughty. "Don't you fool yourself, Estelle. The country's got everything to do with it. It's the haves and the have-nots, that's what it is. James was here in the house first—that's his whole argument—so when I move in, I've got to do exactly as he says, and no matter if it kills me."

"Oh Sally, really!"

"Don't you Sally-really *me*, Estelle. It's the truth and you know it. It should've been my house, if the truth be told. I was the oldest. But everything goes to the men in this country—always has. We might as well

be Negroes. I changed that boy's didies and carried him on my back, I taught him to tie his shoelaces, I led him by the hand back and forth from school, even saved him from Dad's cussed johnny-bull once, and this is the recompense I get! He's got his opinions, and I grant you he's got a right to 'em; but I've got my opinions too, and it's no way to settle it chasing an old woman with a piece of stovewood and locking her up in her bedroom."

"Sally, he didn't!" Estelle exclaimed, merely to show her sympathy. The charge had, Lord knows, the ring of truth. She saw it all as clearly as a picture in a book, and in spite of herself she had to smile.

"Yes he did," Sally said, "and a good deal worse. Threatened my life with a shotgun. He's a drinker, you know."

"No!" Estelle said. It sounded unlikely, he hadn't been known to get drunk in years, but that was unimportant. Sally believed her charges, that was what mattered. Nevertheless, she glanced over at Lewis to see what *he* thought. He shook his head denying it all, but said nothing, merely scraped on. He had the whole molding finished now, and part of the bathroom door.

Sally said, "It's no use making peace with tyranny. If the enemy won't compromise, he gives you no choice; you simply have to take your stand, let come what may."

"Oh dear," Estelle said. She didn't like at all the direction in which the conversation was steering. Not that she didn't believe in principles. Principles were one of the things that made life meaningful—cleanliness, punctuality, a willingness to try to see the other person's side . . . But she'd been down this road too many times; she knew beyond a shadow of a doubt that it led nowhere. "That's all true, I suppose," she said. "But we have to make it *possible* for the other person to compromise, you know. We all have our pride. We have to try to be reasonable and 'do unto others.' "

Even as she said it, her palsied head trembling, her hands clasped together on her knees, Estelle knew it was a useless argument, though a true one. Sally's voice became more adamant than ever. "Let *James* be reasonable," she said. "It's always up to the one in power to be reasonable. It's like the United States after World War II. When Germany and Japan unconditionally surrendered, we reached out and gave them a helping hand, helped them to their feet, like the great nation and model for the world that we're supposed to be, and now Germany and Japan are two of the most decent, most prosperous countries in the world. That's how things should be. That's the *Christian* way. But of course that's not how James sees it—heavens no! He's just like the United States after the war in Viet Nam, stingy and full as a tick with guilt and grudges. He won't turn loose of so much as one thin dime. You'll see what comes of it! You mark my words! Viet Nam will turn elsewhere—and so will Africa and heaven knows who else—and what might have been markets and healthy competitors will be pigs in the parlor."

"Sally, what on earth are you talking about? How can you compare poor James with the whole United States?"

"You'll see," Sally said.

Long as she'd known her, Estelle had never quite realized that Sally was a crank—as much a crank as her brother, it seemed. Perhaps it was something that had come over her since she'd moved back to the farm with James, or perhaps it had been there all along and had simply never come up. When they'd played bridge in the old days, Sally and Horace, Estelle and Ferris, there had been wonderful talk of politics, education, religion—talk about everything under the sun, in fact, or at any rate everything decent people had talked about in those days—but it had been mainly the men who had talked about politics. Sally, whenever she'd taken a side, had taken it firmly, Estelle remembered, thinking back to it now—once, in fact, Sally had surprised them all by becoming quite passionate, even throwing down her cards—but it was rare for things to get that far out of hand when Ferris and Horace were there. Ferris, elegant and handsome, would tell jokes if the evening began to turn serious;

and Horace had had a delightful, almost comic gift for seeing and believing both sides.

Sally was saying, increasingly intense, "People think they can go on exploiting and exploiting forever, and the developing countries will simply have to put up with it, but believe you me that's wrong! There was a program on television, made your hair stand on end. I forget the whole argument—just as clear as two plus two is four—but I remember part of it." Her tone became dogmatic, tinged with self-pity—exactly the tone of the one and only Communist Estelle had ever met —and though Estelle now opened her mouth to object she said nothing, on second thought, but listened in something like amazement. "The handful of plutocrats in the third and fourth world countries," Sally was saying, "the only ones with any money to spend, want nothing but luxury items and bombs, which they get from the first world countries at terrible prices, so the poor people there in the developing countries get poorer and poorer and work harder and harder, and as their countries buy bombs their life becomes more and more dangerous." Estelle glanced at Lewis, who stood, head tipped far over, listening with no expression, like a cat. The voice became more strident. "The situation in the developing countries gets more and more dangerous, so the plutocrats take on more and more power, suspending constitutional government and so forth, just to keep order and protect themselves, oppressing the poor people more and more and buying more and more from the outside world, until it seems there's nothing that can break the—" She paused a moment, hunting for the word. "Spiral. But the plutocrats forget two crucial facts."

"Why Sally," Estelle said, "I never knew you knew about all that!"

"Two crucial facts," Sally said.

"Sally Abbott, you should have been a teacher," Estelle said. "Listen to this, Lewis! Were you aware that Sally had made a study of all this?"

"Aunt Sally's nobody's fool, I've always said that," Lewis said.

"Two facts," said Sally, belligerent.

Estelle sighed and resigned herself. The lecturing voice seemed to be moving around behind the bedroom door, as if Sally were pacing, perhaps keeping track of the two crucial facts on her fingers. Lewis continued to stand with the paint-scraper dangling, all attention on the argument.

"First, just as Walter Cronkite says, they forget the amazing power of 'the Idea of Freedom.' Once people have heard about freedom it's like seventeen seventy-six all over again, they just won't settle for anything less, they'd rather die. It's an idea all the wealth and power in the world can't stop—I can testify to that myself, believe you me!"

"Are you saying—" Lewis began. But she wouldn't be interrupted.

"And the other thing the plutocrats forget is the nature of an army. The plutocrats build up their powerful armies to protect their own interests, but an army's their own worst enemy. In an army people learn discipline, and they learn to be willing to die for what's right. They get educated, more or less—more than they would have back in their villages anyway. And that's the least of it. That many young men brought together in one place makes a natural watchamacallit for ideas —such ideas as freedom and people's natural rights. And pretty soon, just as in Russia and Tanzania and Portugal, *poof!*, revolution!—the dawn of reality and truth!—and all started by the *army*. You tell James Page and all his kind to just give *that* some thought." The bed creaked. She'd apparently seated herself.

"Aunt Sally," Lewis said, but then he reconsidered and merely picked at his moustache and shook his head.

Estelle stared at the bedroom door with an expression of distress, her head jittering and her eyebrows lifted. She wondered if Horace had ever seen poor Sally in such a state. Probably not. These weren't the kinds of thoughts that came up in times of happiness. "My my," Estelle whispered. Whatever the truth might be about James and the United States, or Sally

251

and radicalized armies (or whatever), the truth here in this house was that Sally must be coaxed out of her room before things got worse. An atmosphere of peace and cooperation must be established or they'd never get anywhere. How she wished Ruth Thomas were here! Ruth had always had a way about her. She recited funny poems, told anecdotes, filled every room she entered with such warmth and good feeling it was almost impossible for a person to keep his mind on his grudges. Estelle looked at her watch. My goodness, only quarter to eight! She remembered, the same moment, that Terence, her great-nephew, was still out in the car. "Oh dear," she said aloud.

"Sally," she called, "it doesn't seem right to keep your door locked even against your friends."

"I know it, Estelle," Sally answered. "But I haven't got much choice, do I? I sometimes think—" Her voice became slightly theatrical, the self-pity more distinct, as if she were speaking lines out of Shakespeare or Tennyson: "I sometimes think we're all characters in some book. It's as if our whole lives are plotted from start to finish, so that even if the end should be happy it's poisoned when we get to it."

Estelle's eyes widened. "Sally Abbott, what on earth's got into you?" she said. "Why, that's the silliest thing I ever heard!" She looked over at Lewis. A decision was building in her. "Lewis, dear, help me downstairs," she said. "I need to use the telephone."

He looked alarmed but at once put down the scraper and came to help.

5

James Page stared out his kitchen window in a fury of indignation. "What the *hell?*" he said. He rolled the October *Saturday Evening Post* in his hands as if making it a weapon, his spectacles hanging cockeyed down his nose.

"Company's coming," Dickey called excitedly from the living room.

It was a quarter past eight. James Page's front yard was lit like the parking lot at Mammoth Mart, and pretty near as filled with cars, or so it looked to James.

"Good heavens, I'd better put cocoa on," Virginia said, bursting into the kitchen, cigarette in hand. She'd puffed up her hair and put lipstick on and powder on her cheeks to try to hide the dark circles. Halfway to the pots and pans she stopped. "No," she said, and the cigarette in her hand began wobbling violently, "I'd better see them in." She was thinking, in fact, of the lilac bushes, thinking perhaps she could steer the company off the path and away from them so no one would know.

"I'd like to know what in tunkit's goin on here," her father said.

"Oh, Dad, for heaven's sakes calm down!" she said. She had the door open now, waving and carrying on, yelling "Hi there! Hi there! Over this way!"

Lewis appeared at the foot of the stairway, paint-chips all over him. "Looks like somebody's drove up," he said. He looked guilty as sin.

Estelle Parks said, leaning on both canes, peeking out from the living room—she'd taken her coat and hat off now—"Why, who in the world can that be?"

"You ought to know, you meddlin old buzzard," James Page said, white with anger. "You called 'em youahself, in there on the telephone."

"Why, James!" she said, and then quickly, as if just remembering, "That's true, so I did."

"If that just don't beat hell," he said. He raised the rolled-up *Saturday Evening Post* as if to hit something, found nothing to hit, and lowered it again. A loud crack came from his pipestem. He'd bit clear through it. He spit and put the pipe in his shirt pocket.

"This way! Yoo hoo!, this way!" Virginia was calling. She was off the porch now, herding them away from the lilacs. The car lights were off and the yard was full of happy voices and the sound of feet. He recognized Ed Thomas's hefty Welsh laugh.

James leaned his head toward Estelle, his wide mouth twitching. "Just what in the world you think you're doin?" he said.

"Now easy there, Dad," Lewis said mildly, looking not at his father-in-law but at the painted cap where the stovepipe had once gone. "It's a dahn good idea and you'd ought to go along with it. We'll just have a few people in, that's ah, have a little singin and storytellin—little ahguin, mebby, about politics"—he grinned, "—little sweet smellin food. Ye never know, Aunt Sally might just decide 'Shoot!' and come on down and join us."

"It's an Indian remedy," Estelle said, and smiled. It was a pretty smile, apologetic and kindly, and James was for a moment disconcerted. "When an Iroquois Indian had a tapeworm in him, the medicine doctor would starve the man and then brace the man's jaws open and put out some broth. Pretty soon, out popped the tapeworm."

James' eyes widened. "Great Peter," he barked, and slammed the *Saturday Evening Post* against his leg, *"Sally's* no tapeworm! She does a thing, she's got *reasons* for it." His hands were shaking at the indignity of it all—or so it seemed to Estelle and Lewis, who were suddenly filled with remorse over what they'd done. But the matter was a little more complex than they understood. He was indeed indignant at their treating his sister—however outrageous her behavior might be —as some mindless creature that could be coaxed through fire with a graham cracker. But the thing that had mainly gotten into James Page was Estelle's smile. Old fool that he was—so he put it to himself—for an instant James had felt powerfully attracted to her, emotion rising in his chest as sharp and disturbing as it would in any schoolboy. Even now he was upset and surprised by it. Metaphysically upset, in point of fact, though the word was not one James Page would have used. They were old and ugly, both of them, and the body's harboring of such emotions so long past

254

their time was a cruel affront, a kind of mockery from heaven.

"I'm sorry, James," Estelle said—and damned if the thing didn't leap in him again. But he didn't have long to think about it, or endure it, rather, for now the company was sailing through the door, little Dickey standing there holding it open, grinning like a duck, as if he thought it had suddenly turned Christmas.

"What are *you* doing up, you little whippersnapper?" Ruth Thomas—*née* Jerome—said, tousling Dickey's hair and making her eyes cross. Then, pivoting her three hundred pounds like a dancer, she threw out her arms and embraced the room. "Happy October one and all!" she cried. Her puffy, spotted hands came, graceful as the hands of an actress, to her lips and she blew them all a kiss. From the elbows to the shoulders, her arms were exceedingly fat. Ruth Thomas was, in the old sense, mad. She had a voice like music, for all her years—as remarkable a voice as this world has ever heard, a study in contradictions. It was a clear, ringing voice—or so nature had intended it—a voice built for sweetness and volume, the voice of a singer. For years, indeed, she'd lent her rich, somewhat breathy alto to the Congregational Church Choir in North Bennington, and she'd given more recitals at the McCullough Mansion than anyone now living could remember, including Ruth Thomas. At the same time, her many years as head librarian in the John G. McCullough Free Library—or possibly some other cause—had given her voice a not-quite-dulcet, artificial throatiness that seemed at once studiously cultured and seductive, or at any rate intended to have that effect, unless it was mockery, or self-mockery, or something else. She spoke, or sang, or did both at once, like an unsubmergeably strong piano with the soft pedal pressed to the carpet. She enjoyed good talk—she talked constantly—and had a powerful laugh.

Her body, even now that she was seventy-six, was a creation as curious as her voice. Her walk was no longer spry—she'd limped badly ever since she'd slipped on a shag-rug and broken her hip, six years ago (she had a pin in it now), and her thick gray-stockinged legs were bent just slightly the wrong way at her knees, so that she looked, standing up, like a large deer balanced on its hind legs in an orchard, reaching up for apples. Aside from her walk, her every gesture was the soul of natural grace. For all her weight, she might have been the model of elegance if she'd liked—might, that is, have been a graceful and elegant fat woman—but Ruth was too much the clown for that (for which some people liked her and others did not), delighting in mimickry and buffoonery of every sort, from parody of Queen Victoria to the low bumps and grinds of burlesque halls. This too her years as librarian had tended to modify and inhibit, as was perhaps just as well. She'd learned to limit herself for hours at a time to nothing more outlandish than a clever, perhaps slightly overstated mimickry of prim-ness. Her native impishness showed only, for the most part, as a wicked sparkle in her bright blue eyes and a tendency to make faces. "This book," a visitor to the library might say in high dudgeon, as though it were Ruth Thomas's fault, "is stupid." "Stupid?" Ruth Thomas would exclaim, as if distressed. Before she could stop herself, assuming she wanted to, her upper teeth, or rather dentures, would protrude and her bright blue eyes would cross. With children—or at any rate with most children—it had made her, for years and years, the Queen of North Bennington. On other occasions her curious ability with gestures would slip out—a Jewish shrug, an Italian's flip of the hand for *"eh paesan,"* the silly go-get-em-boys jab and cross of a dim-witted highschool coach.

There was no denying that she could be, at times, an embarrassment. "Ruth, you should be on the stage!" Estelle had told her once. "Or somewhere," Ferris had added dryly. Yet she was, for all that, a tender-hearted, gentle and well-meaning woman, a lover of books, though her taste was odd. She loved "Chaucer," though she had not read him in a while, and she read in modern English; the name "William Shakespeare" she always pronounced in full, with some sort of vaguely British accent; and she would have to think twice, she often said, before choosing between Milton and the gas chamber.

"James," she called out now, bending toward him— she was very tall—"you look like a dog who's eaten fence-nails!"

He shrank back a little. Her breath smelled powerfully of Ovaltine.

The kitchen was now bursting. Behind Ruth Thomas, his hand around her waist, helping to support her, was Ruth's husband Ed Thomas, red-faced, white-haired, cigar-smoking, eighty-year-old Welshman. He looked considerably older than Ruth, partly because of her dyed hair. He was a farmer, a rich one, as large as his wife around the waist and about two-thirds as tall. "Evenin James," he said, "evenin Estelle! Hi there, Lewis, Dickey! Evenin! Evenin!" He swept the unlighted cigar from his mouth and with the same hand took his hat off. Behind him stood his eighteen-year-old grandson DeWitt, carrying a guitar, and behind DeWitt came Roger, close to Dickey's age. Both of the Thomas boys had freckles and dark red hair. "Brought the boys along, 'Stelle," Ed Thomas said. His l's had a kind of click to them, his tongue hitting the teeth on either side. "Witt's in from college for the weekend." He turned to the tall boy: "You remember 'Stelle?" The boy with the guitar bowed formally, shyly. "Roger," Ed Thomas said, "take off yer hat and say How."

Ruth was already plunged deep in conversation with Virginia, who'd just come in.

"Can I see your guitar?" Dickey said.

DeWitt Thomas winked at him, edging away toward the living room, and Dickey followed, glancing apprehensively at his father. Roger moved tentatively after Dickey.

"Well I be damned," James said, whether in anger or in pleasure it was hard to tell.

"Is that you, Ruth?" Sally Abbott's voice called down the stairs.

Reverend Lane Walker was next into the room,

257

his hand on the arm of a stranger, a wicked looking Mexican with a moustache like a cat's. He was fat, with what seemed—to James Page at least—unnaturally and offensively short legs. He wore a brownish green suit that made him look like a frog and had highly polished shoes, the kind of wide-winged shoes you'd expect to be worn, in James' opinion, by an abortionist. Lane Walker was young, maybe thirty, thirty-five. He was Sally's minister in North Bennington, a shy, intellectual sort of man with a horsey wife—wore jodhpurs and carried a ridingwhip even in the grocery store—and three adopted children, Vietnamese. The hair on the top of Rev. Walker's head was cut off like a prisoner's, and under his chin—*under* it, not on it —he had a scraggle of hair like a billygoat's beard or the beard on some Irish elf.

"I asked Lane to come over," Ruth told Estelle. She swept her arm back toward the Mexican, as if to draw him farther in. "Father—" she began, then made a quick face. "Now isn't that silly! I've forgotten your name!" She threw a girlish look at him. He drew back slightly, smiling.

Lane Walker said, bowing and smiling, edging toward James with his hand on the elbow of the Mexican, "Mr. Page, let me introduce an old friend of mine, Father Rafe Hernandez."

"Father, is it," James said unsociably, making no attempt to hide his dislike of foreigners. He had no intention of shaking the man's hand. The Mexican, to James' intense annoyance, did not offer it.

"Rafe will be sufficient," the Mexican said. His voice was oily, soft as a cat's voice, full of insinuation. He slid his black eyes toward the kitchen window as if thinking of stealing it. "Thees is a beautiful setting for a farm," he said.

"S'prised you can see it so well in the dahk," James said.

"Now James," Estelle said.

James smiled acidly, pleased to see that someone had noticed his inhospitality. "You must be one of them new-style priests," he said. He pointed toward

258

his own throat, moving the finger from left to right in a gesture meant to indicate the absence of a clerical collar, but suggesting a throat-cutting.

"Sometimes I wear it, sometimes not," the priest said, impossible to offend.

Lane Walker said, "We were marchers together, Rafe and I." He grinned at the Mexican.

The Mexican nodded. "Selma."

"Is that you, Ruth?" Sally Abbott called down the stairs.

Virginia was over at the stove now, putting on milk, preparing to fix cocoa. In the doorway old Dr. Phelps was calling, leaning on his cane, "Anybody home?"

"Come in, come in and shut the door!" Ruth Thomas bellowed.

"Lo, Doctor!" Ed called grandly waving his cigar. " 'Sthat Margie with you?"

Dr. Phelps' granddaughter was peeking shyly past the doorjamb. She had long blonde hair and timid, faded looking eyes. Dr. Phelps had a face even redder than the Welshman's, and tightly curled white hair. When his granddaughter was in—she seemed to float in her long gray coat like a stick on a stream—Dr. Phelps reached behind him to close the door.

"Don't close it yet!" the Mexican called out, then giggled like a Japanese.

Estelle's grand-nephew Terence was in the doorway, smiling sheepishly, blue with cold.

"Terence!" Estelle cried. "Heavens to Betsy! Come in, child, come in!" She looked at Ruth, smiling and horrified. "He's been out there all this time. I forgot all about him!"

"I was listening to the concert," Terence said, smiling at the floor. "WAMC."

"That's right," Ruth Thomas said, towering near the doorway to the living room. "The Boston Symphony was on. Who won?"

Estelle explained to Rev. Walker, "Terence is a French horn player. He's very good."

"French horn player?" Dr. Phelps asked joyfully,

259

head thrown back like a swordsman's. "Margie here plays the flute. You children know each other?"

They both grinned shyly. They played in the same school orchestra, the same school woodwind quintet.

"You bring your flute tonight, Margie?" Dr. Phelps asked. He was an organizer, also an avid musician.

"It's in the cah," she said. A whisper.

"By cracky, we'll have a concert here, before we're through. I saw DeWitt in there with his guitar. James, we're gonna make your house a concert hall!" He turned around, beaming, to look at James. He wasn't there.

"James?" Estelle said.

"Well don't that beat heck," Dr. Phelps said merrily, lifting his wild white eyebrows and poking his thumbs in his vest.

"Is that you, Dr. Phelps?" Sally Abbott called down.

"Where on earth can he have gone to?" Ruth exclaimed.

In all the commotion, no one had heard the truck start up, but they saw the lights now, careening out toward the road.

"Why that snake in the grass!" cried Ruth Thomas, and made a face.

6

It was a terrible temptation for Sally Page Abbott—as they meant it to be. It reminded her of a thousand happy times, Estelle's piano playing drifting up the stairs, Estelle and the Thomases and Dr. Phelps all singing—*They asked me how I knooooo*—and the glorious smell of cocoa and cinnamon-toast, and in the kitchen people talking, Rev. Walker and some young people and possibly, she couldn't be sure, a stranger. It was the kind of thing she wouldn't have missed for the world, ordinarily, and she was half inclined to think she was a fool to be missing it now, but still she hesitated, standing with her ear to the door-crack, trying to determine what was right, pursing her lips, her palsied old head slightly trembling, her heart full of trouble. If there were a fire, it occurred to her, they'd break her door down and find her looking a sight. Better fix her hair, put on her good bathrobe and slippers just in case.

As she was making her bed, puffing up the pillow, thinking, I must hide those applecores, she heard footsteps coming up the stairs—someone young and light, probably Lewis. She heard whoever it was go into the bathroom and close the door and use the toilet. When he came out she called, "Is that you, Lewis?"

The footsteps stopped, then came somewhat tentatively toward her. "It's Rafe Hernandez, ma'am," a voice said, formal and apparently embarrassed. "You must be Mrs. Abbott?"

Sally looked at the bedroom door as if it had tricked her, then tried to see through the crack. Remembering herself, she said: "How do you do?"

"Very well, thank you," Hernandez said, more formal than before. He had a touch of foreign accent. "Is there anything I can get you?"

She gave a little laugh. "I thought you were my nephew Lewis."

"Ah yes, ha ha. These things will hoppin!"

Her heart beat rapidly. It was difficult to know how to deal with an introduction in these circumstances. No doubt it was hard for Mr. Hernandez too. He merely stood there. She bent down to see if she could see him through the keyhole, but he was standing out of line. She straightened up again, flustered, patting her hair back in place. "Hernandez," she said. "That's a Latin name." She laughed politely, showing interest. "Are you visiting friends here?"

"I'm visiting with Rev. Lane Walker, yes. We knew each other many years ago." He paused, then said— desperate, perhaps, though he hid it well—"He's spoken of you often."

"How kind of you to say so!" She laughed again.

"It's a pleasure to meet you."

She could see him, in her mind's eye, bowing to the door. As a matter of fact she was doing that herself. *"My* pleasure, I'm sure," she said. "Is this your first visit to Vermont?"

"My very first. I must say, it is as beautiful as everybody says!"

"Well yes, *we* like it."

He was silent a moment, no doubt still smiling, bowing at the door.

She picked at her collar with stiff, crooked fingers, hunting for something more to say. It had always been Horace who had the knack for conversation with strangers; she'd smile, delighted, getting by on her looks, and would hurry away to make tea. Theirs had been a wonderfully sociable house, while Horace was alive. He had a way about him. Everyone said so. He had always just finished some interesting book, or heard something curious at his dentist's office, or had acquaintances in common with the stranger. "Pittsburgh!" he would say, "I have a cousin in Pittsburgh! Furniture business." She said: "Where do you call home, Mr. Hernandez?"

"Well, Mexico City, many years ago. At present I have a parish in Tucson."

She felt an instant's panic. She knew no one in either place. "Then you're a priest?" she said.

He laughed rather oddly. "Yes, a man of the cloth."

"Well well," she said. "How interesting!" She leaned closer to the door. "I hope you haven't met with any racial prejudice."

"Oh no," he said, and laughed. "Not at all, not at all."

She smiled and nodded, gratified to hear it, but nevertheless wondered what her wretched brother James might have said. "We're backward, here in Vermont," she confided. "It's because we have no industry, my husband used to say. People don't move in, so we never get to know them. I suppose it's only natural for people to be afraid of the unfamiliar—the 'intruder,' as they think."

"That's natural, yes."

"I've always said we tend to think if we're white, of great, apelike black boys raping poor innocent white girls, you know? We never stop to think how frightening it must be for a black girl to walk down an unfamiliar street filled with white people."

"That's so, yes. That can be very frightening for them. On the other hand, of course . . ."

She nodded to the door, encouraged. "Well, someday all that will be behind us, thank heavens."

"Yes, that's so, no doubt. I hope not too soon."

She tipped her head, suspecting the man might be teasing her. "Not too soon?" she said.

"Individual differences, cultural differences"—she could imagine him thoughtfully gesturing as he spoke —"those are wonderful things. I would hate to see them go."

"Yes, *that's* certainly true." She was nodding emphatically. (How difficult it was to have a serious conversation through a closed door! There was a lesson in that!) Sally said, "They're wonderfully colorful, the minorities. What would we do without our Italians and Jews, or the coloreds with their beautiful, queer speech?" She laughed. She caught a glimpse of her smile in the mirror above the desk.

"Exactly," Mr. Hernandez said happily, "or these wonderful tight-mouthed New Englanders." He flattened his voice and pitched it somewhat higher, mimicking Robert Frost: *"Wheah had ey heahd the wind befoah / Change like this to a deepah roah?"* He laughed, delighted at his own performance. "It's a language I'd hate to see die," he said.

Though she continued to smile, Sally was a little distressed. She had not thought of herself before as one of the colorful minorities. Her people had been here before the Iveses, the Deweys, even the Allens.

The Mexican continued, unaware, it seemed, of her slightly ruffled feelings, "But it all has to go in the end, you're right. Lazy, fat Mexicans, coloreds with their rhythm and beautiful, queer speech, Jews with their skullcaps and keen intelligence, tight-mouthed, tight-fisted New England farmers—"

263

"Some things will probably survive, of course," she said cautiously.

"Yes, I'm sure that's true." He sounded eager to please, yet Sally was increasingly unsure of herself, inclined to be suspicious. As if glad Sally had reminded him of the fact, he said: "As more and more blacks and New Englanders marry and have children, we're sure to see an increase in stubbornness among black people, and a marked relaxation of morals in New England."

Her hands began to shake. She could no longer doubt it. He was attacking her! What had she done? But it wasn't only that. He was a priest. What in the world was wrong with him? They were supposed to be gentle and understanding.

She said, "I'm afraid I don't quite follow you, Father."

His laugh, she thought, was distinctly hostile. "My fault," he said. "You must forgive me. It's the language barrier."

Her heart was pounding and her cheeks felt hot. She had half a mind to unbolt the door and look at him, find out for sure what the trouble was. But before she could decide whether or not to do it, heavy footsteps were coming up the stairs, climbing very slowly, as if with the greatest difficulty, and she knew it was her friend Ruth Thomas.

"Is that you, Ruth?" she called.

"Hello, Sally!" Ruth called back, cheery. And then at once: "Father Rafe, we've missed you. You mustn't stand chatting with this stubborn old woman. We need male voices!" She seemed to have made it to the top of the stairs.

"Yes of course," he said, and his voice, it seemed to Sally, was cheerful again, without a trace of hostility. "I've been having a wonderfully interesting conversation, one of the most interesting I've had in some time." He made it a kind of apology to Sally.

"It's good of you, Father," Sally said, "to come and talk with a stubborn old woman." For Ruth's benefit, or mainly for Ruth's, she put an angry little emphasis on *stubborn*.

"Nonsense," he said lightly. "Stubborn? All human beings are stubborn. It's the reason we're survivors."

"Sally, why don't you come join us?" Ruth called.

Sally hesitated, thinking for the hundredth time of giving in, but before she could decide, Ruth had dismissed her—"Well, do as you like!"—and she heard Ruth go into the bathroom and close the door.

"Goodnight, Mrs. Abbott, I'm glad to have met you," the Mexican said. She heard him going lightly down the stairs.

When Ruth had gone down too, with hardly another word, closing the kitchen door behind her, Sally sat wincing on the edge of the bed, wringing her hands, feeling guilty and misjudged and full of woe. Over and over she asked herself what had happened, what she'd done. She might have guessed—though she didn't—that her brother had intentionally offended the priest. (It would have come as no surprise.) But her mind was filled with a chaos of righteous indignation and distress, perfectly reasonable self-defense and unfair but convincing self-deprecation. The priest—smug and soft-spoken though he'd never laid eyes on her—could have no idea how much she and Horace had done for the poor and underprivileged in their day—how, right to the end, when, aflutter with panic, she knew she was losing everything, she'd kept up her contributions to Foreign Missions. He could not know how she'd listened with sympathy and interest to visitors from tragic inner-city churches and deplored the evils of prejudice in Boston. Yet she knew, for all that, that she was in some way guilty, had unknowingly let some cruel insult slip, had offended the man inside the priest and deserved every bit of his hostility.

Her feeling of distress and confusion grew, pressing in like a cold, invisible creature from outside. The walls of her bedroom hummed with the music and talk below—she could make out not one word of it now, with the door pulled shut at the foot of the stairs—and the light pouring out onto the cars in the front yard, making the glass and metal glint and reminding her faintly of cars parked behind the North Bennington Church at Christmastime, or cars parked around the school on the night of a Sage City concert, stirred her misery still more. Laboriously, she pulled her feet up into the bed and lay back against the pillow. She closed her eyes.

Anguish. How terrible that one must feel it all one's life, from time to time, whatever one might learn, whatever one's decency! Horace had said once, speaking like a novel, cheerfully, though the thought was grim—they'd had a little quarrel—"We humans are all such poor miserable things. However we may hope, we know perfectly well all we have is each other. Pity how we struggle and fight against our own best interests." Horace had frequently said things like that. She'd found his opinions distinctly frightening, and sometimes, lying beside him in bed, feeling completely alone in the universe except for Horace, she would suddenly feel so anxious that, without quite meaning to, she would wake him and get him to talk with her a little. If only they'd had children! She could remember all too vividly—and felt it again now —how it had felt, lying on her back, feeling as if she were endlessly falling, sinking toward death, as if she'd somehow become conscious of the earth's fall through space, her whole body listening to the noise of wind, the creakings of the otherwise silent, falling house. As if to steady herself, pull back against the fall, she would touch her husband's wool-pajama'd arm, but the falling continued, and she would half-realize, with growing alarm, that she was losing the oldest battle in the world, the battle we wage from the moment we're born, when we stretch up our arms, kick our legs, and finally raise up our bodies. She would rouse herself from fear, struggling upward toward the ordinary, and pressing her face against his shoulder would wake her husband up; and as Horace would rise to consciousness, she would mysteriously cheer up, her spirits would lift . . .

Sally blinked and came awake. She pressed up on one elbow, and when it wasn't enough to drive the feeling away, she pivoted her legs off the side of the bed and felt for the floor. She stared down into the yard again, listening to the hum of the party below. She felt giddy, mysteriously endangered, somehow dead wrong. "They give us no choice," she said, tears in her eyes, speaking to the ghost.

Distinctly, as if from right beside her, a voice said sharply, "Sally!"

She was startled half out of her wits. She was absolutely certain it was Horace's voice, though she knew, of course, that it couldn't be. Was she dreaming? She decided then that it must have been Dickey's voice, for he was calling now through the closed door, "Aunt Sally?"

"Is that you, Dickey?" she called back.

"Aunt Sally," he said, "I brought you some cocoa and cinnamon-toast."

"That's sweet of you, dear," she called, feeling suddenly more guilty than ever. She took a step toward the door, hesitated, wadding up her hankie and biting at her lip.

After a moment Dickey called, "I'm sorry I was bad."

"Why Dickey!" she said, surprised, "*you* did nothing wrong!" Sympathy carried her to the door, but with her hand on the knob she paused again.

"I told on Grampa," the child said.

Sally stared, puzzled, at the door. How he could make it all his fault was beyond her, but though she'd had none of her own, she knew the ways of children. "Dickey," she said gently, "it's not your fault at all, and if your grampa James—" She broke off, resisting the temptation to put the blame where it belonged and make the boy's life harder. "Honey, don't you think you're to blame for one minute. It's not your fault at all."

Dickey asked, still dubious, "Can I give you the cocoa and cinnamon-toast?"

It was a terrible dilemma. She stood racking her brains, torn between sympathy and principle. It was wrong, heaven knew, to make the innocent suffer;

267

certainly forcing her to capitulate to her brother's mulish will was the furthest thing from little Dickey's mind. She could see him, in her mind's eye, looking at the floor to avoid looking up imploringly, guilty for no reason, just as his poor uncle Richard had felt, groundlessly guilty all those years—just as she had felt guilty just now with the Mexican priest. How dare she disappoint the child? Nevertheless, the indignity of the thing was a great deal for anyone to ask her to bear. They were all down there partying, making light of the battle—even her dearest and oldest friends—trying to make her give in to James' tyranny, give in as the weak have always given in, as *they* would give in (she thought, with sudden bitterness), accepting the age-old slavery of women and children. No doubt they thought it was purest foolishness, this stand she was taking, and in her heart she could understand their feeling. "Give in! Don't make a scene!" It was the universal cry. How often she'd done just that herself, even with dear Horace. But sooner or later one discovered one had simply had enough, one could give in no longer. They had no idea what it was like, living with a maniac. Someone, sooner or later, had to fight, that or kill themself. Her eyes filled with tears. Oh, she knew how to give in, all right. She could go out and they'd all make a scene over her, praise her and fawn on her exactly as if she'd won, as indeed they'd think she had: won a battle with herself, becoming "sensible." And she could smile shyly, as if admitting she'd been a fool and it was all a funny story, as it would be, someday —a story to her discredit—and she could accept their jokes and compliments, even join in the singing or the cheerful talk, and all would be forgiven. Oh yes! She could see it! James would praise her mulishness, proud of having won, and he might even behave somewhat better for a while, might even grant her, grudgingly, her color TV. But in the end, cut it as you liked, she'd have been beaten, as the weaker sex is always beaten, and she'd cook and clean and keep her opinions to herself, and when James turned cross she'd pretend she didn't see his stupidity, she'd kow-tow and scrape like an Oriental slave, and if anyone was talked of, laughed at, scorned by the gossips—scorned as they scorned that poor Sherbrooke woman, even now, years later, at least in some of the stories —it would be her, that crazy old woman, not sensible James. The image of her cruel and unjust humiliation was stronger than the image of the child at the door, and she said kindly, gently, "It's sweet of you, Dickey, but I'm not hungry. You take it back down, that's a good boy."

"Aunt Sally," Dickey said.

"Run along, dear," she said.

He mumbled something—she couldn't quite hear it —then retreated toward the head of the stairs.

"Thank you, honey!" she called after him. She folded her arms, feeling guilty but nevertheless vic-torious. If she was wrong then very well she was wrong, she could pay in the Afterlife.

Just then wind made the door rumble, and she started. When she glanced out the window she saw branches swaying and leaves brightly tumbling. The wind had come up suddenly, out of nowhere, as it seemed. There were curious noises in the attic above her, and though she knew it was only wind, she felt, welling up more strongly than before, the superstitious alarm she would sometimes feel lying all alone in bed staring into darkness, or had felt, long ago, alone in her bed except for Horace, who could guard her no longer. She crossed to the white wicker table and picked up her paperback book. She stood undecided for a moment, looking out into the night, listening to the hum of the party rising through the walls of the house, keeping it alive, and the groan of the wind-swept darkness outside. It seemed a long time since James had driven off in his pick-up. For an instant she had an image of her brother as a child, bull-necked and petulant, holding her hand. According to the onyx clock on the desk it was quarter to eleven. She'd never known him to stay away so late.

And now an even stranger sensation came over her,

so that her hackles rose in fear. Out by the mailbox, standing perfectly still, there was an old, old man in a long, dark coat, bearded like a rabbi. He stood looking at the house, unaffected by the wind. Her heart leaped in her chest painfully, and she bent closer to the glass. The man was still there, quiet as a statue, alien. She took her blue plastic glasses off and polished them on the front of her bathrobe, then replaced them and quickly looked again. There was no one now. Had it been pure illusion? Someone getting ready for Halloween? Her feeble eyes darted from car to car, shadow to shadow. He'd vanished from the face of the earth.

Below her—though it sounded, at first, far away—someone began playing a French horn.

7

"Somehow it doesn't seem right," Estelle said, "poor Sally up there suffering and James off heaven knows where, fuming, and here we are having a good time!" We should do something, she meant; the plan to coax Sally from her room was getting nowhere. But they chose not to understand her, or the hint was too subtle, or perhaps what she'd *really* meant, she reflected with a sigh, was to excuse her own inaction, keep up the party. She could hardly deny she was enjoying herself. How could she help it, with dear friends around her, Ruth looking larger and more glorious than ever, though she sagged some, these days, if she let herself get overtired—Ruth's husband and Dr. Phelps laughing noisily together, pounding each other's shoulders over stories of the old days— Ruth's handsome red-headed grandson DeWitt hunkered against the wall by the kitchen door singing mournful songs, softly picking his guitar, entertaining the two small boys—and in the back room, James' sitting room and bedroom, Estelle's nephew

270

Terence and Dr. Phelps' granddaughter Margie playing duets on the French horn and flute. How she wished her Ferris could be here now to see it!

Estelle had retreated from the piano some minutes ago. She too tired quickly—they were none of them spring chickens—and it was hard for her to sit for very long on a bench. She'd settled on the couch now, surrounded by pillows, her two canes leaning against her knee. The Mexican priest was on the couch beside her, smelling pleasantly of cologne, and Lane Walker was in the chair by the fireplace, in front of her and to her left.

"Suffering always makes parties more interesting," Lane Walker said, and grinned. He had a habit of speaking mysteriously, perhaps impishly, and smiling like a sphinx. It was flattering in a way, and Estelle enjoyed it—it was pleasant to be treated as one of the knowing—but the truth was, she seldom had the faintest idea what he was talking about. With that cherubic face and that hair-brush beard below his chin, he had the look of an elf, and it would have come as no great surprise to Estelle if she'd learned that all he said was some prank—not irreligious or irreverent: his delight in the ministry was as obvious as his perpetually startled, sky blue eyes, but astonishing and unthinkable all the same, as if Halloween dummies with jack-o-lantern heads should suddenly leap down from their porches—children in disguise!—and begin to frolic. Even his talks to her Sundayschool class left her baffled, though none of her students seemed to mind. It was the same with his sermons. He was fond of building up elaborate, merry structures of logic and Biblical or secular quotation—not so much sermons as prose poems, you might say—and ending with a sudden, quite striking allusion or an echo of something he'd said earlier, so that your heart leaped with pleasure, exactly as it would at some wonderful insight, but when you asked yourself just what it meant you had no idea. Fortunately, tonight Rafe Hernandez was here to help.

"Yes, good point!" he said, and laughed. "It's easy

to take a dark view of such things—" He leaned graciously toward Estelle—his scent became stronger —and explained to her quickly, as if she'd just now stepped in on their conversation, "It's often been observed that suffering has a tendency to give pleasure a special bite, especially, of course, if the suffering is someone else's and not unduly great." His grin was Indian—black eyes, shining teeth—and made her notice that, like other priests she'd met, he had an effeminate, or anyway small-boyish streak. It made her like him more—though it must be said of Estelle that if the man had revealed himself as especially masculine, or even, perhaps, as a disguised chimpanzee, she would also suddenly have liked him more. "We enjoy suffering, at least in small doses," he continued happily. "I saw it in Selma, I've seen it in the lettuce strikes. It makes us feel alert, wide awake. And of course it gives happiness definition."

"Dear me," Estelle said, and laughed nervously. If that was all Lane Walker had meant, she of course understood it. For years she'd been teaching the odes of John Keats. It had probably been someone like Estelle, in fact, who had first made *them,* Lane Walker and Rafe Hernandez, see the meaning of "crush Joy's grape." But she continued to play the surprised innocent, for good fellowship's sake and to make sure that was all Lane had intended.

The priest smiled kindly, exactly like a fat, gentle cat with a human brain, perhaps some protector-beast from the old days. "A cynic might imagine that we *enjoy* the suffering of others. Possibly we do, on occasion—but as a rule it's much simpler. We understand our own well-being by comparison only. What a party it is, inevitably, when the guests are brought together by trouble!"

Ed Thomas sang out from across the room, "My favorite have always been bahn-fire pahties." He held his cigar out dramatically, awaiting the priest's question.

"Barn-fire parties?" Hernandez asked.

"Yes sirree!" he said. To Estelle, his face seemed

abnormally bright, and glancing at Dr. Phelps she got the distinct impression that he was watching his friend Ed Thomas as he might a patient. Ed's cigar wasn't lighted; she couldn't remember that he'd lighted one all night. "Bahn-fire parties!" Ed Thomas sang. "Whenever some poor devil's bahn burns down we always have a pahty just like this one. True, Ruth?" He pointed the cigar at his wife, in the armchair by the piano, demanding confirmation.

Ruth shook her head and laughed. "It's the craziest thing," she said, delighted. Both small boys were looking up at her, grinning, from over near the door with DeWitt. She was aware of it and played as much to them as to Father Hernandez. "Every time some barn burns down, the farmers come barreling in from miles around to try to put the fire out and save the stock—with the help of the Volunteer Fire Department—and when it's all over, one way or the other, we all go barreling to the nearest neighbor's, or sometimes the house of the poor man himself, and out comes the cocoa and cinnamon-toast. It's just like Old Home Week!"

"That's very strange," the priest said, smiling with just his mouth.

"It's not that we got no feelins," Ed Thomas said, grinning still more broadly, his face becoming redder. He grabbed a gulp of air. "We do it as much for the victim as for ennabody else—true, Ruth?"

She shook her head happily. "It's the craziest thing."

He too shook his head, the exact same gesture. "Hi gol," he said.

"Well, different people do things differently," the priest said, apparently to excuse them. He folded his plump hands, and in his slanted black eyes lay the vast superiority of a cat-god.

Estelle said, smiling her forgiveness at the priest, "It's just as you've said yourself, Father. It's a fragile life. One moment we're happy and wonderfully healthy, and our children are all well, and it seems as if nothing can possibly go wrong, and the next some horrible accident has happened, and suddenly we see how things really are and we cling to each other for dear life."

"Hear, hear!" Dr. Phelps said merrily, as if she'd said something funny. They all laughed, understanding his intent. Yet after the moment of laughter the room was unnaturally quiet, as old and insubstantial as the yellowed lace curtains, infirm as the shadows on the fireplace bricks, the whole house still as a grave except for the music of the horn and flute, coming from the sitting room–bedroom. Estelle partly turned her head, listening. They played like young professionals, it seemed to her. Every generation the music in this part of the world got better. Her Terence was studying with Andre Speyer, in Williamstown, who'd played first horn for years with Dimitri Mitropoulos— she had records he'd made and had heard him play once with the Sage City Symphony in North Bennington (formerly Sage City). It was a sound to make your bones tingle, solid and true as a golden cup, full of light and air as love, soaring! It was a sound, when he played, unlike anything else in the orchestra, as if one of the instruments had suddenly come alive, sprouted wings. Her Terence would perhaps play like that someday. He was already very good, at sixteen. But all the children—she hastened to add, as if someone might be listening to her mind and might be offended—all the children in this part of the world had fine teachers these days, musicians from the Albany Symphony, or the Berkshire Symphony, or the Vermont State Symphony. What would the country ever do with so many good musicians? And in the summer there were music camps and conferences nearby—Tanglewood, Kinhaven, Interlocken, Marlboro . . .

It made her heart ache. For a moment she couldn't think why, but then she remembered, of course: listening to the hi-fi with Ferris, in North Bennington, music arching up like a cathedral window. They'd attended High Mass at Notre Dame when they visited France. When they came out it was late and the Seine was still, with colored lights on it, floating like pure, stable voices. She would hardly recognize Paris now, people told her. She smiled. Nor would Paris recognize Estelle Moulds Parks.

All at once she was startled by a memory more harsh. Ferris had thrown a cigarette in the river, and she'd been furious. Was that all? Had there been something more than that? She'd been so angry she couldn't speak. Had he said something, perhaps? Insulted her, made her jealous? As for Ferris, his face had gone white as ivory—he was always rather pale—and his lip had curled up uncontrollably, almost in a sneer. They'd walked like two deadly enemies, in silence, or in silence except for the click of their footsteps, as in a tomb. Such fools they'd been! Such children! The night had been enormous above Notre Dame, as menacing and empty as a gargoyle's eyes—the mad, staring gargoyle that eats a small animal eating its arm. The noise and lights of the cathedral garden, where hucksters sold trinkets, live birds, fruit, relics, had seemed sullen and far away, a shoddy vision of hell. She remembered the lighted cathedral spires against the pitch-black night and imagined herself on the walled sidewalk along the Seine, absolutely alone.

When she stirred from her reverie, she was surprised to hear Ruth reciting, dead serious, as if a party to her thought:

> And we are here as on a darkling plain
> Swept with confused alarms of struggle and flight,
> Where ignorant armies clash by night.

Yes, she said inwardly. She had believed, like old King What's-his-name, that nothing could go wrong. She'd been happy before, or so she'd imagined, but then there was Ferris, beautiful and successful, and traveling with him to France and Germany, Mexico and Japan, she'd discovered that the world was radiant and holy and above all—if they could be true to one another—safe. She remembered walking through a huge Shinto temple in Kyoto. There was almost no one there. Their Japanese friend, Professor Kayoko Kodama, a scholar whom Richard had known at Yale,

275

had told them in his shy, gentle voice about Shinto, how it had legends but no theology—it was the favorite religion of the young, these days—how one clapped in prayer to get the god's attention, though perhaps, he thought, the idea was much older, much deeper than that, had to do with electro-magnetic forces, ancient theories of the body that come down to us, for instance, in acupuncture. Tears came to Professor Kodama's eyes when he spoke of the generosity of the American people to the defeated Japanese. He could not know then (Estelle was thinking of Sally Abbott's indignation), he could not know then what loveless welcome Americans had in store for their allies in Viet Nam. "Very fragile, this world," Professor Kodama had said, "the tiniest rent in the veil, as we say —the tiniest disturbance of the god's sleep . . ." He'd removed his glasses, smiled shyly, brushing tears from his eyes again. Only this instant did it dawn on her that he must have been speaking of some personal grief. Professor Kodama!, she thought, partly in sympathy, partly as a cry for help, as to a spirit-guide. The music of the horn and flute had ended, she realized—perhaps had ended some minutes ago. Virginia was coming through the kitchen door, carrying baked apples.

"Look here!" Dr. Phelps cried. "To the blessed Virgin-ia!" He held up his cup, splashing cocoa. They all laughed and lifted their cups and hoorayed, Estelle among them, though her mind was far away. She registered that the boys were gone from the doorway, registered that their voices came now from the kitchen, squealing something, and she heard DeWitt answer— registered that the dog was moving toward Virginia with an obsequious look, begging for whatever it was she carried on the yellow plastic tray—but she was remembering images from a movie she'd seen with Ferris in Japan, a film about Kamikaze pilots, mere boys, devout Buddhists. She remembered how beautifully they smiled, how they waved with gloved hands, taking off at dawn to die for the Emperor and all they loved in this tragic, fragile world. They wore trailing white silk scarves. *The tiniest disturbance of the god's sleep* . . . Sally and Horace Abbott had saved her life, when Ferris died. If one said it aloud it would sound foolish, but it was true. It would be good to speak, now that she was wiser, with young Professor Kodama.

She accepted the white, cracked china plate offered her and for an instant met Virginia's eyes. She looked down at once at the brown, hot apple with marshmallow on the top and, beside it, a glittering silver spoon. "Oh, Virginia!" she said, and drew the plate closer, to breathe in the smell. For a moment the baked apple, and Virginia's nicotine-stained hand, still steadying the plate, filled all her vision, all her senses, became the whole world.

8
(The Sermon Upstairs)

Lane Walker said, up by the old woman's door, "Mrs. Abbott, come help us carve jack-o-lanterns."

"Reverend Walker," she asked almost timidly, "do you believe in ghosts?"

"Well, *sort* of," he said. "I believe in the Holy Ghost, certainly." Smiling, not in mockery but in enjoyment of the game, he threw his hand down like a bridge-player playing a card, index finger extended, counting off the Holy Ghost as *one*.

From behind the locked door the old woman said —she seemed closer now—"I think I may have seen a ghost."

"Well, it's the season for it," he said, hand lifted again, trying to think of another ghost he could believe in and count off as *two*. "Thing for us to do," he said, "is get out those jack-o-lanterns. Scares the ghosts away." He threw a wink at Lewis Hicks, who stood scraping paint from the closet door beyond the door to Sally Abbott's bedroom. Lewis slightly grinned and ran his tongue around his teeth, not comfortable with ministers, especially this one, who, so far as he could tell, was crazy.

"You think I'm joking, but I'm serious, Reverend," Sally Abbott said.

He could tell well enough by her voice that she was serious, but with the storm outside huffing and puffing like a dragon, window-screens singing, stray objects thumping now and then against the house, it was hard for him to take her as seriously as she might like. "All the more reason to start cutting eyes and mouths in those pumpkins," he said. That, he realized at once, was not as kind as it might have been, and he hurried to make amends. "Tell you what. Unlock the door, and I'll come in and we'll talk about it."

There was a moment's silence. At length she said, "No, that wouldn't be right. I know it seems like nothing to *you* people—"

"Not at all," he said. "It seems to us like a serious problem. That's why we're here." Then once again he spoke too quickly, as he realized as soon as the words were out: "We should try to deal with it like people instead of crazy apes."

There was another brief silence. "I don't think of myself," Sally Abbott said at last, her voice remote, "as a crazy ape."

Lewis was looking at him as if he too, as a relative, was insulted.

"That's not what I meant," Lane Walker said quickly, shrugging and grinning. "I'm sorry. I didn't mean anything like that." He threw a helpless smile at Lewis. Lewis shrugged one shoulder, polite but not assuaged, and turned back to his scraping.

"Oh, don't apologize," Sally said distantly, grandly. "My brother James feels exactly the same. Women aren't human, they're only half evolved."

"Mrs. Abbott," he pleaded, and stretched his hands toward the door, "surely you don't think—" His natural cheerfulness was sinking fast; he made a point now of not looking at Lewis Hicks. One enemy at a time.

"You believe what you believe," Sally Abbott said

with cool charity. "It's only right that you should stick by it."

Though Lane Walker was a small man and congenitally good-natured, one of the elect, John Calvin would have thought—every morning when he woke up, startled back to life by the first small disturbance (the birds, his three noisy children, his wife up already giving riding lessons), he was out of bed at once, with a hundred things he was eager to get busy at, books he had to read, letters he had to write, parishioners to visit, sermons to compose (he loved composing sermons more than anything else and was a master at it) —he knew when he was beaten.

"Mrs. Abbott," he said, "let's start over." He said pleasantly: "The boys and I are making jack-o-lanterns, Mrs. Abbott. Would you care to help?"

"Apes can't make jack-o-lanterns," the old woman said.

He stared at the door, his left hand extended toward it in a gesture of goodwill, then turned his round, elvish head to stare at the back of Lewis Hicks who, for all the cheer of the party downstairs, for all the wailing and buffeting of the windy night outside, stood mechanically scraping off old paint—*gritch, gritch.* The little minister's naturally wide blue eyes widened more, as if he'd suddenly remembered something, his nature, perhaps, and slowly, thoughtfully, he raised a finger and thumb to his leprechaun beard. He turned back to the door, tilted his head back, cast one long foot forward in a jaunty, somewhat theatrical stance, as if mentally detaching himself from the concerns of mortals but willing, like a bent but unbroken Puck, to leave, if humanity would have it, one last helpful bit of instruction and good advice. "Mrs. Abbott," he said, "you're terribly hard on the apes."

"Hmpf!" she said. As a matter of fact, his remark surprised her and she could think of nothing else to come back with.

"You seem to think, like many people, that human beings descended from the apes and show, in some

degree, the traces. That's not true, in fact. Apes descended from human beings."

Lewis Hicks' scraper stopped moving for a moment, then began moving again, as mechanical as before. One could tell by the way his head sat, he was listening with both ears.

"It's true of course," Lane Walker continued loftily, his voice taking on more and more the character of a preacher's, though it still seemed at this point mere spritely mimickry, not the real, dead-serious thing. "It's true of course that the ancestry of man, on one hand, and the apes and monkeys, on the other, has been separate for more than thirty-five million years. Nevertheless, it can easily be demonstrated that man did *not* descend from the apes. It's more correct to say that the apes and monkeys descended from early ancestors of man. The distinction is a real one, and of the greatest moral significance. Man is primitive, apes and monkeys are specialized. We have the most primitive teeth, for example, to be found in the mouth of any featherless biped, discounting 'Platonic man,' as Diogenes put it, that is, plucked birds. We never developed the wonderful, frightening canines of the chimpanzee or gorilla, or their large, knife-sharp incisors. We didn't need them, it seems. We'd probably learned already to cut things with stones, and to frighten off our enemies with spears."

He tipped forward toward the door, clasped his hands behind his back, raised his eyebrows and lowered his voice as if offering the door a tip. "Or take arms and legs. A few million years ago, gibbons had arms and legs of about equal length, just as we do today. But the apes and monkeys—especially the gibbons—developed long arms and short legs specialized for swinging through trees. We, it seems, never needed to. We'd long since ventured out of range of our trees, maybe ten million years ago, boldly invading new territory with our clubs and stones and crafty little heads. Don't think I've made all this up, Mrs. Abbott. It's perfectly standard paleontology—read for example Bjorn Kurtén. If people are going to go around discovering morals in science, they should try to get their science correct."

Again Lewis's scraper paused, and this time his head turned slightly for a glance at the minister. If he was expecting a sternness of expression to match the sternness of Lane Walker's words, he was sadly disappointed. The little man was grinning from ear to ear.

Sally Abbott started to say something—something about ghosts—then thought better of it.

The minister turned from the door, hands still clasped behind him, and set off in the direction of the head of the stairs, then abruptly spun around and came marching back—Lewis Hicks seemed startled —strode past Sally Abbott's door, then spun around again, heading back toward the stairtop, pacing like a tiger. "What," he asked rhetorically, and dramatically raised his right hand, wagging his fingers, "—What are the *real* morals to be drawn from the study of evolution? What does it teach us, that is to say, with regard to social oppression and, in particular, the role of women?"

At this, Lewis Hicks let the hand that held the scraper drop to his side, turned halfway around, and merely stared.

The minister, ignoring him, nodded thoughtfully, as if someone else had asked the question. "Good question," he said, and continued to pace. "First off," he said, "let it be understood that natural selection is still a vital force in human evolution. Natural selection by differential mortality is as important as ever, perhaps more important than it ever was before. Let us consider the dramatic recent history of the red man, the white man, and the black."

While the minister was speaking, warming to his subject more and more, DeWitt Thomas came up the stairs, heading for the bathroom. The minister paid no attention to him, busily pacing and lecturing to the door. DeWitt grinned, nodded in Lewis Hicks' direction, rubbed the side of his nose—a habitual gesture—and went in and closed the bathroom door behind him.

"When the white man came to America," Lane Walker said, "natural selection very nearly wiped out the Indian. No North American Indian liver had ever had to deal with alcohol. Wine, beer, cider, mead, pulque, sake, whiskey—they'd been known for hundreds and hundreds of years over most of this planet, and though they're deadly poisons, a panchromatic race of men had evolved that could take in the pleasures of alcohol and survive. Not so the Indian! His liver and brain went into lunes and shudders, and if he was lucky enough to handle the thing physiologically, he didn't know what to do with it behaviorally. The Vanishing American vanished with his whiskey in one hand and his rifle in the other, and because of the whiskey, neither hand knew what the other was doing—to paraphrase Scripture—and so down he went tail over tincup! Check your history books. It wasn't the United States Cavalry that beat the almighty Apache, it was the supply wagon! Firewater!

"God moves, however, in strange ways. The dying red man got his revenge: with one of the hands that didn't know what it was doing, he gave the white man tobacco!" The bathroom door opened just as the minister was reaching it in his pacing, and Lane Walker jumped back, bowed absentmindedly in DeWitt's direction, pivoted, and paced back toward Lewis Hicks. DeWitt—tall, stoop-shouldered—moved to the head of the stairs but then, instead of going down, stood with his hand on the newel post, a wide, shy grin on his red-headed, freckled face, and listened.

"American Indians"—the minister shook his finger —"had been smoking tobacco for hundreds of years. They'd developed the lungs, the body chemistry, and the social institutions to handle it. The white man, on the other hand—also the black and the Asiatic— having no such defenses, was to find (as he still finds) his race decimated by lung cancer, heart disease, and heaven knows what. One might compare, though

I will not, what happens when the opiates, hash, etcetera,—relatively harmless in the Orient—begin to be popular with young Americans. Those who have the security, wisdom, and strength to resist these poisons against which their bodies are defenseless—whether by rejecting the various drugs completely or by using them only sparingly—*those* are the people who will change the world in the most direct way possible: they will control one whole current in the gene pool."

He paused, both in his speech and in his pacing, and drew himself up. "Now take the most interesting genetic case of all, the black!"

"More interesting than the Chicano?" Rafe Hernandez cried in mock horror, coming up the stairs.

"You are late," Lane Walker said, raising his hand like a traffic policeman, "and like all late-comers you have no rights, so I bid you peace."

The priest touched his chest with his fingertips in protest and made his eyes large. "I was here before Columbus!"

"In that case you are allowed one right," Lane Walker said, bowing. "You may go piss."

The priest smiled happily, bowed from the waist and went, in comic haste, into the bathroom.

"Why Reverend!" Sally Abbott said, more surprised, from the sound of it, than offended.

"We were speaking," he pressed on, blushing, "of the black." He broke in on himself, leaning toward the door: "These are serious matters, you understand. This is no trifling circus entertainment I make you privy to. We were speaking of the morals to be drawn from science, one of the most serious of human investigations, second only, I might say, to Queen Theology. I must ask you to please pay attention." Without turning, he pointed at the bathroom door behind which Father Hernandez was emptying his stream into the toilet. *"Sh!"* Lane Walker commanded sternly, but the noise went on.

"The black," he began, then paused, looking up at the ceiling, hunting for his place. Lewis Hicks looked up too, then down again.

Then, remembering, the minister continued, "One of the most striking things about the blacks, genetically, is the sickle cell. In times past, as you know, one-quarter of the whole black race died of sickle-cell anemia, one-quarter possessed no sickle cells and, in central Africa, died of malaria, and one-half were perfectly healthy and carried on the breed. Expensive, in terms of human lives; but it worked. But what happens, we may ask, when the threat of malaria is ended—as in fact it has, since doctors can now treat it?" He paused, leaning toward the door as if for an answer. "Exactly!" he cried, pretending to have gotten one, and again began pacing. "The so-called 'bad gene' begins to vanish. In a few short generations—think of it—the black race has begun to lose its odd, no longer useful but still-sometimes-deadly gene. Useless adaptations, in short, tend to die, though they never disappear completely—an important point, and one we will return to.

"But consider further. There is hope among scientists at the present time that sickle-cell anemia may soon be overcome, just as we've found medical cures for other heritable diseases or shortcomings. Diabetics, that is to say, can now live a normal life with the help of insulin; nearsighted people can be helped by glasses; the deaf can use hearing aids. Natural selection, in other words, has been 'switched off' once again by our invention of tools. What is the moral to be drawn from this odd fact?" He stared straight at Lewis. It was almost as if he were pointing. "Let us make sure we *understand* this odd fact. With every tool we invent, from the wheel to Vitamin C extract, we *avoid bodily evolution*. The more perfect the Buckminster Fuller dome, the more securely antique its occupant."

Lewis picked at his moustache and looked guilty. At the opposite end of the hallway the bathroom door opened and the priest stuck his head out, seeing if the coast was clear. He stepped out, checked his fly, shot his cuffs, then stood waiting, smiling, palms together as if for prayer. No one even noticed.

"The moral, brothers and sisters," said the minister

—he was now so involved in the thought he was shaping that he was unaware even that Estelle Parks was being helped up the stairs by Virginia Hicks and Dr. Phelps ("What's this?" Estelle was saying, "we've been *missing* something! Why, he's giving a sermon!," and her eyes lit up)—"The moral is that that which was once advanced may prove primitive, and that which was once primitive may suddenly prove advanced, or in the words of that great religious poet Gerard Manley Hopkins, 'Nature is never spent.' We, the most primitive of apes, have proved conquerors of our specialized betters. With our wonderful way of evading the issue—our swollen brains and gift for using tools, and our anachronistic nastiness—we lock them up in zoos and put plates in their heads for our amusement and edification! —Never underestimate, by the way, the importance of nastiness to our progress so far. If intelligence and gentleness were the chief criteria, the planet would be ruled by whales!

" 'But what,' I hear you interject, 'of the sexes?'— for cunning animal that you are, you remember the outline I gave you when I started."

"The sexes?" Estelle said, just starting into the bathroom. Virginia raised her finger to her lips, then waved Estelle on. Estelle went in and closed the bathroom door.

"My friends," the minister said, "in every species in which labor is divided as it was for centuries among creatures of our race—by which I mean the one, sole, indivisible *human* race—we discover a tendency for the female to become small and quick—quick of foot and quick-witted—and highly emotional, and for the male to become large and a trifle slow-witted (consider the gorilla, the orang-utang), for in farmwork and war, to say nothing of hunting, there are certain advantages to—if you will forgive me, gentlemen—stupidity. What male with any sense would be tricked by a small, coy creature's wiles into carrying boulders for a wall to keep her children safe? What crafty Odysseus would stand like a tower against the Trojans, dull-wittedly defending his genetic heritage, as did that huge slow-witted ox Ajax?" A look of confusion came over his face—possibly mere theater. "But then, of course, Odysseus' line also survived, and, unlike Ajax, Odysseus eventually, after a good deal of monkeying around, made it home to his wife. Hmmm."

He pursed his lips and pulled at his beard, and his great slanted eyebrows lowered. The congregation waited with keen interest. It might now quite legitimately be called a congregation. The hallway was so crowded he could no longer pace. There was DeWitt in the corner at the head of the stairs, Virginia and Dr. Phelps beside him, there were the two small boys on the stairway, holding their jack-o-lanterns, there were Lewis and the priest, Sally Abbott behind the door, and there was Estelle, just emerging from the bathroom, leaning on her canes.

Now the minister raised one finger and smiled as if enlightened, making a show of having seen a new angle in the mystery of Ajax and Odysseus. "Let us try putting it another way," he said. "Which is more primitive?—the broad range of tendencies in the X chromosome, or the broad range of tendencies in the Y? In the days when Neanderthals killed with clubs and our own progenitors used spears and darts, a skull of bone solid as a football helmet was an enormous advantage to the Neanderthal fighting a Neanderthal; and a light skull easily jerked from place to place, and easily expanded to make room for more brain, was of similar advantage to *Homo sapiens* when he had to dodge a brother's spearcast. Times change, however, and ice makes men wander. With what sad surprise must the mightiest and bravest of all Neanderthals have faced his first feather-light, dancing *Homo sapiens!* '*Oof!*' the great Ajax among men said mournfully, as the spear slipped lightly through his tank of a body, and with a last, apologetic wave to heaven, the grand beast sank clattering into darkness.

"Times change, then; that is the lesson of our text, God's first great book, as Aquinas called it, 'The Book of Nature.' The carrying of boulders can be done these days by a trim little creature with a gift for pushing buttons, and the creature with the quickest reactions will be queen of the piano, the typewriter, and the jumbo jet. 'Ah ha!,' you say, 'I smell here a female-supremacist!' But not so! As we saw in the case of the sickle cell, even when a thing seems no longer of use, Nature is careful of her old spare parts. We carry, at least in genetic potential, all we ever carried from the time we were Devonian fish. Every man is part female, every woman part male, every mixture of the gene-pool a mixture for the better. Survival in a constantly evolving universe makes no petty-minded distinctions between primitive and advanced. In a word—"

The minister raised his right hand grandly, turning once again to Sally Abbott's door. "In a word, Mrs. Abbott, *Apes—or at least the more primitive apes—can and do make jack-o-lanterns!*"

So saying, he turned to his little congregation in the hallway and on the stairs, bowing and smiling gently, and said, "Amen."

"Amen, amen," said the Mexican priest, and signed the air with a gesture more soft than any butterfly could have made, sitting in the sun, and, smiling and benevolent, fat as a buddha and light as a balloon, *"Ite, missa est,"* he intoned, and then, in another voice, *"Deo gratias!"*

"Bless you, Reverend," Sally Abbott called from behind her door, and judging by her voice, she was deeply moved. "May all these terrible prejudices be driven from the earth!"

"Then you'll come out of your room?" Lane Walker said, delighted.

"Heavens no!" she said. "Why should I?"

Ed Thomas called up from the foot of the stairs, "Hi golly, so *that's* where everybody's gone to! Am I missing something?"

9

While his great-aunt Estelle was thinking of Notre Dame, Terence Parks stood in the old man's sitting room–bedroom, turning the French horn around and around, emptying water from the tubing. He was as shy a boy as ever lived, as shy as the girl seated now on the sagging, old fashioned bed with her hands on the flute in her lap. She, Margie Phelps, gazed steadily at the floor, her silver-blonde hair falling straight past her shoulders, soft as flax. Her face was serious, though she was prepared to smile if he should wish her to. She wore a drab green dress that was long and (he could not know) expensive, striped kneesox, and fashionably clunky shoes. As for Terence, he had brown hair that curled below his ears, glasses without which he was utterly helpless, and a small chin. He had, at least in his own opinion, nothing to recommend him, not even a sense of humor. He therefore dressed, always, with the greatest care—dark blue shirts, never with a shirttail hanging out, black trousers, black shoes and belt. He fitted the mouthpiece back into the horn and glanced at Margie. He had had for some time a great, heart-slaughtering crush on her, though he hadn't told her that, or anyone else. In his secret distress, he was like the only Martian in the world. As if she'd known he would do it, Margie looked up for an instant at exactly the moment he glanced at her, and immediately—blushing—both of them looked down.

He set his horn down carefully on the chair and went over to the window at the foot of the bed to look out. A noisy, blustering wind had come up, pushing large clouds across the sky, a silver-toothed wolf pack moving against the moon, quickly consuming it, throwing the hickory tree, the barn and barnyard into darkness. He could hear what sounded like a gate creaking, metal against metal.

"Is it raining yet?" she asked, her voice almost inaudible.

As she came up timidly behind him, Terence moved over a little to give her room at the window.

Her hand on the windowsill was white, almost blue. He could easily reach over and touch it. In the living room behind them—the door was part way open—the grown-ups were laughing and talking, DeWitt Thomas still picking his guitar and singing. You couldn't hear the words. He looked again at her hand, then at the side of her face, then quickly back out at the night.

"Rain scares me," she said. Though her face turned only a little, he could feel her watching him.

The moon reappeared, the black clouds sweeping along like objects in a flood. Terence put his hand on the windowsill near hers, as if accidentally. He listened for the sound of someone coming into the room and realized only now that the door to his left went to the back entryway and, beyond that, the kitchen. He felt panic, thinking they might go out that door unmissed. Something white blew across the yard, moving slowly, like a form in a dream.

"What's that?" she asked, startled, and put her hand on his. Her head came slightly closer and, despite the violence of the storm in his chest, he smelled her hair.

"Fertilizer bag, I think," he said.

"What?" she said.

He said it again, this time loud enough to hear. She did not draw her hand away, though the touch was light, as if at the slightest sign she would quickly remove it. His mind raced almost as fast as his heart, and he pressed closer to the window, pretending to follow the white thing's ghostly flight. Again he smelled her hair, and now her breath—a warm scent of apple.

As for Dr. Phelps' granddaughter Margie, her heart thudded and her brain tingled; she half believed she might faint. Her friend Jennifer at school had told her weeks ago that Terry Parks had a crush on her, and she hadn't doubted it, though it seemed to her a miracle. When he played his French horn in the school orchestra or at the Sage City Symphony, his playing gave her goosebumps, and when they had answering parts in the woodwind quintet, she blushed. Finding him here at the Pages tonight had been a kind of confirmation of the miracle, and when the grown-ups had suggested that the two of them might play duets together, and had sent them here, so that the adults could talk . . .

Now another cloud, larger than those before it, was swallowing the moon. The noise of the wind half frightened, half thrilled her. The barn stood out stark, sharply outlined. The white thing—fertilizer bag, that was right—was snagged in a fence, gray as bone, suddenly inert.

He moved his hand a little, closing it on hers. She drew her breath in sharply. Was someone coming?

"You kids want baked apples?" Virginia Hicks called from the doorway behind them.

They parted hands quickly and whirled around, frightened and confused.

"I'll leave them here on the bedside table," Virginia said, smiling. She seemed to have seen nothing. "You two make beautiful music together," she said, and smiled again, with a wave of her cigarette.

Neither of them spoke, heads spinning, smiling at the floor. Virginia left them.

Something thudded hard against the house, a small limb, perhaps, but no window broke, the walls did not sway, and so they laughed, embarrassed by their momentary fear. As they laughed they walked toward the bedside table where the baked apples stood oozing juice.

"Mmm, baked apples," Margie said softly. She picked up her plate and seated herself primly on the bedside, eyes cast down. Terence came and sat beside her.

"Listen to that wind," he said. The night howled and thudded like an orchestra gone wrong, dissonant and senseless, dangerous, but Margie was happy, for once in her life utterly without fear, except of him. She laid her hand casually on the cover beside her, conscious of the laughter and talk in the next room and also now a sound like arguing, coming from upstairs. She glanced at Terence and smiled. Smiling back, secretive and careful, he put his hand over hers.

10

Virginia stood smoking a cigarette, filling the sink to wash dishes. People were gathering their coats in the living room, and the thought of their leaving—her father not yet home—filled her with such anxiety she could hardly catch her breath. Perhaps it was the anxiety that made her think of Richard. She thought of him often, though he'd been dead fifteen years. All grief, all trouble, all worry made her think of him, which was strange in a way; he hadn't been all that unhappy, really, or if he had—his suicide made her wonder—she hadn't known it. He'd been a living saint, just like Lewis. She smiled, slightly blushing, remembering the time he'd walked in on them. They'd gone to his house and found the door open, Richard away somewhere—she'd been something like eighteen—and they'd decided to sit on the couch and wait for him. One thing had led to another as it always did with them, and when her brother walked in—they hadn't heard him drive up—there they were on the couch, she with her legs spread wide and Lewis with his pants half off, down around his knees, and Richard had stepped into the dimly lit room, not seeing them at first, and then had seen them and blushed scarlet, as if *he* were the guilty one. "Hi!" he'd said quickly, and hurried through the room to the kitchen. They'd lain there giggling, hardly able to think what to do, and had been tempted to sneak out the door without a word. But it wasn't as if he would yell at them; Richard had never yelled at anyone in his life—except once Aunt Sally when she said a little something about their

293

mother. So they'd gotten themselves arranged—she must have been eighteen, because Richard was twenty-five, it was the last year he lived—and they'd gone in where he was sitting in the kitchen, drinking whiskey and reading the *Banner*. He'd looked up at them and grinned. "I didn't even know you were engaged," he'd said. "Fix you a snort?"

"Mommy, can I have a drink?" Dickey said beside her. Without even rising from her reverie, she took one of the newly washed cups from the drainer, filled it with cold water, and gave it to him.

"What do you say?" she said.

"Thank you," he said and drank. After one swallow he poured out the rest, into her dishwater. She sighed.

She remembered how once when she was four or five Richard had frightened her with a bee. He'd known it was a drone and wouldn't sting—smaller, darker than the rest of the bees; their father had often let Richard play with them—but she hadn't known it couldn't sting and of course had been terrified. She'd screamed, and with a look of alarm he'd grabbed her hand. "It won't sting you, Ginny! Look, it's just a drone!" he'd yelled, trying to make her stop before their father heard. He'd put the bee on her arm, yelling "See? *See?*" And then, coming around the corner of the barn, barrel-chested and terrible, carrying a milk-hose, was their dad.

"Oh God," Richard had said, letting go of her, starting to cry already; and she'd understood she'd gotten him in trouble again. He was always in trouble, though he never did a thing; their father just somehow had it in for him.

"All right," their father said.

"It was just a little drone," he said, and then said no more—in her mind she could see him just as clear as day, a big gawky boy of eleven or twelve, golden-haired in the sunlight, face bright red with shame and anger, crying before he was even hit. All through her childhood, it seemed to her, her father had been beating him for one thing or another. "A lad born for hanging," her father had called him, and again and again laid his belt to him, or a milkhose, or a stick. She knew pretty well what it was in him that made their father furious. He was timid—exactly as their father had been, Aunt Sally said—afraid of the cows, the horses, even of the chickens; afraid of strangers; afraid of cold and of thunder; afraid of ghosts and nightmares; afraid, more than anything else, that one of them might die, or that his father might go crazy, as a man had done once down the road, and might shoot them with his gun. Perhaps if her father had been able to see . . .

Her brother had a wonderful sense of humor, though, even about himself. He knew he was a coward, and made a joke of it. If something made him jump, he'd exaggerate the jump and put mock terror on his face, so you couldn't be sure if he'd really been startled or was just playing; and when he asked their mother for the keys to the car—their gentle, good mother of whom not even mice could conceivably be frightened—he would duck and cringe as if scared she meant to hit him, and she would laugh and catch hold of his hand. He'd once dressed up for a costume party in a horrible outfit—he had a beard and long hair made of white horse's tail, and had a long black coat that had belonged to their father's crazy uncle Ira, and he was carrying an axe with red paint splashed over it. When he came before the party to spring it on their mother, he'd seen himself in the mirror and actually jumped. Even their father had smiled, for once, but all he'd said was, "Don't fahget to clean off that axe when you're through with it." He was something, her father. He was beyond belief! Yet he'd meant no harm. Whatever Uncle Horace and Aunt Sally might think, her mother saw the truth: "He loves that boy more than his own life. That's why he frets so."

Ginny looked at her watch. Where *was* he so long?

"Well, Ginny," Dr. Phelps said behind her, "I guess we better be moseyin on."

"Oh!" Ginny said, and snatched up a towel to dry her hands.

When Ed Thomas got to go up to the bathroom—he had to step back for the descending crowd—he found Lewis Hicks standing at Sally's door scraping off the paint. "Hi gol, Lewis," he said, "you ain't goin down with the others?" He pointed past his shoulder with his partly cut off thumb. "Ye'll be missin the party, boy! Won't last much longer, I can tell ye that fer certain. Ye better get in on it!"

"Well," Lewis said, pausing a moment to reflect on the matter, "I got to get this paintin done, and pahty or no pahty, I hate to drive all this way and just leave it set."

"That's the spirit, boy," Ed Thomas said, and laughed. "Say, what was all that goin on up here?" He pointed past his shoulder again toward where the crowd had gone.

"Talk about apes and women," Lewis said.

"Jokes, ye mean?" Ed asked, squinting, mouth slightly open.

Lewis went on with his scraping. "Not really," he said.

Ed Thomas lowered his head and chuckled. "Apes and women," he said. "Hi golly." He went to the bathroom, and while he was using the toilet, his chest going empty and ringing as if with panic as he urinated, the pain coming out for a look like a woodchuck in February, he got to thinking. When he'd zipped himself up and washed his hands and face and looked himself over in the oval mirror—half the buttons were missing from his washed-out workshirt, missing from the middle toward both ends, as usual, popped by the vast generosity of his belly, but never mine, he was a handsome old dog, as his wife Ruth told him (hair white as sugar, cheeks and nose pink)—he stepped out into the hallway and said, "Doggone it, Lewis, you're a dahn good workman!"

"Thank you, Mr. Thomas," Lewis said. "I always do the best I can."

"That's the truth. I've noticed it. By golly but it's hahd to find a worker these days!"

Lewis nodded and held out the scraper to pick away a few bits of grit. "Yes it is," he said. "It makes you wonder, the way things're goin. People don't seem to have much pride ennamore."

"No pride at all. It's a cryin shame." The Welshman tipped his head, holding up his stomach with his interlaced fingers, and asked pointedly: "That your work, that wall at Peg Ellis's place in Old Bennington, there by the church?"

"Done that this summer, that's right," Lewis said. He added, apologetic, "Hadda use a book. Don't get much oppahtunity to lay stone walls."

Ed Thomas shook his head in admiration. He began to move cautiously, like a fisherman with a bite. He leaned on the bannister and looked approvingly at the newly scraped bathroom door. There was not a gouge, and not a scrap of paint left. It was a job on which some men would have taken days, yet Ed knew it had taken Lewis Hicks no such span; he'd seen how Lewis swept that scraper down Sally Abbott's door. "I imagine you get plenty to keep you busy, a man like you."

Lewis nodded again, but said, "Never make me a tycoon, I guess." He continued to stand dandling the scraper, awkward. He'd never been a man to lounge around, and that was especially true when things had him nervous. His father-in-law had been gone a good long time. It was now, by Lewis's pocketwatch, eleven twenty-five. The people downstairs were making noises about leaving. As they'd gone down after the minister's talk, they'd most of them bade Lewis goodnight.

Ed Thomas pointed at Lewis's chest. He looked him straight in the blue eye, then shifted to the brown one. "Let me ask you somethin straight out, Lewis. How'd you like to come work for me?"

"For you, Mr. Thomas?" He smiled, uneasy, and

ran the index finger of his left hand down the side of Aunt Sally's door. He'd have to persuade her to open the thing or he'd never be able to finish, he thought. He looked at the fingertip, dusty as if with sawdust from a coping saw, and casually, as if speaking to his finger, he said, "No sir, I don't b'lieve I could."

Ed Thomas stood with his mouth open. Not from surprise, necessarily. He usually stood with his mouth open. "Why not?" he said.

"Wal, I got a lot of things lined up," Lewis said. "Can't really affoahd to let my customahs slide." He took another swipe at the door with the scraper. He'd made his point as plain as he cared to. Ed Thomas was famous for being slow to pay. If possible he'd get out of it altogether. That was all right, maybe. Farming wasn't easy for anyone these days. But Lewis would prefer to keep out of it. He listened to the voices coming up from the kitchen. They were definitely moving toward the door, he thought. Ed Thomas would do him a kindness if he'd do that too. He took another swipe at the paint. The scraper snagged; old nail-head. Lewis got out his jackknife.

But Ed stood firm, leaning on the bannister, pursing his lips, breathing shallowly and frowning. He said suddenly, "I don't mean just handyman jobs, Lewis. I want you to be my Number One." He reached into his shirt pocket, got out a cigar, and began peeling off the cellophane. Then, some trouble occurring to him, he changed his mind and left the wrapper on.

"I can't deny that's a good offer," Lewis said, "but I'm no dairyman. I grew up in town." He smiled again.

"Hell, *I'd* tell you what to *do,* Lewis. You're young yet. You got brains. You'll learn the whole business in no time. And I'll tell you what else: If there's one thing a dairyman needs more'n anything else it's an ability to handle any kind of trade—electrician, carpenter, mason, plumber, veterinarian, accountant—"

He shook his head. "Cows bite me, Mr. Thomas. They always have."

"Pshaw," Ed Thomas scoffed. *"Cows* don't bite.

They might bunt, they might kick, but in all my years I never seen a cow bite."

"I been bit, though. And by cows. I never been near a cow that he didn't bite me."

"Then I'll teach ye how to deal with it. You just hit 'em in the nose."

Lewis shook his head. "I appreciate the offer, but no thanks, sir. What about your son?"

"Never do it," Ed said matter-of-factly. "Cholly hates fahmin. So do his boys, though I get a bit of help from 'em when they visit—especially DeWitt. But my boy Cholly, he won't even help when he comes visitin, that's the truth. It's understandable, of course. Cholly's got a good job in Boston, ye know. No reason to get his good shoes dirty." He smiled. "Cholly likes that kind of thing—mowin the lawn, cookin itty-bitty chickens on the backyard bobbycue. But you now, Lewis, you're a Vahmonter. You don't *need* that sort of a life. I b'lieve it'd kill ya."

"That may be so," Lewis said. "All the same, I'm like Cholly. I ain't no fahmer."

"You ain't tried it, though."

All at once Lewis grinned like one of those jack-o-lanterns the boys had carved, for just that instant Ed Thomas looked exactly like the man that had sold him that Chevy. "I ain't tried cyanide either, yet," he said.

The Welshman laughed. He seemed persuaded at last that Lewis meant it. He turned away in the direction of the stairs. "Well, think about it though. You could just about name your terms, I can tell you." He took two steps down, his left hand spread over the top of the newel post. The bedroom and bathroom doors rumbled, catching a sudden draft—the storm outside was getting fiercer by the minute—and abruptly, as if the rumble of the doors had told him something, Ed Thomas stopped and looked up and said, "Truth of the matter is, I could use you, Lewis. I got to get off that fahm or I'm a dead man." His face was serious, redder than usual. He pointed at his chest with the cellophane-wrapped cigar. "It's my ticker," he said. "Doc Phelps'll tell ye." He smiled as if absentmindedly and shook his head. "I work half an hour and by tunkit I got to go in and lie down again. Chores every mornin and night —wrastlin bales, cleanin out gutters—I can't do it anymore, that's the long and the short of it. Doctor asked me, 'You feel pain in your chest, Ed?' 'No sir,' I says, 'just a little discomfit.' 'Well now,' he says 'how *much* discomfit?' 'Well, I wouldn't call it pain,' I says. Well, Doc Phelps looks at me and says, 'People have different ideas about what's pain, Ed.' I says to him, 'What *I* call pain is when you jump right out of your chair.' 'I'd call what you've got pain, then,' says he. 'But I'll tell you this,' he says, 'once winter comes, you might's well just throw that chair away.' By golly it was the truth, too. Here it's only October and the damn thing won't let me sit down. If I work that dairy I'm a dead man sure as I'm standin here." He grinned as if, more than anything else, it was an embarrassment.

Lewis bit his lips together, his cheeks and eyelids tense. "What about your hired men, Ed?"

He shook his head. "Worthless. You know the kind of help a man gets."

Neither of them was looking at the other now. "Maybe you could sell it," Lewis said.

The old man looked down the stairwell. "Ay-uh, I could do that." He began to nod his head slowly, and Lewis sucked in his upper lip and hurriedly looked away. After a moment he touched the old man's forearm. "Ed, we'll talk about it," he said.

Ed Thomas flicked his eyes up, met those strange blue and brown eyes, looked down again, and nodded. He waved the cigar, then grinned mechanically, leaning on the railing, and started down the stairs.

12

"Nothing's perfect," Ruth Thomas was declaiming in the kitchen. On the kitchen table there were two big, saw-toothed jack-o-lanterns, slanted eyes grotesquely staring, black inside. She pointed a long finger ferociously at Dickey, who grinned and shrank back toward his friend Roger and giggled. "You ever hear the poem about the 'possom?," she demanded. Her face was merry, the eye-bags dark. Both boys shook their heads, though Roger, her grandson, had heard it a thousand times.

"Oh yes, Ruth," Estelle cried, eyes twinkling, "do that one!"

Ruth drew herself up to her full height, DeWitt grinning with embarrassment behind her, and in something faintly suggestive of the style of a nineteenth-century orator, she recited for the assembled company—

The Opossum

One day, having nothing much to do, God
Created the Opossum. It was a kind of experiment:
How stupid, ugly, and downright odd
A creature (he wondered) could he possibly invent?
When the 'Possum was created, God shook his head
And grinned. "That's not very good," he said.

But for no real reason he loved the fool thing
And kept the thing functioning age after age.
The dinosaurs died out, or began to sing,
Transformed into birds; apes became the rage;
But the 'Possum trudged on—with some other antiques:
Spiders, sand-crabs, various old freaks.

"Father," said the Son, "that Opossum's a killer—
Murders baby chicks for no reason. He's got to go!
Times have changed, and changed for the better.
He's an anachronism, if I may say so."
God sighed. "Peace and Justice are right," he said,
And whispered to the 'Possum, "Lie down. Play dead."

The company all laughed, as they always did when
Ruth Thomas recited poetry. And as always, they
wouldn't let her off with just one. She was an artist
of a sort almost vanished from the earth—the "country reciter," as William Lyon Phelps, Estelle Parks'
teacher, had called it in his book. "The verse equiv-
alent of the folk-singer." They got their poems from
everywhere, these country reciters—from calendars,
feed-store account books and almanacs, small-town
newspapers, verse-writing aunts, occasionally old
school-books or the *Saturday Evening Post*. No doubt
now and then a reciter wrote some of his verses himself, but there was, in the heyday of the country reciter,
no great honor in that, and he tended to make not too
much of it. Certain poems were, for all reciters, classic,
of course, written by known poets like Eugene Field
and Henry Wadsworth Longfellow, names "now universally scorned by the literate," as Professor Phelps
said, "though one might hesitate to scorn them after
hearing them presented by a reciter."

Ruth Thomas, at least in Estelle's opinion, was as
good a reciter as any to be found in these degenerate
days, though not pure in technique. The faces she
made—bugged eyes, pursed lips—and her tendency
to insist on the different voices when a poem used
dialogue—all these showed she'd been just a touch
corrupted by dramatic monologue and the Broadway
stage. Be that as it may, she was the best you could
hope for, and the effect on the company was not much
worse than in former times, "the true and proper effect
of all art," Professor Phelps had written, "when it is
taken for granted, when no fine distinctions between
bad and good are thought necessary, so that the more-

or-less good has a way of prevailing, unthreatened by
the overreaching snatch at 'the Great' which creates
failed masterworks and devalues the merely excellent,
leaving all the world rubble and a babble of mixed-up
languages." It was a passage Estelle had often quoted
to students and had even used once at a School Board
meeting, in defense of she forgot just what. Even now,
after all these years, it was impossible for Estelle to
hear Ruth recite without thinking of William Lyon
Phelps. She was glad of that, perhaps even forced the
recollection a little. It heightened her pleasure in listening.

"Say another one," Virginia said. "Say the one about
the cat and dog."

"That's a good one," Ruth's grandson DeWitt said,
then blushed.

"The Cat and the Dog," Ruth Thomas began.

Lane Walker poked his Mexican friend in the arm.
"Listen to this," he said.

"Listen closely to this one," Dr. Phelps broke in, the
same moment, "this is a toughie!"

She drew herself up, then broke character to say:
"I recited this once at the McCullough Mansion. John
McCullough had heard me reciting somewhere—I forget where it was—and invited me to do a kind of
poetry concert." She smiled, devilish. "He told me
afterward, 'That's the kind of poem I can only follow
with a pencil.'"

They all laughed. Dr. Phelps' granddaughter smiled
at Estelle's grand-nephew, who stood beside her, and
both of them blushed. (*Ah ha!* thought Estelle.)

Again Ruth drew herself up and took a breath, like
an anthem singer.

The Cat and the Dog

Though he purrs, the Cat's only partly here,
Poised 'tween the hearth and the street outside.
Half-tame, half-wild, he's a walking riddle,
Playing both ends against the middle.

And so Man hangs between Truths he must fear
And the murderous animal under his hide.
The Dog's by nature the best of his friends,
Playing the middle against both ends.

There was a silence when she finished. Then Ed Thomas said, half-joking, face red: "It's true. I need a pencil!"

"Mrs. Thomas," little Margie Phelps said almost inaudibly, "do the one about the bear."

"The bear!" everyone shouted happily. "The bear! The bear!"

For no reason, tears began to stream down Ruth Thomas's cheeks but she said, "The Bear," and drew herself up, more grand than ever.

Estelle whispered, watching her old friend's face in alarm, "Listen to this one, Lewis. This is wonderful."

Ruth Thomas declaimed:

The Bear

If someone offers you a Bear, bow low,
And say "No!"

It was suddenly late. They'd all been aware of it before, which was why they were standing in the kitchen with their coats on, but now they all became conscious at once that the time had come. Virginia Hicks realized that she was frightened. Her father was still not home! But there was nothing she could do, or nothing but light one more cigarette—her throat and lungs on fire—and throw a glance at Lewis, who could give her no help, though she knew he felt it too. If her father had been hurt, the police would call, or the hospital—if they found him, that is. She imagined accidents that would make no sound, rouse no neighbor—the truck slipping softly off the road into the creek, or quietly tipping over on an embankment, vanishing from sight.

"Well, I've had a wonderful time," Dr. Phelps sang heartily, "and so has my Margie, if I mistake not." He winked at her and she blushed, "Come come, my birdy," he said, reaching toward her from across the room. With his red face, his long green scarf wrapped around and around and trailing past his shoulder, he looked like a greetingcard caricature of Christmas. Whispering something—perhaps just "Goodnight"— Margie detached herself from Terence.

"Well, boys?" Ed Thomas said, turning to his grandsons. They shifted slightly to show that they were ready. He turned back to Ruth and slipped his arm around her, preparing to help her walk. "Lewis, my boy," he called out as if casually, "let's don't forget, eh?"

"Yessir," Lewis said, helping Estelle to her feet from the chair by the table.

"Don't call us, we'll call you," Ed Thomas sang out, and laughed.

When Dr. Phelps opened the door it pushed him back a step and wind came bounding into the room like a horse. "Great Christ!" he exclaimed. Whether it was the wind or something darker, a chill went through them, as if the old doctor's cry had in fact been a prayer.

"Wintah's just around the cohner," Lewis Hicks said. No one else spoke.

"Get outta here, you guys!" Ruth Thomas said, addressing the wind, "you think it's Halloween *already*?" No one laughed. She stood tall as a Druid, her head thrown back.

With the door still blown open, the kitchen nearly hushed, there came from somewhere below them on the mountain, surely not more than a half mile away, a sound like the explosion of a bomb.

"What was that?" Estelle whispered.

Virginia put her hand on Dickey's shoulder, her eyes very still.

"Sounds like he didn't make the cohner," Lewis mentioned to the night.

The minister and priest were out the door now, running toward their car.

Sally Abbott, in her room, did not hear the explosion, or if she heard, did not register. She knew only that the house had become quiet, there were just a few people in the kitchen, talking. She couldn't make out what they were saying or even who was there. She listened at the door and then, when she heard cars starting up, went over to look out the window. "They're certainly in a hurry to get away," she said aloud. She went back to the bedroom door to listen, but the voices were quieter than ever now. She went to the edge of the bed and sat down, trembling, feeling strangely alarmed—it was the howling wind, perhaps —and looked at the clock. Past midnight!

She should try to sleep, she knew; but it was out of the question. She glanced at the paperback book and, after a moment's thought, picked it up and found her place. Staring at the page, she saw, as clearly as she had at the time, the ghostly intruder by the mailbox. She leaned back, pulling her feet up into bed with her, and reached clumsily behind her for the pillow. When it was adjusted, no easy matter, she rested her head against it and, with the book still open to her page, closed her eyes. Again she saw the ghost, but mixed with that image, overwhelming it, was the sound of Lane Walker's voice, her sense of the hallway filled with people, above all her embarrassment at having seemed a racist to the Mexican. She opened her eyes and the room was abruptly linear and solid, everything in place. She glanced at the book. Without quite meaning to, she began, once again, to read.

ART AND FREEDOM

Eighteen miles off the Mexican coast, Lost Souls'
Rock rose sharply from the Pacific like a black,
partly fallen natural castle or dark-towered
factory from an abandoned civilization. A nautical mile out, a single greenish spire like a
stalagmite rose from the sea, a welcoming em-

blem, a Statue of Liberty without features or
torch. It was an island strangely hairy, yet bare
in patches, like an animal with mange. Its vege-
tation was all drab brown or gray, fruitless
and nameless—here and there an unsightly,
twisted cactus, elsewhere low thickets of wiry
brush hiding dangerous crevasses, reptile bones,
old beer cans.

"An unsightly place," Santisillia observed, "but a good place for thinking. Nothing to lay demands on you, providing you're well provisioned. Nothing to confuse you in the way Spinoza mentioned."

"Spinoza?" Jane said politely, looking over her glasses.

Santisillia moved his hand as if to touch her, then thought better of it. "Spinoza speaks of how a hungry man or an angry man is not free to think clearly. Only the free man is in a position to be wise."

"Oh, that," she said. She tipped back her red, white, and blue cap, slid her arm through Peter Wagner's, and looked up at the sky as if fixing it in her mind. They were nearing the dark, covered channel mouth.

"It's an ideal place for getting your head straight," Santisillia continued. "Makes you think of Patmos where the man wrote *Revelations*." His smile became rueful. "Of course we never make use of the opportunity."

"*You* make use of it, surely," Jane said, still looking at the sky.

"Maybe this time," he said.

Suddenly a startled look came over her face. "Look!" she cried out, pointing straight up.

Santisillia looked, shading his eyes, but saw nothing. "What is it?"

She was silent for a moment; then: "I'm not sure."

She smiled, unsettled. "I must have imagined it."

"What was it?" he asked.

She shook her head.

Darkness slid over their faces. They had entered the channel.

Chained together, the *Militant* and the *Indomitable* scraped through the winding, covered trough, the clearance, at some points, less than

308

a foot, Peter Wagner maneuvering by torch-
light and echo and the help of his friends—
slowly, laboriously—to where the channel quit
abruptly in a still, roofed-over pool. From
there, taking only necessities, they clambered
up by toe-holds and hand-holds through a shaft
like that of an abandoned mine to a high, sunlit basin where there was still, fresh water,
cupric green and uninviting. Jane held one of
Peter Wagner's arms, the silent Indian held
the other. The only sounds were lizard-eating
birds' low, dissatisfied grunts. The air was warm
and sugary.

Peter Wagner sat with his chin on his fists,
his eyes on nothing. For all he needed, he depended without knowing it on Jane and the
Indian. His mind was not working; the blow
Santisillia had given him had left him with a
concussion, and now, three whole days were as
blank as a mushroom, though second by second
he could function well enough if given con-
tinual instruction on what he was to do. The
gap in his consciousness—the one thing he was
steadily conscious of—made him jumpy. "A
good place for thinking," he mumbled darkly.
"We must all try to think." Jane picked up his
hand and kissed it.

As the hours passed, Jane glanced at him
from time to time, sorry for him but no more
sorry now than at other times. She was writing
cheerful letters—little works of art, in a certain sense—to her mother and Uncle Fred.
*We've put in at a fascinating little Mexican port
that's hardly been spoiled at all by tourists.*
Each time she glanced at Peter Wagner again,
he hadn't moved. Neither had the Indian sitting
like a boulder just beyond him. Luther Santisillia stood down by the stream in his white shirt
and tie, still wearing his dark glasses, smoking.
Just tobacco. Cigars. Dancer lay in the shadow

of the cave, half buried in lizards, smiling in his sleep. He was stoned out of his mind. So was Mr. Goodman, lying among the black rocks by the stream, unaware of the lizards all over him. He was trying to make a large spackled lizard climb a stick. Mr. Nit, if he was still awake, was on watch up on the jutting of rock called the Tower. As for Captain Fist, he sat as he'd been sitting all day, tugging at his ropes and chewing at his gag and rolling his eyes in fury. *Poor Captain Fist*, she thought. According to Dancer, they were going to try the Captain for war crimes.

It was terrible, for the men at least, this waiting. That was always the worst part of these trips. Each time they came, Captain Fist—or, this time, Santisillia—went over to the mainland to arrange the deal, and then they'd all wait—and wait and wait—until the Mexicans came out some night with the load, and then the crew would fill the hold of the *Indomitable*, and they'd ship out before dawn. *Let it be tonight*, she thought.

She stole another look at Peter Wagner. She wished she could remember better the night he'd made love to her. Did he remember it? He'd touched her sometimes, since that night, had even held her in his arms and kissed her, but it wasn't the same. Of course he'd been in a stupor most of the time since then. Nevertheless when he was near she felt hungry and betrayed and a little angry. God, how she needed to be balled! She put down her pen to light a joint. Almost at once the marijuana made her calm, made things sensible. How sad he looked! He reminded her of Uncle Fred the night he had to shoot the ducks. Was that true?, she wondered suddenly. Did he really shoot the ducks, or was that just one of the stories she'd made up, talking in, say, some espresso place in San Francisco?

Peter Wagner stirred out of his daze for a moment, shaking his head and pressing his fingertips to his eyes. The Indian turned his head to watch him. Peter Wagner said, as if desperately, "We've got to get things clear." He nodded, and the nodding went on and on, mechanical. Jane bit her lip, then began to write more rapidly.

Dear God, Mama, I'm so lonely and scared! I'm in love with this man who's suicidal. He's tried to commit suicide several times

She crumpled up the page and began again.

Dear Mama—dear, dear Uncle Fred—I'm so happy! How can I . . .

Mr. Goodman came toward them, staggering slightly, holding out the stick with the lizard on it. He looked absurdly proud, as if he'd just tamed a dinosaur.

"Very good," Jane said.

Mr. Goodman nodded. He looked at Peter Wagner and, little by little, his smile went away.

Jane said, "He thinks too much." Immediately, she felt confused. He was thinking nothing at all, of course. Just blinking and wincing, struggling to get his wits together. For no reason, she felt dizzy. It was true, what Santisillia had said, and Peter Wagner after him: they should think, here where they had time. Get things straight. But when she tried to think, all that came to her was an image of Nebraskan plains, with windmills. She remembered a sky full of dark clouds and lightning, the windmills standing out white as bones, Uncle Fred hurrying to tack down tarpaulins, shouting to her, "Jane, get the horses in!" A great cloud of dust came sweeping toward them, black rain behind it. The sky was full of thunder. The horses were wheeling around her like pinwheels, and though she knew the dog was barking, driving the horses toward the open barn door, she couldn't hear a sound. She ran, breasts bouncing painfully, and her throat was on fire from shouting and hard breathing. All life, that moment, was important, full of meaning. Her mother stood by the kitchen door banging a saucepan with a wooden spoon, every line of her body revealed, stark, under the drab gray dress flattened hard against it by wind. When the last horse ran in, with the dog at his heels, Jane followed, legs wobbly, and, fighting the wind, slid the big door shut. She leaned against it, shaking from head to foot, sucking in big breaths, and then, hearing the rain hit the tin roof, making it roar, she ran through the barn and out the front and across the golden, glowing lawn to the entrance of the shelter, where Uncle Fred stood waiting like a relay runner to grab her and pull her in. She half fell down the stairs. He slammed the door behind her and bolted it. Her mother was waiting there, fists under her chin, face wild as if with joy. The lightbulb flickered, then suddenly went out, and the three of them stood there hugging each other in the musty storm-cellar, and all at the same moment they began to laugh. Rain slammed against the roof, the wild wind howled, and they hugged each other like conquerors.

"It's true of all of us," Mr. Goodman said slowly, bogged down by pot. "We think too much." He touched her hand, then carefully put down the stick, setting the lizard free, and stretched himself out on the ground beside her. He borrowed her matches to relight his pipe, breathed the smoke in and held it in his lungs. They listened to the birds' grunts and watched their winged shadows flit lightly across the stones. So they remained, hardly moving except to smoke, until there were no more shadows and the western wall of rock was jagged black against a red, red sky. Santisillia was fishing, sitting against a rock. Mr. Goodman lay with his eyes closed. She let her hand rest lightly on his stomach and smiled at his chins.

"You must wonder how a person like me ever got in such a business," he said.

Peter Wagner turned his head to look at him, and Jane saw that he was managing to follow at least some of Mr. Goodman's thought. She saw him looking at her hand on Mr. Goodman's belly and felt a pang of guilt but decided not to move it. *Better*, she thought, *to be completely honest.* She *liked* being high, didn't she? She liked having her hand on Mr. Goodman's stomach.

"I grew up more-less middle class," Mr. Goodman said, "and I had what you might call a pretty good job. Detective agency. I guarded things—old factories, museums. Then the kids came along. That changes things, I'll tell you. I had what you'd call a decent salary, but you look at your kids, you see what they could do if they had a little opportunity . . . Lot of people live for the present, I guess. But that's hard to do if you're a thinking man. What *is* the present, anyway? The minute it comes it's already almost gone. You have to live for the future."

Mr. Goodman closed his eyes, thoughtfully nodding, and put the pipe to his lips, sucking in again. "The present moment is for animals," he said. "Life's nothing. It's only the future that counts. I'd do anything for those kids."

Peter Wagner raised his head. The rings under his eyes made him look like a raccoon. Above his right ear there was a horrible purple lump and a broken place. "When'd you last see 'em?" he said.

Mr. Goodman's stomach moved, tightening

under her hand. She moved her fingers farther. "Yes, I know," he said. "I've thought about that."

Peter Wagner shot a look at her, then glanced at the Indian, who turned his face away, looking off into the darkness. He looked at the Indian's knees, his big, still hands, then down and seemed startled to see lizards crawling over his shoes, darting away in all directions when he moved his foot. He rubbed his temples as if trying to stimulate the blood-flow, switch his brain on, and when his fingertips came to the broken place, she saw him wince. He looked up again, first at Jane's hand, then high above her head, at the wide, empty sky where this morning she'd thought for a moment she'd seen a UFO. Her scalp tingled again at the memory. Peter Wagner reached down beside the Indian for something, and his hand came up with a gin bottle. He unscrewed the top and took a sip from it—raw, warm gin—and after a moment he began to talk, as slowly and tortuously as Mr. Goodman had talked. She lay back, carefully, giving the lizards time to scatter, and closed her eyes.

He said: "When I was a kid I sometimes used to visit this individual called my uncle Morton in New York State. He was in sugar-beets, like my father, but he wasn't worth a dime. I admired him for it, but in the end he went crazy —wrote a book about the great Negro-Jewish conspiracy. In the place where he lived, just south of Lake Erie, there were terrible blizzards, sometimes forty below. When the blizzards came they would fill up the roads and make drifts ten, fifteen feet deep over people's yards." He took another swig. "If people were out driving they'd get stuck beside the road and it might be days before the county could get them out. Uncle Morton had a tractor with this big unique iron home-welded snowplow on it. As soon as he'd finished whatever work he had that day, he'd start up the tractor and start clearing out his driveway and then his road, and then he'd start on the neighbors' driveways, and he'd work his way to the county blacktop and he'd start clearing that, because that would be where groups of people would be stuck, maybe freezing to death. I remember how the snow blew like icy dust—I'd be riding beside him on the tractor fender—you couldn't see more than ten feet ahead of you: big trees would suddenly loom up beside you, just dark shadows, letting you know for a minute where you were. He didn't look human, bundled up in coats and three pair of overalls and big wool mittens, and the scarf and hat he had covered his whole face. Me the same. We'd find a car and this crazy individual would stop and get down from the tractor, climb down like a Martian, and he'd shovel to the door and break it open and the people would get out and they'd walk like stiff dolls, you couldn't see their faces, thanking him and hugging him, or swearing at him, asking him where he'd been so long. I must have been twelve or so. They'd come toward the tractor through the whistling wind and the swirls of white dust and they'd get on with me—a crowd of them would get up beside me on the fenders, a crowd would stand on the drawbar, faceless . . . We'd take them to a house and go back again. The road stretched on and on, no way to get to all of them, and nobody trying to help but my poor crazy uncle. 'You want me to send you in to get warm?' he'd yell at me when we came to a house. I'd shake my head, though I was freezing, couldn't move my face. I thought I was part of something wonderful, something heroic and important. We'd plow on, the roar of the tractor deafening in all that white desolation. He looked like a clown, getting off and on, shoveling, jerking the gearshift. He made me think of the clowns in the circus trying to imitate the acrobats. It's as if they're not people, their bodies are stuffed with old rags and straw, you know what I mean? —no minds, no feelings. Ha. God knows what my uncle was imitating. It would get dark, and I'd be hungry, but he couldn't stop. One man couldn't get them all out. He knew it. Other people with tractors should've helped. Then it would be all right. But they didn't. Why should they? They paid taxes for that kind of thing. They stuck together. What could they do, the citizens? They weren't tough or crazy, like my uncle Mort. They weren't heroes. They'd be risking their lives, and for what? Maybe a court case like my uncle Mort's. But I'm ahead of myself."

Peter Wagner paused, staring as if his eyes were frozen. Santisillia had come up from the stream with some fish—black with white squiggles, horrible creatures—and was hunkered down now, a few yards away from him, listening. Mr. Goodman was asleep under Jane's hand. Mr. Nit was still on watch, probably out cold.

Peter Wagner said: "One night we were ramming through heavy drifts, coming to an overpass. He'd been at it all day, getting people out of cars. All of a sudden we hit something— there was a crunch and a sound of glass breaking, and suddenly the tractor tires were spinning and the tractor was skittering sideways. I saw his foot hit the clutch and his mittened paw hit the gearshift at the same time, and the tractor spun back. In the white of the headlights, swirling in the snowstorm like pure white fire, we saw a smashed in car-door, smashed in so far you could see the darkness inside. Everything except the inside of the car was unnaturally bright. After a minute, in the snow underneath where the door was smashed, there was blood. I saw him walking toward it, hands out for balance, wide and awkward as a clown or a bear in the glitter of circus lights, every movement comical, as if somebody was guiding him with long sticks."

He fell silent. No one offered comment. He continued to take pulls at his bottle, though surely it must be burning his mouth out, to say nothing of his brain. Sometimes he passed it to the Indian. Peter Wagner's lips were puckered up as if the taste was terrible, but maybe that was from the story he'd told.

He said, "All books agree. We're wrong for this place. We move through the world like anti-matter, ready to blow up on contact."

When Jane looked over at Dancer she saw that he wasn't asleep after all. He was watching. Overhead the stars were needlesharp bits of ice. She found herself scanning the sky carefully and more or less systematically, looking for that object.

Peter Wagner said—he was rubbing the front of his forehead now, and he no longer had the bottle, the Indian had taken it: "I've read books of all kinds—poetry, anthropology, religion, science—I've read more books than most of the doctors and lawyers I know. And I'll tell you something. There are only two kinds of books in the world—" He raised one finger, a little drunkenly, it seemed to Jane. "There are books that desperately struggle to prove there's some holy, miraculous meaning to it all and desperately deny that everything in the world's mere belts and gears—" he shook out the second finger "—and there are books that say the opposite. After you've read a few, each kind of book is as boring as the other."

"Come now," Luther Santisillia said.

317

But Peter Wagner was adamant. The Indian beside him grew more still and morose. Except for the movement of his arm and throat, his body was motionless. His eyes were filled with rage. Peter Wagner said: "It's all craziness. Hasn't changed in ten thousand years, people still making up gods and devils, out of nothing, not a scrap, nothing but their scrawny need."

"Come now," Santisillia said again. "People don't have to have gods to go on living."

"Not if they're lucky," Peter Wagner answered, "and after you count out the early mortalities and suicides, most people are lucky. That's statistics." He grinned unpleasantly. "Some people aren't, though. Lucky, I mean. I had a sister—or have. I don't mean to make too much of it. Once she was pretty and more or less smart, and rich besides—real catch, you'd say—but she got hit by this fellow who didn't see the light, and now she's ugly and has the brains of a potato, can't even pee without instruments. Such things are common—wrecked promise, obscenity, injustice. Not so common as to make you believe in a god who's evil. Even a man like Chairman Mao, with his sixty million murders—most people survived it. It was just a little ripple, statistically. But if it happens to be you that the bad luck hits, that's different, brother! You reel and stagger and clutch at your head, and if you mean to get up again, you quick make up one kind of idiotic book or the other. You make up some god who can make it all right, or you tell the truth, which takes your mind off it. They'll drive you to suicide in the end, books."

He fell silent. The lizards stood like dogs, looking up at him.

"I'm sorry about your sister," Santisillia said.

Peter Wagner glanced at him, his eyes as

sharp and angry as the Indian's. "Fuck it, man. I made it up."

Then for a long time no one spoke. There were fewer lizards now, though still too many, and those that were left moved more slowly, cooling with the night. At last Santisillia said, almost crossly, "Why don't one of you people make a fire?"

"Good idea," Jane said, and though her lethargy was so heavy she was sure she couldn't move, she found herself getting up.

Captain Fist watched them like an old wolf peeking through trees.

Jane cooked, working a sweat up. The men hunkered around the fire doing nothing, hardly talking—all but Captain Fist, still sitting, tied up, near the cave mouth. Mr. Nit was peevish because no one had come to take over the watch. He sat with his legs crossed, feet under him, elbows on his knees, and glared at the fire. Peter Wagner sat against a rock, smoking pot, gazing at the western rim of stone, or at the stars perhaps, or at nothing.

Santisillia poked the fire, making it flare up, lighting all their faces. "Peter," he said, "let me tell you about Captain Fist."

Peter Wagner turned his head.

"I tell you the story partly because you'll be interested," Santisillia said, "partly because it has a moral. At least I think it does."

Mr. Nit held the marijuana pipe toward him. Santisillia shook his head and looked over at the Captain, then back at Peter Wagner, and smiled. He said:

"Some people get their souls beaten out of them—bad luck, the pressure of events, and so forth. Some lose their souls through carelessness, neglect. But once in a while you have the honor of meeting a man who's sold his soul outright, made a deal with the Devil. Now there's a man worth knowing! And such a man is Captain Fist." He pointed. Fist's eyes squeezed shut. Santisillia grinned, drew out a plastic-tipped cigar, and lit it. "Our Captain Fist is a man deeply versed in philosophy. A stupid man, perhaps, and a vile toad even among stupid men, but nevertheless, well read. He has discovered beyond any shadow of a doubt that all life is mechanics, that faith, hope, and charity are the desperate stratagems of people who would blind themselves to truth. All men, he has come to understand, are victims, objects in fact no more rational than planets; good men, he's discovered by his books, are as much the victims of random concussions in the universe as are bad. All this he will tell you in the greatest detail, quoting the best authorities. And every word he says is in some sense true."

Jane frowned, waiting, then spatula'd the fish and corn meal out of the pan onto their plates and passed them around. Only Dancer thanked her. The others were too intent on Santisillia, or—except for Santisillia—too drugged. She glanced at Captain Fist. He couldn't eat with the gag on, and if they took it off, the night would go black with his obscenities. She decided to let him starve. Mr. Goodman poured and passed out coffee. Santisillia carefully scraped off his cigar, set it on a flat rock beside him, and began to eat.

He said: "I'll tell you how we met. We happened to be in Mexico, at the same time at the same place, on a buying trip. We took it out by road, in those days. Since Dusky's capital was limited, all we had was a car—built-up fenders and so forth, you understand. As for Captain Fist—" He smiled, rolled his eyes up. "Ah, Captain Fist! He had, of all things, a nitro-glycerin truck."

Dancer shook his head. "Lovely."

Santisillia smiled on. "It used to be, in those

days, there'd be convoys of the things, taking the nitro to someplace in Colorado. Fist knew the schedule. There we were, loading up, me and Dusky and Dancer cramming the stuff up in tight little holes, Fist and his apes throwing it in by the forkful, brazen as hell. I just stood there, all amazement. I didn't know what kind of truck it was, he had a canvas on it at the time he loaded. He drives away in front of us, before it's even good and dark, and we think we've seen the last of him in this Vale of Tears —at least Dancer and me do. Dusky's not talking, as usual. Bout ten o'clock we pull out and start north. We drive fifteen minutes, with Dusky taking a little nap in back—cool old man with this long woolly hair—he looked like a sheep was growing out of him—and all of a sudden you'd think the whole Mexican army was on us. *Blam blam blam!* Old car of ours slams into the ditch with fire coming out of her, ready to blow any second, and we jump like a couple of rabbits and yell 'Hey you got us! Señors, you got us! Surrenderons!' And we stand on the road with our hands on our heads. Dusky's gone. No sign of him. He was always like that. Maybe he'd slipped off miles ago. When trouble was around he could smell it. Show up weeks later, and someway talk us into working for him again. So *boom*, goes the car, and it knocks us flat on our faces.

"Then out of the bushes comes Fist and his two apes. 'Get in,' says Fist, and now I see his truck's parked under the trees. We start over, both of us, myself and Dancer, but Fist says, 'Just you,' and points the heat at me. We stare at him, his face all lit up from our burning car, crazy looking. I look at Dancer. 'Hey man,' he says, 'it's twenty miles from noplace.' Far as you can see all there is is those desert bushes and pricklypears and maybe a half-dead burro. 'Get in,' Fist says, and he waves the gun. Since

I got no choice, I do it. I hear him say behind me, 'Start runnin, boy.' I'm scared as hell and I look at the apes. They shake their heads, and when I start to climb out, they grab me. Then I hear the shot and I do climb out, and Fist's there with the muzzle in my belly. So I got to go with him, and I don't know if Dancer's alive or dead. Maybe they've finally snuffed even Dusky. As for Dancer, I find out later old Fist just winged him; so crooked he can't even shoot.

"But I don't know that then. All I know is we go about fifty kilometers and then Fist pulls into some trees again, and we sit waiting. The apes pull the canvas off the truck and shove it down inside with the pot. Along comes the nitro convoy, pretty soon after that, and now they've got me behind the wheel, with the pistol in my ribs, and they make me pull in behind like we're part of the group. He doesn't tell me what's happening—I don't ask; I'm too scared. 'Just drive, boy,' he tells me. 'Misbehave and I'll blast your top half off.' I know he'd do it. He's decided he needs me because there's not many white men drive that load. Just Mexicans and blacks. Any time we come near anybody, these three hombres duck down under the dashboard. I decide he's crazy. Sometimes he even laughs. 'What do I do when they stop me at the border?' I say. 'They won't,' he tells me. I think about it. It makes no sense. We drop back from the convoy, Fist's orders. After a while, about five kilometers short of the border, we come to a town where something's happening— crowd of people in the street, lot of broken out windows, some smoke from a fire, bodies and parts of bodies all around, some of 'em children, and of course a big detour. Everybody runs from the truck, screaming and waving. Old Fist peeks through the window, smiles like crazy, ducks down again. When we come to the border, about five kilometers farther on, Fist tells me 'Talk nice.' I'm ready. They don't even put the gate down in front of us, just wave us through. I'm hip by now. 'How'd you arrange it?' I say. 'That truck that blew up.' 'Never mind,' he says. 'I arranged it.' Man, I believe him."

Santisillia stopped, smiling as if with admiration, and finished off his coffee. He reached down for the cigar he'd started before.

"Is all this true?" Peter Wagner said, looking over at Fist as he would at, say, a dead animal bloated for a week. He looked at Mr. Goodman. "You went along with it?" He glanced at Jane.

I wasn't there, she thought of saying.

"You're crazy, all of you," Peter Wagner said. There was sweat on his forehead. "I mean, innocent people, harmless villagers—You know that about him and—"

"Now, now," Santisillia said. He lit the cigar. "They had no choice, you see—Mr. Nit, that is, and Mr. Goodman. They were accessories and, from a narrow, legalistic point of view, horrible vicious smugglers. They had families to think of. Their children's future. And then too, if they were to turn on their leader and then he should somehow escape the constabulary— vindictive old bastard that they knew him to be . . ." He smiles as if the whole thing delighted him. "And of course we must understand Captain Fist's point of view. A ghastly accident of consciousness in an accidental universe . . ." He let it trail off.

"He should kill himself," Peter Wagner said.

Santisillia laughed. "Ah, but that was not the direction in which he was predetermined." He tipped his head back, blew tobacco smoke at the stars.

Peter Wagner leaned forward a little, studying Jane as if to understand Santisillia by means of her expression. She smiled unhappily to herself and she knew she could be no help—indeed, had no wish to be. She'd stopped thinking about it. Men were forever worrying unanswerable questions. She got up to get their plates, ducking away from the smoke of the fire, and, when she'd collected them, carried them back to scrape into the flames. She kneeled, set the plates in a pile—she'd wash them later—and poured herself another cup of coffee. The fire troubled the rock walls with shadows like bad dreams.

Peter Wagner said to Santisillia, "You don't believe all this. You said yourself, he sold his soul to the Devil."

"Ah, Peter," Santisillia said with a smile, "you know there's no god, no devil."

"Shit," Dancer said.

Peter Wagner turned his head away. He wiped sweat from his forehead and compressed his wide lips, glancing left and right like a cornered rabbit. He knew there was something he had to figure out, but he was drunk and high, too foggy to get it straight.

Jane lit a cigarette, indifferent to it all, and held the marijuana in her lungs. At last she lay back on the flat stone and looked at the stars. Still no movement in the sky, no sign of life. The ground was cool now. The fire had burned down to coals, so that the walls had only a faint glow.

Santisillia said, "Everything's got to be an accident unless you decide there are gods and devils. We do nothing. Peter Wagner's uncle plows out snow and saves freezing people by pure accident, because he's caught in the Sundayschool bag, or his father was a doctor, or God knows what. Captain Fist does all these ungodly things because it happened to rain all through his childhood, or his father was a drunk, or he's an *XXY*, or his blood's deficient in, say, riboflavin. So everybody's a machine, an automaton, unless you decide there are gods and devils and there's some magic way they can get to you."

"Luther, are you telling me there *are* gods and devils?" Peter Wagner said.

"There are no laws but the laws of science," Mr. Nit said.

Dancer looked disgusted. "Shit man, gwon down where you come from."

"A fact," Mr. Nit said.

"An' I say shit."

"Take it easy, Dancer," Santisillia said. "Mr. Nit's right enough, far as he goes. What's physically knowable, science will sooner or later know."

Peter Wagner bowed his head. "I've heard all this," he said dully.

"Everybody has," Santisillia said. "But nobody understands it. Listen. Nothing's knowable but the present and the past. That's the bucket of ashes."

Peter Wagner sighed. "Terrific. Maybe tomorrow there will be gods."

"Exactly!"

Jane looked at Dancer and thought him handsome. Maybe she'd saved his life that night; no telling. Maybe he'd have come around anyway. She got up on one elbow to get her pipe and plastic bag of grass from her tight jeans pocket. Pipes had more oomph.

Santisillia said: "Think about it, though. It disgusts you that Fist blows up Mexican villagers he doesn't even know."

"I understand all that," Peter Wagner broke in impatiently. " 'I assert for all men for all time ta-dum-ta-dum.' "

"Wrong," Santisillia snapped. "It's not some arbitrary, private assertion, like Bluebeard's assertion that murdering wives would be the meaning of his life. Those Mexican villagers

were innocent, vulnerable, like everything alive
—like your imaginary sister crossing the street
when some fat-head wasn't watching the light."

Peter Wagner pressed his hands to his head,
avoiding the sore place. "Say it again. I don't
follow."

Dancer said, pretending he understood,
"Break it down for him, Luther."

Jane leaned upon her elbow again, holding
the lighted pipe out toward Dancer. "You want
some?"

"Grass?" he said.

She nodded.

He took the pipe, held one hand over the
bowl and drew in. When he started to hand it
back she nodded toward Mr. Nit, and Dancer
passed it on. Mr. Goodman got out his own
pipe, loaded it, and lit it. When he'd drawn in, he
passed it to Santisillia. Santisillia waved it off.
"Man, I can't smoke and think," he said. "Shall
I be tempted to infringe my vow in the same
time 'tis made?"

Dancer smiled. He said, "Hey, Luther, we
still gonna try the Captain for atrocities?"

Santisillia shrugged. "How can we? We just
finished proving that nobody's responsible for
anything."

Dancer looked doubtful. "Maybe we could
figure something out, if we once got into it."

Mr. Goodman said soberly, holding out the
pipe again, "I think we should try him."

Again Santisillia laughed, and this time it
sounded, to Jane at least, downright sorrowful.
"Try him, don't try him, what's the difference?"
he said. "Better to shoot him, or let Injun Joe
here strangle him. We were supposed to be
talking about something more important—
justice for the future, how to make gods that
exist."

Peter Wagner continued to sit with his head

down. If he tried to walk, Jane saw, he would be sick.

Mr. Goodman said, "The future's all there is."

"Mr. Goodman," Santisillia said, "you're stoned."

It was true, she saw. He hadn't gotten down from the last one, and was rising again like a balloon at the Zoo. She felt her mind crinkling open like wadded up paper. Maybe she was stoned herself. She tried to remember if she'd ever seen a leprechaun. Whenever she was able to remember it clearly, it was a sign that she was stoned.

They sat for another half hour, or two hours, she had no idea, drifting like a glider, a leaf on a brook. Santisillia kept trying to talk philosophy. She smiled, and eventually even he understood that it was useless. Dancer lay with his head in her lap. She put her feet on Mr. Goodman's chest, her free hand on Dancer's. The bare skin was hairless as a boy's. Peter Wagner looked over at her and suddenly, drunkenly, got to his feet and staggered out to find more sticks. They laughed at him, too high to be bothered by his anger—all but Santisillia—and like a devil, a misanthrope from the woods, he laughed back. After a moment Luther got up, cold sober and graceful, and went to help him. She inched her hand down under Dancer's belt and under the elastic of his underpants. Peter Wagner and Santisillia came back—hours later, it seemed —with their arms loaded, dropped their loads with a crash by the fire, put on a few sticks, and poked it back to life. Then they stretched out on the cool rock a little way away from her, judgmental. Even now Santisillia was trying to make Peter Wagner talk philosophy. *Dear God save us from fanatics*, she thought. "It's a mat-

327

ter of life and death," he was saying. Peter Wagner was rubbing his aching head, watching her. Dancer's hair, under her fingertips, was soft as silk. Her desire was an ache—for Peter and Luther especially. She would, she knew, have to be the one to act, but she was so dopey she could hardly think. She unbuttoned the top buttons of her blouse, smiling sleepily toward Peter and Luther, to show she was theirs if they wanted her, then put her hand back down inside Dancer's pants. She said softly, just loud enough for him to hear, "Peter, come be close to me!" He didn't move at first. Then suddenly, making up his drunken mind, he came to her, took her shoulders in his hands, and kissed her forehead and cheek. She smiled, then lazily raised her head to kiss him on the mouth. She felt as if she were floating, one hand sliding down to close gently on Dancer's enormous crooked penis, the other sliding to Mr. Goodman's. "Luther!" she called softly. "Oh God, Luther, come help!" He thought a moment, then threw his cigar away and crawled toward her, his expression half hunger, half anger.

Quickly Luther and Peter finished unbuttoning her blouse. She felt her breasts tensing more. Their fingertips rang like churchbells on her skin. Peter's lips came to her right nipple, then Luther's to her left. She groaned, then laughed, and in a moment they too were laughing, finally even Luther and Peter. Mr. Nit, over by the fire, was bent like a monkey, jerking frantically, pulling off his pants. Dancer was sliding her jeans and panties off. The laughing gave way to a great, silent tenderness that seemed to her almost holy. She felt herself opening like the Grand Canyon and pulling as if to draw in the whole calm night. She gave herself to them, hardly knowing who was where, as though she were, say, a field of wheat. They hugged each other like lovers as they took her. She felt beautiful, unspeakably alive, loved like a saint in a passionate vision. *This is my body* . . . She thought of poor somber, stiff-necked, ridiculous Nebraska. *Take, eat* . . . She kissed the drunken Indian's tear-stained cheeks.

Then, piled like alligators, they slept. Mr. Nit, small as a boy in her arms, moaned, troubled by bad dreams. She patted his head. *Suffer the little children* . . .

Hours later, Peter Wagner sat up suddenly. There was the drone of an engine—a plane, a boat, he couldn't tell.

"Luther!" he whispered.

Santisillia sat up, shaking his head to clear it. Jane sat up too and snatched about wildly, hunting for her clothes. There were lights and noises over by the shaft that led down to where the boats were hidden. Near the cave, Santisillia hunted naked for the guns. At last Santisillia found the machine gun. "Come on," he called. Peter Wagner followed, jumping as in a sack-race, trying to get into his pants as he ran. On the flat rock at the mouth of the shaft they found a trembling, wild-eyed old man in a wheelchair. There was no one else. Whoever had brought him and the wheelchair was gone.

"My name is John F. Alkahest," the old man whimpered, sniffing the air like a mouse. The eyes behind the thick glasses looked terrified.

Santisillia aimed the machine gun at him but did nothing. "Man, this isn't happening," he said. "This has got to be that grass."

"Got to be," Peter Wagner said. But he had another theory. He was still falling from the Golden Gate Bridge, and all his adventures were a split-second dream, one more cheap illusion of freedom. It came to him that the old man was Death. He smiled and raised one hand to his mouth, a gesture he'd gotten as a child from Little Orphan Annie. Something was wrong. The fingers stank of sex and marijuana.

"No man, I believe, ever had a greater choice
of difficulties and less means to extricate himself from them."

GENERAL GEORGE WASHINGTON,
December, 1776

5

The Old Man and the
Old Woman Choose Violence

1

Teeth clenched together, chest full of wrath, James
Page shot his truck past the cars in his yard, nearly
killing his own chickens, and started down Prospect
Mountain. The right side window was partly open—
it would no longer close—and ice-cold wind sliced in
at him. It would be colder by morning, cold as a cane.
He could smell a change in the weather moving in—
hard wind, likely rain that would tear off the last of
the leaves and turn the pastures drab, make the cows
hang close to the barn, dismal. Locking time, his
uncle Ira had called it. In a day or maybe a week—
or then again a month; there was just no predicting
the weather in Vermont—he'd look out his bedroom
window and the fields would be frosty, and when he
went out to chores there'd be thin panes of ice on the
watertrough. Locking had begun.

The lights of his house were no longer in the mirror. He was coming to what had been the Jerome place twenty-five, thirty years ago—huge barns, huge house; all gone long since, burned to the ground. There'd been a black and white sign, *Horses Stabled: $1.00 per day for Hay Grain & Stabling*. His elder boy Richard had worked there some. The place was grown up in weeds, bone-gray in the glow of his headlights. Sometimes old Jerome—the man's first name escaped him at the moment—sold apples by the peck or bushel crate off a two-wheeled cart by the roadside. Man blew his horn if he wanted to be served. Nobody stole, in those days.

He passed the Crawfords'; he remembered how the Crawfords had used to haul logs, a square Ford truck with hard-rubber tires with chains on 'em, and a sledge behind; a single load brought a thousand board feet. He remembered the sawmills, the slap of the belts, the scream of the big steam-driven saws and the smell of the wood, the sawdust piled up into mountains where he and his friends had played while his father and uncle unloaded. The sawdust would be frozen stiff in winter. He remembered the long-haired horses in the snow—seemed as if winters had been colder then—remembered the flat-cars, the raw-log railroad ties.

He came to the Reynolds place, family all in bed, two limp, unlighted Halloween men propped by the door like sleeping watchmen. They'd raised sheep on the Reynolds place, years ago, called Horned Dorsets. Lambed in September instead of in the spring, lambs born so woolly it was amazing. Vermont had been famous for sheep-farming once. Killed by the Democrats. When the weather warmed, he'd go with his father and uncle to help shear, the two of them long-bearded, sharp of eye and silent, and he remembered as if it was yesterday how surprised he'd been, when he was seven or eight, at how the wool came off all in one piece, like a soft white overcoat. They'd been hit one time, some of those Horned Dorset sheep, by a Bennington & Rutland railroad train. He remembered looking from the cab of the truck, where his father'd

332

had him stay. His uncle stood turning around in a circle, warding off the evil. A crowd of neighbors moved among the dead and dying sheep—there were splashes of blood, bits of clotted wool, there was a whole lot of baaing—and the neighbors would sometimes bend down, sometimes pose for a photograph. They always liked having their picture taken. They'd pose by a wrecked car, a flood, a dead bear . . . When the Jennings house burned, sometime in the twenties, as soon as they found there was somebody had a camera, the people all ran up on the porch and posed, the flames leaping out through the high doors and windows behind them.

That had been a whole different world; gone for good. There weren't many who, like him, remembered. It was a world so forgotten that people now scoffed about "the good old days," made out they were nothing but misery and pain, superstition and narrow-mindedness, and all that was true and firm in them, all that was honest and neighborly and solid as a mountain was some fool illusion. So pygmies hacked the legs off giants—always, of course, for some high-minded purpose, some glorious, bellowing ideal. Like Burr or the State of New York against Ethan Allen. "There's gods of the valleys," Ethan Allen said, "and there's gods of the hills," and scairt them with his eyes. He was ready to make war on the whole United States if they dared steal his land. But the giants were losing to the pygmies, no question. James Page had seen in the paper where somebody claimed it was wrong to have picture-cartoons of Uncle Sam, because America's the melting pot, and Uncle Sam was male and white. Lord God! You couldn't say nigger or Polack anymore, but you could still say WASP. You could write it in the *New York Times*. That was progress. He'd like to see that black-eyed Popish Mexican push ice-crusted logs through a saw sometime, ten hours straight in the freezing cold, the way Wasps used to do in his father's day, before the Jewish and Irish and Italian politicians, the Japanese and Mexicans and the God damned city-slicker Donkey party killed

the lumber business, and then the railroads, and then
finally the farms. It used to be a man took pride in
his work: he built you a wheel or a window-sash, you
could pretty well figure it would last you a while. Not
now. Why? Because nobody cared a mite anymore,
cared not one tunkit, *that* was why. These days they
had unions, and against the law to try and fight 'em.
Whatever kind of work a man might do, you couldn't
turn him out till he'd killed somebody. All that mattered now was seniority and raises. Come to that, if
a man's work happened to be honest, what good did
it do him?—And what point anyways in trying to
make an "honest" disposable syringe—that was all
they had at the hospital anymore. What point in trying
to make a really good, Class A, machine-molded styro-
foam cup? So now if a man bought a chair he'd just
better not set too hard, and if he bought himself a
truck he'd better try it out first in the haylot. No use
anymore to go looking around for a hired man, or a
boy to help out at the grocery store. They'd be in town
joining unions or drawing unemployment, all the smart
ones. Had no choice. Good workmanship hadn't just
died in this country, it had been murdered, shot dead
in its sleep like a bear in the sugarhouse. You take
glass-blowing. Priced right out of the market by strikes
—unions destroying their own workers, and nobody
could stop it. You take coal. —Between the unions and
the city politicians, between crazy demands and confused regulations, the only inalienable right there was
left in this country was the right to Relief. And you
needn't go pointing a finger at where it went wrong—
that want American!

He saw again in his mind's eye the fat, black-eyed
Mexican, standing there gazing around his kitchen as
if thinking of buying it. The old man's jaw—and the
fists closed around the steering wheel—clenched more
tightly. He was guiltily aware that it was not all the
Mexican's fault, exactly. The man had had no real idea
what it was he was treading on. It was Estelle that was to
blame, and Sally, and Ruth Thomas. But in his present
state the old man had no patience for fine distinctions.

He mistrusted Mexicans, that was all—their looks, their smell, the sound of their voices . . . It wasn't a thing he'd defend, wasn't even a thing he approved of. He'd readily admit that all men are created equal, as the *Declaration of Independence* said; but if one of his rights was the pursuit of happiness, he oughtn't to be forced to have equals he happened to despise and detest and know for a fact to be lazy, unclean, and of low moral character—oughtn't to be forced to have Mexicans—right there in his kitchen. It was *not* his kitchen, that was the truth of it—no more than a factory belonged, these days, to the man who'd sweated and risked all he owned to see it built. Fair and just profit was no longer a part of the American Way, nor was dignified labor. The country was in the hands of usurers, and not even American usurers, not even the miserable soft-fingered Jews but the God damned black-eyed Arabs.

He'd thought that leaving the house would calm him. In fact, his anger and frustration were mounting. His cheeks were twitching, his legs were trembling, it was hard for him to get his breath. He felt helpless —everybody did these days, but for him it was new, and a large part of it was physical. The bitterness was that he felt like a young man, trapped inside this wrecked and dying body. He felt as alert as he'd ever been, handsome and full of beans, not at all the hollow-eyed, ghastly white ghost that for an instant stared at him, piteous with appeal, from the windshield. He was like the young parrot at the Arlington House, screaming with holy indignation in his cage while the hotel burned down around him.

Now, as the road broke suddenly from the woods and he could see the lights of the village below, he remembered—as he hadn't remembered in years— how the village had looked in his childhood, before electricity. By horse and buggy it had been a long trip from the farm to this crest where the valley came in view. The sight had been something they'd strongly anticipated—he and Sally and his father and mother and Uncle Ira—and when it came it was earned,

335

like a hard month's wages, or marriage. The lights had been yellow in those days, not white. Only in winter, when there was moonlit snow, could you see the shapes of barns and houses, the square church tower with its four-spike, New England crown. By the river there had been a papermill; place had burned down when he was still a young boy. Whole thing looked like a picture postcard, or one of Grandma Moses' paintings, or the background of one by Norman Rockwell, who'd lived for years up the road a few miles, in Arlington. James Page had known him, by sight that is. Everybody did. Now the first thing that assaulted your eye when you came over that crest was the garish yolk-yellow of the Shell station sign, and the tombstone-and-lightning cold white all around it. He brought his eyes to the road again and jerked the steering wheel, swerving back away from the shoulder. His heart pounded harder, and he slowed down.

At Merton's Hideaway he parked out behind, where he always parked, nosing toward the incinerator. He pulled on the emergency brake and carefully climbed out. There were only a few cars here in back, two of which he didn't recognize, a five or six year old American one, white, with N.Y. State plates, and another white one, expensive looking and foreign. He hawked and spit left, accidentally just missing the foreign car—spit not cleanly but like a sick old man who smoked too much—then made his way, painfully bent over, across gray cinders to the green-lit door. Two windows faced the back, each with a small neon sign in it—Ballantine's, one said, the other said Schlitz. Inside he paused, adjusting to the darkness and the din.

As soon as he could see, his eyes fell at once on the strangers. There was a whole table of them, sitting right next to where he and his friends sat, usually, not far from the bar—grown-ups and children, the whole lot of them as out of place in Merton's Hideaway as Egyptians. He noticed first the women, a black-haired one and a red-haired one, both young or early-middle-aged, gleaming and assured, talking and laughing as if they owned the place, but not loud—no, soft as lambs-wool; in the general rumble of the place he couldn't even hear them. They had perfect teeth and glowing hair, the look of the rich, and so did their children, a blond teen-age boy and a girl, no doubt his sister, and across from them a child in a highchair. The grown-ups were drinking martinis and such, and Merton's girl Emily was bringing in salads. They were lost, he decided. He'd have said they were New York City leaf-lookers, but the foreign-car plate was from here in Vermont. Maybe they'd come from the College, then, and had got off the highway and stopped the first place they could find where a body could get supper.

He saw his own crowd and went toward their booth —Sam Frost, Bill Partridge, Henry Stumpchurch. There were others he knew in booths or at tables or up along the bar—farmers, county road-men, the Ranzona boys, who did light hauling, here and there a woman, most of them unattached, most of them brawlers, trouble-makers, thieves. There was a fifty-year-old, dark-eyed woman named Bea and another one named Laurie, watching from the corner, with burnt-out eyes. As he moved past the group he hadn't seen before, giving their table as wide a berth as he could in all that hub-bub, he glanced at the men among the company. There were three of them. Funny looking devils, he'd have to say. One of them, the quietest, had a suit like a gangster's. In the dim, infernal light of the Hide-away it looked almost pink. He had funny looking ears, a little like a monkey's, and a short, black beard. The second had on boots and an open leather shirt, a man unnaturally handsome in a round-faced, movie-star way. He had coal-black hair, dark skin, black eyes. Talked with an accent. Third one had brittle gray hair to his shoulders and a big gray beard. He had a sagging, red face and huge dark bags under his eyes, though he didn't look old, maybe fifty. His clothes—an old suit with big holes in it and snags— were like a tramp's. None of the three looked human, quite, but this one least of all. With that long gray beard so much lighter than his hair you'd have thought it was artificial, and with that tipped up nose more like a woman's than like a man's, he looked like an elf grown oversize. He flourished a pipe, waving it, pointing it, and he talked somewhat louder than the others, feeling his martinis.

James Page scowled, putting the strangers out of mind, and worked his way to the booth where his friends sat.

"Look what the cat dragged in," Sam Frost piped, grinning.

Bill Partridge, sitting in his hat, said, "Thought you want comin tonight, James." His voice was like a scraper.

"I'm here all right," he said.

"Grab yerself a beer and come rest yer weary bones," Henry Stumpchurch said.

James turned stiffly to catch Emily's eye. She nodded at once, not bothering to smile at him, running her legs off, taking a tray of cheeseburgs over to the Ranzonas, by the jukebox. He took off his cap, got his pipe and tobacco from his jacket pockets, and squeezed in beside Henry Stumpchurch, across from Sam. He had from here a view of the bar and the strangers' table.

"Turned colder out there yet?" Sam asked, and grinned in that foolish way he had, a tic of sorts, in James Page's opinion, a way of making everything he said sound humorous—if you asked him the date and he told you "Today is October the twenty-ninth," he'd wink and give you a poke as he said it, as if the date had salacious implications. But James was used to it—most people never seemed to notice the thing, or so it seemed. Sam meant no harm.

"Not too bad yet," James said. He nodded absently in the direction of the bar, where Merton had seen him and offered his greeting, the little half-salute they'd all used in the war. He was a big man, crew-cut, gray shirt, suspenders. He was leaning on the bar at the darker end, where four, five young toughies sat drinking beer, all regulars from town. Over the bar he had the television on, with the sound off. James filled his pipe. For all his years of milking, his fingers were stiff, uncooperative, scattering bits of black tobacco all over the tabletop. "Not too bad yet," he said again thoughtfully. With his left hand he brushed the tobacco bits over to the table-edge and into his right hand. "Be a damn sight colder by mahnin, and likely rain. Saw the pigs chewin straw."

Now Emily arrived with his Ballantine's. He leaned far over, groped behind his rear end—his fingers had no feeling—and drew out his billfold.

"How's every little thing with *you*?" she said. She gave the table a quick swipe with her cloth. She was thirty, dyed her hair. She had hips like a healthy young stallion, though the rest of her was small.

"Just fine, Emily." He counted out fifteen cents extra. "Keep it."

"Thanks a bunch," she said, and smiled.

He noticed that the stranger with the long gray beard was staring at him.

Bill Partridge said, "Hear you been havin some troubles up there on the mountain."

James poured himself a beer. When the glass was filled, not more than one inch of white on top, he set the bottle back down and said, "Is that what you hear?"

Partridge held his pipe up, an old drugstore Kaywoodie not worth a nickel when the thing was brand new, and Partridge had been smoking it fifteen years, polluting the air and consuming good tobacco to no purpose. His nose was long and thin, malevolent looking, dark as a baboon's at the zoo. His eyes, come to think of it, were also like a baboon's. His voice sounded something between a rusty hinge and a handsaw. "I'm just tellin you what I hear, James," he whined. "I understand your old sister's got a snit on."

"News flies," the old man said and raised his glass as if to toast Sam Frost, then drank.

"You got me, James," Sam Frost said, chuckling, so harmless and amused the old man had no choice but to forgive him on the spot. "I guess the little woman maybe *did* hear somethin on the telephone, and I guess I just may have spilled the beans."

"Well—" James said. He looked around the room. The strangers were eating their T-bone steaks. At the table next to theirs three young villagers sat drinking, glancing at the strangers now and then and smiling. The old man had seen the three many times before and could probably remember who they were if he had to. One of them was fat, with longish black hair. He'd likely be drunk before the night was out, though all he drank, anytime he came, was beer. He was always in jail for one reason or another—singing, mostly, or sleeping in people's cars. He was harmless as a girl. Another one was tall and pock-marked, worked for the phone company. The third one was one of the Grahams, blond-headed and muscular. When he was a boy he'd broke into a barn and mutilated an old blind horse, him and some other boys. They'd nearly had to go to reform school for it. He was trouble, that Graham. Had a look about him. He was what they used to call, in the old days, a lad born to hang.

James sipped his beer. Emily passed close, and Henry Stumpchurch raised his hand, one finger pointing ceilingward, asking for another round. She nodded and hurried on.

"You wonder what in hell the world's comin to," Bill Partridge said, and fit his pipe between his crooked, brown teeth.

"She out of her room yet?" Sam asked, smiling. When James looked puzzled, Sam added: "I mean your sister."

He registered now. "Not yet," he said. "She's gone on a kind of strike, you might say." He sucked at his dentures.

Bill Partridge leaned forward. "She never did!"

The old man nodded again and raised his glass.

Bill Partridge struck one of his wooden matches and held it to his pipe. The light made his eyes glint. "Man couldn't blame you if you threw her right out of the house," he said. "It's just like with old Judah

Sherbrooke that time, when his wife got to carryin on with that organist. Locked her outdoors in the snow barenaked." He grinned for an instant. "Wish to hell I'd seen it."

"And then there's that time when he caught her with the painter in the chickenhouse," Sam Frost said, laughing, and the rest of them joined him. The three of them said at once—James Page remained silent— " 'This what you call makin *Aht,* woman?' " There were hundreds of stories about old Judah Sherbrooke and his teen-ager wife. God only knew if even one of 'em was true. Everybody told them, sometimes even women of known bad character, such as Bea and Laurie, sitting there baggy-eyed like half-drunk Halloween effigies at the bar. Sometimes the stories made the naked young wife a kind of hero of foxiness (in none of the stories was the wife given clothes); how she slipped past the old hawk's eye to make love with the stable-boy when he was "teaching her to ride," or how she made love to a whole string quartet at one time when the old man believed she was practicing the piano. At other times it was the rich old man that the stories praised, how he made her stay all night with the barenaked minister in the Congregational church steeple in the middle of January, and served 'em both right; how he'd made her ride naked from North Bennington to Rutland in the baggage car, where she'd been carrying on. James Page, for one, believed none of the stories and grimly disapproved of people's telling them. Yet he felt at this moment, just as if the stories were true, old Judah's indignation.

"So Sally's gone on strike," Bill Partridge said, and blew smoke out. "What's that woman think she is, I'd like to know?"

Stumpchurch tipped his head, waiting for the answer. Henry was a kind of stupid man, always had been; part Welsh. But his heart was as big as all outdoors, and if once he understood a thing, he was a fair man, fair as any Judge. It occurred to James Page that he'd be interested to know what Stumpchurch thought.

"Well," he said, "the way she sees it there's two different sides to the ahgument. She b'lieves if I let her come live in my house, she's got a right to live ennaway she wants to."

"*That* ain't right," Henry said.

"I dunno," James said. He tipped his long head and poured more beer. It occurred to him beer might help his constipation, and he turned to see if, in all that crowd, he could catch Emily's eye; but she was nowhere to be seen. No matter, it came to him. Henry had signalled for another round already. Wine, it occurred to him, might even be better. He continued thoughtfully:

"It ain't altogether Sally's fault that she's poor, and now that she's in with me, she mostly does her share. I ought to just try and bend more, could be. Whole thing stotted with that television. If it hadn't been for that—" He looked at Henry.

"We heard about that," Sam Frost said, chuckling so hard he bounced.

James said, stern as a minister, "I *hate* that God damn television."

"Don't blame you," Sam Frost said earnestly.

"But then, if I'd give a little maybe then she would too." He pursed his lips. He thought again of that line of his wife's, "Oh James, James." He couldn't summon up how she'd looked when she'd said it. With the rumble of laughter and talk all around him, he wasn't even sure he had her voice right. He could remember the stoneboat his grandfather'd made when he was four years old; he could remember every flicker, every curl of burning white, and how the sky was bright blue when the silo caught fire when he was nine years old; he could remember every board, every barrel and brick of the sugar cabin where the family had made syrup when he was ten; yet his wife's face escaped him.

"Never trust a woman," Bill Partridge said with a significant look.

"Specially that sister of yours," Sam Frost said, and winked.

"What's that mean?" he said.

Now Emily was here with another round. As she scooped up the money, she said, "Ennathin else I can get you men?"

James said with a little stammer, "How much is a bottle of wine?"

She looked baffled. "You want the wine list?"

"I don't need a list, I just like to know what the price is."

"Got a bottle for three dollars if you want," she said. "Taylor's. You want red?"

"I'll take it," he said as if crossly, shocked by the price. "I'll take red." He glanced at the others. "Any you want a glass?"

They looked uneasy, shrugged, smiled, and shook their heads. He was reminded of three talking horses he'd seen in his childhood, time of some election. It occurred to him only this minute to wonder if the horses had really talked. No, of course not, he realized and, sixty years late, felt cheated.

"Just me then," he said. As soon as Emily was out of earshot he leaned forward and explained, "Got a bowels problem." He looked sternly at the table.

A draught of cold air welled around him as someone came in or went out, and he glanced toward the door. Two college girls stood there. They were Bennington girls; you could always spot 'em from a mile away. They usually didn't get out this far from the shadow of Mount Anthony—hung around The Villager in North Bennington, picking up 'lectricians. They stood blinking, letting their eyes adjust, one girl fattish, with a scarf and gray coat and a dark green beret, heavy-lidded eyes, thick lips—Jewish—the other girl tall, pretty except she looked empty as a box. She stood like a lady on a magazine cover or a clothing store ad, one leg thrown forward, elegant as a deer's, hands in the pockets of her long brown leather coat. He pulled his eyes away and pursed his lips, sucking at his dentures with his tongue.

"Well well," Sam Frost said, winking.

James heard one of the girls speak, much nearer than he'd have expected, and turned his head just slightly to look again. They'd come up to the table of strangers to say hello. The tall girl was stretching out her hand to the man with the coarse gray beard— the black-eyed man was introducing them. "I've read all your books," she said. The gray-bearded man got up, almost knocking down his chair, and jokingly seized the girl's hand with both of his. They did more introductions. The man with funny ears was a writer too. Emily came now with the wine and poured a little in his glass. He signalled for her to keep pouring and slid three dollars and twenty-five cents onto the table. Sam Partridge was whining something, ". . . damn place is changing," but James didn't listen. He was listening, ears tingling like a hunting dog's, to the table of strangers and to the Bennington girls, peeling their voices from the surrounding thrum.

The Bennington girls had moved on past the strangers now, over to the three young village men. The voice of the shorter, fatter one said, "You guys want company?"

The black-haired boy said—Albert, his name was, the old man remembered—"Does a bear shit in the woods?"

James sipped his wine. The taste was better than he'd expected, reminded him of something a long time ago—some important memory, but he couldn't quite jump it. He sipped again and then on impulse—his generalized anger, his loss of his own past—he abruptly tipped up the glass and drained it.

"Good wine?" Henry said. He sat with his fingers on the edge of the table, his square, slightly bug-eyed head tilted and thrown forward as if he'd never seen a human being drink wine before.

"You want some?"

Henry raised his hands, palms out.

The fat girl was saying, "What are your interests?"

James Page turned his head again to look. She was talking to the Graham boy. She had her coat off now.

The Graham boy was looking at her. "You really want to know?" he said, grinning.

"That's why I asked."

The tall girl drew herself up and looked at Albert. "Are you for *real?*" she said.

At their table the strangers were gathering up checks, getting ready to leave.

"One more for everybody," the bearded man sang.

The red-headed woman leaned toward him, smiling, but her voice, the old man somehow knew, though he couldn't quite hear it, was like ice.

"Screw yourself," the bearded man answered. The words slipped out as casually as a murderer's knife and easily carried the length of the room. Heads turned. The man seemed not to notice.

The woman blanched and everyone at the table hung hushed and motionless for an instant, like people caught off guard in a photograph. Then the blond, long-haired boy put his hand gently on the drunken man's shoulder and said something.

The bearded man bowed his head and touched his nose, then abruptly pushed his chair back and, helping himself with one hand on the chairback, the other on the table, stood up. The man in the light suit and monkey ears hurried around to steady him, grinning, saying something and making a funny face. The gray-bearded man mumbled something back, apologetic.

James Page poured himself more wine and sipped it, trying to analyze the sensation in his chest. He felt exposed, the whole room mysteriously unsafe. Furtively, he watched them pay Merton at the bar. At the door the bearded man paused for an instant, and it seemed to James that he was about to turn and look back, straight at him; but if that was what was in the man's mind he thought better of it—or in his drunkenness forgot it—and went out. James slowly turned his head. Through the window he watched them help the man over to the foreign car and into the back seat. When the others had gotten in, the motor roared like a race-car engine, the lights went on, then the back-up lights—the lights of the American car went on a second later—the cars backed slowly from their parking places, one after the other, and in a minute both of them were gone.

2

The incident, trifling as it was, had an odd effect on him. Now as his three old friends talked on he was a thousand miles away, going over it in his mind, still trying to identify the deep disquiet in his chest. The man with black eyes was a teacher, he decided—since the Bennington girls knew him—and likely a teacher of literature, like Sally's friend Estelle—since someone had mentioned that his friends the gray-bearded man and the other one wrote books. Maybe all three of them wrote books. James Page was not a great reader of books himself, though he'd bought one, once when he'd driven Estelle and Sally to the Greyhound bus station, because it said on the cover it was a "comic blockbuster," and he was curious to know if it was true or just more empty babble. He'd read about two sentences, had leaped forwards about a hundred pages and had seen it was all sex, and had thrown it in the garbage for the pigs. It was some kind of masterpiece, according to the cover. No doubt the black-eyed teacher and the writers would agree. Those were the books people liked, these days, those were the books people learned, these days, to live from. "Books that tell the truth," they'd no doubt claim, the teacher and the writers. Pure hogslop, same as TV. Where would it end? Bunch of black-eyed Brazilians made a pornographic movie where they finished by actually murdering the actress, and if the acting was right and the language was vile enough, people would be hard put to figure out why it wasn't art.

Outside it was blowing, as if the weather had been following James Page's mood. Two state policemen were hurrying across the parking lot, their coats billowing, their right gloves pressing down their gray fur caps. Behind them, hickories and maples bent back and forth, back and forth, hurrying, black against the mountains, the moon- and cloud-filled hastening sky, and leaves tore loose in shaggy clusters, fluttering in haste through the lighted parking lot and then away again, batlike, fleeing into darkness. When they were halfway to the door, a fat man bundled in an old sheepskin jacket came up to the policemen and stopped them. They talked.

By the light of the Old Grand-Dad clock above the bar it was after eleven. He could hardly believe it, and when he looked at the bottle and discovered he'd drunk more than half of it, the impression was confirmed: Time had shifted gears, or was leaking, like energy from the universe, so he'd heard. He couldn't remember at first where he'd heard it, but then it came to him: Sally's minister. Talk about change! They'd never have allowed such a man to stand up in a church and preach, fifty years ago—or twenty, come to that. They'd have locked him away in an insane asylum. Teachers, ministers . . . It was as if there was a plot against the world's survival, disaster on its way irreversible as a railroad car broken loose on a twenty-mile grade. He filled his glass and drank, heartsick, then excused himself and walked, bent over, to the toilet. His bowels were still jammed, tough as snakewood. He urinated and sat a while with his trousers around his shoes, waiting, then at last gave up.

As he was heading back for the booth, someone said behind him, near the restroom door, "We gotta get home, Fred. We gotta. Drink up."

"Gotta get home," the man agreed—the voice was familiar but James couldn't place it. He kept moving; too much trouble to turn around. "Jeezum," the man said, "look at the time!"

Bill Partridge nodded and touched his hat-brim, coming toward James on his way to the toilet. James nodded back and continued to the booth.

The door at the end of the bar swung open and

347

the policemen came in. Mechanically, Bea and Laurie smiled. One of the policemen mumbled something, and the four of them laughed. The older policeman—James would know his name if he thought about it—went over to talk to Merton. While they talked, leaning together, their faces serious, the younger state policeman went halfway down the bar, just far enough to see the television, then stood, hands hanging at his sides, looking up at it. On the screen a policeman was lifting a child in his arms, face sweating. The child was black, the policeman white. The camera hurried in until all you could see was the two faces. The policeman standing at the bar grinned. Someone spoke to him. He answered without looking from the screen.

Now Partridge was back. James stood up, making way for him. As he was seating himself again, he turned his head slightly, watching the couple pass— a fat young red-headed man—Fred what?—and his wife . . . the name at last came to him: Sylvia. He'd seen them here must be a hundred times, but the last name refused to come. They smiled at him; he nodded back. Then he shook his head, poured the last of the wine, and looked up, startled, as Henry Stumpchurch said: "Right, James?"

"Mmm," he said. Then, with a jerk, he came out of the wine-fog. "What?" he said. A tight muscle in his cheek gave a snap.

Henry Stumpchurch leaned his chin toward him, forehead back aways. "People want to talk about animal cunning, they shouldn't talk about women, they should talk about the beaver."

James looked at him blankly and lifted his wineglass to drink.

"You want to know something?" Henry said. He turned to stare, slightly bug-eyed, at Partridge. "You want to know what a beaver'll do? If the trees are cut down along the edge of the crick where he's decided to build his dam, you know what he'll do?" He sat waiting, head lifted, taller by a foot than the rest of them.

348

"What'll he do," James asked, annoyed.

"He'll dig a canal, by tunkit. That's God's own truth. He'll cut down them trees and trim off the twigs and the whatchamacallums—the crops, that's it, *crops*— and he'll gnaw up the boles and the whatchacallum— branches—into four-foot lengths—more or less four foot—and he'll dig a canal about two foot across and two foot deep—" he measured it out with hands two feet apart, eyeing the gap critically "—and he'll *float* them damn logs to his damsite." He hit the table with his fist.

"*Damn* site," said Partridge, and for a split second grinned.

James shot a look at him, annoyed that he should see fit to mock.

Henry's face reddened. "Listen," he said. "Are you aware that John Jacob Astor made his fortune on beaver, and damn near destroyed the United States?"

"Horsepiss!" Partridge said.

"God's own truth! Caused floods such as never was seen before."

"And then," Sam Frost said, leaning in between them like a referee, "you talk about animal cunning, there's the hog-snake." He chuckled.

"Hog-nosed snake," Henry Stumpchurch said.

"Whatever," Sam said with a sweep of his beer bottle, expansive.

Someone started up the jukebox. James turned to look, but Sam Frost said, "You know about the hog-snake?"

James turned back, raising his glass. It was empty. Emily said at his elbow, "You want another?" It made him jump.

Before he could think, he'd already nodded. No harm. Be good for him.

The tall girl danced past him with the Graham boy. He looked embarrassed, a little defiant. Nobody else in the whole place danced. They never did, it was wrong as an Indian dime, like clapping in church. Everybody watching looked irritated, imposed on, even Merton up by the cash register. What could have made

349

the tall girl think of it, dancing to the jukebox in a place like this?—some movie, maybe? The Ranzonas got up to leave, then Sam and Leonard Pike. Then more people were leaving, not on account of the dancing, in all fairness. He'd ought to be getting on the road himself. But the wine was doing queer things to him. Time was sped up but it was also slowed down. He could stay here forever and no complaints. The edge of some memory kept brushing against his brain, not necessarily a pleasant one.

"The hog-nosed snake," Sam Frost was saying, "is the greatest little actor in the world. This is true."

Partridge nodded sagely.

"Bother the hog-snake," Sam went on, "and he'll coil up his tail and raise up his head and flatten out his neck just exactly like a cobra—flatten it to three times its normal size—I looked it up once with the little woman in the snakebook. He'll hiss at you and strike, though there's nothing in this world will make a hog-snake bite, and if you ain't convinced by the cobra act he'll try his rattlesnake."

Again Partridge nodded.

"That's nothing," Henry said. "You take the common frog—"

Sam forged ahead: "If the hog-snake sees you're not impressed by his rattler, he's got a whole new tactic. He'll open up his mouth and he'll flip into convulsions, and he'll twist and writhe and then roll onto his back with some leaves and little pieces of dirt in his mouth, and he'll stiffen all at once and you could look at him and swear by crimus he's been dead for a week!"

"You take the common frog—"

"Shit, what's a frog do but sit there and wait?" Bill Partridge snapped.

"That ain't so stupid," Henry said. "It's *how* he waits."

"But that's nothing," Sam continued. "Funniest thing about a hog-snake is, you can poke him or swing him or anything you please, and he'll go right on playing dead." He laughed. "Only one little mistake he makes."

350

He laughed harder now. "Snake's got his act down a little too pat. Lay him on his belly and he'll roll right over on his back again, as if nobody could really be dead except lying on his spine."

They laughed, all but James.

"You want animal cunning," Henry Stumpchurch said, sullen but trying to hide it, smiling, "you take your common frog." They leaned toward him like shadows when the light of a fireplace dies low, respectful as they would've been to Mr. Ethan Allen, but before big old Henry had said three words, Sam Frost was squeezing out of the booth, heading for the restroom.

The Bennington girl and the Graham boy swung by again. She was talking about art; seems she was studying art at the College. James turned his head a little, trying to eavesdrop. Art was something he knew about, he'd have said. But the names she mentioned he'd never heard of, and he felt once again caught short, out of date and ridiculous. If the world knew the difference between a cow and a cornknife, he might have reached out his hand and stopped them as they went slithering by—might have said to the girl: "There used to be ahtists on every hand, this pot of the country. I was personally acquainted with a number of 'em. Cousin of mine once sat for Mr. Rockwell, and I met the man many, many times. Also knew Mr. Pelham—did covers for the *Post* . . . Whole bunch of 'em lived right there in Arlington, three, four blocks from my daughter's place. Tell you who else I was acquainted with—Anna Mary Robertson Moses— that's right: 'Grand-ma Moses.' Lived just over the New York State line in Eagle Bridge. Used to work for Peg Ellis, cleaned house for her. But you talk about painters, there's a nun used to live here in Bennington, years ago—"

All this he might have said, and perhaps the young woman would not have laughed, would even have widened her elegant gray eyes in pretended awe; but he chewed his cheek, eyes smouldering, and kept mum.

Both state policemen were watching the TV. On the

screen, two policemen were chasing a big truck. There was an explosion on the highway in front of the police car, and the police went skidding and sliding toward a cliff. There was a shot of the two policemen's faces. Suddenly there was a white-toothed, smiling woman with a yellow box of soap, then two red, rough hands and a butterfly. Sam Frost came back, zipping as he walked.

James was slightly woozy. The crowd had thinned a good deal by now. The roar of talk had for the most part died out, replaced by the music from the juke-box. On the TV a Negro girl was taking a shower, and though the sound was too low for James to hear, he made out that she was singing about some kind of hair-soap. She was naked as old Judah Sherbrooke's wife, the way it looked, though the picture broke off right where the swimsuit might be. Did advertising like that cause rapes? he wondered. Suddenly she turned into a bottle. It made him start. Then there was a picture of a horse, and a man smoking a cigarette. The horse had ear-mites, or a little touch of spavins. There was some writing and then, as if nothing had happened, the police car was skidding around the burning place and coming back onto the road and up even with the truck. An arm with a gun came out the window of the truck and the policeman on the right got his gun out and aimed it, steadying his right hand with his left. He fired and there was a picture of the driver of the truck jerking back with his hand shot half off, pieces flying. The two state policemen at the bar were drinking Cokes, looking at the picture. The policeman in the picture shot his gun again—the car and the truck running side by side, something wrong with the truck's right rear suspension—and this time when the camera looked inside the truck it looked like the driver's whole head had exploded. Suddenly you were looking from behind the car and truck again as they both went crashing into a wall of rock, the truck pushing against the car, and they both exploded. Suddenly you were looking at a woman in a nightclub, singing

352

to a microphone with nothing on but a stocking-like thing and some spangles around her tits and hole.

Emily poured wine into his glass and set the bottle down. He got out money. Henry Stumpchurch and Sam Frost were still talking about frogs, arguing whether it took cunning to just sit till you vanished. "Horsepiss," Bill Partridge said. He sounded a little drunk. Henry said, "In all my sixty-four years—" Bill Partridge said, "I say, Horsepiss!" James drank.

The pock-marked boy and the short, fat Bennington girl went gliding slowly past James Page's table, dancing —or rather hugging each other as they shuffled across the floor. As he looked up, the girl drew her head from the pock-marked boy's chest and said—she was smiling, timid, "You ever read a writer called John *Up*dike?"

Make me do it, make me do it, the jukebox sang.

He thought of Sally and the party up the mountain, and his anger at once boiled up in him again. He had chores in the morning. How was a man to do chores on no sleep? Did they think his damn house was the Walloomsac Hotel? She'd take his money when she needed, she didn't mind that, but when it came to even merely allowing him to work, never mind about helping . . . He'd had fights with his wife, he remembered vaguely, about money and time—and later, fights with his gloomy-hearted, weakling son. His chest gave a jerk as the memory ambushed him, his boy—or rather man, by then—hanging from the gray attic rafter, still as a feedsack, as if he'd never been alive. For days, even months, he'd been unable to believe it: a few harsh words, a quick, impetuous little slap— it seems the boy had been up to something, only God and James' wife Ariah knew what. Seemed to do with whores. He'd refused to speak up, had called James a bastard, hence the little slap, not even hard, mere show of anger with his open hand—"little" it had seemed to James then, that is; he knew better now, for with this stony stillness, this absolute, dead-final victory, his son had avenged himself. Whatever meaning James Page had imagined he'd seen in this pitiful earthly existence he had known that instant for what it was: mere desperate assertion, mere hopeful agreement between two people who could tear up the contract in an instant. He saw the boy standing high on the haywagon, grinning under his hat, sunlight and the wind-fluttered branches of trees wheeling and sliding above his head; and then the old man saw again in his mind the absolute, drab, metaphysical stillness of rafters. He had survived it, he couldn't say how or why. Had worked, had walked on the mountain at night, prowling like a lost bear hunting for the door to the underworld; had drunk some, more than was right, for a span; had written lists of words, little scraps of thought, once a kind of prayer, setting what he had by way of heart in his Agro pocket notebook. At night, when he slept and fell off guard, he would wake up crying. His wife would be holding him.

The old man listened to the rumble around him, a noise like train-wheels, mostly in his brain. He wasn't used to wine, hadn't been for years, and he no longer had, he discovered now, any natural defense against its physical effects and, worse, mental ones. Put off guard by wine, he'd casually wandered into a past he'd locked up tight, and he'd glimpsed there his reason for getting rid of it. Once, standing by the creek, toward dusk, he had looked down at his reflection and said, cold-blooded, however melodramatic: "You're a killer." His voice was flat and lean, knocking against the birches on the creek's far side. The mountain range beyond stretched away out of sight, rolling toward New Hampshire, dwarfing self-hatred as it dwarfed love. *Oh James, James,* his wife's voice whispered in his memory. His eyes filled with flash-tears of anger and grief, and then at once he had forgotten her again —had abruptly forgotten all of it.

Then Emily was there, smiling like a commercial, pouring wine into his glass. He counted out the money; she scooped it up, smiled again. It came to him that he'd drunk too much already. His sensations were as solid and raw as the slats on old apple-crates. Touching his jaw, he felt his whiskers with sharp, numb

clarity, like the bristles of a pig, and felt the toneless-
ness of his flesh. He looked at the clock above the bar
and couldn't make out the hands, not even the blur
of them. He drew his watch out. Quarter to twelve.
That wasn't possible. His friends would have left long
ago, if that was right. Had they stayed because of him?
Carefully, steady as a trivet, he lifted the wineglass to
drink.

"What you goin to do about it?" Partridge said.

Emily was back. She gave the table a swipe with
her cloth, then plunked down the new round of beers.
She picked up the money and then the empties.

"Do?" he said.

"Your sistah," Partridge said.

He drained the glass, some serious thought at the
edge of his mind.

"God knows," he said, and sighed. A fat old man
with a scraggly little beard was dancing with what was
perhaps his wife, circling with tiny little steps two,
three feet from the jukebox. James tried to place
them. They were talking about *Jaws*, holding each
other gently. "*Hell* of a movie," the man said.

Henry Stumpchurch sat now with his chin in his
fists, struggling to keep his eyes open. James turned
briefly for a look at the dancers and saw Stumpchurch
sneak a look at his watch. Merton came over from the
bar with a beer. With two fat fingers he hooked the
back of a chair and dragged it to their booth. He sat
down next to James. "You all right here?" he asked
and grinned.

"We're keepin you," Sam said.

"Hell no," he said. There was no one at the bar.
On the TV there was a spaceship. The picture changed
to a man with pointed ears. Emily went behind the
bar, looking gray as a ghost, and mixed herself a
drink. She looked at the clock, then looked at her
watch, then came over to them, picking up a chair as
she came. James quickly drank and poured another.

Whether or not it would eventually fix his constipation, the wine was playing hell with the rest of his
system. His head felt heavy as a deadman in a pond;

his bladder was in pain. He put down the glass, excused himself, and made his way past Merton and over to the restroom. On the toilet, nothing came but black water. It burned as it came like it was gasoline. He washed his hands, hardly looking at the face peering out at him from the mirror—face like an old bum's begging him for a coin. He went back to the table.

They were talking about Sally, and he should have been interested, but it was as if they'd never met her. His mind kept drifting to the teacher and the writers, the book he'd fed the pigs, his mule-headed sister up there starving in her room, blaming the whole damn world on him, and his spirits grew still heavier, weighed down with self-pity and pity for them all, the whole country sickening by a foolish accident, some deaf misunderstanding. Outside, the wind was ferocious now, and it was beginning to rain. Drops ran down the window, brightening near the neon, then darkening again. He saw in his mind's eye the smile of the Mexican as he gazed around the kitchen, adding up the value of the sink, the stove, the chairs, glass doorknobs, dishes.

The jukebox went off, and the fatter girl and the pock-marked boy, holding hands, went back to their table. The Graham boy and the taller, prettier one were sitting side by side, shoulder against shoulder. She had long, long lashes.

"I like you a lot," the Graham boy said.

"Listen," the girl said, "I like you *too*." She looked at him hard. "*Really*."

The boy with the long black hair—Albert—came vaguely from the restroom and started across to the table then paused, undecided, looking at his friends. He changed his course and came slanting toward the booth, dragging a chair with him. "Mine I join you?" he said. It was barely intelligible. When he sat he'd have fallen if Emily hadn't caught him, laughing.

"Albert, you're drunk," she said.

"When I ever make it with you I wasn' drunk?" he said. He put his hand on her muscular upper thigh and she gently pushed it off. As if to make up for it, she held her drink to him, Scotch or Bourbon. James filled his wineglass, then on second thought let it stand and filled his pipe. Like a mother, Emily was helping Albert drink.

"You got every right to kick her out, by tunkit," Bill Partridge said.

"It's hahd to say," he said. His vision was giving him a good deal of trouble. He looked at Henry Stumpchurch, closing one eye, hoping to get Henry's judgment, but Henry was asleep. Merton sucked at his bottle, then set it down. Albert leaned his head against Emily's shoulder. Gently, laughingly, she pushed it away, balancing him like a toy, and got up to put a quarter in the jukebox. What came out was violins. She came back and picked her glass up, drained it in a gulp, and went back to the bar to fix another. When she was seated with them again, she smiled and moved her chair close to Albert's, then moved his head, with her two hands, to her shoulder.

Merton said absently, studying his bottle, "It's a rare man would put up with it." He nodded to himself.

"She does her pot," James said, "—or did till it come to that TV."

Bill Partridge looked angry. "Hell, James, you *know* that ain't true."

"What?" he said.

"She tricks you, James," Sam Frost said gently, evading his eyes. "You know she does. Been doin it all along."

James raised his glass, waiting. It struck him that he had, in fact, known it all along.

"Never trust a woman," Bill Partridge said. "It's like the time Judah Sherbrooke found his wife in the pottin shed—"

"What you mean, tricks me?" James said. Behind him—troublesome background noise—the fatter of the Bennington girls was saying, "That's a very positive feeling, really."

"Tell him," Merton said.

"Well, you know how it is," Sam Frost said. "The little woman's got a habit of listening on the phone."

James drank, then waited. He stared at his knuckles to keep things in focus.

Sam looked at the table. "That time you took that ad in the *Pennysaver* for someone to help with chores . . . You know why you never got a nibble?"

He waited on, his body growing heavy, heating up with rage.

"Ever time your phone rings *our* phone rings," Sam said, apologetic, "and naturally the little woman listens. You know how women are. Sister of yours claimed you was legally required to hire by 'fair employment.' Wouldn't consider a soul that wasn't Negro or female." He shook his head.

"She'd nevah do that," he said. "Sally's a fair-minded woman, always was." His teeth clamped tight. She'd do it. Hell yes! His childhood burst back over him, his big sister Sally running to the mailbox ahead of him, looking at his mail before he could. He remembered her selfishness, how if she ever got a candy-bar she'd share it with nobody, sneak it away to her room and you'd never know she had it. He'd never have done such a thing in a hundred years. It was animal, someway. Turned his stomach. He remembered how she lied. He'd never known such a liar, he could hardly believe it—neither could his mother or father. He remembered how she'd sneak away to Ralph Beeman and later Horace, go climbing out the window in the middle of the night, and offer him, her little brother James Page, cash money to keep her secret. He'd refused, indignant, and she'd sworn she'd break his arm. He'd believed she'd do it—he believed it yet—and so, though he'd have told if they'd asked him straight out, nobody asked and, ashamed of himself, he *had* kept her secret. He remembered how she'd flounced. She'd been a beauty in those days. Young gentlemen came flocking like dogs around a bitch in heat. And he remembered how she'd sing dirty songs in the kitchen when she was taking her bath, songs their parents didn't know were dirty, though *he* did, because she'd explained them to him, teasing him with sex the way she teased all the others:

I have a little cat, and I'm very fond of that,
But I never had a bow-wow-wow!

Washing her armpit, she'd raise her arm so that her
titty showed, and knowing he was watching she'd roll
her eyes at him and wink. Their mother had had some
sense of it. "James," she'd snap as if the whole thing
was his fault—he was five, maybe six—"get out there
and bring in that kindlin!" James Page's face was burning now, less at his old sister's treachery than at his
own pure damn stupidity. Lucky he hadn't known it
when he chased her up the stairs with the fireplace
log. He'd've popped her one certain.

"That's nothin," Merton said. He sighted down the
hole in his beer bottle.

James' heart was hammering, painful.

Stumpchurch slept on.

Sam Frost took a breath, looked sadly at the ceiling.
"Little woman was in charge of the fund raisin for
the Republican Potty," he said, and sighed again.
"Called you up for help and it was Sally answered."

"Go on," James said. His legs began to tremble.

"Said you want home," Sam Frost said, mournful.
"It want the truth. Little woman could hear you hollerin
in the background."

"She wouldn't do that," James said, eyes bugging.

Sam looked at the table. "Mebby not, mebby not.
Mebby the little woman heard wrong."

James Page turned his head away, shudders running
over him like electric shocks. The Graham boy had
his arm around the taller girl, his hand half an inch
below her breast. "You know what I'd really like?"
he said.

"What would you?" she said.

"I'd really like—" He moved up his hand. "I'd
really like—"

"We're from different worlds, my darling," she said,
and closed her eyes.

Bill Partridge lit his pipe. "Sister of mine did a thing
like that, I'd shoot her," he said.

359

James Page had no slightest intention of shooting his sister when he started up the mountain, though he did have—teeth chattering, legs and arms atremble—the fixed intention of knocking the door down and belting her one.

Driving wasn't easy. The truck kept wandering all over the road, lighting up weeds and trees and fences first on one side, then on the other, and the wind hurled leaves and twigs at his windshield—the rain had stopped, for the time being—and every now and then a gust would catch hold of the truck and throw it sharply toward the ditch. He hung onto the steering wheel with all his might, his left foot riding the clutch, his right foot unsteadily pumping the accelerator, and he kept one eye squeezed tightly shut since the wine, besides souring his stomach and giving him a headache, made him see things in twos. For all his difficulty staying on the road, he was driving so fast he scared himself. The road leaped toward him as if the truck were doing ninety, and once when he went off the shoulder he cried out, yet he refused to slow down, driven on by anger, merely spit to the left and clenched his teeth all the harder and hung on more tightly to the steering wheel. Just past the Crawfords place a motorcycle all at once came out of nowhere, roaring straight at him, so frightening the old man that his hair stood on end. He jerked the steering wheel and plunged off the road on the right-hand side, throwing up leaves left and right like snow, then jerked back just before he came to a tree and shot clear over off the left-hand side—the motorcycle wobbled crazily, slid, shot by him, then righted and steadied itself and roared on down the mountain—and in the nick of time the old man jerked the wheel again and got back onto the road unharmed, or almost unharmed, the left front headlight cocked at an angle, the fender acrumple from snapping off a post. "God damn son of a bitch!" he screamed, and he was shaking from head to foot, yet even now he drove faster than he dared, like a man gone insane.

It was a warning he should have heeded. On the hairpin curve half a mile from his house he gave a hard jerk to the steering wheel and nothing happened—rain had made the concrete pavement slick—and as if in slow-motion he saw the guardrail coming, white as old bone, and with his heart in his mouth, spitting to his left and yelling "Shit, shit, *shit!*" he felt himself going over, the guardrail parting like papier-mâché, and knew that, incredibly, it was curtains. Whether he was thrown from the truck or blown from it when it hit and exploded he would never know; all he knew was that when he came to, blinking, the truck was noisily burning, fifty feet below him, farther down the mountain, and he was sitting, with no damage but a bleeding nose, some bruises and cuts, in the crotch of an apple tree. He was still sitting there, whimpering and swearing—it was raining again, and cold as December—when Sally's minister and the black-eyed Mexican came and found him.

"Good God," the minister said, not swearing but expressing a firm belief, shining the flashlight up into his eyes as if he were an owl on a rafter, "it's a miracle!"

"Miracle my God damn ath," he said, crying. "Pure luck." He felt his mouth with his hand and realized he'd lost his teeth.

The priest was laughing—standing there with his arms hanging down, black eyes glittering from the glow of the fire—laughing at him. "Good luck or bad?" he said. When he thought back to it, later, James Page could see that the Mexican had meant no real harm by it. He must've looked a sight, sitting there in the rain with his shoes off—where they'd gone he had no idea—his false teeth missing, scratches going out from his mouth like a clown's painted frown. Still laughing, the Mexican reached up toward him as his

361

father had done, more than two-thirds of a century ago, inviting him to jump. "I can manage," he said angrily, but found he could not and, in spite of himself, took help.

When he was on the ground, standing in the ice-cold wet in his socks, tears still streaming down his face, he stared at the fire, his jaw working, his legs so trembly he could barely stand up, and saw his whole life there, going up in flames. "Damn truck want even paid for," he wailed.

"Oh come on now, James," Sally's minister said, "that truck's as old as I am!"

"Want *paid* for, I told you," he said, turning on the man, enraged.

"Well, you're still alive. That's all that counts."

"Ith it?" he yelled. "Ith it? *Ith it?* We'll *thee* about that!"

What he meant by it the blind fools had no idea. They understood merely that the accident had made him temporarily crazy, as indeed it had, he himself would know later. What he meant was that his heart had gone black as pitch, and for good reason: the truck was uninsured. He'd worked all his life like a God damn slave and he was poor as a churchmouse, too poor to buy insurance for a God damn used truck, and sick and old and full of pain besides; all that had once made him think life worthwhile was gone, vanished as if it never had been: he'd killed his own first-born miserable son and would have shot himself then if it hadn't been that others were dependent on him; and these smug, rich preachers could stand looking down at his life on fire, stand there in their God damn shiny shoes and their citified suitcoats, immigrants both of them—one of them for sure—living off their wholly fictitious God and the fat of the land, laughing while his God damn life burned up, and above them on the road people gawking like his ruin was a sideshow at the fair, carlights and a blue police-car flasher lighting up the mountain and the cemetery perched among the trees above, stones just the color of the guardrail he'd smashed—under every tombstone the

remains of some poor, once-unhappy human being—
think of it! think of it!—a thousand, thousand ceme-
teries, and under every stone in every one, some poor
damn bastard who'd lived a life of, for the most part,
misery, lied to and cheated and teased by false hopes
. . . What he meant was: he had decided to shoot his
sister.

The Mexican said, "Let me carry you, Mr. Page.
It's steep and you've got no shoes on."

Ed Thomas yelled down from the road, "Is he all
right?"

The minister waved. "He's fine! Few little cuts."

The Mexican was squatting like a frog-monster so
James Page could climb up onto his back.

"I'm fine!" the old man yelled crazily, waving his
trembling, boneless arms, his blue eyes aglitter, on fire
with hatred: "I'm fine!"

4

They drew back from him in horror, eyes and mouths
wide open, squeezing toward the edges of the kitchen.
Estelle, at the table, unable to get up, yelled, "Oh!
Oh!" Her canes went clattering to the floor.

The Mexican squinted, more Indian than ever; all
you could see inside his eyeslits was midnight black.
"Mr. Page," he said, "give me the gun."

"Dad," Ginny said, "for the love of Christ!"

He stood firm, except shaking like a thrashing machine, shaking so badly he was afraid he'd pull the
trigger by accident. He went on swinging the shotgun
from side to side, warning them back, the whole room
red, as if his eyes were full of blood. He was breathing hard and his lips were puffy, and his voice was
so high he might have thought it was somebody else
yelling. "Get out! Get out of my houth! All of you!"

"Mr. Page," the Mexican said, taking a step toward
him.

He jerked the gun up to his shoulder and aimed it straight at him. "You take one more thtep, you greathy bathtahd, and I'll blow off your black-eyed head."

The Mexican considered and decided to believe him.

"Dad, for Christ's sake," Ginny wailed, "you're crazy!" She had her arms around Dickey, who stood staring wide-eyed as if his lids were frozen open.

"He's not crazy," Ruth Thomas said, "he's drunk."

"Don't push him," Sally's minister commanded, stretching his arms out to each side as if to keep the others back. "He's had a terrible experience. Once he's calmed down—"

Ed Thomas stood gulping for air, clutching his chest and groaning.

"Dear heavenly father," Estelle whispered, violently trembling, "it's all my fault!"

"What's the matter?" the Phelps girl said, opening the door a little and timidly jumping, trying to see in.

"Stay outside," someone barked.

Lewis Hicks said, "Get all the kids outside. Dickey, get outside!"

"I haven't got my coat on," Dickey said.

"You get outside, you little bastard," Ginny hissed, pushing him. Then, to her father: "Dad, what's the *matter* with you?"

"Nothin the matter with me," he yelled, forgetting and swinging his eyes in her direction, then instantly snapping them back to the Mexican, the only one in the room he was afraid of.

"You should all go outside," the Mexican said. He spoke without moving his eyes from James' face, peering intently as if to see into the old man's mind. "You people go," he said. "Go quickly. Lane and I will stay and talk with him."

"Nobodyth thtayin," James yelled. "Partyth ovah!"

Lewis Hicks took a step toward him, and James swung the gun more or less in his direction.

"I'm just gonna try and help Estelle," Lewis said. He looked at James, making sure the words registered, then continued over to the table to help her get up.

The Mexican moved his hand and James swung the gun at him, fast. With his left hand James groped toward the table to knock off the plates and jack-o-lanterns, making sure Lewis got no ideas.

"Will you put away that gun if we leave?" Ruth asked. She was drawn up to her full height, and her eyes bulged with indignation, firing daggers.

"I already told you what I'm gonna do," he yelled. "I'm gonna kill Thally." He turned his head and yelled up the stairs, "You hear that, Thally? I'm gonna kill you." He laughed, fake-crazy—or so he intended it. No one but the old man had any doubts that he was crazy.

"Then we're staying," Ruth said.

There was a moment's silence. Then Dr. Phelps said, "That's not a good idea, Ruth. You better think about your husband."

She jerked her head around and saw how Ed was clutching his chest and struggling to get breath.

"My God!" she whispered, and turned her face back to James. She'd gone white. "You fucker!" she said in icy rage. "You *fucker!*" The gun would not have stopped her if she'd decided to come at him. He could have emptied both barrels right into her heart and still, before she was stopped, she'd have torn out his windpipe. But Ruth was moving in the other direction, toward Ed. "DeWitt!" she screamed, "come help me!" The kitchen door opened, shoving against people, and DeWitt was there, as ashen as the rest of them, staring at James. He helped Dr. Phelps and Ruth Thomas get Ed out the door. Others were moving toward the door now. He encouraged them, wagging the shotgun. Soon he was alone with Lane Walker and the Mexican.

"You too," he said. "Out!"

They stood six feet apart, the minister by the door, the priest over by the sink.

Reasonably, gently, the Mexican said, "How will you shoot us both if we jump you the same time?"

"You won't," he said, and smiled. "I'll tell you why. If you jump me, I'm gonna fire at you firtht,

365

Meckthican." He jerked his left thumb at Lane Walker. "It'll be the thame ath if he pulled the trigger."

"Foxy old bastard, ain't he," Lane said.

Out in the yard, a car started up, taking Ed Thomas to the hospital, perhaps, or going for the troopers. He'd never have a chance with just a shotgun against pistols and rifles. He saw in his mind's eye that picture on TV, the truck driver's head exploding when the policeman shot him, and the rage that had begun to flag was back full force.

"Get out," he said. "I got no more time."

Lane Walker looked up at the ceiling, in the direction of Sally's room. "Sally?" he called. There was no answer, and he called again. This time she called back, "I hear you."

"Sally, can you get your bed in front of the door till this maniac calms down? Can you block the door?"

There was no answer.

The minister called, "Did you hear me, Sally?"

After a moment she called, "I hear you."

"Can you do it? He's got a gun."

Again, no answer.

"Thath enough," James snapped. "Get out. I'll count to five. One!"

They hesitated, looking at each other.

"Two!"

"I think he means business," the Mexican said. "Even if he doesn't, by *five* he'll have psyched himself into it." He was looking around as if for something to throw. But his lip was trembling. For the first time, James Page understood that the man was scared to death.

"Three!" he said.

"What good will it do?" Lane Walker said. He was sweating like a blacksmith, and his voice was a whine.

"Four!"

"All right, all right!" the Mexican yelled, almost a squeal. He made a dash for the door. Lane Walker spun around like a basketball player, snatching at the doorknob, and was out ahead of him.

366

"Five!" he screamed, and for pure manic glee he let loose at the top of the door as it slammed shut behind them.

Up in her bedroom, Sally screamed.

5

"It's happened, Horace," Sally said. "You always predicted it would and now it has. He's gone crazy."

She'd screamed in terror when the gun had gone off, but she was over that now. Which one of them he'd killed there was no telling—she hoped not Ginny, not Dickey, not Estelle or Ruth, though she might not mind if it was what's-his-name (again when the old woman tried to think of the name of Ginny's husband, all that would come was that character in her novel, Mr. Nit). After her scream at the sound of the shot, her first full recognition that he indeed meant to kill her, a strange calm had descended on her, and if someone had been there to see her as she set about her preparations—for a plan had come to her—he might have been amazed at how tranquil she was, how logically her mind worked, how her movements and gestures were almost queenly.

Sally Abbott could say truthfully that she had never in her life been afraid of death, though she minded pain and was glad to know her death, if her plan failed, would be a quick one. Nor did she hesitate to admit to herself that, if her death must be by violence, she was glad to have her friends and relations out there, sitting in their cars, anxiously looking up through the rain toward her window, witnessing it. She'd always had, she knew—and Horace had often mentioned—a truly outrageous theatrical streak. Born in another time and place, she might well have been a Broadway actress. She'd been beautiful in her youth, she had photographs to prove it—though with a beauty not fashionable in the present age. She'd worn ringlets

367

and high-necked, floor-length dresses, and had been forced, for the most part, to play demure, though she knew tricks, never doubt it, tricks with her hands, with her eyes and eyelashes, tricks of posture and of voice. Oh Lord but she might have been a wanton, as her father would say, if she'd only had the luck to be born in her own proper time! She regretted now that she hadn't been a good deal more wanton than she was. Years and years ago, when she was seventeen, and the juices flowing so that sometimes she had thought she would simply faint . . . well, never mind. She had had her good times, there was no denying it, though never such times as she might have had. What she wouldn't give to be growing up now, when a girl might go anywhere she pleased and do anything she liked! Those things in that novel, now, how incredible to realize that they were all, in a sense, true! Hundreds of people smoked pot every day, though she'd never gotten a chance to—she could count herself lucky she'd got a bit of sherry!—and hundreds of people had sex orgies. She'd read stories in magazines, seen movies and plays on television. There were even special magazines that brought "adventuresome adults" together—magazines kept locked behind the counter in grim old Vermont. She, Sally Abbott, had missed all that, such were the cruel mechanics of the universe, as her novel would say. Her body—once so beautiful that when she stood in her bedroom, gazing in the mirror, she had thought it tragic that she must cover it with clothes, deny it to men's eyes—that once lovely body was withered away to pure horror now, and virtually unused, unexploited. Not, heaven knows, that she was dissatisfied with her life with Horace, in general. But to think that she had never had the chance to make love with a single, solitary other man, except the Beeman boy—and that (she had to smile) hardly counted. She'd waited too long—it was out in the granary beyond the cowbarn (torn down long since) —and before he could even get it out and into her he'd gone off all over himself, poor silly, and was so embarrassed he wouldn't even touch her though she lay there panting and perspiring and almost dying. It had been a ghastly time, those "good old days" she'd grown up in. Walking home from school with the other boys and girls, she'd see a bull mount a cow, or often a cow mount another cow, and she must stare like an idiot at the ground and say nothing—even if some boy made so bold as to mention it—must bury her talents, hide her light under a bushel. She might have made up for it. She might have had a lover almost anytime she pleased, if she'd chosen to. There had always been attractive young men available— Horace's assistants, people who made deliveries, neighbors, friends—even Estelle's handsome Ferris. He'd eyed her more than once, don't think he hadn't, and she'd smiled, head tilted, not exactly saying "yes" but certainly not saying "watch yourself, buster!"—considering the matter from every angle, watching developments; and in the end, for Estelle's sake, or so she'd always told herself—but more likely, she thought now, because she was tyrannized in a world of unwitting male chauvinists and old fashioned jealous wives—she had neglected to bring that suggestion in the air to a reality. No one was troubled with such scruples nowadays, not the youngsters, anyway. She thought of the party in San Francisco that was mentioned in the book. Incredibly enough, there *were* such parties; one heard of them often, or anyway read of them in magazines. And perhaps there had always been such parties, if it came to that. Ancient Rome, France, England . . . She'd read something somewhere about a Prime Minister in England, many years ago, who'd even had orgies with young boys. Even United States Presidents did it—all of them, probably, except possibly Wilson. Certainly Grover Cleveland and John F. Kennedy, probably Teddy Roosevelt— she'd heard something of the sort, if she wasn't mistaken—and didn't Thomas Jefferson have a beautiful Negro mistress whose name was Sally? God bless you, Sally, she thought, casting her blessing back through time, and smiled. She'd always liked Jefferson—she and Horace had visited Monticello once, and Horace,

369

as usual, had taken wonderful slides. She hoped Thomas Jefferson's Sally was very, very dark, and beautiful and kind. "Would you have minded terribly, Horace?" she whispered to the bedroom's shadows, and thought sadly, "Yes, you would." Well, never mind. The lives she might have lived, the lovers and children she might have had (Horace had gone through World War I and was afraid to have children; the world was, he thought, too dark a place), the career she might have had as an actress on the stage, or even as a prostitute in New Orleans—why not? why not? the young people were right!—she'd missed them all for all eternity, and no use regretting it. Horace had dozens of women, he'd told her. Prostitutes in France. It had hurt her terribly, fool that she'd been. She was glad for him now. Perhaps even then what she'd felt, really, was that his having prostitutes and her having no one but Horace—dear as he was—was bitterly unfair.

It was curious, now that she noticed it: she hadn't thought of sex in quite some time, and here it was rising in her mind almost as strongly as it did when she was young. For that she could thank her trashy novel, and, by heaven, she *did* thank it. Shame was for old biddies! The reawakening was not just in her mind, in fact. Her whole body felt younger, sexually aglow, the girl rediscovering herself in the dry old woman.

There was very little time, but she moved without hurry, climbing the attic stairs, feeling for the string that turned the light on. She groped and groped and was beginning to think it must have broken when at last, lower than she'd expected, it came to her fingers. When she'd turned the light on she continued to the top and crossed, still unhurried, to the apples. One of the crates was less than half full and she picked it up then, changing her mind, set it down on the floor to drag it. It scraped quietly to the top of the stairs and—without hurry, as if time were in the hands of some invisible guardian who would not allow James to move till she

370

was ready—she managed to get the crate down, stair by stair, and over near the foot of the bed.

Now things became more difficult. She stood at the door a moment, listening. He was still in the bathroom. Noises of his going to the toilet came to her, and sometimes a groan—poor old bastard! She saw in the mirror that she was smiling. On the way to the bed she paused and glanced out the window. The cars were still there. "Good," she said aloud. Some of them were running, her friends trying to keep warm, no doubt. The rain was drizzling steadily, now and then shaken by a gust. Surely any moment the police would arrive. She hoped they did of course, yet in this mysterious state of serenity she didn't really care— perhaps she even, with a part of her mind, had a hope that they'd arrive too late.

The bed, fortunately, was on castors, and though it was heavy, and though the floor was slopy and the boards where they butted together not even, she managed to get it to a foot from the door, where, when the time came, she could stand on it. She lifted the applecrate up onto the bed, listened again, then unlocked the door, opened it almost to the bed, put a pair of shoes against it to keep it there, and stood back to inspect. It would do.

Carefully, still feeling the mysterious serenity, she climbed up onto the bed. It was almost impossible, as she'd known it would be, to stand up on the bed and lift the applecrate to the top of the door—it would be something, she thought, if she fell and broke her neck!—but at last, by some miracle, she managed it. Slowly, slowly, as when you put the top block on a tower of blocks, she drew her hands away from each side of the crate. It sat firm, though precarious, tilted from the top of the doorframe—the summerbeam— to the door, and, even when she'd lowered herself to the bed again, it did not fall. She got out of the bed and carefully rolled it to its place against the wall. She smiled. In the mirror above the desk, it seemed to her, she looked positively young.

"Now the lamp," she said. She looked out the window. The cars were still there; no police car.

She moved the white wicker table over to behind the door, where James wouldn't see it and the crate might possibly fall on it if it didn't fall on James, and where in any case the door would bump it when he came barging in; then she went to the washstand for the kerosene lamp. It was nearly full, and the wick was white and new, rising from the brass and sinking into the clean glass bowl. As she picked it up, to carry it to the table, she realized, with a gasp, that she had no matches. At once, all her serenity fell away. She had a vision, clear as a nightmare, of James raising the gun to aim at her, his eyes not human. There would be a thunderous crash that rocked the room— "Oh dear God," she whispered. Her heart was like a hot potato, pounding just behind her throat. She set down the lamp and hurried around the table to the dresser and opened the top draw, then the next and the next. No matches! She looked around wildly, trying to think, then remembered the desk. Of course. Ginny sometimes slept in this room, and Ginny would certainly have matches, she couldn't be without a cigarette two minutes.

She tugged at the front of the desk. It seemed to be locked. She stared at the keyhole in disbelief, then tugged again. Nothing. She turned, listening, imagining she'd heard a footstep, but she'd been wrong, he was still in the bathroom—silent now. Still on the potty? She tugged again. The desk was locked. Then her mind cleared and she realized that for Ginny, too, it would be locked, so the matches must be somewhere else. She pulled at the handles of the desk's top draw. It slid out so easily she almost fell down, and there, lo and behold!, lay a dozen paper matchbooks. She snatched one up and without even closing the draw went back to the lamp on the table. It lit easily, at the first match. She adjusted the wick, then balanced the lamp on the edge of the table, so that the first good bump would send it crashing to the floor. She straightened and looked up at the applecrate—still motionless and dark, waiting for him—and nodded to herself, satisfied.

She knew, of course, that the plan had its risks. She refused to allow herself to think of them. If the applecrate fell on him it would probably kill him, or at very least knock him unconscious; but if he looked up before he came in, and saw it, or if it fell and missed, well, that would be tally-ho Sally, and James not dead with her! So she had no choice but to back up the crate with the kerosene firetrap, and pray that when they saw the flames, if she couldn't get out past them, they'd come and save her. Perhaps they wouldn't, of course, for fear of James' gun . . . She wouldn't think about it. She had lived a full life, a long one anyway. The plan was the only hope she had; it wouldn't fail her; it couldn't. It was like a gift from heaven—not her own plan at all but something that had come out of nowhere, like the plan Peter Wagner had had about knocking off his enemies with eels, in her novel. Not that she wasn't sorry—as Peter Wagner had been—to have to do it. But the world was full of violence these days, nobody even thought twice about it. It wasn't *she* who'd started this war. It was *his* tyranny that started it; *she* was willing enough to live and let live. It was just as Horace had always said, "Enemies in war, in peace friends." Even if it was no one's fault really, she must do what she must. That was simply how she was.

She sat on the edge of the bed, listening. Still no hint of a sound from James! She looked out the window, leaning close to the pane to see better. The cars were still there. By the road there was movement and, squinting hard over the tops of her glasses, she was able to make out a boy and a girl, walking in the rain, holding hands. She stepped from the window, checked her death-trap one more time, then decided she needed to use the bedpan. She pulled the window-shade down and squatted above the pan. Her bowels were like water and made a terrible stink—and there was no place to put the mess, she realized in dismay: she could hardly throw it out the window with her friends all watching. She thought and thought, then carried the pan up to the attic.

When she came down again, bringing with her two apples, which she tossed into the bed, there was still no sign of James. She stood very still, listening, baffled, but there was nothing, no sound in all the house, only the rumble of rain on the attic roof and the howl of wind and then, very faint in the distance, a siren. She hurried to the window. She had, for an instant, an impression that the ghost was back, watching the house from the mailbox, but there was no one. The siren grew louder. A car door opened and someone got out, Ginny's husband, Nit. He went up to stand by the mailbox and wait. Lights appeared down the road and then the state police car was sweeping in, stopping so suddenly it rocked, and the trooper who was driving leaned his head out. He and Mr. Nit talked; she couldn't hear the voices. After a while the police car pulled in farther and parked among the other cars. They just sat there, watching the house, not doing a thing.

According to the onyx clock it was three in the morning. She realized, seeing the time, that she was tired, sick-tired, but not sleepy. Even though it was way up in the attic, and behind the closed attic door, she could smell that bedpan. It was the bedpan, she realized, that she ought to have propped over the door to fall on James.

Smiling like the wicked old witch she was—or so, that moment, she described herself—she got herself into her bed with her trashy book.

Unbeknownst to Sally, though she ought to have guessed, James sat fast asleep on the toilet, his bowels still hard as a Pharaoh's heart, despite the little burst that had brought him here, his trousers at his ankles and his shotgun leaning against the wall.

Down in the yard the Mexican was saying—holding a newspaper over his head to keep the rain off— "What do you think?"

The older of the state policemen shook his head.

"Hate to go in shootin if the man's changed his mind."

"Then again," the younger policeman said, "time we hear somethin it might be too late."

"That's true," the older one said but didn't move. He looked around at the cars. "You people might's well go on home, I guess. No use sittin here in the weather."

"I'll stay," Virginia Hicks called, "I'm his daughter."

"We'll stay too, if you don't mind," Lane Walker said. "I'm a minister. My friend here is a priest."

"Suit yourself," the state policeman said.

The younger one was writing with a ball-point pen. What he was writing on had pages and pages, an inch or more of them clamped together by a black binder.

The Mexican leaned toward the window, trying to see. "That some kind of a report?" he asked.

The older policeman grinned. "Naw," he said. "Damn kid's workin on a *book*."

Sally, up in her room, read:

12

THE PRICE OF PEARL

On the second day after she'd lost track of him, Pearl Wilson slipped her key into Dr. Alkahest's apartment door as she'd done a hundred times before that (the elevator stood open behind her, the grated, shuffling little room peculiarly humble in the presence of the entryhall's cool white walls, the cobalt blue curtains; it had the look of a servant waiting politely, secretly scornful), and as soon as she'd pressed the apartment door open half an inch she knew there was something terrible inside. She hesitated, half expecting the door to be snatched out of her hands and the thing inside, what-

375

ever it was, to snatch her wrist and jerk her inward. Nothing happened. The rational part of her mind moved over the question with careful antennae while the rest conjured demons: Sundayschool horrors and newspaper horrors (she had read last night of a rape that had happened in one of the federal office buildings, and she had suffered then, as she suffered now, in the jungle-shadowy back of her mind, the flame of the intruder's breath, the blue-white fire of his nails and teeth).

She closed her eyes, took a breath. If anything terrible was waiting in the room it would be a man in a suit, legs crossed at the knee, a notebook, a gold ball-point pen. That was the shape things ominous took in apartments like this one.

All this time Pearl stood erect, prim—except for the closed eyes, the intake of breath, no sign of her panic on her face: a lovely young black, perhaps twenty-seven, in a fine, moderately expensive brown coat from Macy's, loosely belted, a discreet brown hat with a vermilion feather three inches long, brown stockings, brown, Italian shoes that perfectly matched her purse, her hat, her gloves. Her form was magnificent, her face like a carving, not soft and pliable but elegant, poised. Her lips were full and sharply lined, undecorated. Her lashes, natural, were finer and darker than Japanese black silk. One might have wondered, peeking out at her in what she took for the empty entryhall, "Where does such a creature belong?" In some university, perhaps, regally poised at her student desk in a red dress open at the neck, narrow V'd, taking notes in her round hand on history or literature or microbes; but Pearl had done badly at State and had quit—though her speech was faultless and she liked to read, she'd gotten C's in English, even worse in math—and she never wore red.

In some shop then? Some nifty gentlewomen's shoppe like the ones where she bought her shoes, her brown silk scarf? But Pearl had tried that. Her mind would click off while the supervisor was speaking with her, and in a moment she would see, as if from infinitely far away, the fat little woman's lips shaking, her tiny blue eyes unnaturally light, one fat pink hand pressed to her heart. "Girl, why you got to be so uppidy?" her mother used to wail when she was still alive. Pearl would walk away. She wasn't uppity. She knew what was deserved and what was not—knew, exactly to the penny, her worth.

So she cleaned house like a Nubian slave, though a born princess, because the money was good, so that she could live in approximately the way she wished—could buy records and books, new clothes for church, an occasional lithograph, reproductions of paintings—could keep up the noble old traditions she in fact had never known. If traditions made you safe, gave stability, identity—or at least the illusion of secure identity—she would be safe, though she knew there was no safety, finally. She'd had a friend once, a young minister. He had taken his religion seriously—had taken it to the streets, to the druggies, the drunks and small-time thieves. But it was expensive and, besides, unseemly, taking religion to the ugly and fierce; religion was community, and they preyed on community. Soon he'd found he had behind him only his beliefs, no church. His beliefs had changed. He had seemed to her once beautiful and vulnerable, the two inextricable in his character, or perhaps the beauty *was* the vulnerability. If she were to meet him now, she knew, she would be afraid of him.

Still there had come no sound from the room. Strong as it was, she dismissed the intuition and opened the apartment door wide.

Nothing was changed. If he'd been back while she was away, he'd left no sign. The gray-white monkscloth curtains were drawn, making the place a crypt. She opened them, then opened the window a crack to get rid of the scent of —what? Without removing her coat, as if the intuition she'd dismissed was still with her, she walked through the never-used dining room to the kitchen. There was nothing changed there either: no sign that he'd eaten or even entered the place. Yet she hesitated, troubled by an inexplicable sense that, once again, the jungle had inched closer. She caught that smell again, like escaping gas, and knew even before she checked the range that that was not where it came from. Moving quickly all at once, she went back into the dining room and opened the bathroom door. She caught her breath. On the white sink, the white formica top beside it, there were black handprints. She shot a look behind her, but the dining room was empty. "Jesus," Pearl whispered. There was a towel on the floor, black and horrible, and the room was full of a smell like rottenness. Worse. There were smudges of filth on the floor too, and on the bathtub and toilet. She knew now what the black stuff was, though the word escaped her. Was the creature still here. Her roommate would be at work, not reachable till five. She remembered then the telephone number in her purse. Leonard had insisted that she take it, his neighbor's number; they knew where to get him if she needed him. "Phone up, now," he'd said, urgent yet casual, like the boyfriend in one of those sunlit, big-city horror films. "No jive, baby. Phone up." She felt better, as if the phone number were Leonard himself, curled up snug in her purse ready to leap out into the room with a howl of *Banzai!* to defend her.

Because of the confidence the number gave her, she hurried to the bedroom, where a worse

surprise awaited her. The bed, not slept in, had
black stains on it, and on the carpet beside it
lay a black pile of clothes. She only looked at
first, steadying herself on the doorframe. Then
she bent down to touch the mess, and the word
suddenly popped into her mind: *sewer*. He'd
fallen in the sewer, or someone had thrown
him there, then brought him back, for some
reason, and changed his clothes, or else he'd
crawled back himself—or, no, hired someone
to carry him—and he'd changed and returned
to—wherever—without a word. Before she knew
she'd do it she had slipped her gloves off and
was going through his pockets, gritty outside,
slimy inside. Everything was gone but a few
slips of dirt blackened paper. She took them
to the bathroom and held them, one by one,
under the faucet. The first was a note in ink,
and whatever it said went down the pipes to
the darkness it came from. The second was a
note in pencil. She set it on the windowledge
to dry a little. The third was a sales receipt
which she didn't even finish cleaning when she
saw that it was nothing. She looked again at
the pencil note. *The Indom* (something) *off
mexico lost souls r.*

In the elevator she suddenly changed her
mind and pressed the button that would take
her up, not down. She felt unreal, a little wild,
like the heroine in a scary movie. The door
closed and she felt the sudden lift that would
take her to the tower. The first thing she saw
when the elevator opened was that the gin
cupboard was ajar. It was someone else, then,
she thought, and they had robbed him. Her
skin prickled as it always did when she was
reminded of the intruder, and she clenched her
fists.

But the black metal box was still there—
though some of the gin was gone, several bot-

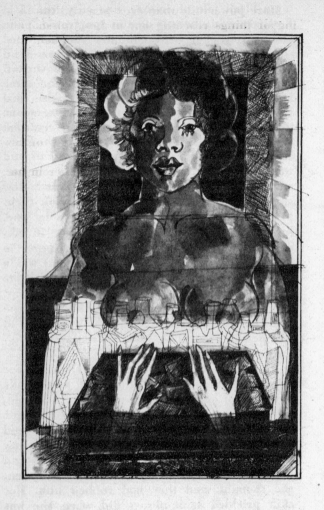

tles. She lifted the box and it was heavy, the money still inside, or certainly most of it.

More powerfully than ever, she had the feeling of things reaching out at her, misshapen, pale as a flicker of witchcraft. She held the box in her two hands. He was gone, perhaps dead, perhaps sunk to some mad depravity of drugs. Gone, in any case, abandoning the house, the sunlit world of rooftops, chimneys, the double spires in the distance. And she too was abandoned, then, who cleaned for him, who said nothing of his eccentricities, the scent of his flesh and gin, his wine and oysters.

She thought of the telephone number in her purse. Leonard could advise her, Leonard with his kind and vulnerable eyes, his ridiculous street-talk, his darkie shuffle. He would know what to do. His very normalness would save her. But it flashed through her mind that in the big cheap building where they had lived—ten, twelve people in one apartment—Beverly Hollander had gone to the basement with Leonard More, sometimes to the roof, so people said . . . Her mind went blank. There were books above the gin cupboard, dark green leather bindings, *The Complete Works of Chas. Dickens.* A title caught her eye, *The Pickwick Papers*, a book she'd read, and for an instant she saw an English landscape clearly, as if she'd really been there, and a huge old lumbering carriage, old gentlemen laughing.

She turned, looked out the window. The lines of the houses were as clean and precise as the hands of clocks, and the streets moved over the hills like well-planned arguments. She moved closer to the window, narrowing her eyes, her face prickling. It was Saturday, but there was no sign of life in the house where the herd of hippies lived. Asleep, probably—tangled together on their filthy mattresses. She hated them, drunkards and carriers of disease, yet at the thought of them lying there together like lost children, bare arms draped off the mattress-sides, no decent food, in the drawer where the silverware should be, guns and gun-parts, she felt a pang, not sorrow for them specially but for all lost lives, all wrecked souls past feeling pain.

The metal box in her hands was warm, as if the money inside it were on fire. The street directly below her was black with new asphalt, black and warm, beautiful in the sun, like a huge sleeping serpent that meant no harm. She strained to think. She stared at the street as if waiting for the blackness to explain itself, alive in the sunlight, warm and regular, maybe deep-rooted as a desert tree, reaching down like a fist into the earth. But no—

She would steal the money. That was what was lurking in her mind, she knew: the thought watching her, biding its time like a lion in high grass. There was enough to last her a lifetime, and in a way she had a right to it. Whether he was dead right now or not, he was a dead man. On some mad whim he'd stepped off the path of the possible, and he'd left no other heir. It would save her, unprotected as she was, alone, without any vow to keep and no one to keep to any vow.

The sharp-lined roofs in the sunlight were like dusty jewels. Houses in the distance were as wealthy white as houses on a travel poster. A face, gray like a fish, appeared at a window in the hippie house, then vanished again as if swallowed. She remembered, for no reason—unless it was the white wisp of smoke in the distance—the scent of garbage burning. Christ was crucified in a city dump, someone had told her. In church? She saw the three crosses rising shadowy blue, out of blue-gray smoke. The small crowd coughed, moved back. Red flame-less fire seeped out of mounds near the tilting, shaggy crosses. Christ's death was an accident, someone had told her. They mistook him for a politician.

Her eyes narrowed as if offended, and she touched her lower lip lightly with her upper teeth. She replaced the box, closed the cupboard, and carefully drew on her gloves.

Mr. Fiorenzi sat in his gray suit, wringing his soft hands and shaking his head. "This is terrible," he said. "And how terrible for you! How terrible you must feel."

Just perceptibly, for politeness, Pearl nodded.

"And here just a day or two ago," Mr. Fiorenzi continued, his amazement growing, "there he sat, right where you're sitting, more or less." He looked at the little piece of cardboard she'd given him. "Can I keep this?" he said.

"You can copy it, if you want," she said. "I need it."

"Yes of course. Good idea!" He hunted through the papers on his desk for a pencil or pen, then opened his drawer. "Damn," he said. He hunted on the top of the desk again and at last found a small green felt-tip. He found his notepad, ran his tongue around his lips, and began to copy the note. She looked over at the flag, the suitcase at the foot of it. She would try Mrs. Waggoner again, if she ever managed to get away from Mr. Fiorenzi. He was a kind enough man, there was no denying that; it was a pity he couldn't be, also, a little competent.

"There!" he said, "that's got it." He pushed back his chair and stood up, came around the desk, and handed her the note she'd found at Dr. Alkahest's.

"Thank you," she said, and dropped the note into her coinpurse. She stood up.

There was a gap of several pages. The novel resumed:

. . . Waggoner was out but would be back in
ten minutes; they'd have her return the call.
Pearl waited for an hour, then gave up.

"Lady," the Commissioner said, "you're
wasting my time. I talked with your employer
myself just three, four days ago. I grant you
he's interested in the drug problem, that much
is true. Lot of people are, these days. Popular
issue." He blew out smoke and sucked for air.
"But as to his being snuffed, or tied up with—"
he laughed, then coughed, still laughing, then
smoked again, and coughed. His face was so
fat it made his eyes want to shut.

But Pearl had waited forever to see him, had
refused to go away, and though he waved
toward the door, coughing too hard to be able
to dismiss her, she sat tight, stiffly erect in her
chair, knees clamped together, brown purse
in her lap. As if for help, she stared at the
collection on the gray-green wall behind him.
She opened the purse then and drew out the clip
of paper she'd found. He merely looked at it,
not reaching for it, forcing her to rise partly
out of her chair to hand it to him. *Racist*, she
thought, and felt better.

"Look here," he said, "got no time for this."
He glanced at the paper, dismissed it.

"Read it," she said.

He scowled, a man to whom respect was due.
But he read it, then jerked it closer and read
it again. He reached for the telephone and
dialed a number, at the same time calling to
the man in the reception room. "Sergeant
Mawkin!"

"Yes sir?" the man said, behind her.

"Hold this woman, and get me State Narcotics."

"What charge, sir?" Mawkin said.

"Suspicion," he said. He looked cross-eyed into the telephone receiver. "Hello? Hello?"

"Suspicion of what?"

"Murder!" the Commissioner squealed, "Murder One!—And just between you and me, it's drug related."

The Commissioner, though not a soft-hearted man, was competent.

She was half out of her chair, reaching toward his desk. "What do you mean? What are you saying?"

"Lady, you come in here with this cocka-mamie story about a citizen's duty and—hee hee!—" His eyes crossed again, snapping back to the telephone receiver. "Hello, Governor?" He sucked in air, blew it out again, leaned back.

13

HOSANNAH! GLORY TO THE HIGHEST!

"Don't let me interrupt you," Dr. Alkahest said. "Whatever you were doing before I arrived, go right ahead with it!" He was so excited he could hardly sit still. The whole volcano basin was filled with potsmoke like a bowl of heaven's grace. He looked around him, twitching, dead knees jerking. Part of the group stood over by the cave-mouth, holding their clothes up in front of them. "Go ahead!" he said, waving, giggling. "Go right ahead! Feel Free!" Handsome young men, a beautiful young maiden . . . Was it possible he'd arrived too late, missed all the fucking? But they were young, yes, wonderful! Surely . . . "I'm here to buy your shit," he cried out.

The bearded black man handed the machine gun to the brown-haired man and went to the flat rock near the fire to snatch up his clothes.

"Who knows you came?" he demanded.

"Not a soul!" Dr. Alkahest said, leaning forward in his chair. "Nobody but the old Negro gentleman who brought me. An old fisherman, he told me. Great silver, woolly head of hair. He's been fishing these waters since nineteen hundred and five." He chuckled. "He's nobody's fool, I can tell you. Charged me two hundred dollars."

"Dusky," Santisillia whispered. Some thought teased his brain . . .

There was another gap in the novel, a dozen or more pages, and Sally stared at it in dismay, reaching out toward the wicker table with her left hand for an apple exactly as Ginny, in distress, would reach for her cigarettes, or Richard, in his last years, would have reached for his glass. It didn't matter to the old woman that she was missing the adventures of Dr. Alkahest. She disliked the character and did not believe in him—recognized him, without knowing the term, as a gothic cliché, one more version of the age-old mad scientist, here put to use for some satirical purpose which she grasped only dimly and felt no sympathy with. But she did feel concern about Dr. Alkahest's cleaning woman, Pearl. Already too much of Pearl's story had been lost to missing pages. How, she wondered, could they accuse Pearl of murder? It made no sense! Sally Abbott of course knew perfectly well that one could not ask too much of a novel, a weightless trifle even in comparison to what was happening right here in this house tonight; but her dismay refused to be driven away by reason. Did all turn out well with Pearl Wilson or didn't it?

As she thought back over the story, hoping to find a clue—knowing that quite possibly it would all be revealed in the part she hadn't read yet, but knowing too that, given all those missing pages, she'd do well to be prepared to catch the slightest hint—she noticed an odd pattern. Pearl Wilson was frightened by animalness, which had gotten mixed up in her mind with movies of African savages with bones in their noses, with the jungle-like quality of her life in the ghetto, and with love. The intruder who'd broken into her apartment had become related in her mind with the white man who'd raped her, until in the end all intrusions, even the innocent words "What's happenin?" were alarming to her. The more Sally Abbott thought about it, glancing back now through the earlier pages, making sure she was right, the more elaborate the pattern became. She doubted that the author had intended it, but that was unimportant; it was definitely there, and vaguely, only half aware that she was doing it, Sally began to muse on it. It was a kind of puzzle, tantalizing because she had a curious feeling that it had crept into the book from the real world, so that to solve it would be to know something—reach some point of wisdom she had perhaps reached already in dim intuition; otherwise why this curious feeling of distress?

There was no one in this world, however mighty of will—her own life was proof—not capable of being robbed, or raped, or murdered, not capable of being attacked from nowhere, for no real reason, by the mindless bestiality of things—her drunken brother with his shotgun. And also there was no one not capable of slipping toward the bestial himself, as Pearl had done when she considered taking the money from Dr. Alkahest, or as the people who frightened Pearl did, stealing or breathing obscenities to some stranger on the phone. It was that—both those things—that made it terrible to be alone: one's potential for becoming an innocent victim, and one's potential for becoming a destroyer. One had to be a kind of mad hero, like Peter Wagner's old uncle with the snowplow, to go it alone, and even he had been a destroyer— though not from bestiality. Was Pearl, then, a hero? —acting all alone, by the highest code she knew, the behavior of women in movies and books, and a version of Christian righteousness? Her way of acting hadn't saved her—unless it was yet to come. Would any heroic way of acting save her? Sally did not believe one bit in the character of the Missing Persons man or in that of the fat Police Commissioner, but she'd lived around James L. Page too long to have complete confidence in regulations, impersonal agencies, officials. Better for Pearl, then, to huddle safe with the ordinary people, better to have phoned Leonard, submitting to commonness, the touch of bestiality in the life she'd escaped. Why not?

She looked hard at the crate above her bedroom door and frowned. *No!,* she thought. As soon say that she, Sally Page Abbott, should come out of her room and let all she had fought for be a joke at her expense and a glory to James because his violence had won! As soon say Horace had been wrong to give Richard support in his rebellion against his father! No, no, no, no siree! But if submission was wrong . . .

She glanced at the page beyond the gap, took a bite from her apple, and uneasily, decided to read on.

. . . life evil. What I mean—when my moment of Conversion came . . ." He jerked his head around, as if he were seeing something strange in the heavens. Mr. Goodman, just about to hand him the pipe, reconsidered, smoking it himself, looking up.

"What's that?" Dr. Alkahest cried out, pointing.

They all had the solid impression, for an instant, that directly above them hung a huge flying saucer. It vanished. "Did you see what *I* saw?" they all said at once. They couldn't believe they'd really seen it. "The pot," they said. "It *must* be." But they talked in hushed voices, awed by a whole new world of possibility.

Dr. Alkahest told them he wanted to buy their pot. Not just a little. All of it.

"Man, you are a gas," Dancer said.

"I'm in earnest, young man," Dr. Alkahest said. "Look." He fumbled with his moneybelt, then dipped his fingertips in and drew out a thousand-dollar bill.

Dancer snatched it, held it over the fire where he could see it. His eyes bugged. "It's real!" He looked from one to another of them. His face became indignant. "What you doin, carrying around thousan' dollar bills? What if I was a thief or somethin? You tryin to lead me to temptation?" He put the money in his pocket.

Dr. Alkahest watched with a startled grin. He'd been robbed—they'd all seen it. Perhaps he'd be beaten—perhaps he'd be stripped and bound and gagged, perhaps even made a human sacrifice. "He he he!" Dr. Alkahest laughed ecstatically. What a place! What a company! No limits!

"Don't laugh," Santisillia said, misunderstanding, "he really is a thief. Grew up in Harlem. Can't help himself. They made him a transom man when he was four."

Dr. Alkahest trembled, dizzy with happiness. The bearded man was a moralist. All the better! "Don't you people have any standards?" he cackled, and crazily flopped his head from side to side. They hadn't yet noticed that he was seated on a cushion of moneybags.

They all looked at him, a little puzzled. Dancer said, as if trying it out, "You're rich, I'm poor." He poked his white-T-shirted chest with his big black thumb. "You got a responsibility for me."

Dr. Alkahest squealed with laughter, and

Dancer looked around at his friends again, hoping for clarification. Gradually the doctor got control of himself. He'd remembered that he must settle the arrangements while he still had the wit. With a quick little jerk, he got out his flask and drank. He said, "When does the shipment arrive?"

"Any time," Santisillia said. "We don't know. They'll bring it over from the mainland some night, probably early in the morning. What time you got, Peter?"

Peter Wagner looked at his watch. "Two a.m."

"If it's tonight, they'll be along soon," Santisillia said. "Otherwise we wait until tomorrow night, or the night after that—"

"They come by boat?" Dr. Alkahest said.

He nodded.

"Then maybe that's them." The old cripple cocked his head.

Santisillia looked doubtful, glanced at Peter Wagner. "You hear anything?"

"Not me," Peter Wagner said.

The Indian, who'd been sitting as still as a boulder, put his hand to his ear, then shook his head.

"I have excellent hearing," Dr. Alkahest said. "I assure you somebody's loading a boat, back that way." He pointed.

"Crazy," Dancer said. A wicked smile showed at the corner of his mouth. "Hey listen, I'll make you a bet. A thousand dollars."

"Oh come on," Peter Wagner said.

"No deal, but I'll bet you a nickel," Dr. Alkahest said.

Dancer sagged. "Shit man, who's got a nickel?"

An hour later they heard the rumble of the Mexicans' boats.

"They're coming! He could really hear them!" Jane said.

"Then my part in the comedy is over," Peter Wagner said. "I've brought you to your Mexicans. Adieu, adieu, night-night, ta ta!" He snatched up the rifle.

"Stop it!" Santisillia said. "You going to shoot yourself right in front of *us*, boy? You got no *feelings?*"

Peter Wagner sighed and put it down.

By now the Mexicans were inside the cave, climbing out of the boats. Their yells of greeting—coming up through the shaft they sounded more like groans—rose to the basin, and a moment later their heads began appearing. Soon the volcano basin was full of them, a huddled mass if ever there was one, people crippled, maimed, bloated, wart-faced, dwarfed, blind, deaf, voiceless, some of them on wooden legs, some of them on skate-boards; Dr. Alkahest fainted, bowled over by the scent.

"Let's go! Let's load up!" Santisillia said.

But Dancer leaped up. "Wait! We forgot the trial!" He stood with his arms raised, like a wildman praying.

Ominously, as if in support of his earnestness, the earth grumbled.

"Aw, come on, Dancer," Peter Wagner said.

Jane said, "Outlaws can't hold trials."

"It's illogical," Mr. Nit said.

The Indian nodded, solemn.

The crowd of Mexicans watched them, bright eyed and agreeable. A fat one with gunbelts crossing his chest, two of his upper teeth missing, said, *¿Qué es? ¿Una misa?*" Those behind him pressed closer.

Dr. Alkahest opened his eyes and cried, "Welcome friends! God bless you," then passed out again, though he wanted to say more.

"*¿Qué es?*," the fat man said. He leaned forward, staring with his eyebrows lifted, like a man looking into an aquarium at a curious fish. He pointed at the doctor.

"He's high," Peter Wagner explained. "He's found happiness."

"*High*," the Mexican said to those behind him. They passed it back.

Santisillia was looking at the sky, troubled. It would be morning soon. If they didn't get the boats loaded and move out, they'd have to sit here another whole day. It was time they didn't have. If the old man had found them, others knew. And if it was true that Dusky had brought Dr. Alkahest and was near, staying out of sight, given that infallible sixth sense he had . . .

Suddenly Luther Santisillia hit himself on the forehead and whispered, "Shit! What a fool!" It wasn't by some uncanny sixth sense that Dusky always knew where Fist was, where the Feds were, where everything was! Old Dusky had the whole fucking picture: he was a *Narc!* Santisillia began to laugh, his muscles going weak. Old Dusky had played his dumb niggers like a ju-ju man—he'd said a little pig-Latin backwards and they'd believed! *Beware the stories yo mama tells you*, he thought. *Beware the man with the fictions!*

He raised his arms for attention. "Listen," he said, "we gotta leave. We been fucked. Dusky's out there—he brought the old man in. He's a Narc."

They looked at him.

"No Narc," the Indian said.

"He's a Narc, I tell you. It's incredible none of us thought of it. All the time he's been settin us up, playin us that tune about his infallible sixth sense—"

"Setting us up why?" the Indian said.

"Who knows why? *You* understand the mind of a government agent?"

"Some kind of rip-off maybe," Peter Wagner said. "Ends against the middle."

"No Narc," the Indian said. He folded his

arms like an Indian in the movies. "We take the load."

Santisillia flashed anger for an instant, then laughed. He felt something give in his head. It was too late anyway. Ah, that Dusky!

"Maybe he's a Narc and maybe not," Mr. Goodman said. "But to walk away from a load like this one—"

"We could load fast," Mr. Nit said.

Santisillia held out his arms, palms up, as if to plead, then laughed again. It made no difference. "OK," he said, "let's load."

The crowd stirred slightly in the direction of the entrance, then stopped. Dancer was waving the machine gun. "No!" he yelled. "First the trial! Captain Fist shot me in the leg! I ain't had my vengeance!"

"Hey, cool it man," Santisillia said. "It's all over." He took a step, casual, smiling, then jerked back with a yelp. Bullets chopped up the stone just in front of his feet.

"We gonna have a trial. That's final," Dancer said.

They looked at him.

The Mexicans all scratched their heads and smiled. It always takes time to learn new customs. Nobody spoke.

Peter Wagner said at last, wearily, "Why, Dancer? Why so petty? What if it turns out Luther's right—what if the Narcs are on the way right now?"

Dancer stamped his foot. "Man, you're crazy! Dusky's a gentleman, pride of the people. How come you bastards always tryin to undermine a young person's heroes and ideals?"

"All the same," Peter Wagner said reasonably, "we could hold the trial later—be on the safe side."

"Safety is for chickens," Dancer snapped.

"Makes no difference," Santisillia said. "It's all over but the shooting anyway."

Dancer shook his head furiously, as if to drive away gnats. "I want you peoples to get ready for this trial."

"With the Narcs coming?" Peter Wagner asked.

"No Narcs coming, God damn you," Dancer yelled. "The Narc is a mythological beast. One more word about Narcs, I gonna shoot you for contempt of this court."

Jane touched his arm. "Why have it now though, really?"

"We gonna find out," Dancer said. "That's all, man. We just gonna find out."

They all looked over at Captain Fist, still bound and gagged. Jane said innocently, "Find out what?"

"What's the matter you, ofay?" Dancer said, turning the machine gun toward her. "What you *spose* to find out when you try a man? We gone find out if he's guilty, you understan? We gone put that ole motherfucker on trial and try him and see if he's guilty. What the fuck you expect?"

"Man," Santisillia said, smiling at the sky, "what's guilt? You never killed nobody?"

But Dancer wasn't hearing.

"Hey Alkahest!" he yelled. He poked the old man in the chest with his machine gun. "Wake up, man. We havin some justice."

The doctor slept on, both drugged and drunk, mumbling in his sleep, "What fun for the Sons of Liberty!"

"Let him be," Santisillia said. "He's way up in the sky. He can't get down."

"I say he's comin *down*," Dancer said. He leaned over and shouted in Alkahest's ear. "Wake up and look sober or I'll blast your faggotty head off. What you mean, man, settin there, ignorin your social responsibility?" He held the gun three inches away from the tip of Dr. Alkahest's nose. Dr. Alkahest opened first one eye, then the other, and abruptly smiled from ear to ear.

"Are you going to kill me?" he asked coyly.

Santisillia said, "You want to murder the Captain, why don't you just *shoot* him?"

Alkahest was making a powerful effort to keep his eyes open. If he was to die, it was important that he feel it, actually hurt for an instant, get the whole sensation. It was his inalienable right. He shook his head, batting his lashes and rolling his half-closed eyes, smiling widely.

"That's better, rich man," Dancer said. Alkahest trembled with excitement, pinching himself, picking at himself. Dancer chattered on. "I appreciate your sittin up and doin your duty. And to show my appreciation I'm gonna confer a honor upon you, understand? I gonna glorify you, Jack. On account of I can see you're one smarrrrt doood, and you been educated and all that shit, and also because I have happened to observe you are higher than Jesus, I'm makin you Attorney for the Defense." He pointed at Captain Fist. "Now get ready to defend him."

Alkahest looked at Fist—still bound and gagged—then back at Dancer. At the sight of the Captain's wicked little eyes, fouler than plague, Dr. Alkahest smiled and went woozy. "I'll do my best," he brought out, and giggled.

Dancer nodded. "You gonna have to."

———

"A question was once, somehow or other, started between Collins and me, of the propriety of educating the female sex in learning, and their abilities for study. He was of opinion that it was improper, and that they were naturally unequal to it. I took the contrary side, perhaps a little for dispute's sake."

The Autobiography of
Benjamin Franklin, 1757

6

Truces and Human Considerations Rejected, the War Rages On

1

Despite the discomfort of his sleeping position, James Page awakened late. Out by the barn, the cows were noisily bellowing to be milked. The sunlight, what there was of it, luminous gray as a month-old boiled egg, came spilling into the bathroom not horizontally but from fifty degrees up. He was sick and full of pain. His head was splitting, his scratches, bumps, and cuts were all whimpering, his dry lips were strangely stuck together, so that parting them made slivers of the skin tear off. As if his eyes had been open before he came awake, he was aware abruptly, without

transition from sleep, of the sink and its pitted pipes
and trap, the blistering gray wall behind it. All he
saw was unnaturally motionless, unreal, as if it were
a cunningly built model of itself, or as if the world
had gone through some catastrophe and, surviving,
was at perfect rest, regathering its strength. His rear
end was numb, his neck stiff and painful, his gray-
haired bare legs freezing.

He couldn't remember at first what had happened
or why he was here, sitting above foul waters his
swollen and blood-clotted nose couldn't smell. But by
lifelong habit he was disturbed by the mooing of the
cows by the barn, the cackling of the chickens, troubled, maybe, by one of these 'possums that had been
moving into New England these last few years, settling
like a plague; and he blinked, turned his head, and
reached with his left hand for the wall, with his right
for the sink, intending to raise himself. He saw the
shotgun and looked hard at it, registered its weight, its
curious purity of purpose and line, the two shiny
triggers, the pock-marked stock—many's the woodchuck and skunk he'd shot with it—then remembered
what he'd done. His heart went out from under him.
He ached too much to feel, just now, the full shame
or shock; what he felt was worse, and duller: simple
and absolute despair and the farmer's bred-in knowledge that whatever his misery, however profound his
self-hatred and sense of life's mortal injustice, he
must get up and go milk the cows, feed the pigs and
horses and, if he could get to it, winter the bees.

He bent forward and pulled up his trousers, then,
knees screaming, straightened up. With stiff, numb
fingers he hooked the top fly-button, hooked his belt,
then worked, slowly, clumsily, at the rest of the buttons. He took two steps forward, put his hands on the
sink, and carefully, for fear he might pull it off the
wall, leaned on the edge. He glanced at the mirror
and was arrested. On the side of his head stood a
pearshaped black lump, black as an eggplant, with
cracks running out from the center like the faults on
a broken tomato, radiating spokes of split-open flesh,

bloodless, as if the wound were an old one and he'd picked the scab. Scratches went out from each side of his mouth, and on his upper lip dark clotted blood formed a moustache. His nose, below the swollen black ridge, was as red with burst vessels as an old, half-dead wino's. *All this damage in one night!*, he thought. He assumed that his nose would be like this henceforth, the ruin looked final; but in this, he would find, he was mistaken; in a week the nose would be practically normal. Surprisingly enough, the old man was not distressed by the ruin. By virtue of the depth of his self-hatred he was beyond that, almost welcomed it as justice.

He became aware again of the cows' mooing, and leaned to look out through the window. Outside, the world was gray, the glory of foliage all gone, no leaves still clinging but the dull brown of oakleaves, the gossamer tan leaves of beeches. The pastures were as drab as the barn walls, no color but here and there the maroon of a brier. The rain had again, for the time being, stopped. He turned on the faucets, pushed in the plug, splashed cold water on his face, and began to wash up. When the blackish, caked blood was almost all washed away, he groped along the rack for a towel and dried himself. He was reaching for the door when he remembered the shotgun. He took it up and broke it, removed the empty shell and the loaded one, put both in his pocket, and, closing the gun, indifferently leaned it once more against the wall.

He had a dizzy moment, pain that went through him like a brash yell, and it made him yell himself. Out in the barnyard the cows mooed more loudly, as if they'd heard him.

He rubbed the sides of his face with his fingertips—the old man never used pain-killers—and, having no choice, he moved on.

At the top of the stairs he hesitated, his clogged nostrils catching some peculiar scent, and after a moment he turned again, bent half double, and walked to his sister's door. He stood there looking in, having no intention of entering, though the door was open as if in invitation. The smell was stronger, something burning, a smell from his childhood. Through the door's foot-wide opening he saw Sally in bed, sleeping with her hands over a paperback book. Her dentures were in and had slipped out of position—the uppers hung crookedly between her dry, crinkled lips like the wax vampire-teeth children wore, dressed for a Halloween party. He again had a picture of Sally as a teenager, taking her bath in the kitchen tub. He nodded as if someone had spoken.

He was staring at her door, and it came to him that somebody—Lewis, of course—had scraped off the paint. He remembered now that he'd heard him doing it. He was saddened. They deserved no kindness, Sally and he, though he was grateful. His eyes traveled up the door cross, admiring his son-in-law's workmanship, and with a jerk of his heart he saw, perched above, the crate of apples. It seemed to take on weight as he stared at it—the weight, perhaps, of her murderous intent. Despite his headache, despite his wild alarm, he smiled. He looked again at his old, sleeping sister.

"Thally?" he said.

She was dead to the world.

He recognized the smell as insurance oil—kerosene, that is; but for years in Vermont, because of the Democrats, its main use had been getting back money out of fire insurance. On the bedroom walls he could make out a hint of the flame's yellow flickering. After a moment he spit on the floor to his left for luck, then carefully, carefully put his head through the open door to look. His heart pounded once, like a blow from outside, when he saw the lamp. It was burned almost out, no more than an inch of kerosene in the bottom of the grayish glass bowl. He could let it burn on; it had burned all night without accident. But even as he thought it he knew it was no good. The gods take care of fools and children for only so long; they eventually look away. He took a deep breath and straightened up—pains shot through his abdomen— and inched far enough through the door to reach the lamp. With his fingertips he pushed it from the edge onto the table, clear to the middle, where it wouldn't fall even if the applecrate fell; then carefully, balanced like an acrobat, he drew his hand away and edged himself back into the hall. He let his breath out.

Sally slept on.

He went to the head of the stairs, then, gripping the bannister firmly with his left hand, started down. The cows mooed more urgently. "I hear you," he said. With his right hand he rubbed his forehead, then his right temple.

The kitchen startled him: broken plates on the floor, and the jack-o-lanterns; one of them leering up at him. He bent over to pick up some pieces of plate, put them on the table, then decided to let it go. First the chores, or he'd have himself a barn full of mastitis. He went to the back door to put on his coat and boots, then paused, thinking back, and because he'd changed his mind about which door to leave by, turned himself around to the left three times, then crossed the kitchen, awkwardly cocked forward, to open the front door and look out into the yard. The state police car was still sitting there, the policemen asleep, and a few feet away Lewis Hicks' car, empty. The others were gone.

He looked at the headlights of the police car a while, steeling himself, then opened the door farther and went out. The stoop was still wet—the rain had apparently stopped not long since—and the ground, when he stepped on it, was mushy. He walked over with long, squishy steps and knocked on the window of the police car. He knocked again. The man in the driver's seat opened his eyes and turned his head, not startled, not thinking anything at all, the way it looked. The old man yelled, "Mahnin!"

The state policeman nodded, then rolled down his window. He looked at James, saying nothing.

"Mahnin," James said.

The state policeman nodded.

James said, "Ith all over."

The policeman looked at the house. At last, pointedly not speaking, he reached for the radio mike to the right of his steering wheel. Now the younger one woke up, looked startled, then relaxed.

"Mahnin," James said.

He nodded.

"Winterth put-near here," James said. His voice knocked against the trees, high and plain. He looked around the yard. The limbs were bare—all in one night. He shut his eyes. The luminous sky behind the bare branches even now sent pain shogging through him.

The driver was saying on the radio, "It's ok here. We're comin in."

"You don't want to arreth me?" James said.

The driver looked at him, still holding the radio microphone. "Go milk your cows," he said.

James nodded and started to turn away.

"Me ask you somethin," the policeman said.

He half turned back.

The policeman looked at him, severe but not quite meeting his eyes. "You sure this is over?"

"Ith over," James said.

The policeman hung up the radio mike, professionally uncivil. Despite the day's dimness, he reached for his dark glasses on the dashboard, opened them, and hooked them on his ears.

It crossed James' mind that he could shoot his cows, then himself; but it was an idle thought.

"Thankth," he said.

The policeman started up the motor.

When he was back in the kitchen, intending to walk through it and out to the barn to begin his chores, he remembered that Ginny's husband's car was still here, out there sitting in the yard, and stopped in his tracks, looking down at the ripply linoleum, then turned and went over to the living-room door. It creaked as he opened it, but they remained fast asleep, Ginny on the couch, Dickey in front of the burned-cold fireplace, Lewis sitting up in the armchair next to the TV. Ginny lay crumpled and gray-faced, her coat and another one, a black one, over her, the black one from his closet. He recognized it as the one his

401

son Richard had worn when he dressed up once as an axe-murderer for some party—a good joke, they'd all agreed, Richard included. All his life he'd been one of those people ascairt of his own shadow. Dickey too had two coats on, Lewis's and his own. Lewis had only the afghan James' wife Ariah had made when she was dying. He remembered for an instant how she'd worked on it, lying with her eyes closed, listening while Ginny read to her. Ariah would hardly speak to James, would look away when he came in. Well, he could endure it, just as she was enduring; anyway, she hadn't been herself, with all those drugs. There were droplets on Ariah's forehead, but she never once complained. It was assumed you'd try to be brave, in those days. When you were gone, people would tell stories of how you died, so you better not kick and whine and whinny like the man Judah Sherbrooke shot.

The momentary sharp memory of his wife was gone now; his years with her frozen up as solidly as ever. The old man stood miserably gazing at his family, all that was left of it not counting Sally, his head splitting, the light in the room fluorescent gray, the child not even their own true blood but adopted, the spawn of God knew what—though there were of course times when James loved the child, whatever that meant—and the image before him he would have called, if he'd known the word, symbolic: poor miserable creatures not beautiful in any way, uncomfortably sleeping in an ugly room, lit by such weather as only October had the gall to fob off on dismal humanity—though that was unfair, October would be bluer than blue again soon—dense, sharp daylight, the last thing left alive —and his heart ached, that instant, even more than his head. He listened to the bellowing of the cows in their pain and with part of his mind heard the dog scratching, locked, for some reason, in the cellar. He backed out of the room and softly closed the door, then went to let the dog in. It leaped up on him, wet-muzzled. He pushed it away roughly, with a snarl not human, and went, with the cowering animal beside him—

pushing up against him and wagging its tail—to the woodshed to put down food for the dog and cat. As soon as he shook the Purina box, the cat appeared from nowhere, racing, then switched to slow-motion, as if disdainful and not his dependent. Like Sally. "Come on, Thpot," he said gruffly, for the dog held back, fearful of a kick. The dog snivelled up and ate timidly, looking up at him, large *U*'s of white below his eyes. The cat settled calmly, tail slowly switching, aware that he could vanish in an instant, or snarl, hiss, scratch, stay King of the Mountain and James Page be cussed. A foolish image, a kind of daydream, came into his head of putting down food for Henry Stumpchurch, Henry smiling, surprised and pleased. He thought of Henry's theory of the cunning of the common frog, and his eyes slipped out of focus for a moment, dreaming again. Then the horses called to him, and, gingerly rubbing the sides of his head, the old man started for the barn.

2

Ginny started suddenly, waking with a snap from a nightmare of being eaten. It was freezing cold and her right arm was so numb it felt dead. She opened her eyes.

"Mahnin, sweet-hot," Lewis said, looking at her forehead as if afraid he might offend. He was kneeling at the fireplace, trying to start a fire. The room was full of billowing smoke. She flapped her left hand in front of her and made a face. Dickey said something —"I'm hungry"—but she didn't quite register the words. She sat up abruptly, pushing up on one arm, the numb one, her left hand still flapping at the smoke. A kind of pain, almost a shock, went up the arm that was asleep. "What time is it?" The light coming through the smoke from the windows and off the walls

405

was dull, as if the sun were dying. "Christ," she said.

"Almost noon," Lewis said.

"Why's it so cold?"

Lewis blew a time or two more, down on his hands and knees. "Seems like the furnace wasn't stoked," he said.

"I'm hungry," Dickey said.

"Just a minute, honey," she said. "Let Mama wake up."

"Lots of wood down there," Lewis said. "Only trouble is, it's wet."

She rubbed her eyes, smarting from the smoke, then looked at Lewis again. "You're not starting that fire with Dad's good magazines! You know he saves 'em!"

"Well, I could've used the wah-paper," he said.

It was as harsh as he ever got, and she was warned. "I suppose he'll never notice. —Almost noon, you say? Aren't you supposed to be working for Mrs. Ellis?"

"I called her up on the telephone," he said.

"Oh."

She swung her legs over the side of the couch, yawned and stretched, thought of smoking a cigarette, then changed her mind. Sometimes he made comments (distant and indirect) when she smoked first thing in the morning. She straightened out her coat, draped it around her shoulders, and remembered she had cigarettes in the pocket. She threw a look at him. On the back of his head a shock of hair stood up. Guiltily, she reached for the cigarettes, shook one out, and opened the pack of matches tucked inside the cellophane.

"God *damn* smoke," Lewis said, rubbing his eyes. He turned and looked at her, or, rather, not at her, at the cigarette in her hand. "Whant you fix Dickey some breakfast," he suggested. He made it sound like an alternative.

"I will," she said. "Don't I always?" She steeled herself against his tyranny and lit the cigarette.

Suddenly last night came over her, in its full horror, her father gone insane, waving the gun at them, his

406

face a horrible leer above the jack-o-lanterns on the table. "Oh God!" she said.

"What's the matter?"

"I was thinking of last night." The wallpaper was light-gray and dark-gray, diamond-shapes with roses. She remembered staring at it as a child, when the colors were fresh and it had seemed to her pretty. Christ, what a ruin! Waking up in the living room was like learning you were dead.

"Never mine," Lewis said. He was fanning the fire with a magazine now. "Yoah dad was drunk, that's ah."

"He was going to kill her!"

"I wouldn't think too much about it."

She stood up, sucking hard at the cigarette. It was like Kleenex in her throat, and in her back, just under the shoulder-blade, there was a sharp pain. Oh, Jesus, she thought. Oh, Christ. She started for the kitchen door. "Come on, Dickey."

"I'm cold," Dickey said.

"Jump up and down," she said. "Hurry up! Come on!" At the door she turned her head, raising her hand and running it through her stiff, oily hair. "You had breakfast, Lewis?"

"Not yet," he said, careful, as if avoiding a fight.

"Jesus," she said angrily, and hit the door with just the heel of her hand, the cigarette between two fingers. "Dickey, go up and use the bathroom," she said.

"I don't need to, Mom."

"Go try! Go on before I clobber you!"

He went, dawdling, and when he returned she had breakfast on.

While they were eating—she wasn't hungry—she went up to the bathroom and the first thing she saw was that damn shotgun. Her cheeks went fiery, mainly because Dickey had just been here and might have killed himself, and if she could have thought of a way to destroy it that instant, she'd have done so. Instead, she sat down to go to the bathroom and while she was seated there picked up the shotgun to see if she could open it and make sure it was empty. It was heavy. She felt an urge to empty it by pulling the triggers, shooting out the little square bathroom window, but it was only a passing thought, not a real temptation, and she continued to study the shotgun looking for a release. She found one on the top, where the barrels began, and the minute she touched it the gun broke, smoothly and silently, sending a shiver up her back—the pure efficiency of the thing. Once when her father had been hunting woodchucks with the shotgun and his dog, they'd cornered one against an old stone wall, and when the woodchuck had tried to attack the dog her father had poked the gun-barrel at it. The woodchuck had bit at the gun—had the barrel in his mouth—when her father pulled the trigger. You could hardly find the pieces.

There were no shells where she knew they should be and she snapped the gun shut again. Perhaps there'd been no shells from the beginning, she thought, but then remembered the explosion when the minister and priest came diving out the door. Another job for Lewis. The pellets had not only demolished the plaster, they'd blasted away the lath.

"Crazy!" she whispered, and felt tears welling up. How would she ever dare face them again, all those people! Again she felt her cheeks go hot with anger, this time at Lewis—superior bastard. But instantly, flushing the toilet, she was ashamed of the feeling. It wasn't his fault. He'd been born that way, a damned saint. He really was! She arranged herself, splashed water on her face, and looked in the mirror. She looked, she thought, like an old village whore—hair sticking up crookedly where she'd slept on it, big circles under her eyes. She heard her father shouting and looked out the window. He was chasing the bull with a pitchfork, slipping and sliding in the mess of the barnyard. Chickens stood watching. He'd kill the damn thing before he knew it and be out a thousand dollars. "Stupid bastard," she whispered. Tears welled up in her eyes again, and she splashed more water on her face. In the medicine chest above the sink she found an orange plastic comb with half the teeth gone.

She held it under the faucet to wet it, then ran it through her hair. She looked as bad as before when she was finished, but gave up and put the comb back and angrily dried her hands. She felt some unconscious, habitual dissatisfaction and remembered she'd left her cigarettes downstairs.

As she was about to go down it struck her like a thunderbolt that Aunt Sally's door was open. She stood a moment staring in disbelief, then went striding down the hallway to reach it before Aunt Sally could slam it shut. She saw her aunt asleep on her back, snoring, her flabby brown and light-blue speckled arms outside the covers, and she felt something wrong—*danger!,* her body said, jerking her to a halt. She smelled kerosene smoke and stood perfectly still, or still except that she was tentatively pushing at the door. Suddenly, from nowhere, something heavy and sharp slammed down hard on her head—she felt a flash of unspeakable, splintering pain—and Aunt Sally's eyes popped open. There was a roar like an explosion, a terrible, dark rumbling, the room shone with glittering pinwheels and stars, and she went hurtling, as· if at the speed of light, into blackness.

3

Dickey sat motionless, carefully balanced like a bird on a wire, his knife and fork in his fists—he'd been trying to cut his toast and egg—his eyes wide. (*Good boys don't cut their toast like that.*) The dog sat beside him, nose at the edge of the table, begging— he himself had let it in; in that too he knew he was wrong. His father's leaping from the table and running up the stairs when everything went smashing and clattering had left the room dangerous and accusing. *Be a good boy!,* the hole in the ceiling warned. *Be like the girl with the umbrella!,* said the round, blue salt box. He stared at the round thing where once,

he'd been told, a stovepipe had gone—there was a picture on it, a red barn, a white house, and a creek (it was winter)—and listened with all his might. There were no shouts, no voices; what had happened he could not guess.

Carefully, eyes still wide, he got down from his chair, looked around to be sure he was unwatched, and went on tip-toe to the foot of the stairs, then up three steps, then up four more. When he was high enough to see into the upstairs hallway through the bannister, what he saw was apples all over the floor and his father kneeling over his mother, who didn't move. Around her head there was blood. Aunt Sally was leaning through her bedroom door, holding her hand over her mouth, silent.

"Ginny, sweet-hot?" his father said softly, as though nothing were wrong, there was no hurry. "Ginny?"

In the kitchen below he heard the plate crash and knew the dog had gotten it. His father showed no sign of noticing. "Ginny?" he said again. He lifted her head with his right hand and felt through the hair with his left. There was blood everywhere, a lake of it. It was all over his father's coveralls and hands and was coming in a slow rivulet toward the stairwell. His father put his mother's head down again and put his two arms under her, bit down with his upper teeth on his lower lip, and lifted her up. He gave a jerk, trying to stand, and slipped in the blood and almost let her head hit the wall. Aunt Sally just watched with her hand over her mouth, not saying a word. His father, holding his mother in his arms, walked on his knees out of the lake of blood and tried again to stand up. He did it this time, the muscles of his face bulging. He leaned on the wall, trying to wipe off the soles of his shoes, holding her—her arms hung down—then lifted her higher, trying to get her on his shoulder. He grabbed at her seat with his right arm and made a grunting noise, lifting—she was bigger than he was, and heavier—and her skirt slid up so that her underpants showed—but he grabbed again, his arm under her seat, and now he got her over his shoulder. Her head hung over

412

his back, bleeding, and her eyes were open. As if he'd known Dickey was there all along, he said, "Get to the cah. Get the coats."

Dickey turned like lightning, running down the stairs for the coats. On the table he saw his mother's cigarettes and grabbed them—the dog looked up at him for food—and ran on to the living room where the coats were. He threw them over his shoulder and ran back to the kitchen. His father was down the stairs now, carrying his mother, and he ran to the front door to open it. He kicked away plaster so his father wouldn't trip. His father's face was red and showed nothing but how heavy she was. He was biting so hard on his bottom lip it looked as if it hurt. His father went through the door and as soon as he was down off the stoop, Dickey leaped off and ran ahead of him to open the car door.

"Back one," his father said.

He widened his eyes as if in horror at his mistake, shut the front one, and opened the back one. He quickly pushed the folded tarpaulin and the paintbrushes off the seat and jumped back out of the way. His father set his mother's rear end against the seat and gently laid her down, then got in and pulled her farther, then bent her knees to make room for the door to close. She made a farting noise. "Get in," his father said.

Quickly Dickey jumped in in front and closed the door while his father walked around to his side. His father opened his door and slid in and turned a little sideways to get his keys from his pocket, then put them in the switch. He turned the keys and the car made a little grunt, but nothing happened.

"You better stot," his father said quietly, as if, if it didn't start, he was going to shoot it.

He turned the keys again. There wasn't even a grunt.

"Go to the bahn and get your grampa," his father said.

The car smelled of blood, the exact same smell as

413

when Aunt Sally cut the heads off chickens. He opened the door and jumped out, shut the door, and ran toward the end of the house, heading for the barn. He smelled the doodie in the bushes from Aunt Sally's bedroom. Suddenly the car made a roaring noise behind him, and white smoke rolled up, a huge cloud of it. He spun around and ran back.

"Lock your door," his father said, as soon as he was in. While his finger was still on the lock button, the car began backing toward the road, not fast but definite, like the charge of a bull.

His father drove no faster than usual, saying not a word. Dickey got up on his one knee to look back at his mother. Her eyes were still open, and there was blood all over the seat. He wanted to ask if she was dead.

"Sit down," his father said.

He lowered himself again and put his hands in his lap.

When they were coming down into the valley he looked over at his father and said, "It's because of that book."

His father said nothing.

He squeezed his hands together. "I found a dirty book in the pigpen," he said. "I put it in my pocket, but my pocket's got a hole." He reached his hand through the pocket and lining of his overcoat, showing his father how it was all torn away.

"Who told you it was dutty?" his father said.

"It had a dirty picture." He plunged on: "I couldn't read it. It had big words and little tiny printing."

"How you *know* it was a dutty pitcha?" his father asked.

"It just was." He added: "I lost the book up in Aunt Sally's room."

His father glanced down but said nothing. He looked back at the road.

When they'd driven on a little farther, Dickey said, "I lost the book the same night Grampa and Aunt Sally had the fight."

His father went on looking through the windshield. He sighed. "Your mother was hit by an applecrate," he said. "It want your book."

4

A little after noon Estelle called Ruth Thomas at Putnam Hospital. "How is he?" she asked.

Ruth's voice had no spunk. "He's in the oxygen tent," she said. "Dr. Phelps says we'll just have to see."

"Oh dear. Oh dear," Estelle said. "Oh, I feel so awful!"

"Well, he's got the best care in the world. We can be thankful for that."

"I feel as if it's all my fault," Estelle said.

"Well it isn't," she said. "You can put that right out of your mind." Her tone had an edge like a butcher knife, and Estelle said, understanding:

"Oh, Ruth!"

"I don't care," Ruth said. "I blame him, and that's all there is to it."

"You can't, dear! You mustn't! Think what poor James had been through!"

"Through a whole lot of liquor, that's how it smelled to me."

"Oh, but dearest, that's not fair!"

"Fair!" Ruth said.

Estelle could see her in her mind, eyes bugging, head drawn up in righteous indignation. You couldn't blame her, heaven knows; she'd be the same herself, probably, if it had been Ferris and not Ed. She thought of how wonderfully everything had gone before James got home—how pitiful and apart from them all he'd looked when he'd got there, not himself, all banged up and not in his right mind. "I'm so sorry," she said, the palsy coming over her, making her head jiggle. "It makes me just sick. Is there anything I can do?"

415

"You can pray," Ruth said. "That's all any of us can do."

"I will. You know that. I've been praying all morning."

There was a pause. Estelle said, thinking in sudden distress of more difficulties, "Are the boys still there with you?"

"They've gone home, thank goodness," Ruth said, and sighed. "Chief Young was there, at the hospital. He drove them over to the bus station for us. He'd come in with a boy had an accident in the graveyard by the old First Church. Beaten up, it seems. It was the youngest Flynn boy, or Porter, whichever they're calling themselves now. Ethain's son?"

"Oh good heavens!"

"It was nothing, just scratches," Ruth said quickly, "though they're keeping him over for observation. It was a blessing to have Chief Young on hand, believe me. It was Providential!"

"I should think so," Estelle said. Then: "They've gone home then. That's good. What a terrible thing for everyone!"

"Lucky thing there was a bus," Ruth said.

Estelle said, "You really should blame me, not James. It was my meddling—"

There was a silence.

"Well it's no use blaming anyone, I suppose," Ruth said. "I certainly can't blame you. It's true he was drunk, so he wasn't himself; but you know how we are in our family about drink."

"And you're perfectly right," Estelle said. "Of course you are!" Her mind began to race. Why had Ruth so suddenly changed her tune, holding back all at once, beginning to play charitable? She looked hard at the curtains, as if the pattern in the lace might have words for her to read, then looked down at her hands, small and liver-spotted, trembling. She looked up again at once. On the street beyond the curtains, John G. McCullough was driving by in his big, frog-green, old fashioned Marmon, John sitting straight and red-eared in the cold—the top was down—going to some meeting of the city fathers, probably, or to visit his bank, or to slip through a side door at Mt. Anthony High and have a word with poor silly Mr. Pelkie about music in the schools. There ought to be courses about people like John McCullough. Education should be real and personal. He was a direct descendent of Lady Godiva, and an important and valuable man in his own right—a patron of the arts, an important publisher, or had been for years, with his brother-in-law William C. Scott. Why, she wondered for the thousandth time, were the McCulloughs and Deweys not friendly? But all the while, just under the surface of her hurrying thoughts, she was working on why Ruth had changed her tune. And she was saying, meanwhile, "He's not really a drunkard, it's the stress. You know how it was when his son died."

"He was certainly a drunkard *then,* poor boy!"

She gave a little laugh. "Poor boy indeed! But he got hold of himself."

"Poor Ariah, I'd say."

"Well," Estelle said, nodding at the phone, "it wasn't easy for either one of them."

"No, that's true," Ruth said. "I don't mean to criticize. I know how fond you always were of him."

Estelle felt a curious sensation, then lost her thread. She waited for Ruth to speak.

Ruth said darkly, "I suppose you've heard about Virginia?"

"Virginia?" Estelle said. At Ruth's tone of voice she was suddenly wide awake again, tingling with alarm.

"His daughter Virginia Hicks is here in the hospital," Ruth said.

"No!"

"Yes indeedy! Husband Lewis brought her in." She said ominously: "Nobody's saying what happened to her."

"Good heavens!" Estelle said.

"Cut on the head, apparently," Ruth said. "I understand she's been unconscious for hours."

"No," Estelle whispered.

"Well, we'll just have to see what we see," Ruth said. "It's a funny world."

Estelle nodded, then shook her head, saying nothing. The pattern on the curtains was sharper all at once. If there were anything there to read, she could have read it. It's my fault, she thought, all my fault. She'd known she shouldn't interfere. But no fool like an old fool. She said: "Is that all they're saying? A cut on the head?"

"You know how they are in hospitals," Ruth said.

Estelle's head was jittering more troublesomely now with the stupid palsy. "How tired you must be," she said. "Ruth, have you slept?"

There were noises for a moment in the background, and in a changed voice Ruth said, "Oh! Here's Dr. Phelps and Dr. Sung. I'll have to hang up now. It's so good of you to call."

"Of course. Don't mention it! Do keep me posted, and if there's anything I can do—"

"I'll keep in touch, dear. It's so good to talk to you!"

"Heavens, not at all!"

"Good-bye," Ruth said. "Thank you." The phone clicked.

"Good-bye," Estelle said to the humming line. She hung up the receiver and slowly brought her fingertips to her mouth.

5
(Terence on Pure and Subservient Art)

Terence Parks sat in the corner chair in the green living room of his parents' house, three houses down from his aunt Estelle's, listening to the Tippett Sonata for Four Horns and trying to think, or rather struggling with a chaos of old and new feelings, in a sense old and new ideas. Evening was coming on, filling him with restlessness and a queer sense of dread, a sensa-

418

tion difficult to get ahold of, put a name to, worse than anything he could remember since childhood, though in a general way, of course, he understood it. James Page, waving his shotgun last night, had changed everything.

Nothing in his father's large record collection was more familiar to Terence than the Tippett Sonata: happy music, he'd always thought; but tonight it had dark implications he'd never before noticed. Not that the music wasn't happy even now—in general, at least—and not that he wasn't himself feeling something like happiness, or at any rate feeling stirred up, uplifted by excitement—though at the same time fearful. Even talking with Margie last night he hadn't worked out the exact way to say it, but he was onto something. He had made, or perhaps was on the verge of making, a discovery. It had to do, it seemed to him now, with walking in the rain with Margie Phelps, and with the mad old man's shotgun, and with music.

When her grandfather had had to go to the hospital with the Thomases—Ed Thomas groaning, his wife sick with fear, and even old Dr. Phelps alarmed—Terence had suggested that he and his aunt Estelle drive Margie home. The grown-ups had accepted his suggestion at once, like panic-fuddled children who'd been waiting for advice, and though he'd been surprised at their listening to him—treating him, abruptly and without thinking, as an equal—he'd known instantly that their listening was right. It was not so much a thought as suddenly ripe knowledge, like the knowledge that one day comes to a young bull when by chance he knocks down the farmer.

That was only the beginning. As soon as the Thomases were out of the yard, his aunt had changed her mind about starting down the mountain. They must wait, she insisted, at least until the police came. She sat with her head lowered, lips clamped tight, watching the house. She was as pale and shaky as Ed Thomas had been—for which Terence couldn't blame her, he was shaky himself—yet there was something more to her distress than ordinary fear, he sensed. Whimpering, touching her face with both hands, now praying that poor James might be brought to his senses, now praying for Sally's life, she showed a side Terence had never before seen in her and couldn't understand, found distasteful. Her emotion seemed to him extreme, theatrical in fact, and, what was worse, unbalanced: there was no one to impress with her pious concern except himself and Margie—and Aunt Estelle seemed hardly to be conscious of their existence. Pulling at her face, whimpering and whispering, she struck him as a little like a madwoman: nothing in the real world (nothing he could think of) could provoke all this, though of course it was possible that the fault was his, that he too should feel grief and concern but was cruelly insensitive. It did not occur to him, since he knew them only as cranky and old, even at their best moments "difficult," that his great-aunt Estelle in fact loved James Page and Sally Abbott, dearly loved both of them, remembering them young—remembering how James had been wide of chest, cocksure and quick-witted, and how Sally had been a remarkable beauty and, sometimes in spite of her instincts, a faithful friend.

Margie, too, had been uncomfortable in the car. All at once she'd said, practically a whisper, "I think I'll get out and walk a little, if you don't mind. I love walking in the rain. *Do* you mind?" His aunt had said, "Why, child, you'll catch your death!" But her attention was elsewhere, eyes straining toward the lighted upstairs window. "I'm used to it, really," Margie had said, and though her smile and the tilt of her head were meek, she was already opening the door. His aunt could say only, "Really? In this weather?" "I'll keep her company," Terence had said, making it sound half reluctant, a duty.

The thought, or memory, of walking through darkness, holding her hand, was pleasant beyond comparison, and he was fully aware that his pleasure last night had been intensified by the horror earlier—the old man waving his shotgun, his mad eyes darting, mouth shaking, and then Ed Thomas's heart attack,

Aunt Estelle's strange behavior in the car. He thought again of Margie's voice, the smell of her hair. He'd wanted to ask her for a picture—it had seemed important, mysteriously so—a way of keeping clear, as if by voodoo, her exact quality and, in a way, his own—a way of welding both their natures firmly to the urgent, as if timeless quality of that moment: the alarming darkness of trees, the groan of wind.

He closed his eyes, listening to the Tippett and summoning up her image, a light, still core in a swirl of change, chaos and dissonance, leaping darkness. When her hair had come a little loose under the rainhat she wore and she'd reached up to slide out the bobby pins, pushing her hair back to fall under her collar, he had almost asked her for one of the bobby pins, but he couldn't find the nerve. He'd have been glad to get anything at all that was hers (he smiled at himself, thinking of it)—a bit of wood, an old bone, a dead chicken's foot . . .

He scroonched lower in the chair, until his head was just above the level of his knees, his large hands in his lap, folded. His father, who was for the most part a wise and gentle man, a psychiatrist, sat on the couch across the room from him, leafing without interest through a magazine. His mother was in the room off the kitchen sorting laundry. Terence could just hear her singing, a sign that she was cross.

Terence had listened to the Tippett often. In the beginning he couldn't have said why except, of course, that it was for horns, and he was a hornist. It was not "thrilling" or in the usual sense "beautiful" or any of the things that make particular pieces "universally appealing," as his teacher at school would say. The Sonata was simply something that—knowing really nothing about music except what he knew about playing French horn—he had "taken a shine to," as his mother would put it—an Alabamian. It was a piece to daydream by—or to remember by, as he was remembering now (but with unusual intensity), his consciousness closed like a fist around last night. And

421

also the music had been for him a kind of puzzle, one he was reworking now, this moment.

When he had first begun to listen to it, once having gotten past his interest in the tone, the hurry of sixteenth notes, he had asked himself what it was that the music reminded him of—the first movement, for instance, with its medieval opening and surprisingly quick flight from any trace of the medieval, a hustle-bustle of sweetly dissonant liquid sounds, sometimes such a flurry that you'd swear there were dozens of horns, not just four—and he'd tried various ideas: the idea that the image was of threatening apes, harmless ones, small ones, chittering and flapping unbelligerent arms in a brightly lit jungle; the idea that the picture was of children at the beach in sped-up motion . . .

Then it had come to him as a startling revelation— though he couldn't explain even to his horn teacher Andre Speyer why it was that he found the discovery startling—that the music meant nothing at all but what it was: panting, puffing, comically hurrying French horns. That had been, ever since—until to-night—what he saw when he closed his eyes and listened: horns, sometimes horn players, but mainly horn sounds, the very *nature* of horn sounds, puffing, hurrying, getting in each other's way yet in wonderful agreement finally, as if by accident. Sometimes, listening, he would smile, and his father would say quizzically, "What's with you?" It was the same when he listened to the other movements: What he saw was French horns, that is, the music. The moods changed, things happened, but only to French horns, French horn sounds. There was a four-note theme in the second movement that sounded like "Oh When the Saints," a theme that shifted from key to key, sung with great confidence by a solo horn, answered by a kind of scornful gibberish from the second, third, and fourth, as if the first horn's opinion was ridiculous and they knew what they knew. Or the slow movement: As if they'd finally stopped and thought it out, the horns played together, a three-note broken chord several times repeated, and then the first horn taking off as if at the suggestion of the broken chord and flying like a gull—except *not* like a gull, nothing like that, flying like only a solo French horn. Now the flying solo became the others' suggestion and the chord began to undulate, and all four horns together were saying something, almost words, first a mournful sound like *Maybe* and then later a desperate *Oh yes I think so,* except to give it words was to change it utterly: it was exactly what it was, as clear as day—or a moonlit lake where strange creatures lurk—and nothing could describe it but itself. It wasn't sad, the slow movement; only troubled, hesitant, exactly as he often felt himself. Then came—and he would sometimes laugh aloud—the final, fast movement. Though the slow movement's question had never quite been answered, all the threat was still there, the fast movement started with absurd self-confidence, with some huffings and puffings, and then the first horn set off with delightful bravado, like a fat man on skates who hadn't skated in years (but *not* like a fat man on skates, like nothing but itself), *Woo-woo-woo-woops!* and the spectator horns laughed *tiggledy-tiggledy-tiggledy!,* or that was vaguely the idea —every slightly wrong chord, every swoop, every hand-stop changed everything completely . . . It was impossible to say what, precisely, he meant.

He had been told in school that Beethoven's *Pastoral Symphony* made you think of the country. It wasn't true—or else his mind worked differently from the minds of other people. It was itself, or anyway that was all he'd cared for it to be, its note-by-note self, not sunrises or storms, though it was true that, when told to, he could imagine a storm for the storm passage, though also when listening to a real storm he could imagine a train. It was no doubt true that Beethoven had meant it to remind you of a storm, just as, of course, he intended his setting of the "Ode to Joy" to sound joyful. Beethoven's intention was a matter of record, and Beethoven was the one great master, everyone agreed. Well . . .

Perhaps, he'd decided, it would all come clearer to him later, as people were always telling you things would. But if what he'd discovered was misinformation, the fact was—had been—that he preferred it to the truth. There were in this world, he'd gradually discerned, two kinds of music: real music and work music. The setting of poems, even the best poems, was work music. What the music might have done if it followed its own will was prohibited, the music was enslaved. Ballet was work music, violins trapped inside the narrow limits of swans, though ballet dancers could of course—and sometimes did—interpret real music with their bodies. And then there was the worst work music of all, picture music, the kind they kept having to play at school, *The Pines of Rome, Pictures at an Exhibition.* Real music, on the other hand, was music liberated, free to be itself. For these theories he'd had proofs.

His mother was always listening to Bach's *Well-Tempered Klavier,* and as soon as he'd noticed there was a piece for each key he had understood—so Terence had believed—the whole meaning of the piece. The meaning of the section in D minor was D minor, as if Bach should say to his numerous children, "Listen, my children, to what *D minor* makes me play!" What Terence had discovered about music was not quite respectable, he'd realized. Narrow minded, perhaps snobbish, not easy to defend. There were places in Mahler where the drums insisted on your thinking of an army, or the violins made you think of . . . whatever. Then he'd deal with Mahler and Beethoven later. For now, he'd decided, it was enough to understand firmly what he understood, that Tippett's Sonata for Four Horns was entirely about horns.

So he'd decided. But as he listened this time, thinking of the music and of Margie Phelps, thinking of battered and bruised James Page in the house with his shotgun—down the mountain, not far from where the suicide had been, the garnet glow of his still-burning truck—Terence's stomach was suddenly all butterflies, as if something terrible were about to happen, some great evil, some monster in the music, about to emerge. *Whiffle-whiffle-whiffle!* went the second, third, and fourth, humorous but threatening, perceptibly malevolent, the tip of a dangerous iceberg. The first horn sailed over them, oblivious as a child or fool, in an entirely wrong key.

Last night Terence had explained his theory, as he'd had it worked out then, to Margie Phelps, realizing as he talked that he was talking about *her*—the scent of her, the way her hands moved, the way she walked just a little pigeon-toed (he wouldn't have her walk any other way), unique as a snowflake and, in Terence's eyes, infinitely more beautiful. "I mean, everything should be what it is," he'd said, "you know? *Absolutely free.*"

With a solemn expression she'd looked up at his face—she'd been watching the ground as he told her all this, not speaking except now and then to ask a question: "How do you think of things like that?" she'd said. "I could think for a million years and never come up with it!" Only now, in retrospect, was he fully aware of the darkness all around them and swirling up within them, two innocents chattering, while the old man schemed murder and Aunt Estelle, in the car, sat trembling.

Margie's words, her perfectly serious expression, had transformed him, given him value and potential. So it had seemed to him and seemed to him now. She had *seen* him, seen his seeing of the music, and he had therefore seen himself.

Something stirred in the music, darting from dark place to dark place. His eyes snapped open. Had he slept for an instant? For an instant at most; yet he seemed to have dreamed of the suicide—the story his aunt had told him years ago of the young man hanging calm as stone in his attic, in the house below him, Mozart. In the dream—or perhaps inside Tippett's music—Terence had stared at the faceless, still figure and had realized someone was in terrible danger, drifting out of key, out of orbit toward nothingness, toward emptiness and itself. *Margie?,* he wondered in brief panic. *Ed Thomas? Aunt Estelle?* For a split

425

second he understood everything, life's monstrosity and beauty. Then he was listening to the horns again.

His father, on the couch, opened the center-page foldout and looked at it without interest, then raised his eyes and looked at Terence. "What's the matter?" he said, grinning.

"Nothing," Terence said, and blushed.

6

"You mean to thay you ain't comin out even now?" James called in.

She was silent a moment, hugging herself against the cold and watching herself as she might a stranger, seeing if she'd relent. "Nothing's changed," she said.

"Nothingth *changed!*" he yelled. "By God, Thally, you're the meaneth, thtubborneth, bitchieth, mule-headedeth, vengefulleth cold-blooded therpent in the Thtate of Vermont!"

"That may be true, and I don't say I'm proud of it, but it don't change the facts one iota." She stood with her chin lifted, her two hands holding the bath-robe together, one of them clutching the paperback book, her whole being braced against the world, against God and all His angels if need be.

James was hopping mad. She could see him, in her mind's eye, bent over the doorknob, wild blue eyes bulging from his black-and-blue, scratched up face. Well rant on, Lucifer! *She* hadn't made him get crazy drunk and drive that truck off the road—smash up his truck till there was nothing left of it and he couldn't even drive to the hospital to visit his daughter.

"Ith a lucky thing for you they don't thtill burn witcheth!" he yelled. "You theen the blood out here? Little Ginnyth half-dead in the hothpital and that don't change *nothing?*"

"Applecrate want meant for her and you know it," she snapped. "It was *you* started wavin that gun around, James Page. I was just setting here mindin my own business, and *you* went—"

"And eatin appleth!" he yelled.

"What?" she said.

"You wath juth thettin there mindin your own bithneth and eatin *appleth!* Pretendin you wath goin on a hunger thtrike like Mahatma Gandhi, and all the time you wath cheatin like you've cheated me all your life! You wath livin on appleth!"

The old woman clamped her lips together and her eyes flashed. "That's not the argument we're havin," she yelled, faster and sharper than a horsewhip snapping, "and don't you go slitherin from one thing to another like I don't know a cow from a cornknife. If your idea is to bring up every speck and mite of dirt you can think of from fifty, sixty years ago, why let me just warn you I can bring to mind a few little incidents myself that I'd be pleased to tell you, so if I was you I'd drop that, and faster'n you'd ever drop a bumblebee!"

"Damn!" he yelled. He stamped his foot. "Damn if you don't make me want to come in there and thute you all ovah again! You jith won't quit! Therth my little Ginny in the hothpital—"

"God knows that applecrate want meant for Ginny. If you'd took it on the head yourself as you was meant to—"

He was incredulous. His voice went up two octaves. "Ye'd have *killed* me, Thally! *Damn* if you wouldn't. I'm an old man! Ye'd have thmathed my head like an eggthell and broken my back! Who'd ye gone and lived off then, damn it?"

"I never started it, believe you me, and I don't see the need for all this swearin and coarse language. If your daughter's in the hospital it's nobody put her there but you, James Page, same as you put old Ed Thomas in the hospital and would've put me in the hospital if not in my grave if I hadn't defended myself. You can rant and rail till the cows come home, and try to make me feel guilty and come clean up your mess for you—all the blood you spilt and the

427

dishes you broke and I don't know what-all—but the situation hasn't changed one iota, or if it has it's for the worse: I came into this room because you chased me with stovewood, and ye'd like to have killed me then and there if I hadn't stepped lively. That's how you do things, that's all you know. You think the whole world's just a herd of milkcows that you can drive wheresoever you please by hittin 'em with a stick or throwin some stones or maybe sickin the dog on 'em. Well believe you me it won't work on Sally Abbott and that's all there is to it, so here I *sit!*" When she finished, far stronger and firmer than she'd started, rising on her anger and rhetoric to conviction—becoming like her mother in her final years, Rebekah Page, tall and unyielding, sober-eyed and stern as Old Testament Justice—and also like her grandmother Leah Starke, who had borne sixteen children, most of whom died young, and had survived to the age of a hundred and three, much of that time in the Old Folks' Home—her voice was ringing like an old-time orator's, so that the silence that followed was like a sudden courtroom hush. She waited for him to answer, half alarmed by her own gall. Instead, she heard him moving away.

"James," she said sternly, fiercely—though her wish was to keep him there.

"I got work to do," he said. "Gotta thtot the furnace." He continued down the hall. "Anytime you want to come out, you jith come out." It was a whimper. She saw that she'd hurt him, and though she had meant to, she was distressed at having managed it so well.

She heard him reach the head of the stairs and start slowly down, and she thought, in brief panic, of calling to him again, then decided against it. She laid the book on the bed and rubbed her palms together in front of her chin, frowning, sharp-eyed, thinking of her grandmother. There was no reason she herself should not live that long—at very *least* that long, if James didn't kill her. Despite the image of her niece fallen and stock-still in the doorway—on the hall floor

428

behind her blood-spattered apples, blood pouring down from Ginny's scalp as from a hose (but that had not frightened her, at least not unduly: there was always a good deal of bleeding with a scalp wound)—she must, she saw again, hold firm, stick tight to her principles. Days, months, years passed quickly when you were old, but even so, twenty years of life was a span worth getting decent terms for. She'd been cheated long enough.

When the telephone rang, James Page was in the kitchen, frying himself an egg. He jumped, not because it surprised him but because he'd been expecting it, turned off the heat under the pan, and hurried as fast as he could go to the living room to pick up the receiver. As he did so he drew out his watch and looked at it. Nearly four o'clock. He spit to his left.

"Ay-uh?" he called.

"H'lo," Lewis called back—neither of the two had full confidence in wire—"this is Lewis."

"H'lo," he said. "I recognitheth your voith." He thought of asking What's the news? but hesitated out of fear.

"You ah right up there?" Lewis asked.

"Fine. We're jith fine. Howth everything down there?"

"Ginny's ah right," he said. "Doctor says she's got a haihline fracture on her skull, but she'll be fine."

"Thath good newth!" he said. His hands shook.

"If you wanta come see her I'll come get you," Lewis said. He didn't sound eager. You couldn't blame him.

"Oh?" he said. "Can thee have vithitorth, then?" He realized that he was, strange to say, stalling. It wasn't that he didn't want to see her. Ever since he'd come in after finishing chores and had come upon the blood and apples in the upstairs hallway, he had wanted to see with his own eyes that she was alive and would be well—had wanted to hold her hand as he would when she was a child and feverish, wanted to watch till she came back to consciousness, be

429

there when she opened her eyes. He'd called Putnam Hospital from time to time and had gotten reports—she'd regained consciousness a little after two—and he'd even gone so far as to consider calling some neighbor, maybe Sam Frost, and asking for a ride down to Bennington. But it was a long way, more imposition than he could bring himself to make, so he'd dismissed the idea, had gone up to the bathroom and had tried to ease his mind by talking with Sally—fool that he was! She was a pure hell-fire demon, always had been! The country could fall to the Communist Chinese and she'd still be settin there, locked in her bedroom, demandin her rights!

Lewis said, "Ay-uh, doctor says there's no hahm in her havin visitors. She won't recognize you, though. Little foggy from that bump on the head."

"Foggy, ith thee?"

"What?" Lewis said.

"I thaid Ginnyth foggy."

"Oh, foggy. Ay-uh." Lewis seemed to consider. At last he said, "I could come on up and get you if you want me to. Ed Thomas is here in the hospital too, ye know."

He bent his head more and pulled his arms against his chest, steadying them. "Howth Ed?"

"He's better. Ruth's gone home."

"Thank God for that—that heeth better."

"Thank somebody, ah right." It was not meant to be ironic. It was merely that Lewis disbelieved in God. There was a silence. At length, Lewis said, "Well, what you think, Dad. You want me to come get you?"

"I don' think tho, no," he said, and frowned, feeling guilty. "Ginny wouldn't know me, and Ed jith ath thoon not thee me, I gueth—"

"Ed what?"

He said it again.

"I wouldn't worry about that," Lewis drawled. "Ed don't hold grudges. I talked to him some. He's out of the oxygen tent, by the way."

"Oh?" he said, and waited.

"They got him restin now."

The old man could think of no way to ask right out what Ed might have said about his behavior last night. Every time he thought of it, the more intense his shame was. He'd be glad to get some idea how the others looked at it. Even to know that they hated him would be something. He'd had in his lifetime more than one or two that had hated him.

"Edth better, then, hey?"

"He'll be ah right. They got him restin."

James nodded to the phone. When he was sure Lewis would say no more about Ed Thomas, he asked, "You got Dickey there with you?"

"He's at the sitter's," Lewis said.

"Thath good." He nodded to the phone again. Finally he said, "If ye'd come up and get me tomorrow, I'd be glad. Maybe I'll have Thally out of her room by then." He laughed.

"I wouldn't bet my ahm on it," Lewis said.

When they'd said good-bye and hung up, he sat looking out the window a while, his mind just drifting. The afternoon was as gray as the morning had been, no life but a few chickens in the yard, and he realized that this was the season he'd always forgotten, all his life, had neglected to prepare for until suddenly it was upon him, the gap between the glory of fall and the serenity of winter in Vermont, the deep soft snow of November and December, the long blue shadows of January . . . Though it was only last night that the storm had torn them off, the leaves seemed to have lost their vitality already, their yellow dulling to a yellowish gray, the red dimming down towards orange. It was the light, perhaps, that made the leaves seem half-rotted, but if the rot hadn't really set in yet today, it would be there for sure tomorrow or the next day, and the gap of drab weather, no life but in the sky, would drag on and on, the days growing shorter, more uncomfortable, more unhealthy, no pleasure but a few butternuts the squirrels had missed —perhaps a glimpse of a fox—until getting out of bed was the hardest of his chores, and getting back into it at night was unconditional surrender. The gap might last for weeks—gray pastures, gray skies, even the crows in the birches looking up—and then when he began to believe he would never get through it alive, there suddenly, one morning, would be the world transformed, knee deep in snow, and even if the sky was gray, the farm would be beautiful.

He sat feeling his gums with his tongue-tip, tasting his mouth, then leaned forward in his chair, pressed down on his knees, and got up. He walked to the kitchen and remembered the egg he'd been frying. He turned the electric burner back on and, because it would be slow to heat, thought he'd go to the bathroom. When he did so, it was almost not worth the trouble; yet his stomach for some reason wasn't paining him especially right now—the pains came and went, though mostly they were there, dug in good, either stabbing like hot spears or rumbling, burning on low, but burning. He rinsed off his hands, wiped them on the towel, and started back downstairs. He called to Sally as he took the first step down.

"That wath Lewith on the phone. Ginnyth all right. Little foggy from the bump."

"Thank heavens," Sally called. "Is Ed Thomas better?"

"Edth better too," he said, and took another step.

"I'm glad to hear it."

He took another step down.

She called, "James?"

He waited.

"What you going to do about that truck? You can't get through the winter without a truck."

"*I'll* worry about that." There were always the horses.

"Well we can't just set here on the mountain all winter long, ye know. And what about your teeth? How you going to pay for new teeth?"

"Maybe jith ath well," he said crossly, "I don't get no teeth I can't *bite* nobody."

"Thath right," she mimicked. "You can drown 'em to death in thpit!"

He went angrily down the stairs—she could smell his fried eggs burning—and from the way he grunted with every step she knew he was bent like a gorilla. She was doing none too well herself. She'd brought the bedpan back down from the attic, not just because now that the cars were gone she could empty it out the window, but also because she had to use it every fifteen minutes or so—she kept it with her in the bed—and every time she used it her diarrhea was worse. She was so sore and stinging that doing her business made her eyes well up. If anything broke her spirit, she knew, it would be the pain of those bowel movements. If it weren't for the pain she knew *he* was in, tied in knots by constipation, she'd have abandoned the fort long since. She would run out of Kleenex in another day, but she'd manage. She could tear up sheets.

For half an hour she walked back and forth from the window to the attic door to the window, keeping herself in shape. She bent twenty times to touch her knees, put her hands behind her head and wagged her elbows back and forth, clapped her hands above her head until her arms were tired, then climbed up in bed and ate an apple and, at last, settled to her book. She'd been looking forward to it. She was close to the end, where you expected some excitement. And what did they give you? A long, boring chapter full of some queer irony, the whole thing preachy, preachy, preachy! Luckily, much of it was missing. She looked up from time to time in angry indignation, feeling cheated, fiddled with. "Oh!" she cried out once, clapping the book shut and half inclined to tear out more pages. She read on, in the end, only to find out how far these people would dare go.

14

THE TRIAL OF CAPTAIN FIST

Again the earth rumbled and a tremor went through the rocks. "It's nothing," said Mr. Nit. "—I think."

Dancer stood on a table of rock near the entrance to the cave, with Captain Fist bound and gagged on his right, and all the people seated in front of him and to his left, a great, dark multitude watching and listening, though none of the Mexicans knew English. The barren basin of Lost Souls' Rock was full of the deep red flicker of torches. Santisillia, the Indian, and the crew of the *Indomitable* sat in front, looking at neither Dancer nor the Captain.

"Brothers and sisters," Dancer said, "we gathered together this day for the purpose of blasting this here Captain Fist. But first we gonna give him a fair trial and see if he's guilty. Now I'm gonna tell you in the first place, since I'm the prosecution, I've had some experience with this man myself, and in my experience he's a shit-eatin, motherfuckin, baby-killin, lady-rapin *faggot*." He whirled to point at Fist. "He's a lowborn unprincipled traitor against humanity, and a false ideal for youth, if you understan me. He's a subhuman animal that stinks worsen shit or even hair burning. He's murdered people and he's buggered people, and all he is is putrefaction, and I mean he ain't fit to commingle with even damn vermin, so we're here to justice the dude." He paused, chin lifted, dark glasses in his hand, his violent black eyes flashing. Abruptly, he pointed at Santisillia. "Firs witness!"

Santisillia stood up, smiling a little oddly, marijuana in his pipe.

"Raise your hand," Dancer said. "You swear to tell the truth the whole truth and nothin but the truth so help you God?"

Santisillia shrugged. "Man, who wants truth?"

"Truth and the whole truth," Dancer said. "Start talkin." He sat down, furious, watching like a wolf. The firelight turned his dark glasses red.

Santisillia turned toward the people and stood looking, shaking his head as if this couldn't be happening. At last he spoke. He put on the stage accent like a ceremonial mask.

"I read in a book once, 'Let a man be either a hero or a saint. In between lies, not wisdom, but banality.'"

He smoked and seemed to think about it, looking at the Captain.

"But what is a hero? If there were truths independent of the currents of being, there could be no history of truths. And what is a saint? If there were one single eternally right religion, religious history would be an inconceivable idea. However well developed a man's consciousness may be, it is nevertheless something stretched like a membrane over his developing life, perfused by the pulsing blood, even betraying the hidden power of cosmic directness. It is the destiny of each moment of awareness to be a cast of Time's net over Space."

Dancer half rose, aiming the machine gun in Santisillia's direction. "Hey, quit that. Lay down what he done."

Santisillia nodded.

"I don't mean that eternal truths don't exist," he said. "Every man possesses them—a thousand of them—to the extent that he exists and exercises the understanding faculty in a world of thoughts, in the connected ensemble of which they are, in and for the instant of thought, unalterable fixtures—ironbound as cause-effect combinations in hoops of premises and conclusions. Nothing in this disposition . . .

There was a gap of several pages.

. . . influence. Captain Fist is Lucifer himself, the ultimate revolutionary. Or worse. —Or better. —Depending on your point of view. He does not revolt in the name of good. He denies the system, rejects its laws, reduces its history to nothingness by a resounding *Deus sum!* Behold the true Son of Liberty! There are no laws but the laws of Captain Fist. There can be no just and lawful judgment but the judgment handed down by Captain Fist! Would you try a man by a system he never subscribed to, never believed in for a minute? How can you call a man guilty except by the laws he acknowledged and broke? Is a lion guilty? A scorpion? Killing is the work of animals. Why should I philosophize the bestiality of a certain society's 'justice' into 'reasonable' law? Much that was criminal a hundred years ago is not criminal in the same society today. Much that is criminal today will be legal, I assure you, the day after tomorrow. God's laws are not our laws."

He stood as if awaiting an answer. At last, he took a puff from his pipe, shook his head, and sat down.

Dancer said, "What the fuck?" Then: "How come you on his side, you crazy Luther? Man, this is beautiful!"

He turned to the people angrily, as if Santisillia's speech were entirely their fault.

436

"Listen! This Captain Fist shot me, understand? He blown up this here nitro-glycerin truck and they was peoples laid out like it was wartime, man, and Russians was throwing round atomic bombs. He wrecked our car one time, another time he sunk this boat we had. He got us arrested one time, and another time he come up and got us in a alley and beat us black and blue and made us go wif him, all except Dusky, because Dusky got away, like he always does, and Fist made us go help him bail out his motherfucking boat. It's beautiful, man! He makes people do his work and he makes 'em slave till their noses bleed, and if they die of it, man, he don' give a damn purple-green shit. Now you gonna tell me that ain't against the law?

"Listen! People's got hopes and aspirations, that's only natural. And a man comes along and he stands in the way there, and he won't let 'em get at their hopes and aspirations—well that *ain't* natural. We all in this together, you understand? And this man sets himself up like God, you dig? and he says, 'All you people here's working for me, and you got no rights and privileges, dig? because I'm God, Jack, and you people just human beings, worsen animals, right? and you're all crazy slobberin sex maniacs and lazy good-for-nothings and you ain't no better than dogshit.' We gonna take that, brothers? You gonna say that's the law? Now I want you people to get yourself together and make some sense. I'm gonna call my next witness." He turned on Peter Wagner. "*You!*"

Peter Wagner looked grieved, faintly dopey, like a man roused out of sleep. He stretched his hands out helplessly. "Why don't you just go ahead and shoot him?"

Dancer waited.

Peter Wagner stood up, silent, puffing at his pipe. The Mexicans all smiled, clapping, stomping their feet, encouraging him. He glanced at Dancer's machine gun, then at Jane. "Very well," he said. He put one hand on his hip and extended the other.

"Luther's told you the Captain's an existentialist," he said, "a man who defines the whole universe by the fact that he happens to be in it. He's told you the only laws the Captain knows are the ones he makes up. You all understand, of course, that we could fix that. Simple. We could all vote and make up a set of laws and demand that the Captain obey them or get out. In other words, we could start the whole process of civilization over. It's an amusing idea." He smiled, showing his teeth. He didn't look amused. "That's how the whole thing probably started in the first place—a bunch of outlaws in some prehistoric jungle or valley, bored to tears by always getting their stuff swiped, their children getting killed, certain people doing all the talking . . . But we've been through all that now, we understand the problem. Societies evolve. The freedom that law hands out is always yesterday's freedom. Freedom for the few, or the freedom of a horse with blinders, otherwise called blinkers: he's free to look straight ahead. The only real free state is the one governed, second by second, exactly as each man within it wants it to be governed that second. Which is impossible. So you and I, sensible people, have become anarchists. Outlaws. Or rather we have become, like everyone else, scoff-laws. You people more or . . .

Another gap.

438

. . . a world so feminized that revolutionaries with slogans of death and home-made atomic bombs are softly analyzed, generously understood. Imagine a whole planet of big-boobed girl Congressmen——"

"That's enough!" Santisillia broke in. He was on his feet, angrily shaking his fist. "He's crazy. His testimony's useless. He's got a woman thing."

"That's not true," Peter Wagner shouted. "I'm presenting Captain Fist's point of view."

Dancer scratched his head. "Man, somebody got to present the *other* side."

"I'm saying he hates women," Peter Wagner said. "I'm saying he only had two choices, to turn on them and on everything that reminded him of them with rage and scorn, or accept them, be swallowed up like the rest of us in effeminate softness and confusion—give in to a world where 'The best lack all conviction, while the worst——' "

"I *still* say he's got a woman thing," Santisillia said.

"You're crazy," Peter Wagner shouted. "Women are my gods, my eternal torment. You, you got a *theology* thing!"

Dancer thought about it, scowling intensely. Finally he made his decision. "Sit down, you faggot."

Peter Wagner sat down.

Mr. Nit's testimony was short and to the point. "The whole thing is a matter of mechanics," he said. He popped his knuckles, suffering from stage-fright. "The Captain was born ugly, which got him into fights, which left him uglier and uglier, by perceptible degrees. Finally he was so horrible he had to live by his wits. As a general proposition, it is safe to say that all causes and effects are physical, and that every so-called moral cause can eventually be factored to a willow switch or a pat on the cheek. This has been shown in laboratories. It is possible to teach the highest pitch of religious zeal to a war ant, or something indistinguishable from tender affection to a fruitfly. I might take, for example, the example of eels——"

"That won't be necessary," Dancer said. He pushed him away. "You all crazy. You're God damn fuckheads!" He called Jane to the stand.

She said, after a moment's hesitation, "Listen, Dancer, why don't we simply *ask* Captain Fist if he's guilty?" She asked it so innocently, so sweetly, her comic-book blue eyes so wide, that Dancer was stopped.

"That's stupid," he said without conviction. "You're as crazy as they are! He'd just lie."

"What's the difference?" she said. "It's his trial, after all. How would you feel if it was your trial, and they kept you tied up like that all the way through it and never even let you speak?"

"If that man goes and contempts this court——" Dancer said.

"Oh come on, Dance," she said. She put her hand on his shoulder.

He glanced at the others. The Mexicans all smiled and clapped. He took a deep breath. His face squeezed.

"Somebody go take the gag off the motherfucking Captain and drag his ass over."

Tears of perhaps gratitude rolled down the Captain's cheeks.

The people stirred approvingly as Santisillia and Mr. Nit carried the Captain forward, bound hand and foot, tied up from end to end like a bundle of rags. The women whispered among themselves or hushed their crying babies. (As soon as his face had come out of the shadows, the babies had all begun to cry.) The men said nothing. They'd had dealings with him and

440

regretted that he wasn't in more pain. At last he was standing on the speaker's rock, his bound hands clinging to the head of his cane, leaning on it slightly. His feet were so tightly tied together that he couldn't move an inch. Santisillia threw more wood on the fire. It flared up, lighting the underside of Captain Fist's jaw and his tumor-fat belly. The crowd fell silent.

"Ladies and gentlemen," Captain Fist said, "I thank you for this opportunity." His voice was a whisper, full of emotion. His whiskered, horrible face twitched and jerked as if the muscles were fish in a sack. Tears streamed down his cheeks, his shaggy eyebrows glistened with sweat. People hissed. He endured it in silence, with a pained, dignified smile, tears streaming down his cheeks and nose. At last the crowd was still again.

"I have been deeply moved by these men's defense of me." People booed. Again he waited.

"Excuse me," he said, looking mournfully at Dancer, "might I get you to untie my feet? I like to pace when I talk. When I can't pace I can't think. Actually, it's not fair, in a sense. It's like asking a man to defend himself when he's drunk."

Dancer stood still, as if he hadn't heard, but he was thinking about it. At last, with a ferocious jerk, he crossed to the Captain and, in the spirit of fair play, flipped his switchblade from his pocket, and cut the ropes that bound the foul old man from the waist to the feet. Then he went back to his place without a word and stood waiting, casually aiming the machine gun at Captain Fist's head.

"Thank you," Captain Fist said, a catch in his voice.

"I've been very interested in all that these gentlemen have said. They make me feel humble, that's the truth. They make me feel I'm part of a great movement—the whole progress of man. They make me stop and think. I'm always grateful to a man for that. They've made me see this Vale of Tears from a whole new perspective.

"I'm not a formally educated man." He simpered and bowed. "Almost the only philosophers I know are the ones I read in the Harvard Classics. But I will say this: the ones I know I know well, the way we know our dearest friends. They have been my constant companions, in dingy hotels, in jails, on the seven seas . . . They have been, I might say, among the closest friends I have." He simpered and sniffed, deeply touched, then suddenly remembered that his legs were free and he could pace. He lifted one stiff leg, set it down, lurched over onto it, then did the same with the other. Soon he was more or less walking, jerking stiffly back and forth, keeping his balance with the cane.

"Among my favorite philosophers," he said, simpering again, "is Jean Jacques Rousseau. A number of things these gentlemen have said have turned my mind to that great man's writings—for example, his discourse on the question 'Whether the Progress of the Sciences and of Letters Has Tended to Corrupt or to Elevate Morals,' and also, for example, his 'Discourse on Inequality.' I should like, with your permission, to dedicate these few remarks of mine, this little *apologia*, to that great, high-minded philosopher to whom all of us here in America owe so much."

He bowed his head, memorial. When he raised it he turned it slowly, mournfully, like a cannon turning on a battleship, to Dancer. "Would you mind if I had my right hand free?" he asked. "It's so difficult to talk without gestures."

Dancer sighed and shook his head, then went

over and untied the Captain's right hand. Jane brought him a glass of water.

"Thank you," the Captain said.

"Let us reflect once again on the savage," he said. He took a sip of water, put it down on the rock, and paced again.

"The body being the only instrument that savage man is acquainted with, he naturally employs it to different uses, of which ours, for want of practice, are incapable." He nodded, thinking it over, seeing that it was so. "Had the savage a hatchet, would his hand so easily snap from an oak so stout a branch? Had he a sling, would his hand dart a stone so far? Or had he a ladder, would he run up, so nimbly, a tree? Give civilized man but time to collect his mechanisms, and no doubt he would be an overmatch for the savage. But if you care to see a contest even more unequal, place the two naked and unarmed one opposite the other—" He struck a pose: "—Nature against Art!

"An animal is a mere machine, to which nature hath given senses to wind itself up and guard, to a degree, its life. The human machine is the same, with this difference, that nature alone works the workings of the animal, whereas man, as a free agent, has a share in his. One chooses by instinct, the other—I must here disagree with my friends—by an act of liberty; for which reason the beast cannot deviate from the rules that have been prescribed to it, even in cases where such deviation might prove useful. Thus a pigeon might starve near a fine, rare steak, or a cat beside a bowl of ripe cherries!

"Nature speaks to all animals, and beasts obey her voice. Man feels the same impression, but he at the same time perceives that he is free to resist or acquiesce. And it is surely in consciousness of this liberty that the spirituality of his soul chiefly arises: for natural philosophy explains, in some measure, the mechanism of the senses and the formation of ideas; but in the power of willing, or rather of choosing, and in the consciousness of this power, nothing can be discovered but acts outside the laws of mechanics. Let me add, for the benefit of my friend Mr. Nit, that even if all a man's deeds are ultimately mechanical (as he so persuasively maintains), his consciousness that he might do otherwise, and his anxiety at being unable to do both, are sufficient signs of his liberty. I am as deeply impressed as is Mr. Nit (I presume) that the root pressure of a common tomato can throw a one-inch column of water a hundred and eighty-two feet straight up. But a man who did the same would be *proud* of it, or, in another situation, chagrined.

"However, I digress."

Dancer was shaking his head and moaning.

The Captain slipped his free hand inside the lapel of his overcoat and stood, like Sam Adams, with one fat leg thrust forward.

"To see and to feel would be the first conditions of savage man, which he would enjoy in common with other animals. To will and not to will, to wish and to fear, would be the first and only operations of his soul. Let professors say what they will, my friends—blathering of 'models' like Hektor and Akhelleus, heroes who reveal to us the ways of the gods—the human understanding is profoundly indebted to the passions. It is by their activity that our reason improves: we covet knowledge merely because we covet pleasure, and it is impossible to conceive why a man exempt from fears and desires should take the trouble to reason. The passions, in their turn, owe their origin to our wants, and their increase to our progress in science. For we cannot desire or fear anything but in consequence of the *ideas* we have of it, and savage man, ideally considered, destitute of every species of knowledge . . .

Another gap.

. . . And what are all these, to speak more directly, but empathy—the unconscious outreach of soul to soul, the direct, precognitive experience of another man's toothache?

"Obviously this identification must have been infinitely more perfect in the state of nature than in the state of reason. It is reason that makes man keep aloof from every thing that can bother him. So psychologists tell us, whose whole occupation is to get us back in touch with our emotions. It is philosophy that destroys our connections with other men. What can disturb the calm sleep of the philosopher and force him from his bed? One man may slit another's throat with impunity under his open window: the philosopher needs only to clap his hands to his ears, argue with himself a little, and rest. In riots and street brawls, the lowest and meanest of the populace flock together, the prudent sneak off.

"And I might add in support of Mr. Wagner's perhaps somewhat antifeminist position—" he made a depreciatory little gesture, as if to say everyone has his little faults "—that all I've said concerning empathy can be said as well of so-called sexual love. The physical part of love is easily enough dismissed: the general desire which prompts the two sexes to unite. A form of empathy rewarded. But what is the 'moral' part of love? The 'moral' part, as all truly modern men perceive, is a factitious not to say meretricious sentiment, dismissed by feminists

445

while it suits their whim and fleshly greed, then later cried up by them, with great care and address, in order that they may establish their empire and secure command for the sex which ought rightly to obey. How decadently civilized, how advanced and reasonable, is this 'moral' love whose signs and proofs are jealous rages, murdered philanderers, the sorrows and sicknesses of whorehouses, and the black shame of death by abortion—yes, I say, *death by abortion!*"

Captain Fist paused, heaving and panting, surveying his audience. They were visibly shaken. He looked all but distraught.

"Perhaps you are asking yourselves, 'What has all this to do with Captain Fist?' I will tell you. You see before you, in my humble person, the extreme of the civilized philosopher, dread image (if you'll forgive me) of your own too ironic, too self-conscious selves: a man so distant from the simple and lovable emotions of the savage that nothing makes him weep but a nicely constructed argument, true or false; a man who, tossing in his bed, instead of counting sheep, invents bland, sophisticated chatter on world-wide starvation. I am deeply, deeply aware of this fault. As a matter of fact, I carry newspaper clippings in my pocket—touching and uplifting things that I think it might do my soul good to peruse from time to time; for believe me, my fellow Americans and guests, philosophy will not save us! Intelligence will not save us! *Art* will not save us! We must find our way back to authentic emotion, back to the Spirit that carried our forefathers through Valley Forge, and the Battle of the Marne, and Okinawa! It is our *hearts* that must save us, our pure and uncomplicated Yankee emotion—Ben Franklin, Mark Twain, Norman Rockwell! I carry such clippings as this, for instance—"

He reached clumsily with his right hand for his left hip pocket, but unluckily he was much too fat, and neither by going around front nor by going around back could he get his wriggling, fat-pink-spider fingers near the pocket. "Excuse me," he said to Dancer with a look of sorrow, "would you object to untying my left hand?"

Dancer did so.

"Ah, thank you!" he said. The clippings were not in the left hip pocket after all, but eventually, by patting all his pockets—trousers, shirt, suitcoat, overcoat—he found them and unfolded them. He sorted through them, glancing them over. "Ah!" he said. "Listen!"

FATHER WHO JOINED SON
IN HOLDUP GETS PROBATION

Thomas Pepper, 51, San Diego, was placed on five-year probation today by Judge John Claypole in circuit court, San Diego.

Pepper pleaded guilty to armed robbery of the San Diego American Legion Club Dec. 5, 1960.

In issuing his opinion, Claypole said, "The fact that 17 people appeared in the courtroom on a day when temperatures were below 60 outside and less than 70 in the courtroom, several of them war veterans and people of means, and strongly recommended probation for the defendant, shows, I think, that their request must be taken seriously."

Pepper was joined in the robbery by his 16-year-old son, Thomas Jr. The youth was committed to the California Youth Commission and then released for military service when he expressed a desire to serve his country.

"Now isn't that something?" Captain Fist said. "Is that how America works or isn't it? By God, my fellow countrymen and guests, I tell you wherever you please to look, from Seattle to Miami, from New York to San Francisco, *by God that's America!*"

A thrill went through them and they applauded. As for the Captain, for some reason as he spoke his final words his face shattered into laughter. They all stopped applauding and looked at him. He laughed harder and harder. "That's America!" he squealed. They tipped their heads, looking, and the corners of their mouths began to wiggle. He'd lost all control now. He hooted, howled, bawled, gasped, guffawed and wet his pants; and gradually, after glancing at one another, the others began laughing too, first Jane and Mr. Goodman and Mr. Nit.

"That's Nebraska!" cried Jane, and laughed more shrilly. Then Dancer and Santisillia and Peter Wagner grinned, then began to laugh, and finally all the Mexicans joined in, rolling around, slapping the ground with their sombreros. The laughter swelled until the whole volcanic basin roared and rumbled and wheeped with it. For a moment the walls themselves shook, and a roar as of terrible laughter came booming from below. Captain Fist was on the jittering, cracking ground, lying on his humped back, kicking like a ladybug, clutching his belly, clawing at his eyes and nose. Dancer gasped and reeled and coughed, so weak he had to drop his machine gun. Captain Fist snatched at it as soon as it fell, but he was laughing so hard his fingers had no strength. Dancer tried to drag the machine gun out of the Captain's reach, but he lurched and gasped and couldn't pick it up. Santisillia tried to grab it but he fell down, helplessly laughing, and soon they were all, or almost all, piled up together, hitting each other's backs with great resounding wallops, hooting, howling, bawling, gasping, and guffawing. This went on for some time.

When the hilarity passed—the earthquake had also stopped, temporarily—they lay exhausted for a while, only giggling now and then, or giving a little chortle, and then at last they began to extricate themselves from the heap, giving each other a friendly hand. When everyone who had been in the pile was on his feet, it began to appear that Captain Fist was not among them.

15

THIS PROVES
YE ARE ABOVE, YE JUSTICERS!

The lights went on early in the Governor's high chambers. Many of those present had been informed only at the last minute of what was to transpire—had been assembled in such haste that some still had on their nightgowns beneath their coats. Only the Governor, the State and Federal Narcotics officials, the CIA, the FBI, several U.S. Senators, and the representatives of the military had been in on the plan from the beginning. They'd been here with the Governor, working out strategy and keeping touch with Washington, the various agencies jockeying for position, since midnight. There had been shouting and some violence and even one such threat of violence as had not been heard between government officials since Ethan Allen and Aaron Burr debated on who should be Governor of Fort Ticonderoga. All that, however, had been behind closed doors. Now, in public view, the whole assembly sat hushed and solemn in wide semi-circular rows facing the television set, the Governor and various

449

politicos in front, serious men with large paunches . . .

Another gap. She took a bite of her apple.

. . . "That's it, Chief," the Governor's aide said, and gave him a little poke.

The Governor jerked as if he'd nodded off, then said into his mike: "Go, boys! God bless!"

The fat aide beside him pressed his palms together as if praying.

Over the TV came now the roar of engines.

In his murky living room, the Police Commissioner of San Francisco, tiny eyes staring at the black and white TV, reached over to shake the cosmic flank of his wife beside him. "Zero hour," he said. She opened one eye, raised her beer, and wriggled her nose. "God be with them," she said. "Amen," he said. "Amen," they said together.

Sally Abbott looked up from her book. "That's stupid," he said. Then, pursing her lips, she looked down again.

Now in the Governor's high chambers everyone sat on the edge of his chair as, in the blood red light of early morning, fifteen miles from San Diego, the big planes lifted off one by one and droned in V-formation south-southwest. A reporter was talking with a bombardier. The emergency call, the bombardier said, had not awakened the post. There had been a party going on. The troops had snatched up their bottles and brought them along.

"Are you afraid?" the reporter asked, and again held the mike to the bombardier.

"Not too bad," the bombardier said, grinning boyishly.

Twenty minutes into the mission, after some talk and commercials, the camera picked up the lead pilot, Commander Purcel, who was checking the roll. All the planes were still with him. He nodded satisfaction to his co-pilot, a woman, and smiled, showing perfect little teeth. He was an older man, veteran of World War II. He had shaggy white hair pushing out around his helmet, and his leather jacket was covered, like the chest of a Czar, with ribbons and medals. "Our Father, which are in Heaven," he said. He flicked on the radio button so the others could hear him. "Hallowed be Thy name."

Far in the distance, black against the red of the sky, towered Lost Souls' Rock. The Governor abruptly leaned forward in his chair, snatching off his glasses, and squinting at the television. "What the hell is that?" he bellowed.

His aide said, "Holy cow! It looks like—"

A few thousand feet above Lost Souls' Rock, motionless and gleaming, hung a huge and serene flying saucer.

"No sir! No *siree!*" Sally Abbott cried, jerking her head up. "Oh, really! For mercy's sakes!" She stared at the book as if right in front of her eyes it had changed into a garden snake, then threw it so hard that when it hit it made a crack in the panel of the bedroom door. She was surprised her arm had such strength left in it—must have hit the panel just exactly right. She sat wide-eyed and shaking, so angry she

451

could have cursed. What kind of person would *write* such slop? she'd like to know. And not only that, some company had *published* it! Had those people no *shame?* A thought still more terrible came to her: there were people out there who *read* these things. It made her sit up and put her feet over the side, her hand on her heart, though what she meant to do, once she was up, she was hard put to say. She looked out into the evening darkness, trying to imagine what debauched, sick people would believe such foolishness amusing. "Gracious!" she breathed.

What came to her mind first was the ugly old men she would sometimes notice at bus stations, when she went on her yearly spree with Estelle to New York: old blear-eyed bums, tobacco running down their whiskered chins, fingernails black, trousers unbuttoned, perhaps one eye poked out and grown over below the lid. But she knew at once that, ugly as they were, they weren't the ones. Such people never read, or if they did, read only newspapers, following along under the words with their fingers, jerking and muttering, finding in everything they stumbled on new and evermore bitter confirmation of what their lives had taught them long ago, that sorrow and disease are the lot of all animals, so that perhaps they'd been right, after all, to give in, become these mindless and despairing husks that they knew very well they'd become. No, they were not the ones; no. Her own brother James might become such a man without much labor, violent, stubborn, and self-critical as he was, beset with more troubles than a cranberry merchant; and though he was her enemy, for now at least—"in war enemies, in peace friends," as Horace would say— James and miserable people like him were not the evil she'd hurled from her bed. Young people, then?

She pursed her lips and pulled at a strand of her hair, considering. It was possible, of course. She half-turned and felt behind her on the bed for the bedpan. Some young people, heaven knew, were arrogant fools, always sneering at their elders, sure they knew far more than anybody. It wasn't true of the young people she knew just now; but she had known such children from time to time. And one thought of people like Patricia Hearst, or those people who blew up banks and stores, or those Manson people—terrifying things!—Satanists who lived off the garbage of hotels—so she'd heard on the news—and at night crept into people's houses and chopped them up horribly, no one knew why. But it was hard to believe such people as poor Patricia or those others read novels, though perhaps they read Communist tracts— perhaps they read even honest books about the troubles in the world, and because they were young and hadn't yet noticed that for the most part grown-ups are merely stupid, not purposely evil (though some were that too), they took things into their own young, foolish hands. They were idealists, in a certain sad, terrible way. Some of them had gotten good grades in college, she'd seen on TV, and if you could believe what they said—and Sally was inclined to believe what people said, even when she knew they were partly lying— their whole purpose was to call attention to social injustices and destroy what they saw as the System. She would not care to be friends with such people (it might be interesting—though Horace would be shocked—to talk with one, briefly), but she could not believe it was for them her book was meant. They had better things to do—self-pity to revel in and plots to hatch, sticking pins into candle-lit maps somewhere down cellar. The book would bore them, even though they might well agree with its sour opinions.

Who then?

She finished with the bedpan, opened the window and dumped it out, closed the window again, and noticing only now how cold the floor was, pushed her feet into her slippers. She absently took an apple and began to eat it, pacing in an *L* back and forth around the bed, back and forth between the window and the attic door. The night was very quiet. Out in the barn she could hear James' milking machines chugging. She paused, sucking a piece of apple from her dentures and thinking of him moving from cow to

453

cow, hunched over, hauling heavy cans, laboring on though his life, he must know if he looked at it, had no longer any hint of rhyme or reason—laboring on by senseless habit, or for the cows' sake and, by accident, half against his will, for hers.

She turned in haste from the window and the thought. There was only one place that thought could lead, she knew: capitulation. She'd find herself giving in to his senseless tyranny, a life not worth living, as far as she was concerned, plain and dreary as a plank in the barn—giving in for no better reason than James had for milking his cows. She glanced past her shoulder at the book on the floor, face down, as she'd have looked at a crushed brown spider that might not be dead.

She returned to her pacing, touching the bedpost each time she went by. Who else was there, she asked herself, that read books? Suddenly and mysteriously— though she did not notice the mystery—a picture came to her, clearer than a picture on television, of people on a bus. It was a gloomy bus with knife-slashed seats and, outside the windows, dull rain and the lights of a city. Perhaps it was a bus she'd really seen, in New York for instance, or perhaps she was only imagining it, as she imagined things while reading; either way, the image was crystal clear, so clear that, except for curious blurs and uncertainties, she could study the faces one by one.

She studied a large, middle-aged black woman. The woman was tired, her head tipped back, the flesh of her face all hanging, it seemed, from the shiny bridge of her nose. Her eyes were closed, her fingers interlaced, her workshoes worn over on the outsides. She had a paper bag, wrinkled as if she'd carried things home in it many times. She had with her no newspaper, no books. If she ever read anything, it was the Bible. There were people these days—mostly young; people that never read it—who claimed the Bible was an enslaver of women like this one, this . . . From nowhere the weird thought came back that the black woman's name was Sally. How odd! . . . Perhaps

it was true (her mind hurried on) that the Bible enslaved the poor and oppressed, such as women, inclining them to acceptance; but Sally Abbott for one did not believe it. She was a true Christian woman if ever one lived, though she said so herself, and *she* was no slave. Some things, of course, one had to accept without whimpering, such as old age. But as for human tyranny ... Sally Abbott smiled, her eyes closed tightly, studying the black woman. For all her weariness, all her burdens of family, poverty, uncertainty, and the weight of her flesh, she was no cowed dog, no weakling. Her black eyes could flash, she could lash out with words or with her hand or with the end of her broom ...

She studied the young, light-skinned black girl beside the fat woman, no relation. The girl was beautiful and generous of heart, though it seemed to her troubled in some way, dissatisfied or frightened. She had a brown leather purse, an elegant brown coat, and probably, at home in her apartment, good books, novels translated from French, poetry by Langston Hughes, biographies perhaps, also records and prints ... Her face was motionless, hiding all her thoughts. Her hands, too—in brown gloves—were motionless. Sally realized with a start that the girl was Pearl Wilson, from her novel.

But she did not stop her little game with her mind merely because her mind had tricked her. She pressed her fingertips to her eyelids until colors came, but also an image. Behind them sat ... a rabbi with a tangled beard. She smiled—he somehow pleased her —but passed over him at once, remembering her purpose. He, certainly, would waste no time on such a novel.

There was a countrified girl with bad skin, a cheap overcoat of electric purple, a piece of gum in her cheek, and in her squat, slightly spatulate hands she had, Sally saw, a paperback novel. But it was a novel about a nurse, some silly, frumpy book that could surely do no harm, no more harm than a daydream, a cup of hot milk—or at any rate no harm beyond making her snap at her husband, if she should be lucky enough to catch one, some innocent drudge like Ginny's Mr. Nit—no harm beyond making her criticize the man, or use tears against him because he failed to measure up to the doctor who loved the nurse (Jennifer) in her book.

There was a Jewish girl with a bad cold, shy and lightly moustached, thick glasses on her nose—not flattering to her red and swollen eyes—a scratchy woven bag drooping down from her shoulder and, peeking from the top, along with other college books, a Russian novel. Beside her sat a man in a shabby raincoat. He had a large, long-nostrilled nose and tiny eyes, a black hat with a pinkish purple band and feather. His hands were pushed down in the raincoat pockets, and for an instant Sally thought, in alarm, that he was going to expose himself. She watched with distaste and fascination, but the man did nothing, merely stared with an expression of storekeeper-annoyance at the rabbi's huge ears, then at length turned his head and watched, as he would a potential shoplifter, the street.

The picture had been as sharp as a vision all this time—it was like a conscious and intentional dream—but now it dimmed, and she was seeing, just as clearly, as if it came from the same queer back room of her mind, an image of the crowd of Mexicans at Captain Fist's trial, and Dancer with his machine gun.

Abruptly, Sally stooped for the book. She put the applecore on the dresser, found the place where she'd left off, and, pursing her lips with disapproval, began walking back and forth between the window and the door to the attic, continuing her reading.

Meanwhile on Lost Souls' Rock, the vast crowd —all but invisible in smoke, a cloud of marijuana as thick as London fog—was deliberating on the case of Captain Fist, though he was nowhere to be seen. Perhaps they assumed he'd show up, in time; perhaps, high as the moon, they saw the case as academic.

"He's an eloquent speaker," Santisillia said, sprawled on the ground, laboring to keep his eyes open. Slowly he brought out, "Be a shame to kill a man who can orate like that, even though we know it's all bullshit. Captain's an artist."

"I say blow him away," Dancer said, smiling and wagging both hands. "That's what we *had* this trial for, isn't it?"

Peter Wagner sighed.

"Man, what's the difference?" Dancer said. "Everybody knocks off, sooner or later. That's the thing none of you dudes will face. The ultimate death rate of the human animal is fantastic."

Jane said, "You know what? I'm tired of this, I don't know about you people. Anyway, we've got to hang around all day. Why can't we decide it later? Let's ball." She relit her pipe and unfastened the top buttons of her shirt. Mr. Goodman watched her, thought about things, and then relit his pipe too. "Do unto others—that's what I say," he said. The eyes of the Mexicans came to life and they all relit their pipes, though most of them were still going. Children and toothless old women, smiling, passed through the crowd with torches.

Dr. Alkahest opened his eyes for an instant, smiled, tongue lolling, and fainted. His moneybelt and all his moneybags were empty. Except Dr. Alkahest, who'd already experienced it, everyone in the crowd was rich.

The volcano basin filled still more thickly with smoke. There was laughter and lovemaking on every hand, everyone doing what he liked to do. Some were having knife fights. Peter Wagner, profoundly at peace, gazed inward, savoring images of poison-bottles, hangingropes, knives, guns, razors, vats of acid. He saw

458

golden-winged angels, all female. Vaguely, though it seemed to him his mind was clear, he mused on the Captain's speech. It was a queer thing that the Captain, vicious as he was, could express such wonderful sentiments. One of the angels pressed her cool, wet lips on Peter Wagner's, then pushed her tongue into his mouth.

Santisillia recited dramatically:

When I consider Life, 'tis all a Cheat;
Yet, Fool'd by Hope, men favour the Deceit,
Trust on, and think Tomorrow will repay!
Tomorrow's false than the former Day . . .

It was that instant that the earthquake broke loose in earnest. Peter Wagner rolled blindly, a fissure opening directly underneath him, sending up a roar from the earth's twisted guts. He snatched Jane's slick, naked body and rolled her with him——he wasn't even sure that the body was Jane's——instinctively driving toward what ought to be the safety of the cave and the basin's only exit. Lizards flew back and forth crazily, flopping and hissing like snakes.

"Stay down! Stay down!" Santisillia yelled. He slammed himself over them, locking them cruelly to the shuddering, booming floor. In a split second they realized why. Dancer was firing the machine gun crazily; they were never to know what it was that set him off. The Indian, hit in the stomach and enraged, seized the barrel——more bullets now slamming into his chest ——and tore the weapon from Dancer's hands. "I'm sorry!" Dancer howled, making out at last, through the thick smoke, who he'd shot. The Indian, staggering, was turning the gun around to let loose at Dancer, steamy blood gushing out of his belly and chest, but by the time he had his hand on the trigger he was blind, in fact dead, though still standing, and it was into

459

the legs and belly of old Dr. Alkahest that he emptied the gun. Dr. Alkahest opened his eyes in stark terror, suddenly cold sober, and bawled like a goat.

Despite the roar, the trembling and cracking and grinding of the rocks, despite the smoke and now billowing steam, the leaping, spinning, stampeding lizards, the Mexicans made out that the gringos were shooting, and in terror for their lives snatched out pistols and rifles and started firing. Dancer screamed, flesh flying from his hip, then his chest, and then the side of his head. Mr. Goodman, buck naked, ran six feet, yelling, before his arms flew out sideways with a mechanical jerk, his back arched sharply, and he slammed down face first into the lizards and lay still as a rock. "Not me! Please, not me!" Mr. Nit screamed, covering his face with his left hand, his penis with his right. Something knocked his head off, hand and all, and he fell backward, twitching.

"Don't move," Santisillia kept whispering, soothing as a parent: "Don't move!"

Old Alkahest screeched above the roar of the earthquake, the Mexicans' guns, "I'm a cripple! Please, I'm innocent! I'm a cripple!" But they understood no English. Volley after volley they emptied into him, the old man screaming till they shot out his throat, his wheelchair bucking and spinning with every hit.

The Mexicans had now all run past Santisillia, Peter Wagner, and Jane, pouring toward the cave and the exit. "This way—quick!" Santisillia said urgently, pulling Peter Wagner and the girl to their feet, Jane naked except for her patriotic cap, and dragging them away from the cave toward the cracking outer wall: "It's our only chance!" They reached the wall unseen and scrambled upward toward the blood-red sky, the Mexicans' screams of terror and confusion echoing behind them. All at once the screams stopped. The cave roof had fallen.

The sky became redder now, less filtered by marijuana smoke. As they climbed still higher, the smoke and the sick-sweet smell dropped away entirely. They reached the top, the rim of the basin, the thin shelf jarring and jumping with each shudder of the earthquake. Behind them the basin was a hell of fire and smoke. Ahead of them . . . They gasped and flinched back, dizzy.

"Dead end," Santisillia whispered. "We're finished!"

The rock wall fell straight as a plumbline, impossible to scale, for a thousand feet.

Peter Wagner stood up on the narrow rim and helped Jane up beside him, protectively clamping his arm around her naked waist. Santisillia, a few feet to their left, stood up too. Like Peter Wagner, he had on only his shirt and shoes.

Then they saw the planes. The whole northeast was full of them, like an invasion force. They stared in disbelief.

"B-fifty-two's," Santisillia said. "Bombers!"

"It can't be," Jane whispered, tightening her arms around Peter Wagner's waist. "Peter," she wailed, tears rushing down her cheeks, "I don't want to die! I'm young!"

"Be quiet," he commanded, closing his arm still more tightly around her.

Her eyes widened. She too had heard it: a gentle hum like music, just above their heads. They looked up and saw it the same instant: an enormous, perfectly still flying saucer.

"I don't believe it," Santisillia whispered.

"My God," Peter Wagner breathed.

Jane cried out wildly, "Hey, wow! We're saved!"

They began to wave frantically.

"Help!" Jane cried. "Help us! Please!"

"Beam us up!" Peter Wagner shouted. "Beam us up!"

The saucer lowered toward them a little, as if shyly.

That moment, the island gave a violent shudder like the spasm of an enormous, dying animal, and without a sound, as it seemed to Peter Wagner, a vast stretch of the wall to their left sank crashing toward the sea. Luther Santisillia, without so much as a cry of alarm, had vanished—he seemed simply to vanish into air.

The planes were much nearer now, absolutely silent, coming at well above the speed of sound. The two survivors looked up hungrily at the saucer.

"They'll save us, Peter," Jane whispered earnestly, gazing at the hushed, silver stranger. "Don't worry, my darling, they'll save us!"

"Save us!" Peter Wagner shouted. "We're innocent! Beam us up!"

So the book ended. Sally Abbott shook her head and put it down. She turned to the window, staring at her reflection and the darkness beyond.

"Horace," she said wearily, "that's the kind of thing this world's come to."

7

The Old Woman Relents
and Unlocks Her Door

1

When Lewis found him, the old man was out by the beehives, the shotgun propped up against the nearest of the group—brought along, Lewis knew, on the chance that there might be a skunk on the prowl, hunting some bees for his supper. The old man had no guards on; he claimed the bees knew him. It was true enough that he rarely got stung, and maybe they did know his smell, his endless mutterings to them, all his troubles and all the world's troubles. On a wooden tray near his feet he had bottles of sugar-water. He stood hunched over, arms covered with bees like living gloves, drawing out the combs, replacing them with sugar-water, then corking up the hives. The hives were dingy, cocked left and right by years of ground-swell; they reminded you some of old tombstones.

"Winterin the bees then, are ye?" he said.

"Ay-uh," the old man said, not looking up.

"Seems eahly," Lewis said. "Last year it want till November ye sealed up the hives."

463

The old man worked on, apparently assuming the remark required no comment.

"Ye think it'll be an eahly winter, then?"

James nodded. After a time: "Oak-appleth theem to think tho. Woolly-bearth too." He added, after a little thought: "My Dad uthe to thay, 'Only the Good Lord knowth about the weather, and therth timeth when I wonder if even He ith real thertain.' " He straightened up a little, arms held out from his sides. "Howth Ginny?"

"That's what I come up about," Lewis said. "I'm pickin her up at the hospital this mahnin. Thought you might like to come along."

James studied him, then glanced at the hives. "Lot of work here yet."

"You don't wanna come then?"

"I didn't thay that." He pursed his lips, looked down at the coating of bees on his arms. "Let me clean up here a little," he said. "You go up and thay hello to Aunt Thally."

Lewis smiled, not enough for the old man to catch it. "Ay-uh," he said. "I'll do that." He stood watching a moment longer, then started toward the house.

Leaning toward Aunt Sally's door he said, "You awake, Aunt Sally?"

"Good morning, Lewis," she answered brightly. "What are you doing here so early? How's Virginia?"

"Ginny's fine," he said. "Mind's still fuzzy, might be she'll stay that way for days, but nothin serious wrong with her, so they tell me. May come out of it any time."

"Thank God for that!"

"Thank somebody," he said.

"My goodness but you are stubborn," she said. "When you get to Heaven and find there's a good Lord that all this time you should've thanked for your blessings, and now, woe is you—"

"You think he's really all that pretty?" Lewis asked, ever mild.

She said nothing and Lewis smiled, uneasy, pulling again at his moustache. He said "Aunt Sally?"

"I'm still here," she said. The cheerfulness with which she'd first greeted him was now gone utterly. "You think I jumped out the window?"

It crossed his mind what she'd land in if she did, but he said only: "I come up to ask you if you want to ride in with me to town. I got to pick up Ginny at the hospital."

"You're bringing her up here?"

"I thought I might. Few little things I got to do around the place."

Again she was silent, and again, uncomfortably, he smiled. He could imagine her pursing her lips, sorely tempted, though he knew pretty well she'd say no.

"No," she said. "I realize nobody understands—"

"Oh, I wouldn't say that."

"If James would just show some respect for my rights—"

"Well, you do what you think's best," he said.

"Poor Ginny," she said. "It's good you're bringing her here. I'll be glad to see her."

Below, the woodshed door opened. A chicken squawked. The old man was coming in, grumbling something at the dog.

"Well, I got to go now," Lewis said. He took a step toward the stairs.

"Do drive carefully, Lewis," she said. The old woman's voice was both cranky and urgent, as if she had no idea herself what she felt or meant.

"I will," he said.

From the foot of the stairs the old man called, "We thtill goin, Lewith, or did you change your mind?"

"I never knew a soul in this family to change his mind," Lewis mentioned to the air.

All the way to town, the old man sat with his lips sucked in and kept mum.

When they'd parked the car and were walking up the steps to the hospital, Lewis said, "Whant you visit Ed Thomas while I see if Ginny's ready?"

James had been afraid he'd say that. But immediately, as if he'd already decided it, he said, "Thath a good idea."

They stopped at the desk, and Lewis made sure Ed Thomas's room number was the same as before. They'd talked of moving him to a double, let him have more company to pick up his spirits.

James Page, bent forward, his face unshaven, his cap in his hands, said cautiously to the nurse, "Ith all right if he hath vithitorth, then?"

"Perfectly all right," she said, and smiled.

James nodded, glanced at Lewis. "I thought tho," he said.

They walked to the elevator, Lewis Hicks fiddling at his moustache with two fingers as usual, the old man nervously chewing on his mouth. They reached the elevator—stainless-steel doors—and Lewis pushed the button. They put their hands behind their backs and waited, the old man from time to time glancing at his son-in-law, once even clearing his throat to speak; but when the elevator arrived and the doors hummed open, neither of them had yet broken silence. Two doctors of some sort were on the elevator already, coming up from the basement, a tall blond doctor and a short Oriental one, both in green outfits with green caps and little green masks hanging loose below their chins. "The really hard part," one of them said, "is keeping yourself from saying 'Woops!' when you slice through a nerve." They both laughed. The door hummed open and they got off. James started to follow. "We go one more, Dad," Lewis said. James came back in, eyes darting like an animal's. Lewis looked up at the ceiling, hands behind his back. They reached their floor.

Such guilt was coursing through the old man's veins he could hardly breathe. He felt as he'd felt when his son had killed himself, or, long years before, when he'd found his uncle Ira in the woods. It was a little while after his parents' funeral—they'd been killed in a car wreck when Richard was something like nine years old and Ginny was still small enough to sit in a highchair. Why Ira had done it he would never know; there was no telling with Uncle Ira, even for James, who had probably known him better than anyone else except possibly James' father. Perhaps, though he showed nothing, it was sorrow that had done it, old Ira rattling around in the suddenly empty house; or perhaps it was anger at their leaving the house to James and Ariah, not him; or perhaps it had been what he took, in his crazy, half-animal mind, for a kindness to them: if he was dead, they could move up from the smaller house Ariah's parents had bought them and take the family place. Whatever it was, there the old man lay, everything above his beard shot to hell, his right foot bare—with the barrels in his mouth he'd pulled the triggers (he'd rammed down both of them) with his toe. On a stump right beside him sat the snake's skull, an ash stick, and the claw of a bear. James, though a grown man, had kneeled beside the body, crying in great whoops. He'd pointed the place out to Richard, years later, when Richard was maybe twenty. James had mentioned, without making too much of it, how he'd wept. Richard had asked, "What was Uncle Ira like?" James had shook his head and had been close to tears again. "He was crazy," he'd said and, remembering, had smiled. "He was the bravest, toughest man I ever knew. Man shot him one time, some drunken Irish. Shot him in the chest. Tracked that man nine miles through the snow, it was the dead of December, and would have killed him for sure but luckily he lost so much blood he passed out. My father caught up to him and dragged him home, and two days later Uncle Ira was back at the chores." Richard had said, "He never talked much, they say." "No, that's true," James said. "I guess most people talk because they're lonely or there's somethin they're not clear on. That wasn't his case, or if it was he never knew it." Richard had asked, looking up into the trees, "Was his mind clear when he—shot himself?" James had glanced at his son, wanting to reach out and touch him but holding back, half sick with love for his big, handsome child and confused by the feeling, as he'd always been, though he'd never had trouble showing love to little Ginny; and then he'd looked down at the ground thoughtfully, fingering the snake's head in his pocket as if thinking of giving it to the boy. "I suppose he must've *thought* his mind was clear," he at last brought out.

He'd remembered all that, standing in the attic when he'd found his son, and he'd thought of the empty whiskey bottle on the table downstairs, the whiskey Uncle Ira hadn't needed, as of course Richard knew. If his son could come back—if some magic could happen in the world just once, and his son could slip back through the secret door—he would say to him: "Richard, never mind about the whiskey. It's all right."

But there was, of course, no secret door; that was the single most important fact in the universe. Mistakes were final—the ladder against the barn, the story about the death of Uncle Ira that he shouldn't have told. He felt himself fingering the snake's head again, scraping the tip of his bobbed finger against the one remaining tooth, and a brief flush of some queer emotion went through him—not anger, exactly; perhaps a brief flicker of understanding. There was a wastebasket standing by the table in the corridor ahead of them, and he drew out the snake's head and, when he came to the wastebasket, dropped it in. "Thorry," he said aloud. Lewis glanced at him.

Ed Thomas's door was partly closed. Lewis, after a moment's thought, leaned over toward it and lightly knocked.

"Come in!" someone called, possibly Ed Thomas's voice gone light.

Lewis pushed the door a little, stepping back from it as if he thought it might have a crate on top. "I'll go see about Ginny," he said.

James sucked his mouth in, his eyes darting in alarm once more, then nodded. "Ay-uh," he said. "Well . . . I be here."

Far down the corridor there was a middle-aged red-headed woman he thought he knew. She was heavy, rumpled from sleeplessness. She did not seem to see him.

3
(Ed's Song)

No one had prepared him for how Ed Thomas looked. He was better, Lewis had said, and it was true he was out of the oxygen tent—it was over by the wall, ready to be used again if he should need it—but he was no better than he might be. His skin had gone transparent, the blood in his veins looked the blue of snowy shadows in January, his eyes had sunken, and one got the impression that in a few hours he'd lost weight. Though he was weak—his voice, above all, had lost energy—he lit up with pleasure as James came in. It was an effect difficult to pin to any physical particulars: though he was weak as a baby, too feeble even for a full-fledged smile, his mind, perhaps spirit, seemed as lively as ever, locked inside.

"James, boy," he said, almost a whisper. "Hi golly there!"

"Mahnin, Ed." He approached the bed timidly, his cap in the two hands in front of him like a rabbit's, chin arching over it, meek as Ethan Allen when Jedediah Dewey got through with him for shootin at the churchbell, before Ticonderoga.

It was a single room—a chest, a lamp, a standing bed-table, some closets, a door to a bathroom, one chair, and one long window looking out at the Bennington Monument and the mountain beyond. Ed was in pajamas Ruth had brought him, dark red with black collar, Japanese-looking. His white hair was cocked up at curious angles; along the hairline there were tiny beads of sweat. He held out his hand for James to shake, though neither one of them was a handshaker, and both would have thought it, any other time, affected, citified, and morally dubious, like the smiles of a salesman. Ed made an effort to squeeze heartily; the effect showed only on his face.

"Hi golly," he said again. "Lewis told me he'd trick you up here!"

"Didn't take him no trickin, Ed. Ith good to thee you better."

"Sorry bout the way I went and crumpled there." Ed smiled feebly and slightly shook his head. "Own damn fault. Thirty years they been tellin me to quit those cigars."

James met his eyes, tasted his lips, getting courage up, then changed his mind and looked down.

"Damned embarrassin to be sick," Ed said. "Raises hob with the fahmwork. But then—" He rolled his eyes toward the window without turning his head. "I guess if I ain't made a fortune by now, I might's well tell it to the bees."

"You know how it ith in Vermont," James said. "Mebby neth year."

Ed nodded, half-smiled. "Mebby." For a moment he closed his eyes. When he opened them he said, "I spose you're hopin that boy Lewis will take over the fahm for you, one day."

"I dunno. Don't much matter. I put him in my will —after Thally." He smiled, seeing the irony in that, and glanced at Ed. "I thould have cut off that ole woman without a thin dime."

Ed smiled back. "It's a funny world," he said.

James nodded thoughtfully, pushing his hands into his overalls pockets, then abruptly shook his head. "That Thallyth the Devilth own thtepmother," he said.

As if he'd heard something completely different— or as if he knew James had meant something different

470

—he said, "She was a beautiful woman all right." His voice all at once had turned surprisingly sad. He rolled his head sideways to look more comfortably at the monument and mountain. James said nothing, hardly knowing what to say, and after a time Ed said, "I'll be sorry to miss the elections on TV."

James' eyebrows lifted.

"Never live to see 'em," Ed said, not making much of it. "Man knows about these things, sometimes. Got no reason to complain, never said I do, but I always enjoyed a good election."

"Now wait a minute, Ed—"

He waved it away, half smiling. "No, never mine that. They'll let me inta Heaven. Only real sin they can lay on me is I never did a dollar's worth of sin in my life." He smiled again. "Oh, I've thought a few. Maybe they'll count that."

The Bennington Monument was creamy white, with the sunlight falling full on it. On the crest of its high hill, surrounded by mountains, it ruled the valley. Despite its pure color, its imposing height, it was an ugly structure, most people with a modicum of sense maintained. James Page was among them, though he loved the thing anyway, patriot that he was, and in fact thought it fitting—massive, countrified, a towering but somewhat orotund obelisk constructed not of Vermont marble but of New York State limestone, plain and raw as the people memorialized: Col. Stark, for instance, one of James' ancestors, famous for standing on a farmer's pair of fence-bars and sighting the enemy and yelling to his men: "There's the British, and they're ours, or tonight Molly Stark sleeps a widow!" Mount Anthony was grayish blue to the west of it, here and there a patch of green, or a single tree with yellow leaves still on it, a poplar maybe, among the last to go. Overhead, the sky was bright blue.

Ed rolled his head back—lying with it turned to look out was too much strain—and closed his eyes. He went on talking, and James Page listened, unable to think of a word he could say except lies, and it wasn't a good time for lies.

"I always enjoyed a good election," he said. "It was better in the old days, when you and I was young. There'd be bunting in the villages, streets full of buggies, some fancy politician come to hammer on our ears. You remember the election of nineteen twelve? Teddy Roosevelt came and made a speech there in Bennington, that was the year of the Bull Moose campaign. I dunno what he said, I was too young to listen, but I remember, by tunkit, that man was *big*. You look at his picture, you'd think he was some little bespectacled doctor or college professor, and you read all the stories of how he overcame sickness and whatnot, you might get the idea he was one of those little Napoleons proving his stuff. But hi golly, that man stood a whole head taller than John G. McCullough in his prime, and more solid than one of George Ellis's Marmons. I remember that same year President William Howard Taft came to Manchester, fat as a hippopotamus—played golf with my uncle—I member the President had a floppy white hat. He was no good, that Taft. See it in his eyes. Back-slappin hand-claspin stogie-puffin bandit, so fat if you'd put a wick in him, you could have burned him for a candle." He smiled.

"I member one year at election time there was a man came to town had a white bear."

"I remember that!" James Page said, startled.

"You oughtta remember it," Ed said with a laugh—his eyes remained closed—"it was dahn near the end of your Ariah."

James frowned. "Now that pot I *don't* remember."

"You don't? Why son of a dog! Ariah was thirteen years old at the time. Prettiest thing in all the Shires. Eyes blue as skies in October and yellah yellah hair. Got darker later, but when Ariah was thirteen, it was still about the color of thrashin straw. She was over at her aunt's on the Monument Road, there by the Drake place, and she got it in her mind she'd take a ride in the buggy. Hoss they had was skittish, but Ariah was pretty good at handlin the thing, and her aunt never gave it two thoughts, I guess. So they hitched up the buggy and away she went.

"Half an hour later, just about time it was gettin down toward dark, aunt was out in the yahd and what should she behold but that man with that cussed white bear go by, bear sittin there in the buggy-seat just like a human, right next to the man. Well the aunt knew pretty well what that hoss was gonna think when he looked at that bear, so she goes flying down the road yelling 'Ha-a-a-lp! Ha-a-a-lp!' and every neighbor from far or near come flyin to the rescue. Happened my father was there in the vicinity in his trap, and me there beside him, and as soon as he leahnt what was happenin, away we flew to overtake 'em.

"Well we never saw the bear, as it happened; all we saw was that hoss and little Ariah come flyin down the road towahds us, and my father whipped around and went fast he could go in the same direction as that runaway hoss, and finally he captured it. Found out later what happened was, the man had heard Ariah's hoss comin, when she was comin through the shale line on Monument Road, and he'd run his buggy up in some weeds and got the bear down and sat on the thing till the hoss went by. But Ariah's hoss had smelled the bear, and that was ah it took. You fahgot that story?"

"No," James said, "I remember now." His eyes had filled with tears, though he was not aware of any feeling.

"Those was fine elections," Ed Thomas said and nodded, still not opening his eyes. "But they's too many people for such elections now. I don't begrudge it. I like those TV elections too. Believe you me! I remember the John F. Kennedy election. First time I ever understood what was really goin on at those things—cameras pokin out every cranny and nook, talkin to delegates when they was drunk and half crazy —it was an eye-opener. Demonstrations on the floor, they would've fooled me easy, but there was Walter Cronkite explainin what was happenin, or Huntley or what-have-you, and I tell you it made me more excited than I ever was before about a public election. People

475

groan abut the modahn world, but let me tell you, I've been proud, sometimes, watchin the elections.

"People scoff at TV. I b'lieve *you* do, James. But let me tell you, we don't vote like we used to. Whole country could be swayed by a tame white bear, or one time three hosses that supposably could talk. It was fun, by tunkit, but it's over; the world's grown up. People are thinkin and ahguin like they never did previous to this present age, and it's the idiot-box more'n ennathin else that made it happen.

"Well, I'll miss the election." He shook his head, opening his eyes for a moment, then letting them close again. James gazed out at the monument, waiting, hoping for something, he could hardly have said what. He wiped his wet eyes.

"I'll tell you some other things I'll miss, if you ask me."

James stirred himself to ask, but Ed went on:

"I'll miss walkin out these last days of October, when the land's dyin and the sky's oversharp, and findin where the deer are on their hind legs pickin wild apples. And I'll miss winter, by guard. I've never gotten over how much snow can fall in just five short months of winter. Never mind November, stot with the dark time, December. Blackest month of the year it is, and steadily increasin in blackness as the month draws on. Vermont's a lot farther north than most people realize, ye know. A man I knew left the State a few years ago and moved south. Where he went was Canada, city of London, Ontario, to be precise, which is a hundred and twenty-five miles south of where he stotted, which was St. Albans, Vermont. If he'd gone on to Kingsville, he would've been two hundred miles south, swelterin in the sun.

"But the dahkness at least increases in a known and predictable way, and furthermore, by the end of the month the days reach their shottest and stot growin again. The cold's trickier. Month begins gently, but one day—I've known it to be as early as the fifth and as late as the twentieth—you wake up cold and pull up another blanket. No use—you're still cold. In the mahnin you look at the thehmometer and it's eight below. Yestehday the Walloomsac was open water; today it's solid ice. Then January. That's the month of the snow. I don't mean more snow falls, because it doesn't—so cold that even the clouds lock up tight—but there's snow there always, not a speck of bare ground, nothin alive but some deer and rabbits and snowmobiles." He opened his eyes to meet James'. "Lot of people don't care much for snowmobiles," he said accusingly, "and I grant you they're loud, besides nocturnal. But I tell you this: I use to go lookin at the scenery round my place on skis or snowshoes. Now I just walk in the snowmobile tracks. Funny thing about snowmobiles. They're stupid little animals, but they know where the sights are, better than a deer.

"Then February. The days are longer then, the sun is higher, the snow's more dramatic. An evening flurry will come down in huge, wet flakes, so thick and fast you're convinced in an hour your fahm will be buried like Pompeii. But the flurry stops in ten minutes or so, leavin maybe two inches of good snowball snow, big feathery flakes. The mahnin after such a snow as that is what gave rise to picture postcards in the first place. The sky's clear, air still and cold but not too cold. From every chimney you see the smoke goes up straight as a stick. You pass through a valley with an unfrozen brook, and such vapor comes up through the fifteen degrees that for fifty yards on each side of it, the branches, the bob-wire, the weeds that poke up through the snow are ah covered with jewelry.

"But I'll tell you what I'll miss more than ah the rest, and that's 'unlocking.' Fools call it 'mud season,' and I don't dare deny you, there's a good deal of mud, because the first thing unlocks is the ground. I'll tell you the first sign. It's easily missed. Every year one of the first four or five days in March is going to be warm and sunny, with the temperature rising, for a little while, to somewhere between fifty and sixty. Look hard at a birch or red maple that day, you'll see a peculiar haze of color in the upper branches: yellow on birch, red on a red maple. Look again the next day and the color is gone, nothing but dark, bare branches and, likely, a sleet storm. All the same, unlocking's stotted. Dirt roads unlock first—the only ground not covered with snow. Each warm day the top inch or two of road touched by the sun thaws out. First cah goes by makes a couple of inch-deep ruts that'll freeze by evening. You can pretty well count on getting stuck once or twice. I never count on it, myself, but I always do.

"Rivers unlock next. The two I know best—the Walloomsac and the Hoosac—both stot the same way. You first see two small streams running on top of the ice, one near each frozen bank. Then one day towards the middle of March, a patch of open water appears, then another. On the Walloomsac, which has a good many dams and slow water, the patches slowly enlarge for a week, until one day you notice an open channel with a line of ice floes sailing solemnly down the middle like Pharaoh's boats.

"Meanwhile, two other kinds of unlocking have stotted. One's the town meeting, where, you know yourself, what we mostly do is block progress—keep to our old covered bridges, for instance, though the richest and smartest people in town want concrete for their darn trucks and bulldozers. The other's done with a brace and bit, and it's called sugarin.

"The weather's capricious, around sugarin time— the more capricious the better. The more Miss Spring dances in and backs out again, the more syrup you get. People in cars get furious when they're stopped by a late, wet April snow, but in the sugarbush that's a cause for rejoicing. Most of the season you do well to get three four inches of sap in the bottom of each bucket over twenty-four hours, but on the day of a sugar snow, your best buckets fill to the brim and run over. That night you boil to midnight, and it seems like a holiday.

"That's a life, James, I'll tell you, not as if you didn't know—standin out there in the maple grove countin up your buckets like a banker, and lookin out over the hills as the whole world outside and inside

478

unlocks. First the pussy willows come, and the rivers run emerald green. Then the deer come out. After a winter of eating just tree buds, and not too many of even them, they're mad for grass. They come boldly into the fields to eat last year's withered stems. One mornin last April I saw fourteen of the things in the pasture behind my house.

"Then the robins arrive, sometimes in flocks of two or three hundred, brightening the bare brown southern cants. About the same time, spring peepers stot up. Then fields begin to green. Some reason, the green always appears first where the snow's melted last. And one day after the first green tips appear, the first woodchuck pops up. Woodchucks are great gourmets, I'll tell you, and they ain't about to eat that old winter-killed hay the way the deer do. In April their brown fur has reddish glints to it, and for a couple of weeks, until the grass gets long or some neighbor's son comes out with his twenty-two rifle, they dot the fields like flowers. By that time, of course, it's no longer un-lockin time; it's spring.

"I'll miss that, this year, or ennaway take pot in it in a way I never did before. But I can't complain."

He smiled.

"James, how come you're listenin to all this?"

James thought about it. "Becauth," he said at last, "ith true."

Ed's smile widened. "That's what I tell my Ruth," he said. "She's got good poems and bad poems, and she'll swear on the Bible she can't tell which is which. I explain to her only the good poems are exactly true."

"Like a good window-thash," James said, "or horth."

"That's it," Ed said. "You got it."

479

"Look who's here!" Ruth Thomas sang out, coming into the room, and whether she meant James, and intended the greeting to show that she had no hard feelings now, or meant, instead, the minister and the priest, whom she'd discovered in one of the hospital corridors and now brought into the room with her, James Page could not certainly determine.

"H'lo, Ruth," he said, and could hardly meet her eyes. For which reason, perhaps, she looked at him harder, all at once, and her face became serious, and she said:

"James, I'm so glad you could come! You know, we've been worried about you. Is Sally out yet?"

"Not yet," he said. "But we're here to pick up Ginny, and I got an idea old Thally'll come out when we git Ginny home."

"Drat!" Ruth said, and clapped her hands. "If I'd known you'd be here I'd have brought Sally's plant book."

"Plant book?" James said.

"For her coleus, you know."

"Coleuth?"

"Really, James! Sally's precious coleus that's been dying for months. I got a plant book out of the library for her, so maybe she can find out what's wrong with the poor thing and doctor it. She's tried everything she knows, so she tells me—more water, less water, moving it around the room—"

"Thallyth got a coleuth in her room?" James said, head cocked.

"That's what I just said."

James nodded. "It'll die."

"It *is* dying." She looked at him. "Why?"

"Ith them appleth," he said. "Planth can't live around appleth. We got appleth in the attic."

"He's right," Ed said, opening his eyes.

"Why James, you should have told her!" Ruth said, indignant.

"Thee didn't athk," James said.

"Hello there, James," Lane Walker said.

James looked around Ruth and nodded his greeting, and the minister smiled and bowed as if that adventure in the kitchen had slipped his mind entirely. That was a curious trait in human beings, James had noticed, a trait they seemed to share with no other animal he was acquainted with excepting dogs. Hit a horse on the nose, and even a cussed chicken, he'd take a good while to make up with you, but a human being that could keep his mind firmly on a grudge (if he knew beforehand your better as well as your worse side) had to be—like Sally—exceptional. The priest's smile was a good deal more reserved, which was not, of course, too surprising. You couldn't say they'd hit it off, that one and only night they'd ever met. On the other hand, James, for one, had revised his opinion some. He remembered how the man had stood there facing him, even when the shotgun was up at James' shoulder and pointing at his head. Any ordinary man would have clim the wall. Not only that, in the time since that evening James had come even to admire the man's standing there laughing at him, there when the truck burned and he was sitting in the tree. A man who slinked and cowered had never been the old man's favorite kind of animal—it was the one thing he'd hated in his son Richard—nor did he care for a man in the obsequious professions—ministers, dentists, and undertakers—who advertised his calling on his face. Unfortunately, being not well equipped when it came to social graces, James Page had no way of communicating this change of opinion to the Mexican, who seemed to him now to be watching him exactly as he might a black insect in a jar. James' nod was so cautious—unbeknownst to James—that the Mexican didn't even see it and assumed James intended to be offensive. He looked above James' head, giving him no

481

sign of greeting, then pointedly smiled at Ed Thomas and went over to the bed.

"Feeling better today?" he said.

"Not really," Ed said.

"I'm sorry to hee-ur that!"

James Page lightly tapped his mouth with his fist, watching Ed and the Mexican and feeling guiltier by the minute. Lane Walker had gone now to the end of the room to bring the green vinyl visitor's chair to Ruth. James, with a look of surprise, hurried after him. "Here," he said, "let me help you with that!" The minister hardly needed help, the chair-legs had taps and slid easily across the thick, highly polished linoleum, but he accepted, with a private grin, the old man's help. Lane Walker thought: Trying to make up, are we? Having second thoughts like old Adam? A curious fact about Lane Walker's character was that he thought theologically all the time, exactly as writers think always as writers and first-rate businessmen think only of business.

"Here, Ruth," James said, "have a theat."

"Why thank you, James," Ruth said, preparing to sit and glancing at Lane Walker. "What are *you* smiling at?" she said. "You look like the cat that ate the canary!"

"Well I'll tell you," Lane said, making, suddenly, another impish decision. "I was thinking how guilty some people feel if they're poor benighted souls and not true, orthodox, educated Christians who are joyfully aware their salvation is fully accomplished and no questions asked if they'll just turn to Jesus."

"What in the world are you talking about?" Ruth said, and because the man's elvish grin was infectious, she too began to smile.

"I'm talking about people who turn to *drink* in their troubles, and not to Jesus. I'm talkin about people who harden their hearts about their brothers and even sisters!"

Her eyes widened. "Why Lane!" she said, "stop that!"

But he wouldn't be stopped. "And talkin bout people, even ministers of the Lord, who won't reach out to those poor benighted people in the darkness of their misery and benightedness and say, 'Brother, the Lord forgives you and even *I* forgive you.' "

James glanced in panic at the Mexican. The man was smiling, looking like a huge sheepish frog. By accident their eyes met, James' and the priest's, and automatically they nodded.

"Ah!" Lane said. "Signs of hope! Forms of civility! Hallaluja!"

Ed Thomas grinned, then closed his eyes.

"I swear," Ruth said, "it's a wonder they don't defrock you, the way you mock religion!"

"He wasn't mocking," the priest said—and even James Page understood that it was true—"that *is* religion."

5

When Lewis arrived with Ginny, they all fell silent; for a moment not even Ruth Thomas could think what to say. Ginny seemed transformed by the accident, and though in fact she would soon be her former self —except in one respect, as only Lewis was as yet aware—it was hard to believe, as they looked at her now, that she would ever again be the same. She was white as a sheet; part of her right eyebrow had been shaved; and from the eyebrow to her scalp-line ran an ugly, tightly sewed up gash. If the crate had struck three inches farther back, the doctor had told Lewis, if it had struck her, that is, on the temple, she would have been killed.

It was James who spoke first. "Hi, Ginny," he said, going to her, reaching out to touch her.

She smiled vaguely, as if almost but not quite recognizing him.

"The poor thing!" Ruth said, pushing down on the chair-arms, laboring to rise.

"Don't get up," Lewis said, still holding his wife's hand. "We got to go ennaway. Got to pick up Dickey." Then he called past her, "Hi there, Ed. Any better?"

"Gettin there," Ed said, and raised his arm a few inches as if to wave.

"You'll show 'em," Lewis said. He glanced at Lane Walker and then at Rafe Hernandez, bobbing his head to each of them, shy and eager to be away. "Mahnin, Reverend. Mahnin, sir."

As they greeted him he backed toward the door. Ginny turned, looked at him uncomprehendingly as he pulled at her arm, then docilely followed. James bowed good-byes and left behind her.

In the car the old man took the back seat, the left-hand side, and rode leaning far forward so that his forearms lay flat on the back of Lewis's seat, so that he could watch his daughter, sitting on the right in front. Nobody spoke. Ginny rode staring straight in front of her, on her face an expression frightening because it was not an expression, a kind of smile without humor or even life in it. Her throat was—as Ed's face had been, back at the hospital—bluish white, that same blue of shadows on the January snow.

"They thay Ginny be ah right, hey Lewis?"

"That's what they said."

"Well then I gueth thee will be."

"I guess so," Lewis said.

They turned onto Pleasant Street. Small, shabby houses; by the curb an old Volkswagen with one fender the wrong color.

"Where we going?" James said.

"Got to pick up Dickey," Lewis said.

"Oh, thath right. I fahgot."

He stopped in front of a dark green house and got out. James continued to look at Ginny. He leaned farther forward and said, "Doth it hurt, honey?"

After a moment, she turned her head slowly and looked at him. Please, God, he whispered inside his mind. It was his first prayer in years, the first since his wife died, when he'd carefully, tortuously written down in his Agro book his prayer for punishment, or understanding, or at least death. It was nothing like death that he prayed for now.

Then Lewis came out, holding Dickey's hand—there was a young, thin woman in a housecoat at the door, or perhaps not a woman but a child, the old man couldn't tell for sure—and Dickey got in with them, sitting in back on the right. Exhaust fumes came pouring in while Dickey had the door open.

"Ah you ok, Mommy?" he said.

"Hi, honey," she said. It made them all start. But the next instant she was as far away as ever.

"She knew me!" Dickey said, keeping his father from closing the door.

"I saw," Lewis said. "Draw yer head in."

The old man batted away exhaust fumes. Lewis slammed the door and walked around to the driver's seat, got in, closed the door, and nosed back out into the street.

"Ith a funny thing thee'd know Dickey and not her own father," James said.

Lewis smiled and drove in silence.

James' mind went back to Ed, lying there in the hospital, maybe dying. So he believed, and so it looked. All because of him, James Page, and his sister Sally. He thought about the story of the white bear. It was a queer thing to have forgotten. He must've heard it a hundred times. As Ed was telling it he'd seen her plain, flying in the buggy behind the runaway horse, with her yellow, yellow hair. He remembered picking her up one time in his own buggy—remembered the black-tailed, chestnut horse, the shine of lines hanging down over the thill. He remembered Ariah's round, smiling face, two dimples cut into it, a small, pretty nose. She had not been strikingly beautiful, like Sally, but she had been good—loving and lovable—in a way Sally would have no way even of perceiving. He stared hard at the frozen mental image: Ariah in sunlight looking up at him, the lines hanging down—which meant that he was soon to jump down from the buggy and help her up in—but, strangely, he couldn't remember jumping down, couldn't remember what it was he'd just said that had made her smile, if that was why she was smiling, couldn't remember where, or when . . .

The sky was still the same clear blue; the valley below where the road climbed, and the mountain range beyond, were scratchy with trees; in the middle of the valley, the village sat like a village of toy houses, a Christmas village waiting for fake snow and lights. He thought of Merton's Hideaway and of the drunken writer, thought of how the man had turned to stare at him, stared as if to consume him, put him in some book. Nothing wrong with that, of course, James reflected, dubious. Mr. Rockwell put people in his pictures —real people, many of whom James Page had known: his cousin Sharon O'Neil a time or two, Lee Marsh's wife and Mrs. Crofut, once or twice Grandma Moses herself. No harm. But of course Mr. Rockwell had always meant no harm, which was why he'd achieved it. He'd meant to paint the way things could be, he'd explained once to the schoolchildren, and to paint how some of the time, if people will stay awake, things actually are. People always thought of him as a happy man, and he had been, in a way—all his friends right there around him, and getting paid for doing what he would've done anyway—but there was another, less cheerful side to him, they said in Arlington; there were times he seemed weighed down with grief, they said, and James had some evidence that it was true.

Perhaps all Vermonters were inclined to be pessimists, but the painter had not only expected the worst, he'd brooded on it. "The country's ill," he'd said one time, sitting on the porch at Pelham's place, James Page standing below him with a glass of ice-tea. (James had come to Pelham's delivering wood, and Mrs. Pelham had asked him if he'd mind a little tea.) "The country's ill," the man had said. "Christianity's ill. Sometimes I feel a little shaggy myself." They'd all laughed, including the painter. But a few minutes later, getting into his truck, James had looked at the tall, skinny artist, and he'd understood by the expression on the man's face in repose that he'd been dead serious, at least about the country and Christianity: that for all his easy ways, his security in this safe, sun-lit village in Vermont where they were still in the nineteenth century, he was worried, smoking day and night just like Ginny, and now and then frowning the way Ginny would sometimes do when she wasn't aware you were watching her. The man had painted as if he had a devil in him, so people said that knew him, sit-ting or standing there legs akimbo, straight pipe clenched in his long, yellow teeth, small blue eyes glittering. Painted as if his pictures might check the decay—decay that, in those days, most people hadn't yet glimpsed.

"Tell me the story about the parson," Dickey said.

James turned, eyebrows lowered, shifting his gaze reluctantly from his daughter's face. "Parthon?"

Dickey nodded. He had his hands in his lap, as if making a point, for James' benefit, of his excellent behavior. "You know," he said, "The one about Parson Dewey and the hero.

"Ah!" James said. "*That* parthon." He sat back a little, to give the story proper weight. "On the Thunday right after the battle of Fort Ticonderoga, when Ethan Allen hit the Redcoath from behind, thneakin up on 'em by climbing a cliff and dragging up hith cannonth —an impothable feat, moth people will agree—and that thon-of-a-gun hunk of rock Ethan Allen did it *drunk*—Jedediah Dewey wath thaying a long prayer in the pulpit, thanking God for the victory at Fort Ticonderoga, and giving God all the credit for it. Ethan Allen couldn't thtand it, and finally he jumped up— all thix-foot-thix of him—and thouted to the minithter, 'Parthon Dewey! Parthon Dewey!' Three timeth he thouted it. 'Parthon Dewey!' he thouted. Jedediah blinked and come out of his tranth and thaid, 'Thir?' Ethan Allen thaid, 'Would ye pleath mention to the Lord about my being there?' "

Dickey laughed, as usual—possibly, James knew, as a kindness.

"Is that story s'posed to be true?" Lewis said.

"Everythin they tell about Ethan Allen ith true," James said. "That what maketh a hero."

6

The old woman came out of her room for many reasons, the least of which was that, in a technical sense, at least, she won the war. In fact, she hardly noticed the victory when it came. James had come up to use the bathroom—Lewis was in the hallway, painting, and her door was unlocked, because Lewis said he couldn't finish scraping if she wouldn't please open it —and James, after he was finished in the bathroom, came over and said: "Ed Thomath tellth me TV ith a wonderful invention, around electhion time. I hadn't thought of that. —Heeth not too well, by the way. Himthelf, he don't think he'll pull through."

"What?" she said, alarmed, opening the door more and looking at his face.

"He lookth bad, truth of it."

She cocked her head out to look at Lewis. "He took a turn for the worse?" She brought her hand up to her heart.

Lewis kept his eye on the paintbrush. He was painting the doorframe shiny white; hadn't even asked her what color she'd prefer. But despite her irritation she returned her mind to Ed, and to poor Ruth. Lewis said, "He's awful pale, looks to me. Weak as a kitten."

Before she knew it, she was out in the hall. "Poor Ruth," she said. She remembered vividly, for the thousandth time, how she'd wept and wept, that terrible Halloween twenty years ago, half in fear, half from loss. She'd found him sitting in his chair, still warm, his record caught in a groove—it was that that had made her come in. She found herself speaking of it, looking at James, at the same time seeing Ruth in her mind's eye. "I remember how it was when Horace died. I thought I'd die myself, of crying. At least, with Ruth, there'll be no mystery to it, nothing to be afraid of."

"Mythtery?" he asked blankly.

"The door was open, you remember," she said. "That may have had nothing to do with it, he may have just then given some child his treat—it happened on Halloween—and before he got the door closed, he had his attack. But I kept thinking at the time—I sometimes think now . . ."

James was squinting, waiting as if alarmed.

"I keep thinking, what if he'd just seen something— or someone—and whatever it was *meant* to frighten him, and gave him that heart attack. They must have known, if that's what happened, but they ran, let him stagger over to his chair and . . . A child, I suppose. But how could a child—" She broke off, looking at him. "What, James?"

The old man was twitching, feeling his chin with his fingertips, one muscle ticking rapidly in his cheek as if some control had snapped. Now the side of his neck began to throb as if his heart had sped up, and there was something around his face, or for an instant so it seemed, a dark light.

Lewis came nearer, watching from behind her shoulder.

James said, turning away to the right as if unaware he was doing it, beginning a slow, complete circle, "You never told me the door wath open."

"I told the police." A shiver went up her back, and the hallway snapped into sharper focus, exactly as if this were a dream, not really happening—a dream that had been sunlit and pleasant and now suddenly was changing.

"But you never told *me*," he yelled.

"James," she said, voice low in fear of him, "tell me what you're thinking?"

He seemed far away, still making his circle, rubbing the sides of his chest. "I will," he said, "don't worry. Let me think."

She turned to glance at Lewis. Without speaking or moving he convinced her it was best not to press, give the old man his time.

James, having completed his full circle, turned to the right again as if to make another, but this time he came out of it and moved toward the head of the stairs and then, after some thought, slowly down to the kitchen.

"I'll get dressed," Sally said.

Lewis nodded.

James, stepping into the kitchen, could hardly see. He rubbed away tears with his fingertips—he couldn't tell whether they were tears of fear or sorrow or shame or what. Maybe all of that, or maybe mere words were too narrow for the feeling charging through him like a fire. It was as if, suddenly, he had fallen back into the world, found the magic door. He saw Ariah's face clearly, as he hadn't remembered it for a long time— saw her as a young woman, laughing with just a touch of fright in her voice as he pushed her on the swing; saw her laughing again, a few years older, sitting around the table at (it must have been) Thanksgiving time at the Blackmer house, hearing old man Dewey, Jedediah's great-great-grandson, tell the story of the time the sleigh tipped over, and all the Dewey women were hurled into the street and it was revealed to all Bennington that under their long black skirts they wore petticoats splashed with every color in the rainbow. He saw her in her last illness reaching to touch his cheek, saying *Oh James, James,* forgiving him— and forgiving herself—though he, even when she was dying, could forgive neither one of them. More pictures of her rose, one after another, it was as if he had suddenly been given back his life, and, still weeping, groping ahead of himself with one hand, he moved as quickly as he could toward the living room, because it was there that the albums were, and he wanted to look, find out if the pictures had come alive again.

Ginny was on the couch, sitting perfectly still. Dickey snuggled up beside her, holding her hand.

"Hi, honey," James said, and again he brushed away the tears, wanting to see her.

She smiled, and this time he knew that, for a minute, anyway, she'd known him. Thank God. Thank God!

"She can talk," Dickey said. "She talked to me."

"Thank God," he said.

And then, because he could do nothing for Ginny that Dickey wasn't doing, and maybe doing better than he could now, he moved on past them and over to the bookshelf to the left of the fireplace and bent down and drew out the albums. He opened the oldest of them—dust flew, and it seemed that the paper itself was partly made of dust—opened it hungrily, and the first picture of her he saw leaped alive in his mind as if her ghost had come back to remind him that life had been good once, of course it had been, and that life *was* good, as poor Ed Thomas understood now more clearly than ever, now that he was dying. He saw a picture of her standing in snowshoes, grinning, a dog beside her—even the dog's name came back to him: Angus. There she was on a tractor, and there looking out from the porch they'd had on the house at that time, she was leaning coyly against the pillar. He remembered the time. Remembered all the times. Also this: she was sewing, sitting in an island of light. As he came into the room, having just finished chores and brought the milk in, she looked up and said suddenly, as if otherwise she mightn't get it out, "Richard's sick, James. Ill."

"Richard?" he'd said.

She'd looked down then, face flushing. "It's something he's done," she said almost inaudibly. "Five years ago."

"That's why he's turned to a drunkahd?"

"I suppose so." Still her head was bowed, light pouring over it, the hair brown, streaked with gray, yet pretty, that instant.

491

"What was it?"

"It's better if Richard tells you, when he comes over."

"What was it?" he'd insisted. "Women?" He'd seen one at his house one time, staring out the window.

She shook her head, tears running down her cheeks. "I can't tell you," she'd answered, not rising, not even looking up at him, yet for all that standing up to him; it wasn't usually her way. She said, "I told him I wouldn't." It was she who'd made the boy weak. She said so.

When he'd come the next day and James had demanded to know what he'd done, what was wrong with him—his son had whiskey on his breath, as usual—the boy had blanched and refused to say a word except, "Tell you, you old bastahd?" He gave a kind of laugh, that cowardly-sounding laugh he'd had all his life, and he'd brought out, already ducking like a gun-shy dog, "I'd die first," laughing again. It was because of the laugh and because he was ducking already that James had slapped him. The boy had stared, as if some terrible suspicion was confirmed, and had abruptly walked away. He'd gone over to his own house and gotten himself drunk—he'd never have had the nerve for it otherwise—and he'd hanged himself. When he was dead, Ariah wouldn't tell what it was he'd done, clinging foolishly to the promise she'd given him, even now when he was dead and it meant nothing, promise to a manure pile. "It's too late," she'd said, and had made James understand—whether or not it was what she meant him to understand— that she would not stop blaming him for the boy's death, even in her grave. If they'd had time no doubt they'd have softened, both of them, though a year after his suicide she had still not said a word. Then one day there were bumps in her armpits and the backs of her knees. Four months later she was buried, and even in his grief he had found he couldn't picture her in his mind.

Now he knew and could see that he'd misunderstood completely. The boy had had reason to be afraid to give an answer. James would have told Sally, would have taken the boy by the scruff of the neck for all his twenty-five years and would have made him face up. The boy had known, as his mother had known, because all his life, he understood now, James Page had had a petty-minded notion of truth, had been a dangerous fool.

Guilt. All this time he'd carried it, a burden that had bent his whole life double and when he caught it and held it in his two hands and opened them, there was nothing there. He'd been benighted, just as the minister said. And she too, poor Ariah, had gone to her grave full of guilt because, having told James, she blamed herself for the suicide. And the boy—James brushed away tears again, crossly—it had not been rage at his father, had not been revenge, or only a little of it was that. It had been the burden of five years' nurtured guilt at the fact that, in some foolish or maybe drunken prank—Richard had been twenty, a grown man, or so Richard would have thought, though no man of seventy-two would allow that a boy of twenty was grown—the boy had frightened his uncle to death, and, cowardly all his life (whipped all his life, threatened and hollered at and told he was a coward—James would face all of it, now that he'd come to), he had not even stayed or cried out to his aunt for help, but had been true to the image James Page had created for him to live by, or both James and Ariah and even little Ginny—they'd all been in on the conspiracy—and had fled. Benighted, the lot of them, himself worst of all. He'd prayed for punishment, and had been punished well: punished years before the prayer.

Tears streamed down the old man's face, though what he felt did not even seem sorrow, seemed merely knowledge, knowledge of them all from inside, understanding of the waste. Again he wiped his eyes, drying them on his sleeve. When he could see again, Ginny was looking at him. Her mind had cleared.

"Dad!" she said, starting to rise, then sinking back again. "Are you all right?"

"Ginny, you're better!" he cried.

She tried again to get up from the couch—Dickey drew back—and for an instant the fog was there again, but then again her eyes cleared. She raised two fingers to her forehead to touch the wound. "What happened?" she exclaimed.

"Ith all right," James told her, going to her. "Crate of appleth fell down on ye."

"Aunt Sally made a trap for Grampa," Dickey said eagerly, then glanced at James to see if it was all right.

"And you walked into it," James said.

Now Lewis and Aunt Sally were there, pleased to see her rational again.

"Ginny, my poor darling!" Sally said, hurrying to her.

"Boy, do I feel funny!" Ginny said. She looked around the room. "Anybody seen my cigarettes?"

"I got 'em," Lewis said.

"Thank heavens! Toss me one, would you, sweetie?"

"No," he said. He looked over at the wall, not straight at her.

"What?" she said.

"You're quittin."

She stared at him—so did Sally—and for a moment it seemed that the fog had come back over Ginny. Then she said, blistering, "Lewis Hicks who in the hell do you think you are?"

"Never mind," he said, "you're quittin."

"Why?" she demanded. "Is this a free country or *isn't* it?"

He looked over at the other wall. "No," he said.

7
(The Intruder)

Out by the hives, where he was finishing up with what he'd started that morning, taking the last of the honey out, removing the thick wax that meant a queen bee— she'd steal half the hive if he left her free to hatch— putting in sugar-water, then sealing up the hives —James Page had a strange experience. He was working in a daze, the shotgun leaning against a hive ten feet away from him, his hands automatic, his mind still engaged in savoring the pleasures and sorrows of memory. It had begun with a drone: looking at it, as he'd looked at drones thousands of times in his life, he'd remembered how sometimes he'd given Richard and Virginia drones to play with, when they were young— since drones would not sting and had only a short life anyway. He could see them both just as clear as day, and remembered they had both had, like their mother, yellow yellow hair. While he was staring at this image of his two children—his second son hadn't yet been born at this time—he'd moved through the image of them to another, a memory of his wife.

He'd come to pick her up in the buggy. It was a bright, bright day. He had no thought then of marrying; it would be years before he could afford to support a family—his father was at that time still running the farm, or his father and his uncle. And if he had thought of marrying, it would probably not have been Ariah he'd have thought of getting married to, supposing someone should have asked him, that moment, to make his choice. She was his good, delightful friend, from a family much better off than his, better educated, richer. There was no way on earth he could have asked her to marry him—except the way he did. She came running toward the buggy, smiling, glad to see him as she always was—it was a curious thing, what fun they'd had together all their lives, though of course they'd had their spats, mostly, he knew now, because of his excessive Yankee pride in workmanship, his greed, his refusal to stop and simply look, the way Ed Thomas had looked, or play—and he'd dropped the lines over the thill to get down from the buggy and help her. She'd stopped abruptly, four feet from the wheel, and said, "James Page you've got a mighty funny look on you. Tell me what you were thinking right then." Before he knew he'd say it—from the pure, benighted habit of absolute honesty (when he heard himself saying it, it was as if it was coming from the sun above his head, or from God Himself, tricking him to happiness): "I was thinking I wish we could get married," he said. She tipped her head sideways, smiling, showing her dimples, and said, "Let's!" Three years later, they did.

So the unlocking of his heart continued. He remembered the death of his younger son—that had been the first death—remembered Sally's horror and indignation when Ginny got engaged to that strange looking Lewis Hicks. "He don't seem a bad sort," James had said. Sally had said, "She's selling herself cheap. Our Ginny's a wonderful and intelligent girl. Have you noticed that boy's eyes?" "You don't like him," James had said smugly, "because he's part Indian." That had pleased him—pleased him still, thinking back to it.

While he was savoring his memories, by this time standing there motionless as a frog, snowy head bowed, something came up behind him or materialized from invisibility and draped its shadow over him. His blood ran cold—there was a smell of wildness—and slowly, expecting God knows what, he turned to look. Five feet away from him, between him and the gun, there stood what must've been—judging by the tracks when he examined them later—a six hundred pound black bear. Perhaps it had not realized the old man was here; perhaps it was sick, or paying no attention . . . It was an old bear, that much he knew at once, observing dispassionately even as his knees banged together. Around the bear's muzzle the hair had all turned gray, and it seemed to James Page that there was something not quite right about the eyes.

The two ancient creatures stared at one another, both of them standing more or less upright—the bear considerably more upright than the man—the old man unable to do a thing to defend himself, too weak-kneed to try running or even jump for the gun, his heart so hammering at the root of his throat that he could not even make a sound. He often thought, going over it later, how that Britisher must have felt when he looked up at the top of the wall by the cliff, there at Fort Ticonderoga, and beheld that stone man Ethan Allen towering against the stars and gray dawn, filling the sky with his obscenities. He, the Britisher, had been an ordinary man, as James Page, here among his hives, was only an ordinary man. Ethan Allen had been put upon the earth like Hercules, to show an impression of things beyond it. So it was with this enormous old bear that stood sniffing at the wind and studying him, uncertain what heaven had in mind. A full minute passed, and still the bear stood considering, as if baffled by where the old man had come from and what his purpose could be, creeping up on him. Then at last the bear went down on all fours again, turned to where the containers for the honeycombs sat, and began—as if he had all day and had forgotten James' existence—to eat. James made for the gun and, despite the weakness of his legs, reached it. The bear turned, a low growl coming from low in his throat, then went back calmly to his business. James with wildly trembling hands raised the gun to his shoulder and aimed it at the back of the bear's head. What happened then he could not clearly remember afterward. As he was about to pull the trigger, something jerked the gun straight up—possibly, of course, his own arm. He fired at the sky, as if warning a burglar. The bear jumped three feet into the air and began shaking exactly as the old man was doing, snatched up an armload of honeycombs, and began to back off.

"And you didn't shoot at him?" Lewis said, looking

thoughtfully past him with that one blue eye, one brown eye.

"I fahgot!" James said, squeezing his lower lip between his right-hand finger and thumb.

"It theemed like—" He broke off, realizing he must have, for an instant, fallen into a dream. It had seemed to the old man that the bear had said something, had said to him distinctly, reproachfully, *Oh James, James!*

JOHN GARDNER has received great acclaim for his novels, THE RESURRECTION, THE WRECK-AGE OF AGATHON, GRENDEL, THE SUN-LIGHT DIALOGUES, NICKEL MOUNTAIN, FREDDY'S BOOK, and IN THE SUICIDE MOUN-TAINS; for his biography, THE LIFE AND TIMES OF CHAUCER; for his epic poem, JASON AND MEDEIA; for his collection of stories, THE KING'S INDIAN; for his books of fairy tales for children, GUDGEKIN THE THISTLE GIRL, THE KING OF THE HUMMINGBIRDS, and DRAGON, DRAGON; and for his criticism, ON MORAL FICTION. He has taught medieval literature at Oberlin, San Franciso State, Northwestern, Southern Illinois, and Bennington, and is currently teaching at SUNY-Binghamton. Mr. Gardner was born in 1933 in Batavia, New York.

The best
in modern fiction from
BALLANTINE